Sometimes beautiful things come from odd pieces of fabric, and it doesn't matter if they're a little tattered, they still keep you warm. Just like family.

Annabelle Hubbard thinks she has good reason to be exhausted all the time: she's the caretaker for three good-hearted but challenging grandkids and a three-legged cat named Ms. Pickles, plus she feels awkward about settling like a charity case into her grandmother's home, now owned by her wealthy cousin Regina in Wichita, Kansas.

Regina and Annabelle have never been close, and Regina begrudged her beleaguered cousin every bit of help until the past two years. Family is family! After all, Annabelle supports Regina's romance with silver-haired Wichita attorney Sam Duncan, who encourages Regina to believe in herself again after years with a cheating husband.

But Regina and Annabelle's new-found kinship is put to the test when Annabelle's ex-con son-in-law shows up demanding to get to know his kids, and the shock brings on Annabelle's mild heart attack.

The day Annabelle returns from the hospital, her youngest grandchild, Megan, is in a car accident. Regina returns to the family home as temporary caregiver, while Annabelle and Megan recuperate, and the older teens struggle with issues about their reformed but rough-edged dad. As Annabelle sets out on a healthy new lifestyle while accepting the romantic advances of a retired coach, Regina wrestles with Sam's marriage proposal, and the dramas of their quickly stitched-together family tug at the seams.

Will this patchwork family survive?

Praise for *Patchwork Family*

"PATCHWORK FAMILY by Bonnie Tharp is an absolutely wonderful story about family, strength, and the power of love. I savored every single word!"
—*Dorothea Benton Frank, author of* The Last Original Wife

"Patchwork Family draws us into the tender, cranky, loving lives of the Morgans . . . Bonnie Tharp's depiction of the Morgans pulls the reader in to feel the pain and love that keeps family together as the world fights to wrench it apart."
—*C. Hope Clark, author of* The Carolina Slade Mystery Series

Patchwork Family

by

Bonnie Tharp

Bell Bridge Books

Bell Bridge Books
PO BOX 300921
Memphis, TN 38130
Print ISBN: 978-1-61194-472-3

Bell Bridge Books is an Imprint of BelleBooks, Inc.

Copyright © 2014 by Bonnie D. Tharp DBA Scribble, LLC

Printed and bound in the United States of America.

We at BelleBooks enjoy hearing from readers.
Visit our websites
BelleBooks.com
BellBridgeBooks.com.
ImaJinnBooks.com

10 9 8 7 6 5 4 3 2 1

Cover design: Debra Dixon
Interior design: Hank Smith
Photo/Art credits:
Still life © Kiril Stanchev | Dreamstime.com
Wallpaper texture (manipulated) © Jodielee | Dreamstime.com

:Lfpo:01:

Chapter 1

SIPPING HER COFFEE, Annabelle Morgan Hubbard glanced at her friend over the cup. "I don't know why you put up with me, Tillie. I'm sixty-seven years old and I can't cook. I'm not much of a housekeeper, I've never held a job, and about the only talent I have is with a needle and thread."

"I envy you that talent, dear friend. But I must tell you that the way to win the heart of a man is with sticky cinnamon nut rolls."

Sighing, Annabelle said, "Then I'm doomed. I don't bake any better than I cook. Don't you remember the cherry pie disaster last year?"

Tillie Linden laughed, "Who can forget? Salt instead of sugar, what a nasty mess. Uh, no offense . . ." She reached out to pat Annabelle's arm.

I've had enough of the wrong man to last me a lifetime. Who needs the heartache?

"Besides, there are no male prospects in my future and frankly I don't want any. How long has it been for you and Joe?"

"I can't believe I've been married over a year already," Tillie said. The tiny, fifty-eight-year-old woman pulled her fingers through her white curls. "And I've got hair again! I was hoping more of the blonde would show when I was done with chemo, but nope, it's white as a marshmallow."

"I told you it would grow back. And it's pretty. Now if I could just do something with this mop." Annabelle patted her own fuzzy, styleless locks, leaned against the ladder-back chair and turned to face her friend.

"Ah, honey, it's just luck," Tillie said. "I got some great hair genes, but I'll trade all this and half my teeth to be entirely shed of the cancer genes." Tillie squeezed Annabelle's hand.

"How long has it been since your last chemo treatment?"

"Thirteen months, sixteen days, but who's counting?" Tillie's dark chocolate-brown eyes sparkled. She sipped her coffee and grimaced before setting the cup back on the table.

"That's wonderful; I'd be counting, too." Annabelle noticed her friend's frown. "Are you feeling okay?"

Although Tillie's face was pale, her friend's requisite khaki slacks, slogan t-shirt and walking shoes made her appear healthy to the casual eye. But they'd been through a lot together this past year, what with her daughter Liddy's death, Tillie's mastectomy, the grandchildren moving in and Regina moving out. Tillie had been a trooper through it all. Annabelle and her cousin Regina couldn't ask for a more loyal friend.

"I feel fit as an Amazon warrior, even if I am only five-foot-nothing." Tillie flexed her arm like a muscleman.

"If you weren't a warrior, you wouldn't have beat that disease and captured the heart of a nice man like Joe Linden." When the handsome retired Air Force officer moved into the house across the street, Annabelle, Regina and Tillie felt excitement in the air. But Joe only had eyes for Tillie, the feistiest of the bunch. Taking a deep breath, Annabelle felt tightness in her chest. She tucked her shaking hands into her ample lap. "Would you like more coffee?"

"No, thanks. Between Joe's wake-up nudge, a two-mile walk and a mug of your motor oil java, I've had enough stimulation to keep me going for the rest of the day." Tillie took her cup to the sink, pouring the last half down the drain.

"Is my coffee that bad?" Annabelle sniffed the contents of her cup and frowned.

"Not really, Belle, it's just that Joe's spoiled me rotten. He makes better coffee than the mega-million-dollar coffee shops. Nobody can compete. Walk me to the door?" Tillie waited for her friend.

"Sure." Rising, Annabelle said, "It still feels odd to be in this old house without Regina complaining about the mess or me or the grandkids. Even after a year."

Though Annabelle was the oldest of the cousins by eight years, Regina had inherited their Grandmother Morgan's house. The century-old Victorian home nestled in the Riverside area of Wichita had been in the Morgan family for generations. Regina's snobbish mother, Victoria, raised her like a porcelain doll—never to be played with or risk getting dirty. Victoria's sister, Rose, the youngest and Annabelle's mother, dreamt of living in the country. Recalling her happy childhood, Annabelle knew she'd been raised with love, but little money. Quite the contrast with her well-to-do cousin's upbringing, and the major rift between them.

They walked through the formal dining room on their way to the front door. Annabelle glanced at the Morgan family crystal and china.

Becoming the steward of the Morgan family heirlooms probably left Aunt Victoria smoldering in her grave. She would never have allowed such an unworthy person as myself care for them.

"Speaking of the grandkids, how are the little darlings?"

Entering the cluttered parlor, Annabelle could almost hear Regina snort in disgust. Magazines, books, shoes, assorted children's clothing littered the room, looking like a small explosion had distributed the debris at random.

"They took Ms. Pickles for a walk this morning and almost missed their buses."

"You're kidding, right?" Tillie asked. "You don't walk a cat, especially not a three-legged cat."

Annabelle smiled. "We know that, but tell it to a ten-year-old. I imagine that Megan carried Ms. Pickles so Tad didn't step on her with his huge feet. He's fourteen and I'm afraid that's what size his feet will be if he doesn't stop growing."

"Think of it this way—he's got a firm foundation," Tillie said. "And Peg? Where was she in all this?" They stopped in the foyer. The front door was flanked by floor to ceiling windows covered in sheer curtains. The spring sunlight filtered onto the hard wood floor, casting rectangular pools.

"Peggy spent the night at her friend Malissa's. They probably fixed each other's hair, slathered on makeup and called boys."

"My Lord. I guess she is almost sixteen. What on earth are you going to do when she starts dating alone instead of in groups?" Tillie opened the oak door and paused.

Annabelle's hand clutched the front of her dress. "Have a heart attack."

"If it were me, my hair would be gone again, one handful at a time." Tillie stepped onto the wrap-around porch, calling over her shoulder. "You take care of yourself. Don't let the kids get you down. Joe and I are just across the street if you need us. And Regina is only a phone call away."

"Thanks, Tillie. I appreciate everything you and Joe have done for us. You're good friends. I probably should give Regina a call. Maybe we'll have her and Sam over for dinner, but not before the kids and I clean the place up."

Tillie turned and winked. "Wise woman. See you later."

Watching Tillie's energetic march across the yard made Annabelle's breath catch. "I'm only sixty-seven, and I can hardly walk across the room without sitting down for a rest. It's time to go back on a diet. Maybe Doc will take pity on me and give me something to help the process along. Good thing I have an appointment today. I'm too young to feel this rough." She shook her head when she realized she'd been talking to herself—again. "Get a grip."

Her three grandkids were a mess, but she loved them. It had been a challenging year. The pain of their mother's accidental death had faded along with the bruises her abuse had inflicted on them. Tad's broken arm had healed quickly, as young bones often do, but the nightmare of his mother breaking it had not. At least he no longer woke up screaming with fear. Tillie had suggested they check into family therapy at the Child Guidance Center. At the time, Annabelle resisted, afraid the cost would be prohibitive, but after six months of therapy they reaped the benefits.

Annabelle was getting her chance to make things right, to undo the mistakes she'd made with her daughter Liddy, their mother.

The phone rang in the kitchen, disrupting Annabelle's thoughts. She shuffled down the hall and snatched up the receiver. "Heh . . . low?" She panted, gulping for air.

"Annabelle? Is that you?" Regina asked.

"Hello. Sorry, I was just saying goodbye to Tillie."

"What did you do, race her to the door?"

Annabelle chuckled, "No. And I'm fine, thanks for asking." She knew her cousin would ignore the sarcasm.

"You don't sound fine. I called to make sure the family home was still standing and to ask you to watch Sugar for the weekend."

"This house may be more than a hundred-years-old, but it's sturdy. It'll even survive us. We'd love to see Sugar. Tad's crazy about that dog." She hesitated. "Ms. Pickles isn't too fond of her, but Megan will see that no harm comes to the cat or the dog's nose." Annabelle twirled the phone cord around her finger.

We really should upgrade this phone. Ah, well, this one still works.

"Great. We'll bring her by Friday after Sam gets home from the office and pick her up Sunday afternoon."

Taking slow calming breaths, Annabelle could still feel her heart pounding. "That'll be fine. Don't forget to bring plenty of dog food. We ran out last time. Ms. Pickles had a fit when her cat food disappeared."

"That cat has no sense of humor." Regina laughed. "See you Friday."

"Bye." Annabelle eased down onto the kitchen chair, pressing her closed fist to her chest. "Probably heartburn. Too much coffee and cookie dough," she said. The mantle clock struck the half hour. "Oh, it's eight-thirty. I have to go if I'm going to make my appointment."

She changed her dress, pulled on a cardigan, grabbed her pocketbook and was out the back door in minutes. The former carriage house now doubled as a garage with a playroom overhead for the kids. Fumbling for the button, she pressed the garage door opener and walked up to her shiny 1970 Rambler Rebel.

Tillie and Joe had given it to her as a house-warming present after Joe replaced the engine. "No self-respecting grandmother can be without wheels with three grandkids to taxi around," Joe had said.

A real beauty, too, metallic gold outside with an aging tan interior, once driven by the proverbial "little old lady from Wichita" and garaged all its life. And who wouldn't love a car named "Rebel," something she had never really been.

Annabelle had sewn new seat covers out of an old bedspread she'd found in the attic, making the seats warm and comfortable. No one liked the feel of vinyl on bare skin.

Regina had laughed when she saw them. "Mother's ghost probably haunted you for a week after you ransacked the attic, desecrating her property. Where did you find the fabric?"

"In Grandmother Morgan's cedar chest," Annabelle said. "Going to waste."

"The cabbage rose pattern is *so* you."

Annabelle had thought so, too. She drove to Dr. Miller's office with both hands clutching the steering wheel, shoulders hunched. Doc had retired six months ago, but not before he'd taken on a handsome young partner, Dr. Joshua Stamp. The sign still said Miller and Stamp, but Doc Miller spent his days on the golf course—rain or shine. She pulled up in front of the strip mall that housed their office and parked by the door.

Heaving a sigh, she scooped up her purse and went inside, five minutes early. A buzzer sounded in the back as she entered the empty waiting room. Annabelle noticed the intermingled aromas of flowers, antiseptic and the receptionist's perfume.

She must bathe in the stuff, like an eighty-year-old Avon lady. I'm glad we're not in an elevator . . .

"That you, Annabelle?" Rachel called from the back. "Be right there."

Annabelle sat in front of the window watching the cars zip by on West Thirteenth Street. She glanced toward the back hallway where Rachel emerged, popping a wad of pink gum.

What a bad habit for a woman in her fifties.

Medium height and chunky, Rachel had brown streaks through her gray hair. She dressed nicely, but she always had gum in her mouth that showed when she talked.

"Hi there. Come on back to room two. Doc will be in with you in a minute." Motioning Annabelle to follow, Rachel held open the door, slipping a chart in the slot outside.

'Pop' goes Rachel's gum and my last nerve.

Once inside the tiny room, Annabelle sat on the visitor's chair instead of the exam table with its cold metal stirrups. She clutched her purse in her lap, taking slow deep breaths. "What in the devil are you afraid of?"

The door clicked open and a Johnny Depp look-alike walked in. He held out his hand to her, "Good morning, Annabelle. How's my favorite patient?"

She felt heat rise in her cheeks.

He's so cute.

"I'm fine, Dr. Josh."

"I don't think so."

"I suppose." She slipped a tissue from her bag, folded it and began dabbing her damp palms.

"Tell me, how are you really?" He used his feet to roll his stool to a spot a scant foot in front of her.

"I'm tired all the time." She fisted her hands.

"Understandable, you've got three grandchildren at home. You're supposed to be enjoying your empty nest years, not traipsing all over town herding teens." He took her chin in his hand, quickly flashing a light in one eye then the other. "What else?"

"I've been having a lot of heart burn."

"Are you eating spicy foods?" He checked each ear.

"Not really. I just feel pressure in my chest. Sometimes, I find it hard to breathe." She watched as he scooted across the room, grabbed a wooden tongue depressor and crab walked back, never rising from the stool.

"Say, 'Ah'." He looked inside her mouth.

"I think it's time we did some tests. Let's make sure there's nothing seriously wrong. Once we rule out the bad stuff, then we'll see what kind of annoying little thing it could be." He pulled a pen out of his pocket to write in her chart.

"When?" Annabelle asked.

"How about now?"

"So soon?" She watched him roll his stool back into the corner of the room and open the door.

"Rachel, get Shelley for me please. Annabelle needs a few tests."

Annabelle stared, her heartbeat thudding in her ears.

What now?

Chapter 2

LONG BLACK-AND-SILVER waves of hair cascaded over the pillow and onto the sheets. Regina smiled at the ceiling, content, while Sam circled her nipple with his huge finger. In the past year she had learned how to love, not only the bear-like man beside her, but love herself as a woman. At fifty-nine, she'd discarded the men's pajamas she'd always preferred. Now, she reveled in the feel of cool cotton sheets upon her warm, bare skin and the feel of hot flesh against flesh.

Warm moist breath sent goose bumps shimmering up her body.

"Go away, Sugar, you're distracting the object of my attention," Sam said.

Regina scratched the Labrador Retriever under her silky neck. "Good morning, sweetie."

The white haired hunk beside her snorted, "Fine, say good morning to the canine and just ignore me." The bed rocked as he turned away.

"Go lay down, baby girl, I have something to attend to," Regina said. Taking her time, she rolled to face Sam. Sliding her arms around his waist, she scooted into his warm back, tucking her knees behind his.

"Good morning." Her breath blew on the back of his neck.

"Hi."

Wiggling against his backside, she felt his breath catch, then escape with a sigh.

"You're happy, aren't you, Reg?" He cradled her arm against his body.

"Ahuh." She kissed his broad shoulder.

"You know I love you."

"I know. I love you, too." She stroked his stomach.

"Then, marry me." He turned his head to look over his shoulder.

"Sam, darling, we are married." She kissed his cheek.

"Not legally." He sighed then turned away.

"Common law marriage is legal in the state of Kansas, is it not?"

"Yes, but we have to pool our resources, present ourselves as a married couple, file joint tax returns and cohabitate. The latter we do, but . . ."

"No, buts, Mister. We don't need a piece of paper to declare our love. So what if we each have our own money? Financial security isn't an issue.

What *is* the problem, my fine man?" She found herself inching away, the cool air a shock to the fire between their bodies.

Regina felt her ardor start to cool. How a man of Sam's strength could be insecure, she'd never understand.

"It just feels temporary, that's all."

"Darling, we're almost sixty, and life is temporary. Let's enjoy each other and not complicate things with papers and promises. For the first time in my life, I feel real love. That won't go away."

He rolled over to face her. "You're right, of course. I have to go to work today. Want to make me breakfast?" He slipped a lock of her hair behind her ear.

"How do you want your Grape Nuts? With milk or yogurt?"

"Surprise me." Rolling out of bed, he headed toward the shower.

Regina stretched, smiling at the creaks in her knees. She might be considered mature, but she was pretty fit. She'd always been blessed with a tall slender frame, unlike her chunky cousin, Annabelle.

Sugar padded back into the room and gave a quiet *woof.*

"I'll bet you're ready for breakfast, too, aren't you, girl?" Regina rolled onto her feet, slipping Sam's tee shirt over her head. It hung off of one shoulder, covered her to mid thigh, smelling of aftershave and his wonderful scent.

It doesn't get much better than this.

She put the coffee on and set out a bowl of cereal. Regina leaned against the counter braiding her hair into one long rope of black and gray, watching Sugar gobble her kibble until Sam joined them in the kitchen.

"You look pretty good in my undershirt, woman." He slipped his arm around her waist, kissing her neck.

Eying the starched shirt, crisp gray slacks and polished loafers, Regina grinned. "You don't look bad yourself."

He patted her behind then raised an eyebrow. "My, you're getting quite liberated. No panties for Regal Regina?"

Chuckling, she said, "It's about time, don't you think? Mother never allowed me out of my room without 'proper attire.'"

"I'm glad my dad was her lawyer. I don't think I would've liked your mother much. She was gone when I took over the business. I've heard you and Annabelle both speak of her coldness. I just can't see how such a frigid woman could have borne such a hot daughter." His blue eyes crinkled, but he forced the corners of his mouth from turning up too far.

"Flattery will get you everywhere." Regina sat down beside him. She sipped her coffee while he ate.

"Beautiful, elegant, Mother was like a porcelain doll. Deep down I really wanted to be more like her sister. Aunt Rose was more free-spirited."

"More like you are now." Sam picked up her hand and kissed the palm. "You're a beautiful mix of both."

"Thank you, Sam. That's the best compliment I could ever have." Her sly smile suggested she'd be willing to thank him properly if only he'd ask.

"Now, don't you do that, or you'll have me cuddling up with you and not getting to work on time." He reached out, cupping her chin.

"Very well, off with you then. I'll see you later, but don't expect me to fix dinner, too. We'll eat out or you'll have to grill something. I have a blank canvas upstairs, with a picture forming in my brain as we speak."

"Very well, I'm off." Sam kissed the top of her head on his way out.

She sat for a few more minutes, enjoying the slurping sounds Sugar made over her bowl. Regina's paintings had been modestly successful, adding to the money her parents left her. She'd never wanted for anything in her entire life, except their affection. They were too busy with "society" to nurture their own child.

When the Lab finished, she tried to nuzzle Regina's arm.

"Oh, no you don't, Miss Slobber Lips. Let's wipe your mouth and get to work." Regina could just imagine her mother's cross words about filthy animals in the house. Victoria never knew the joy of animal companionship. Come to think of it, she couldn't recall her mother enjoying anything. Victoria had been a cold fish, and Regina had spent most of her life trying to be just like her.

What a waste.

Chapter 3

PEGGY TIPTOED UP the stair edges, hoping to avoid the squeaks. It's a good thing she'd checked herself in the mirror. Her grandmother would have a fit if she saw the state of her clothing and hair. She'd lost her brush. Finger combing had been useless. Her lips were swollen, her cheeks red. It had only taken Miles fifteen minutes to muss her up when they stopped to "make out" before he dropped her off on the corner.

Looking over her shoulder to check that the coast was clear, Peggy missed the last step. She dropped her books on a formerly sleeping Ms. Pickles, whose feline squall could be heard for blocks.

"Hello?" Annabelle called from the kitchen. "Peg, is that you?"

"Damn," Peggy cursed under her breath. Scooping up her books, she dropped her purse near the hissing cat. "Sorry, Ms. Pickles. Hi, Gram."

"You're a little late," Annabelle called from the parlor. "Did you miss the bus?"

"Yes," Peggy called over her shoulder. "I got a ride home."

"How was your day?"

"Fine." Peggy sprinted into her room and shut the door. Leaning against it, her chest heaved.

A soft knock made her jump.

"Peg, is something wrong?"

"No, Gram, I'm fine. I just need a few minutes alone. Tough day, you know?" The throbbing of her heart filled her ears.

"All right. I've got fresh chocolate chip cookies in the kitchen if you want some."

"Thanks." Peggy crossed to the dressing table, looking at herself in the mirror. What she saw looked guilty and thoroughly kissed. "Oh my god." Looking more closely at her neck, she gasped. *A hickey. I'll kill Miles Asher, I swear I will.*

Pulling off her wrinkled shirt, she searched for something with a collar. Discovering a white cotton button down with short sleeves in the back of her closet, she looked at her developing bust and grimaced. *It probably won't fit. Cripes. Gram is gonna kill me.*

I'll be sixteen in a few months and able to date without a crowd. I want to be alone with Miles. Now.

She placed a safety pin between the buttons, but the fabric still gapped. Brushing her hair over her ears, she turned her head to see if the hickey still showed. Hidden in the shadow of her collar, she had to be careful not to tuck her hair behind her ears. Megan and Tad would be home soon. While Tad did the male gender proud with his lack of observation skills, Megan made up for it. She noticed everything. In the past year she'd gotten more and more vocal about things, too. Her baby sister was coming out of her shell. Peggy hoped Megan would be too preoccupied to notice her neck, or at least be quiet about it. She took one last look in the mirror before heading downstairs to the kitchen.

The aroma of fresh baked cookies wafted to her. "How could I have missed this?" Taking a deep whiff, Peggy crossed the linoleum to the fridge to get the milk. The front door slammed, followed by a rush of feet coming down the hallway.

"I smell cookies!" Megan said.

Peggy began to pour three glasses of milk. "Do you want a glass, Gram?"

"No, thank you, hon, I'm fine." Annabelle paused to look thoroughly at her eldest grandchild.

Feeling the heat flood her face, Peggy dropped her chin so her hair would fall forward, hiding her throat.

Tad tossed his backpack in the corner of the room, flopping into a chair. "Hey, Gram." He gave her a lopsided grin, running his fingers through his spiked blond hair.

"Hey, yourself, young man. Did you wait for Megan's bus?"

"Yeah, ours was running late so I just hung out on the corner."

"Hi Gram, did you have a good day?" Megan asked.

"Busy, but much better now that you children are home."

Megan watched her grandmother lower herself to the empty seat.

"Did you miss us?" Tad said, stuffing his mouth with a cookie. "Too quiet around here?" It came out a jumble that was easily understood.

Peggy sat back in silence, afraid of drawing attention to her swollen lips.

"You look tired," Megan said. "Can we help you with anything?"

Snorting, Tad said, "Gee, thanks, Meg, I really needed you to volunteer me for chores."

When Tad started complaining, Peggy couldn't keep still. "It's about time you did something around here, Tadpole."

"Bite me," he responded.

"Tad!" Annabelle said. "I don't want to hear you say that again."

"Sorry." His eyes narrowed as Peggy smirked.

"It would help a lot if you three would put your things away. The clutter is getting a bit deep." Annabelle sighed, looking in the direction of the backpack. "We're dog-sitting this weekend. I don't want Regina to see this place like it is right now. She'd pitch a fit."

Tad dragged a finger across his throat.

Megan giggled and bit into her cookie, a milk mustache decorating her upper lip.

"You should know," Peggy said. "I thought she'd clobber you when you messed with her paintings last year. Adding mustaches to all the portraits was the stupidest thing you could do."

"She was kinda mad," he said, his ears reddening.

"More like scary." Megan shivered. "But Tillie showed us how to clean them off without ruining the faces."

Their grandmother interrupted the conversation before it got out of hand. "Never mind, that was a long time ago. It doesn't pay to look back. We aren't going that way." Annabelle looked off into space.

"Wow, Gram. You're, like, philosophical," Peggy said.

"Not really, hon, just realistic. That was one of my Grandmother Morgan's favorite sayings."

The children finished off the plate of cookies, draining their milk, being quiet for a change. Annabelle felt numb, totally preoccupied with her own concerns.

After being reminded, they deposited the dirty dishes in the dishwasher. The younger kids headed up the stairs, the noise level decreasing as they went.

Hanging back, Peggy stood in the doorway looking at her grandmother. "You okay?"

"I'm a little tired. Maybe we'll order pizza tonight."

"Better order two. Tad seems to be trying to fill his size twenty feet. He'll be taller than me before long."

And I don't need him towering over me. I am the oldest.

"You're all growing up so fast." Annabelle struggled to smile.

"I'm sorry we don't help as much as we should. I'll talk to the kids. We'll do better, I promise." Peggy crossed the room in quick strides, wrapping her arms around her grandmother's soft neck. "We love you, Gram."

"Oh, hon," Annabelle said, patting her thin arm. "I love you three very much. This past year's been wonderful, but it's gone by so fast. You'll all be grown up and gone before I know it. Then I'll be a lonely old woman with a three-legged cat."

Ms. Pickles raised her head from the curl she'd made of her body on the rag rug and sneezed.

"Unless Megan takes the cat, that is." Annabelle smiled.

"Don't worry. We'll be around quite awhile yet. So will you."

"You're probably right. I'm just a little past middle age, *if* I live to be a hundred and thirty." Annabelle planted a kiss on her granddaughter's cheek. "Thank you."

Peggy unwrapped herself and followed after her siblings.

Gram looks worried. I wonder if she saw my hickey? Surely she would've said something if she had.

Shaking her head, Peggy moved down the hallway to her brother's room. "Tad, let's help more around here. Gram looks beat."

He studied his sister's face before responding. "She is kind of old, isn't she? I'll try to be more careful about leaving my stuff lying around, but I'm a guy you know. How long is this going to take? I can't like, change who I am."

"You can try, dweeb."

Going back to the room she shared with Megan, Peggy closed the door, crossing to the bed. The room smelled like freshly washed cotton.

The therapist said Megan's old enough to have her own room, but whenever she tries to sleep in another room she has bad dreams, ending right back here with me. We're both older now. I need my space. I'll see if Megan is ready to try again.

Her sister sat in the middle of the pillows, a book in her hand and a faded, stuffed dog under her arm. Her eyes were open wide.

"Something's wrong with Gram," Megan said.

"She's just tired. We need to help her more, that's all." Peggy lay down on the pillow beside her little sister.

"It's more, I can feel it. She's hurting."

Gazing into her little sister's gentle brown eyes, Peggy wondered just how much she really felt. Gram took care of Megan from the time she was born, when their father had split for good and their mom was at work. When she came home, she drank. Stale sweat, cigarettes and liquor hung on her mother like a cloud. Those were the smells she associated with Liddy. That, and the sound of glasses breaking in the sink where they'd been thrown, or the bone in Tad's arm when she'd snapped it.

"I hope she's not."

Handing her sister the stuffed animal, Megan stuck her thumb in her mouth, curling into Peggy's side.

"Come on, Megan, don't suck you're thumb. You're *way* too big for that."

She pulled her thumb out of her mouth and hugged her big sister.

Patting Megan's back, Peggy fought the unshed tears. "It'll be okay, don't worry." But, Peggy's chest felt tight and her stomach began to hurt.

What now? And what am I going to do about Miles? I'm not sure I'm ready to give in, but he makes me feel so . . . special.

Chapter 4

THE NEXT MORNING, Annabelle parked a block away from the law office with the hope that if Regina drove by she wouldn't notice the Rambler. Shuffling down the sidewalk, moisture dampened her upper lip. Breathing was a challenge.

A buzzer sounded when she entered the front door of the offices of Duncan & Duncan, Attorneys At Law. Rising from her chair, the receptionist frowned as Annabelle approached. "Hello, my name is Annabelle Hubbard. I'd like to see Sam Duncan, if he has a couple of minutes, please."

"I don't believe you have an appointment." The woman looked down her skinny nose with a disapproving frown. The nameplate on her desk read "Marvel."

What kind of a name is Marvel?

Straightening her spine, Annabelle said, "No, I don't. It shouldn't take long, if you'd just let him know I'm here." Obviously, this woman screened would-be clients. She'd only seen Sam once professionally, a little over a year ago to get custody of the grandchildren, so this woman didn't know she and Regina were related.

Marvel picked up her phone with long, well-manicured fingers. "Mr. Duncan, there's an Annabelle Hubbard to see you. She *doesn't* have an appointment." Her frown deepened, "Very well." She patted her lacquered brown hair then smoothed her pencil skirt before coming around the desk. "Come with me, please."

Annabelle followed the stick thin receptionist down a short hallway to the first door on the left, feeling all of her years and then some. Maybe she was further beyond the midway mark in her life, a scary thought. Looking down, she frowned at her comfortable shoes and baggy slacks.

I certainly dress like an old lady. I'd better rethink my fashion statement if I don't want to feel a thousand years old and look that way, too.

With a quick knock, Marvel opened the door, motioning for Annabelle to enter then clicked it shut behind her.

"Annabelle!" Sam met her at the door, enveloping her in a huge bear hug. "How nice of you to drop by." He looked closely into her face then led her to one of the leather visitor chairs in front of a massive cherry wood desk. "Have a seat. Would you like a glass of water? You look a little flushed."

Giving her lip a quick pat with her ever-present tissue, Annabelle smiled. "That would be nice, thank you."

Walking to the credenza where a silver coffee service and crystal pitcher of water perched, he poured her a glass, returning to sit in the visitor chair across from the one Annabelle now occupied. "Here you go. Now tell me, what's up? You weren't just in the neighborhood, were you? Are the kids okay?"

She hesitated. "The kids are fine, but I'm not. I haven't been feeling well, so I went to see the doctor. He says my heart is in bad shape. I'm supposed to talk with a cardiologist tomorrow."

"Oh, Annabelle." He clasped her hands in his. "I'm sorry. What can I do to help? Do you want me to talk with Regina?"

"No. Not yet, anyway." Her tissue was now a twisted rope around her fingers. "What I want is a will. The kids have to be taken care of legally."

He sat back in the chair, pulling a pen from his pocket and a pad from the top of his desk. "Don't worry, we'll work something out to take care of the kids."

"It has to be Regina. She's the only family they have left." Annabelle's hand shook as she took a drink.

Scrubbing through his thick white hair, Sam said, "Have you talked with her about this?"

"There hasn't been time."

"What about right now?" He reached over to get the receiver.

"No. I think she's painting. Sam, there isn't anyone else. Regina's strong enough to protect the kids. It's got to be her. But, I can't face her right now."

"What about their father? He's still living, isn't he?"

"Tom's been gone ten years. Why would he come back after this long?" Tears slipped down Annabelle's cheeks.

"I'm not sure I should be doing this. It could be a conflict of interest, especially considering my relationship with Regina. I'll recommend someone else to you."

Annabelle tried to stem the flow with her already soggy tissue.

They can't tell you no if it's already done.

"Please, won't you draw something up right away? I'll call Regina, I promise."

"Surely you can wait a couple of days? Talk to the cardiologist. See what he has to say. I'll call Bob Schultz, he's a good friend of mine. He'll help you draw up a Power of Attorney with an Appointment of Guardian." Sam patted her clutched fingers.

"But he's not family like you are, Sam. I'm afraid to wait. Please do this for me. If the doctor says it's a false alarm, we can talk to this Schultz fellow. I'll call Regina, but in the mean time I want to make sure the kids are protected." She straightened her spine and lifted her chin. "Please."

With a sigh, Sam squeezed her hands. He walked around the desk and sat, pulling a form from one of the bottom drawers. He began writing then lifted his head to look her in the eye. "Are you sure you can't wait?"

"No. Now, please," she whispered.

You've really worked yourself into a tizzy. Now calm down before you scare the man to death. You aren't dead yet.

He put his pen to the paper, filled out the requisite information then pushed it across the desk toward her. "This is a basic Power of Attorney, which stipulates that if anything should prevent you from functioning to full capacity, Regina Morgan-Smith will be appointed as attorney and for the care of Peggy, Tad and Megan Malone."

"Fine." Annabelle glanced over the form. "Where do I sign?"

He picked up the phone and hit a number on the keypad. "Marvel, please come into my office to witness a signature. Bring Jim, the file clerk, will you?" He held Annabelle's gaze for a moment until she dropped her eyes to her lap.

"As soon as Marvel and Jim come in, you can sign at the bottom. Then they'll sign it."

The door opened to admit the frowning receptionist and a strapping young man. They stepped up beside the desk, watched as Annabelle signed the document and slid it over to them.

Marvel sniffed, signing with a stiff hand. Annabelle then handed it to Sam who added his signature. "Thank you, Marvel and Jim, that will be all."

Waiting until they were alone again, Sam and Annabelle stared at each other.

She stuffed her tissue in her purse. "Thank you."

"You know, if your heart doesn't kill you, Regina will."

She couldn't meet his eyes. "I know. I'm sorry. I've put you into a bad position. I'll explain it all to her later, I promise."

"It'll be okay, don't worry. Go home and rest. Make sure to give Regina a call today." He stood, offering her his hand. "Do you need us to change our plans for the weekend?"

She allowed him to help her stand. "I'm probably being overly dramatic. The kids would love to see your dog. Please don't let my paranoia ruin your weekend."

Giving her hand an affectionate squeeze, he said, "If you're sure. We'll be over Friday to drop off Sugar. But if anything changes, let us know."

"Thanks." She smiled up at his warm face. "I forgot to ask, what are you two planning?"

"We're heading to Kansas City for a stage play and there's an exhibition at the Nelson-Atkins Art Gallery we plan to see."

"Sounds nice. Thanks, I feel better just knowing the kids are taken care of."

He dipped his head in a slight bow. "Everything will be fine."

"Bye." Annabelle exited the office.

Once outside she took a deep breath, squinting into the sun. "He's a good man." She walked down the street to her car, slid in behind the wheel and pressed a fist into her chest. "Hang in there, goof ball. You'll have an anxiety attack if you don't calm down."

On the drive home she noticed the time on the bank sign. She had an hour to rest before the kids got home from school. Leaving the car in the driveway, she mounted the front steps, her keys already in hand. The phone rang. She unlocked the door, leaving it open as she dashed for the extension in the parlor.

"Heh . . . low," she panted.

"Hello," a deep male voice responded. "Is this Mrs. Annabelle Hubbard?"

She gulped for air thinking he sounded familiar, but she couldn't quite place the voice.

"Mrs. Hubbard?"

"Yes. Who is this?"

"This is Assistant Principal Johnston, from the high school."

The hairs rose on Annabelle's arms. "Is Peggy okay?"

"I'm afraid Peggy has been skipping classes."

"What?" Annabelle sank down onto the sofa. "Do you know where she went? Or who she was with?"

"She's in my office now with Miles Asher. They will both have to serve detention either before or after school. I recall from last year that there was some trouble at home and she rides the bus. Would you be able to come into my office tomorrow so we can discuss a detention schedule?"

"Of course, what time?"

"Would ten o'clock work for you?"

"Fine, thank you for calling." She hung up the phone, sighing.

What is Peggy thinking? What is she doing with Miles? What in the world is going on with that girl?

The phone rang again and she jumped, fumbling for the receiver.

"Hello."

"Hello." A raspy male voice responded. "Is this Mother Annabelle?"

"Pardon?"

Two strange men calling in one day is quite a record.

He cleared his throat. "Is this Annabelle Hubbard?"

"Yes. Who is this?"

"Don't you recognize my voice? It's your son-in-law, Tom."

Sweat broke out on her brow. "Tom?"

"That's right. I'm sorry I haven't called sooner. I just heard that Liddy died. Are the kids okay?"

"They're fine." Annabelle laid her head back. She pictured him in her mind. Tall, thin but muscular, his brown hair thick and his gray eyes the color of storm clouds. "What do you want?"

"I want to see my kids."

"They've gotten along fine without you for ten years." Annabelle ground her teeth together. "What do you really want?"

"They're my kids." Tom sighed. "Didn't you get my letters?"

"What letters?"

"Huh. Well, I wrote a dozen times at least."

Her head began to ache and an invisible hippo just settled on her chest. "We never got them. Where have you been?" She couldn't keep the bitterness from her voice.

"Oh, man. To hell and back is the best way to describe it."

"And why are you here now? It's been years. The kids are doing good—your returning will just confuse them."

Her imagination began running wild. She couldn't let him get his hands on the children. Megan didn't even know him and was beginning to blossom. Tad would be vulnerable to whatever this loser would expose him to. Peggy was just discovering herself. Granted she was on the verge of discovering the power of her sexuality, but Tom would probably—she really had no idea what he would do or not do.

"I'm the kids' legal guardian, Tom. You can't have them. It's not enough to just make the babies. Go away." Annabelle dropped the receiver into the cradle.

Lord, her head was splitting. She hurt all over. Sliding down on the sofa, she tried to calm her breathing. Leaning on one elbow, Annabelle reached for the phone. Her fingers remembered Tillie's number.

"Hey, there," Tillie said.

Annabelle gasped and the receiver toppled to the floor. The heel of her hand pressed on her chest to hold her heart in. The last thing she heard over the pounding of her heart was Tillie's voice calling her name before everything went black.

Chapter 5

PEGGY MET TAD as he jumped off the bus at the corner of Riverside Drive near the park. The pear trees had bloomed out and now were turning green. The tiny white petals littered the ground like flattened snowflakes.

"Are you crazy?" Tad asked his older sister.

"About what?" His tone startled her.

"Letting Miles leave a mark on your neck."

She pulled her hair forward to cover the fading hickey.

"I didn't know he was leaving a mark. Jeez, Tad, you're not that much younger than me. Haven't you ever kissed a girl and gotten carried away?" They walked down the sidewalk toward the three-story Victorian they called home.

"I never tried to suck her blood through her skin! Besides, it's none of your business what I've done or not done. You're not my mom." He stepped off of the sidewalk, putting more space between them.

"I'm the oldest. I'm supposed to keep you out of trouble," Peggy said, straightening her shoulders.

"I'm not the one with a purple neck or the one who needs a keeper. Maybe Butch "the Bruiser" Butkas can be your body-guard." His grin troubled his sister.

Their long legs ate up the length of the sidewalk, bringing them to the front porch.

"Don't you dare say anything to Butch. He's a lunatic. Just drop it, please. I'll be more careful." Her finger made an "X" across her chest. "Promise. Besides, right now that's the least of my problems."

"What did you do now?"

"I got caught skipping today. The AP called Gram." He didn't need to know who she'd been with.

"Oh, man, you do need a keeper. Were you with Miles?"

She looked at her feet. "Yeah."

"Idiot." He shook his head.

They mounted the steps to find their neighbor and friend, Joe Linden, sitting alone on the porch swing in the shadows. Although retired from the Air Force, he was still fit, wearing his gray hair cut short.

"Hiya, Joe," Tad said. "You lost?"

He stopped the swing, but remained seated. The grim look on Joe's handsome face penetrated Peggy's self-absorption.

"Where's Tillie? What's wrong?" Peggy threw open the door. "Gram? Gram! We're home." She dashed inside, her panicked voice seeming to echo off of the walls. She stopped to listen for a response, hearing her brother's words instead.

"What's going on?"

Joe rose from the creaky swing. "Let's go get your sister."

The man and boy stepped inside and met Peggy at the bottom of the staircase.

Her cheeks were hot, her skin moist with perspiration. "What's happened?"

"Let's go into the living room for a minute," Joe said.

"NO! Tell us what's wrong!" Peggy began to sweat even more.

I didn't mean to get into trouble. Could Gram have gotten mad enough to leave?

"Your grandmother's had a heart attack. She's at *Via Christ St. Francis.*"

Collapsing at the bottom of the stairs, Peggy sobbed. "Is she . . . dead?"

We've already lost our mom. Dad's been MIA for a decade. We can't lose Gram now, too.

"No, but she's in critical condition," Joe said.

"Can we go to her?" Tad asked.

"Not quite yet. Let's let the doctors do their jobs. We'll go to see her when she's stable." Joe squeezed Tad's shoulder.

Using his sleeve, Tad wiped the silent tears that fell.

They all turned when they heard footsteps on the porch.

"Megan." Peggy stood, brushed the tears off of her cheeks, and straightened her t-shirt.

Their little sister's smile faded as she stepped into the foyer. "What's going on?" Her brown eyes were huge in her small round face.

Joe squatted down in front of her, holding her cool hand in his. "Your Gram is sick."

"Is she in the hospital?" Megan asked.

"Yes. Tillie is with her."

Withdrawing her hand, Megan walked into the room, hung her backpack on the newel post and sat on the bottom step. Peggy and Tad sat down on either side of her, like bookends. They put their arms around her. Megan's solemn face was devoid of tears.

Peggy smoothed her little sister's brown hair.

"Will you take us to see her?" Megan asked.

"I don't think they'll let us see her for a while," Joe said.

Her eyes glistened, but no tears fell. "We need to be there. Before it's too late."

"She'll be okay." Tad patted her knee. "She's a tough lady."

"Yeah, she's handled tougher stuff than this." Peggy spoke with a confidence she didn't feel.

Megan slipped her hand into Joe's. "Please take us now, Uncle Joe. She needs us."

Picking her up into a big hug, Joe blinked back tears. "Okay, sweetie, we'll go, but they might not let us see her for a little while."

Following them out of the house, Peggy locked the front door. She wiped her eyes, stomping down the porch stairs to cross the street.

All we've ever been able to count on is each other and Gram. What will happen to us now?

"Life sucks." Tad kicked a stone from his path before sliding into the front passenger seat of Joe's SUV.

"Did someone call Regina?" Peggy asked.

"I'm pretty sure Tillie did, honey. She'll probably meet us at the hospital."

Megan squirmed in the back seat. "I forgot to check on Ms. Pickles."

"I'm sure she's fine," Joe said.

Her hands clasped in her lap, Megan said, "She'll be worried about Gram, too."

Peggy and Tad exchanged a glance.

Questions filled Peggy's mind.

What did their little sister really understand? Was she so close to their Gram that she could feel their grandmother's pain? That was too weird to even think about.

Joe looked into the rearview mirror. "Try not to worry."

"Yeah, right." Tad slapped the front seat. "It's probably that hickey that broke her heart."

"Shut up, Tad," Peggy said, anger building.

"Hickey?" Joe glanced at the older kids.

"What's a hickey?" Megan asked.

"Oh, God." Peggy covered her face with her hands, her purple nail polish stark against the white skin of her fingers.

"What's a hickey?" Megan asked again.

Joe cleared his throat. "It's kind of a bruise."

"Oh. That doesn't make any sense. How can Peggy's bruise hurt Gram's heart?"

Tad's head snapped around as he stared at his baby sister, "You don't make sense, either."

"Leave Megan alone." Peggy was glad the focus had shifted from her.

Megan sniffed back tears.

Putting his head down, Tad moaned. "They're both crazy."

"Everyone's just upset," Joe said. "We'll find out what happened when we talk with the doctor."

They rode the last few minutes in silence. When Joe pulled into the emergency room parking lot, Tad jumped out, dashing through the sliding glass doors. By the time the girls and Joe arrived, Tad sat in a waiting room chair beside Tillie, sulking.

"They won't let us see her," he said.

"She can't have visitors right now," Tillie confirmed.

"Then we'll wait." Joe sat down beside Tillie, putting his arm around her.

Megan sat beside her brother, but didn't speak. Heaving a sigh, she settled in to wait.

Pacing the room, Peggy fought back tears. "What's going on?"

"Let's go up to CICU and park in their waiting room. It's closer to your grandmother," Tillie said. "I just came down here to wait for you guys. It's altogether too quiet up there alone."

The sliding glass doors swished as Regina strode in, flipping her braid back over her shoulder. Sam was right behind her, a scowl on his face. She stopped in front of Tillie, put her hands on her hips. "Where's Annabelle? And what in the hell happened?"

Standing as tall as her five feet would allow, Tillie laid a hand on her friend's chest. "She's in CICU. She's had a heart attack, and that's about all we know. We're going upstairs to wait. Care to join us?"

Regina stepped over to the elevators. "Let's go."

Grasping Regina's arm, Sam whispered in her ear. "Wait just a moment, please. I have to speak with you."

She looked into his eyes, recognizing the seriousness of his request. Regina turned to Tillie. "We'll meet you upstairs in just a minute."

Megan tugged on Regina's hand. "We have to hurry. She's really bad."

Hunkering down, she hugged the young girl. "Don't you worry, honey. Your grandmother's a Morgan. We're made of sturdy stock. We'll see you up there in just a moment." She kissed Megan's cheek and turned her toward the elevator doors as they opened.

After they closed, she turned back to Sam and crossed her arms over her chest. "What is so urgent that it couldn't wait until after we've seen about Annabelle?"

A group of medical personnel were walking toward them. Sam motioned her into an alcove with a window overlooking the parking lot. He waited for the staff to leave, cleared his throat and gripped her hand. "You need to talk with Annabelle, right away."

"About what?"

"All I can tell you is—she has something to tell you."

"Did she call you? Why not Tillie, or me, for that matter?" She pulled her hand free, clenching it in a fist. "What is going on?"

Shoving his hands in his pockets, he stared into her flashing blue eyes. "Talk to Annabelle. She has something to tell you."

"What? Why? Sam, talk to me." Regina laid her hand on his broad chest. "Please, tell me."

"Honey, attorney-client privilege prevents me from telling you, I'm sorry." Taking her hand in both of his, he swallowed. "You have to trust me."

She pulled her hand free. "What the hell is this?"

"Honey, you have to talk to Annabelle."

Regina turned her back on him and faced the glass. "What could be so important that you can't talk about it? Unless . . ." Spinning on her heel, she faced him. "Is it the house? The kids? What?"

"You have to talk to *her.*" His normally ruddy complexion drained of color.

"Did she do something illegal?"

"No." He gently grasped her shoulders. "She can explain it to you, but I can't."

Regina twisted out of his grasp. The smell of cleansers and sickness clogged her nose.

"For pity's sake . . ." She twisted the end of her braid around her finger. "I don't have time for this nonsense."

"Just talk to her, okay? And trust me." His hands hung at his sides.

"How can I trust you when I don't even know what's going on? Cripes." Regina straightened to her full five-feet-nine-inches. "Tell me."

"I can't, you know that."

"Convenient." She pushed past him, jabbing the elevator button. "I'd appreciate it if you didn't come up with me just now." The bell dinged as the doors opened. "By the time I get up there . . . I don't want the kids to see . . . I need time to think, Sam, and right now you make that impossible."

"Okay. I'll see you at home tonight." Sorrow filled his eyes.

Regina punched the floor number, the doors closing on her last words. "Or not."

Her reflection in the brass wall plaque showed a grim woman. "Oh, hell." She patted her hair and wiped the tears she didn't realize had fallen.

When the doors opened, she exited into a quiet hallway. Turning toward the sound of voices, she proceeded to the waiting room. Joe stood when she entered.

"Where's Sam?" he asked.

"Called away," Regina lied. "Has the doctor been in?"

"Not yet," Tillie said. "We let them know at the nurse's station that we were here. I said we'd wait until we could speak to the doctor."

"Good." Regina crossed the room, squeezing between Megan and Peggy on the sofa. Tad sat alone in the corner. Joe and Tillie were in the chairs closest to the phone. A game show was on the television suspended from the ceiling, the sound turned low. Taking Megan's hand, Regina patted it. Megan laid her head on her shoulder, closing her eyes. "Don't worry, honey, she's tough."

Peggy slumped against Regina's other side. Regina reached up and smoothed her fine blonde hair. For nearly an hour they sat in silence, swirling in a whirlpool of their own thoughts.

The swishing sounds of paper-covered shoes preceded the doctor's entrance. "Are you Mrs. Hubbard's family?" he asked.

The expulsion of their collective breaths was audible. Regina stood. "Yes. How is she?"

He pulled the paper cover off of his hair and sat down on the sturdy coffee table. "She's stable. We found a blockage and inserted a stint."

"Will she recover?" Regina asked.

"She should, but we'll know better in the morning. For now, you should all go home, have dinner, and get some rest. I'll be around until she comes out from under the anesthesia."

"Can we see her?" Peggy asked.

"Not right now. If you want to come back after dinner . . . you can see her for a few minutes. And not all at once." He stood. "She needs to rest."

"Thank you, doctor," Tillie said. She put her arm around Peggy's shoulder.

Megan stood, reaching her hand out for the doctor to shake. "Thank you, sir." She turned, looking up at Regina. "She's sleeping. Let's come back later and bring her favorite nightgown."

A corner of Regina's lips lifted. "Good idea."

They filed out of the room, Tad bringing up the rear.

"Come on, Tad," Regina said. "Let's go get something to eat. I'll pack some things for your grandmother."

Tillie and Joe whispered to one another then asked, "May we join you?"

"Of course," Regina said.

Sliding up beside her friend, Tillie gave her a quick hug. "Hang in there, Regina Louise, I know how you hate hospitals."

"I do. And if she survives this, I'm going to kill her."

"What's got your knickers in such a twist?" Tillie asked.

"Not sure yet. For now, let's just get through the night."

Chapter 6

THEY PUSHED THE food from one side to the other on their plates, with very little consumed. Conversation didn't exist, but the kids couldn't sit still for a second. The occasional sigh or sniffle broke the silence. Ms. Pickles sat guard in the doorway.

"Would you children please stop wiggling and eat your dinner? Or would you prefer to eat out of the hospital vending machines?"

"Stop being such a grouch, Regina. They're just anxious," Tillie said.

Regina scowled at her best friend.

When the clock struck eight, Peggy spoke for the first time. "Can we go to the hospital now? I'd really like to see Gram."

"Sure, honey, but visiting hours may be over," said Regina. "We'll clear the table and go."

The children scraped and bagged the trash in record time.

Joe stood at the door. "We'll drive the SUV. Any of you kids want to ride with us?"

"I do." Tad followed them out.

Picking up her purse, Regina led the two girls to her bright red Cadillac.

The ride to the hospital was quick and quiet. The two groups met up in the parking garage and continued to the elevators, then up to the eighth floor. Regina pushed the buzzer.

"CICU, may I help you?" said the disembodied woman's voice.

Regina spoke into the intercom. "Annabelle Hubbard's family to see her."

"How many are there?"

"Four family, two friends," Regina replied.

"Only two family members at a time for no more than fifteen minutes. Only family is allowed in CICU."

"Very well." Regina turned to face the others.

"Tillie and Joe are family." Megan took Tillie's hand in hers.

"Thank you, sweetheart," Tillie said. "We can see her later. Right now, we'll just hang around in case you need anything."

"Okay." Megan said.

The door lock clicked.

Peggy took Tad's hand. "We'd like to go first."

"All right. Megan and I will wait for you," Regina said.

PEGGY FELT SMALL entering the hallway filled with the quiet whirs and beeps of machinery. And it smelled like heavy-duty cleaner. Curtained alcoves lined one wall, while rooms with windows lined the other. The nurse's station stood sentinel midway between them. Tad and Peggy approached the desk.

"Annabelle Hubbard, please," Peggy said, straightening to her full height.

A middle-aged woman in turquoise scrubs pointed across the hall toward a green and white striped curtain. "Are you eighteen? Children must be accompanied by an adult."

"Yes," Peggy whispered, her eyes warning Tad to keep his mouth shut.

The nurse spoke, "Keep your voices down. Don't stay longer than fifteen minutes."

Peggy nodded, pulling Tad in the direction the nurse had pointed. Grasping the curtain, the young woman hesitated before easing it back enough to see the person lying in the bed. "Gram?"

Their grandmother lay with tubes coming out of her nose and arms. Monitors surrounded the bed with yellow numbers, lines that blinked or moved across the screens.

Her hair stuck straight up in the back from lying so long on the pillow, looking blue in the lights of the machines. Annabelle's skin was as colorless as the sheet. Opening her eyes, she blinked as if to clear the fog. "Peg? Tad?"

"We're here, Gram," Peggy said. They crossed to the bedside. Peggy's shaking hand paused in mid-air, as if a force field prevented her from touching the wrinkled fingers she loved. Neither one of her grandmother's hands were unencumbered by gadgetry.

Tad laid his head on his grandmother's stomach, hugging her.

Annabelle lifted her hand a couple of inches off the bed and Peggy gave it a squeeze. "How ya doing?" Peggy asked.

Their grandmother cleared her throat but her voice came out raw. "I've had better days." She patted Tad's head, tugging at the tape and tubing. "Don't fret. You'll be fine."

An angry scowl on his face, Tad said, "We're not worried about us. What about you?"

"Shush. The doctor said I'd be okay. Where's Regina?"

"She's outside with Megan," Peggy said. "We can only stay fifteen minutes, then they'll kick us out. Is there anything we can do for you?"

"No, just be good for Regina." She stroked Tad's spiky hair.

"We brought your nightgown," he said. "Figured it'd be nicer than those stupid hospital things that show your . . . behind." He disengaged himself from his grandmother and straightened his shoulders.

She smiled. "That's sweet. Thank you."

"Did we do something wrong?" Tad asked, looking at Peggy, disapproval emanating from every pore.

"What?" One of the lines on the monitor spiked.

"Is it because of us that you had a heart attack?" He stared at his older sister.

"No. You kids had nothing to do with it." The lines on the monitor rose and fell like the etching of a mountain range.

Watching her face, Tad nodded. "We're sorry."

"It's not your fault." She attempted to lick her lips. "Ice . . . please."

Peggy grabbed the cup and gave her grandmother a spoonful. Peggy felt hot, unable to look either of them in the eye.

Maybe I'm coming down with something. Can guilt cause a cold?

Annabelle's lids drooped as she let the ice melt in her mouth. "Thanks."

"Do you want us to bring your slippers, too?" Peggy asked.

Tad thinks it's my fault.

"That would be nice." Annabelle didn't open her eyes.

The curtain slid back and the desk nurse entered. "Time's up." She put her fingers on Annabelle's wrist, and looked at the clock.

"Love you, Gram," Peggy said.

"We'll be back," Tad said. "With your slippers."

"Love you both." Annabelle watched the blood pressure cuff fill with air.

They hurried out of the curtained room and down the hall to the double doors. The lock disengaged so the wooden portal could open. They were both anxious to be shed of the antiseptic smell and mechanical sounds. Tad made a dash for the waiting room to pour himself onto the sofa. Pacing the length of the room, Peggy hugged her chest and struggled to keep from crying.

It's my fault. If I hadn't got caught skipping school, this might not have happened.

"Fifteen minutes isn't any time at all," Tad said. "It's not fair. We should be able to stay with her if she wants us to."

"And I'm sure she does, but she needs to sleep, too." Regina patted his arm. "Come on, Megan, let's go say a quick hello."

"Watch out for the nurse. She's tough," Tad said. "She'll time ya."

Peggy sat down beside Tillie who squeezed her hand.

I'll make it up to you, Gram. I swear I will.

MEGAN TOOK REGINA'S hand, accompanying her to the entry to CICU. After they were buzzed in and found Annabelle, they slipped behind the curtain. Without a word, Annabelle reached out a hand to Megan, who climbed onto the hospital bed. She wiggled under the tubes in her grandmother's arm. Snuggling up to her grandmother's stomach, Megan sighed.

Standing at the foot of the bed, Regina spoke, "A heart attack? You've really done it this time. When were you going to tell me you had a weak heart?" She swept her arm around the room, encompassing the machines before finally settling her hand near Megan and dropping it to her side.

"Don't scold. Didn't have a chance to talk to you before this . . ."

"What's going on?" Regina crossed her arms over her chest.

"Where's Sam?" Annabelle asked.

"Off somewhere keeping secrets." Regina's hand made a dismissive flip in the air.

Laying her hand over Megan's ear, Annabelle whispered. "School called. Peggy's skipping classes. I'm supposed to meet with the assistant principal tomorrow."

"Oh?" Regina gripped the foot of the bed. "Is that what set this off?"

"I don't think so." Annabelle shook her head. "The second call was the real shocker."

"Who called the second time?"

"Tom."

"The kids' father?" Regina whispered. Megan's eyes were still closed, but she doubted her ears were. And getting her to leave her grandmother's side so they could talk privately was totally out of the question. "What did he want?"

"To see the kids." The lines on the monitor jumped up and down.

Regina shook her head, her dangly earrings tinkled. "After ten years?"

Megan lifted her head. "Why? He doesn't care about us."

Patting her cheek, Annabelle sniffed. "I don't know. Don't worry. You kids will be fine."

The little girl smiled. "I know that." Cuddling back into Annabelle's awkward embrace, she closed her eyes. "I'm not worried."

Exchanging looks over Megan's head, the cousins knew trouble wasn't just coming—it was already messing with the family. "Is this what you talked to Sam about?"

"No, I talked to him before, I mean, after the doctor told me . . . I asked him for a power of attorney. And for you to be guardian."

Shit.

"Time's up." The nurse said, pulling back the curtain. "What the . . . ? Young lady, you shouldn't be in that bed. Your grandmother's a very sick woman." Hands on turquoise covered hips, she glared at the visitors.

Megan hugged her grandmother's middle and whispered, "I love you," before scooting off the bed.

"No harm done. She was very careful." Regina took Megan's hand and turned to Annabelle. "We'll talk later. Right now, behave yourself."

"Take good care of my Gram," Megan said. She squeezed Regina's hand as they passed through the curtains and back out to the hallway. "That nurse sure is grumpy."

"That's her job. She's making sure no one tires out her patients."

"She's very good at it."

Coughing to hide her chuckle, Regina led her small charge to the waiting room and the anxious group.

Joe stood, giving Regina his seat. "How's our girl?"

"Oh, Joseph," Regina said, "She's weak and tired. We didn't see the doctor, so I don't know anything new."

"We saw the nurse," Megan said. "You're right, Tad. She's tough. Gram's going to be all right, I just know it."

The confidence in Megan's voice made Regina wonder what was going on inside that little girl's mind. Of the three children, Megan had always been the most like Annabelle, soft hearted. Regina said a silent prayer.

I hope for all their sakes Annabelle recovers and soon.

Tad shook his head. "Little sister, you are very weird, but in a good way." He dodged Peggy's punch, but not by much.

"Can we see her again later?" Peggy asked.

"Let's go home and let her rest. We'll come up in the morning before school," Regina said. "Tillie, do you and Joe want to come by the house for a while?"

Shaking her head, Tillie hugged her friend. "No, I think my man and I will go home. It's been a tough day for all of us."

"About tomorrow, I have a commitment, but if you want me to, I can cancel," Joe said.

"No, I'll come up after I finish at the bistro. You don't have to change your plans. Annabelle will probably be here a few days," Tillie said.

"Probably," Regina agreed. "Let's go kids."

"Go where?" Tad asked.

Megan slipped her hand back into Regina's. "Home."

Tad and Peggy got up from the waiting room couch.

"It'll seem weird without Gram," Tad whispered.

"A-huh. Nobody's been in Cousin Regina's room since she left. I'll bet the dust is pretty deep."

"Nope. Gram dusts it every week," Tad said. "I've seen her. It's weird, like she's been waiting for her to come back or something."

"Well, it *is* Regina's house."

"Do you think Regina will ever kick us out?" Tad asked Peggy.

"I don't know, but she could." Peggy caught up with Regina and Megan at the car.

"Don't worry, you two. We'll be back tomorrow," Regina said.

Megan got into the front passenger seat and buckled her seat belt. "Will you stay with us until Gram is all better?"

"Do you want me to?"

"Yes."

Looking in the rear view mirror, Regina saw Tad and Peggy exchange a look, but didn't know what it meant. She couldn't anticipate what might happen next in a house with two teens and a tween.

It's past time to have a long conversation with my cousin, Annabelle.

Chapter 7

THE HOUSE WAS quiet except for the ticking of the mantle clock. When it chimed two, Regina decided she'd lain awake long enough. Donning her robe, she slipped out of her room, pausing before Tad's door. Hearing no sounds, she stepped to the girls' door next.

Nothing.

Gliding down the stairs, Regina avoided the creaky spots and hoped no new ones had developed since she'd moved out. She'd missed the voice of the family house. It had kept her company for many lonely years after her parents then her husband died. Stepping into the parlor, Regina saw that the light of the moon had turned the room gray. The house seemed the same as the night she'd left. The portrait of her mother she had removed from the mantel had not been returned. That was the night Regina took control of her life, gave her family home to her cousins and moved in with Sam. Regina never had a single regret, until now.

"Oh, Sam." She pulled the robe closer around her. "Why couldn't you tell me what's going on?"

I can't think about Sam now.

Her thoughts roamed to when Annabelle showed up on the doorstep, battered and homeless, two years ago.

This family has had too much pain and loss.

Feeling a chill, Regina lifted the afghan off the sofa, wrapping it around her shoulders.

Maybe tea or warm milk will help.

Stopping in the kitchen doorway, her eyes scanned the cluttered room. Daylight would reveal just how much things had altered. "It doesn't matter. This isn't my home anymore."

Crossing to the cabinet, she pulled out a pan to warm the milk. "I'll use Tillie's recipe for a good night's sleep."

Reaching up to the top shelf behind the cookbooks, she took down a bottle of brandy that had been stored there forever. First, Grandmere had kept a bottle, her mother, then Tillie, now Annabelle. "Nice to see some traditions still exist."

Pouring a splash in the glass, she sniffed the amber liquid then downed it in one gulp. Liquid heat burned her throat, sliding down through her chest, into her stomach. She shivered at the sensation, capped the bottle and restored it to its hiding place.

The smell of warming milk told her it would scorch soon. So, she took her cup to the stove and turned off the burner. A tiny motor sounded as a silky gray form stepped between her feet.

"Hello there, cat. I see your nose works." Regina bent down to stroke the kitty's now arching back. "Sucking up? No need, I'll share." She poured part of the milk into the cat's bowl on the floor. The remainder went into her cup with a pinch of nutmeg and honey. "We ought to sleep after this, eh, Ms. Pickles?"

Pausing from her snack, tiny beads of milk dotted her whiskers. Ms. Pickles mewed in agreement before she resumed lapping.

"I miss Sam and Sugar." Regina pulled the afghan tighter and sat on the floor with her back to the cabinets. When Ms. Pickles finished, she balanced on her remaining back leg and used her front paws to clean her whiskers.

"You are a bit more tidy than Sugar, but I miss her none the less. Doubt you do, though. I've seen you watch her from a safe distance, of course. She just wants to play, you know."

Shifting her gaze to Regina's face, the cat sneezed in disagreement.

"Whatever. Let's get to bed." Regina got up from the floor, put her cup in the dishwasher, and led the way up the stairs. "If I can't sleep with Sam, I'll sleep alone, thank you." And she shut the bedroom door in the cat's whiskered face.

THE RINGING PHONE woke Regina. She glanced at the clock but couldn't read the numbers. She picked up the receiver. "This better be good."

"Excuse me," said a male voice she didn't recognize. "Who is this?"

"If you don't know who I am, then you've got a wrong number." Regina slammed down the phone. She had no more than pulled up the covers when it rang again. Snatching it up, she said through clenched teeth, "You have the wrong number."

"Doesn't Annabelle Hubbard live there?"

Regina sat up in the bed. "Yes. Who is this?"

"I'm her son-in-law, Tom Malone."

"What do you want at this hour?"

"Where's Annabelle? Is everything okay?" Tom asked.

"I was sleeping before some cretin called at dawn." She swiped the hair out of her eyes.

"Cretin? Aren't you Rebecca or Rosalind or something with an 'R'?

You were at Liddy's and my wedding."

"Yes, not that it matters, now. What do you want?"

He chuckled. "I want to see my kids."

"Bull! You just want trouble or money." Her hand clenched the receiver.

"I could definitely use some money. I'm between jobs. But I *am* family and I haven't seen my kids in a long time."

"Sperm donors don't count. Go away. Get a job. Then you can move somewhere tropical." She waved her hand in dismissal even though he couldn't see it.

"See, that's just the problem. Potential employers just aren't that understanding . . ."

"About what? Drinking? Drugs?" Regina knew full well that Tom had been either drunk or stoned while he'd lived with Annabelle's daughter, Lydia.

"Nah, I've been clean ten years now. But I do enjoy an ice-cold beer, now and again."

She rolled her eyes heavenward. "Go away, Tom. Hustle someone else." Regina hung up the phone.

It rang immediately. In full temper, she shouted into the receiver, "Leave us alone!"

"Regina?"

Sam's warm tone penetrated her anger.

"Sam?"

"Are you alright?" His voice was like cashmere, rich and soft.

"Yes. No. I'm sorry. I thought . . ." She folded the blanket back.

"You thought what? What's happened? What's wrong?"

"Nothing. I'm sorry I shouted." She sighed.

"I couldn't sleep so I went by the hospital early and caught the doctor."

She swung her legs over the side of the bed. "He talked to you? What did he say?"

"Yeah, I told him I was a cousin. He said that Annabelle's stable. But this was a warning."

"Damn. What did he suggest?"

"Bed rest for the next few days. No stress. When she's on her feet again she's supposed to start walking. Nothing strenuous. He'll send her home in a day or two if she continues to improve, but she'll need help with the house, the kids . . ." he trailed off.

"I'll do it." Regina fingered the cord.

"Sugar and I'll miss you. Regina?"

"Ahuh." Her thoughts jumped to Annabelle and the secret his oath had prevented him from revealing.

"Everything happened so fast . . ."

"I know. She told me." Regina smiled.

He'd always be there for her, for all of them.

"Do you forgive me?"

"What's to forgive? You did what she asked you to do. Now I'm glad you did." She walked to the window to see the morning break.

"You are?"

"Yes. The children's father called. That's who I thought was on the phone just now."

"I'm coming over."

"No, that's not necessary. We're going to the hospital before I take the kids to school. Annabelle had a meeting with the assistant principal later this morning, which I'll take for her. It would seem that on top of everything else, Peggy has been skipping classes."

"Then I'll bring Sugar. She'll protect you during the day. I'll come by each evening after work." Warmness filled her heart.

"Sam. Thank you, but no. I'll alert Joe and Tillie. They'll keep watch from across the street."

"What did Malone want?"

"The kids. Money, I think."

"There's not much the law can do unless he poses a threat."

"I know." She crossed the room and lay back across the bed.

"Reg, did you talk to Annabelle?"

"Yes, but Nurse Ratchet shooed us out before we could finish."

"Talk to her when you think she's strong enough, okay. Let me know if you need me to do something about Tom."

"If the bastard tries to get the kids, Ms. Pickles and I will scratch his eyes out." She glared at the ceiling, blue gray with predawn light.

"If he bothers any of you, call the police. Isn't he a substance abuser?"

"He used to be. I don't know about now. It's been a decade since anyone's seen or heard from him." Regina hugged the comforter, pulling it to her chin.

"Make sure the doors are locked and tell the kids to . . ."

"He's their father. What do I tell them?" She twisted the corner of the blanket around her fist.

"Talk to Annabelle, and see what she thinks. She knows the kids better than anyone."

"Good idea. I'll speak to her this morning. Will I see you later?"

"Damn right, woman. I love you."

"I love you, too." Regina hung up the phone. She sat up on the edge of the bed, worrying that they expected too much from Annabelle. If her cousin couldn't make a decision about Tom, she would be forced to do it for her. And what about Peggy? What did Regina know about teenagers? She didn't feel as though she'd ever even been one.

I would never have dared skip school. In fact, I never missed school at all. Time to pay more attention. If Annabelle's heart gives out, I'll be their guardian. Crap on a cupcake. I don't think I'm prepared for this. I can't just wing it. How does Annabelle do this day after day? No wonder her heart is tired. She's tougher than I ever gave her credit for. Now it's time to see what I'm really made of . . .

Chapter 8

DECIDING WHAT TO tell the kids weighed on Regina's mind.

How much should I say about Annabelle's condition? What should I say to Peggy? Should I mention their father? Will they want to see him after all this time? Too many questions and no answers.

"Regina?" Megan asked.

"Yes, dear?" Regina sat down her coffee cup and smiled.

"I tore the hem of my jacket. Could you sew it for me?" She held up the dangling edge.

"I'm afraid not. That's your grandmother's skill, not mine. Here, let's put a safety pin in it until she can fix it properly."

"Okay, thanks."

The little girl watched while Regina dug a safety pin out of the kitchen drawer, pinning the fabric back together. Tad and Peggy joined them at the table with wet heads and sleepy eyes.

"Let's sit down and eat a quick bite of breakfast. I need to talk to all of you." Regina straightened her gauzy skirt before relating the conversation Sam had with Annabelle's doctor.

She could almost see their minds churn as they listened to her retell what Sam had learned from the doctor.

"What else?" Peggy finally asked.

"It'll take a while to get her strength back," Regina said.

"What does that mean?" Tad crumpled his napkin.

"She'll have to go slow, taking it easy." Scanning their faces, Regina saw storm clouds building on Tad's.

"What do we have to do?" Tad asked, tossing the napkin on the table.

"We'll need to do the heavy lifting, laundry baskets and groceries." Regina said. "You'll need to keep your things picked up. We don't want to risk her falling."

"When will she be better?" Megan asked.

"If we can encourage her to take walks, she'll get stronger more quickly. And we'll have to revise the menu. No more pizza or high fat foods like burgers and fries. They're bad for the heart."

"I can't live without pizza." Tad scowled. "And no burgers or fries is un-American."

Regina struggled not to roll her eyes. The kids grabbed their backpacks and followed her out to the car.

"More fruits and vegetables, too, I'll bet," Peggy said.

"I don't like to eat green stuff. It always tastes like dirt." He glared at his giggling baby sister.

"Maybe we can make a grocery list once we find out the doctor's orders," Regina suggested.

"What about cookies?" Megan asked. "Would oatmeal raisin be okay? Gram says they're healthy."

"Well, maybe." Regina smiled.

Probably wouldn't hurt me to eat healthier, either.

Megan sat in the backseat, gazing through the window at the passing scenery. "Maybe she can help me walk Ms. Pickles."

"And she can walk with Tillie," Peggy said.

"Tillie hustles." Tad pumped his arms to illustrate. "She doesn't just walk."

Regina sent an icy stare over her shoulder. "She will probably slow down until your grandmother gets stronger."

Arriving at the hospital, they stopped at the information desk to get Annabelle's new room number.

"She's on the cardiac ward," the receptionist explained, writing the room number on a map for them.

"At least she's out of CICU," Peggy said. "We'll be able to stay longer."

"That's a good sign," Regina said. "We don't want to tire her out, though. Rest will help her body to heal."

"I thought we grow when we sleep," Megan said.

Regina smiled. "That's true for children, sweetie, but your grandmother's already grown."

"That makes sense. Can we take her flowers?"

"Absolutely. The gift shop is just around the next corner."

After making their purchases, Regina preceded the children into Annabelle's room. Each child had chosen something different. Tad placed a vase of yellow daisies on her nightstand. Peggy set an arrangement of purple Dutch irises and pink carnations on the windowsill. Megan's red rose bud took up residence on the bed tray.

"Oh, how beautiful," Annabelle said. "They smell so good. Thank you."

The children surrounded the bed while Regina stood to the side.

"Are you feeling better?" Peggy asked. "You look better without all those tubes everywhere."

Annabelle's eyes glistened. "I'm better now that I see your smiling faces."

"Is the food any good?" Tad asked.

She wrinkled her nose at him. "Not particularly."

"When will they let you come home?" Peggy asked.

"Soon."

"Regina thinks we'll all have to go on a diet and eat green things," Megan said.

"Oh, dear. I . . . well . . . I don't quite know . . . a nutritionist is supposed to come visit me."

"Will it make your heart better if we eat more cauliflower?" Megan said. "I don't like cauliflower. I think it smells funny and looks like the picture of a brain in my science book. I couldn't eat a brain."

Annabelle clutched a pillow to her chest and laughed so hard tears fell down her pink cheeks.

"Kids." Regina rifled her hobo bag for money. "Go back down to the gift shop. Get your grandmother a magazine and a crossword."

Peggy took the money at Regina's nod.

"But we just got here," Megan said. "I want to stay with Gram."

"I don't know anything about old lady magazines." Tad crossed his arms over his chest. "Why do I have to go?"

Peggy grabbed her siblings' arms and pulled. "We'll be back in a few minutes."

After the kids slipped out of the room, Regina waited for the elevator bell to ding before speaking.

"Sam talked with your doctor this morning. This episode was a serious warning."

"I know." Annabelle closed her eyes. "Don't scold."

Leaning over the bed rail, Regina said, "You're going to have to make some lifestyle changes immediately or the next one could be fatal."

"You're right, but it's not fair to the kids to make them eat baked chicken and steamed vegetables every day." Annabelle frowned.

"It can't hurt the kids to eat a more healthy diet." Regina straightened her spine. "I took inventory. You all eat way too much junk food. They can have it for special occasions, but every day isn't good for any of you. See what the nutritionist suggests."

"So, you're taking over for me?" Annabelle's eyes filled.

"No, it's just my opinion. Ask the doctor." Regina dropped her arms. "We'll get Tillie to help us create some heart healthy recipes that taste good."

"Okay. But . . ." Annabelle closed her eyes.

Reaching out, Regina patted her cousin's hand, the opaque skin splashed with age spots. "It won't be so bad."

"Tillie can make anything delicious." The corners of Annabelle's mouth lifted. The drab room brightened as the morning sun peeked around the building.

"Absolutely. The kids won't be deprived. They're smart. They'll adjust."

"Thanks."

Pulling up a chair, she leaned toward the bed.

"Tom called this morning."

"Oh, mercy," Annabelle said. "Maybe, we're being too critical." She turned to face her cousin, her frizzy hair flattened from lying on the pillow. "But, he can't have the kids. They don't even know him. I'm afraid, Regina. I'm in no condition to handle him right now."

"Don't worry. I'll be around. So will Sam. If that doesn't work, we'll sic Tillie on him." She squeezed her cousin's hand with care. "What do you want me to do about Peggy skipping school?"

With surprise, Annabelle's mouth dropped open. "You're asking me, not telling me?"

"Yes, but, if you want my opinion, I'll give it."

Annabelle closed her eyes for a moment before responding.

"I think Peg's afraid she may have caused my heart attack, so she's suffering right now. She already has to spend time in school detention. Let's see if that cures the skipping before we do anything more."

Nodding her head, Regina sighed. "We never would've dreamed of doing something like this when we were children."

When Annabelle opened her eyes, they were sad.

"That's true. When I get home I'll give the therapist a call. She may know what's going on in Peg's head. I'm just not sure."

Regina got up and paced the small space between the bed and the window.

"Okay. One more thing, what did you ask Sam to do? And why were you in such a hurry?" She wrapped her arms around her body.

"Doc Josh's warning scared my panty hose off. I got really paranoid and asked Sam to draw up a Power of Attorney."

"And?"

"And, make you guardian of the kids if I'm gone." Annabelle struggled to scoot up in the bed.

"That's what I thought you said yesterday. Good thing you're in here or I might just clobber you."

"I'm sorry." Annabelle stared at her cousin.

With a nod, Regina sighed. "I understand."

The elevator bell dinged and the children's voices and squeaking tennis shoes echoed down the hallway.

"Kids," Regina muttered, looking toward the ceiling, her hands upraised.

Tad and Megan tussled over the bag as they came into the room. Peggy snatched it out of their hands. "Kids," she said, handing it to her grandmother. "Smells good in here, like a flower shop."

Regina struggled not to smile. "Come on, you're going to be late for school."

"Can't we skip?" Tad asked, winking at his older sister.

"No, you can't." Regina and Annabelle said in unison.

Peggy's cheeks were crimson.

"Fine. It was just a thought, you know . . ." He stuffed his hands in his pockets.

The children each gave Annabelle a kiss and went out into the hall.

"We'll be back later." Regina followed them out. There was more activity in the hallways than when they'd arrived earlier. The smells of institutional food and antiseptic made her stomach flip-flop. "What a way to start the day."

"Did you say something?" Peggy asked.

"Not really. We'd better hurry."

Megan ran to keep up with the long strides of her companions, so Regina slowed her pace. "We'll drop you and Tad first, little one. I have business in the office at the high school."

She heard Peggy's intake of breath but kept her eyes straight ahead, leading her charges with purpose and no small amount of dread.

Chapter 9

TWO DAYS PASSED quickly for Regina, but not so for Peggy's detention. Wednesday broke with a mild drizzle and sixty-four degrees, the perfect temperature for spring in Kansas. Daffodils were popping their yellow heads and the greening tree buds almost made them look full again. Regina felt glad that Peggy could finally ride the bus and wondered what Annabelle's return home would bring. Joe and Tillie volunteered to pick her up from the hospital so Regina could stay at home to wait for the kids' buses.

She laid chocolate sandwich cookies in concentric circles on a china plate, placing it on the kitchen table. Pulling down four plastic tumblers, a necessary addition to the household since the children had broken most of the glasses, she smiled. Her mother never would've dreamed of using plastic. *"How gauche!"*

The clock struck three. She sat down in the window seat and watched for the two older kids. The neighbor's pear tree, now in full leaf, obscured her view to the corner. Through the crack in the open window, she smelled the sweetness of spring.

She heard the two teens long before she saw them pass by the tree. They were laughing. When they came into view they seemed to bounce down the sidewalk. Tad dodged the backpack Peggy swung at his head. Regina moved to the porch swing, hidden by the shadows and smiled again. *You missed out, Mother. Kids can be great fun.*

Peggy had resumed wearing her hair in a ponytail since her not-so-secret hickey—that no one spoke about—had disappeared. It swayed back and forth with each step. Regina worried that raging hormones would get the best of Peggy.

The corn colored spikes that normally crowned the top of Tad's head had wilted, but a smile lit up his face.

"Oh, stop." Peggy giggled. "You made that up."

"I did not." Tad thrust his chest out. "Katie said I was cute and kissed me. I swear." He pounded his chest with his fist.

"Well, Katie is a dope." Peggy pushed past her brother. "Hi Regina."

"Hello, you two." She stood and led them into the house.

The screen slammed, just missing Tad's heels. "Katie says I'm a hunk for my age."

"A hunk of what? Cheese?" His sister cackled.

Regina called over her shoulder. "How was your day?"

"Fun, no detention," Peggy said. "Thank God it's nearly summer. I need a tan."

"Yeah, whatever. We're finishing up stuff, cleaning and running relays during PE. I'll probably win a medal," Tad said.

"Right, the geek medal."

Regina hid her smile behind her hand. "There are cookies in the kitchen. Why don't you pour some milk, please, Peg?"

"Cookies? You baked? That's scary." Tad turned toward the food.

His sister poked him in the ribs. "Great. Thanks, Regina." She took her brother's arm and he dragged her through the dining room, the magnetic pull of sugar propelling them both. The time for pushing her "little" brother around was nearly gone. Peggy hissed between her teeth.

"What did I say?" Tad asked.

Regina heard the next bus, knowing Megan would be along shortly. All three of the children were different. Had her daughter Beth lived, she would be a few years older than Peggy and probably in college.

"Regina?" Peggy watched her brother's cheeks protrude from the number cookies he'd popped in his mouth at once.

"Hum?"

"Do you have a cell phone?" Peggy asked.

"No, but Sam does. He uses it for business. Why?"

"All of my friends have them. They're so nice for checking in and stuff. Don't you think I should have one for my birthday?"

"Gram can't afford it," Tad said, chocolate cookie coating his teeth.

The enthusiasm slid off the young woman's face. "You're probably right . . ."

A squeal of car tires drew her out of her musings. "What the devil was that?"

The older children were still verbally fencing in the kitchen when the clock struck the quarter hour. Something wasn't right. Regina pressed the heel of her hand on the knot forming in her stomach. Walking out on the porch, she went down the steps and followed the short walk to the curb. Once she'd cleared the neighbor's bushy pear tree, she looked down the street. The bus was still parked at the corner, its warning lights flashing. She checked her watch. Three-seventeen. "Where is that child?"

The screen door banged against the jamb.

"Isn't that Megan's bus?" Peggy asked.

"Whassup?" Tad said.

Regina shaded her eyes with her hand, her forehead creased.

The three of them started walking down the sidewalk, the pace picking up with each step. A crowd of neighbors gathered as kids spilled from the bus. The sound of a siren some distance away caused them to break into a run, Regina trailing behind. Tad's long legs ate up the distance to the corner in a hurry. Panting, Regina caught up to the older siblings.

"Excuse me, excuse me." Tad shoved his way forward, Peggy at his heels.

"Where's Megan?" Peggy shouted.

Even with all her height, Regina couldn't see what lay in the street. *Oh my God . . .*

She wouldn't finish the thought. Regina shouldered her way through the crowd. Sweat and accumulated body odor assaulted her nose.

Peggy and Tad were kneeling over the prone body of their little sister. Tad stroked Megan's hair while Peggy held her inert hand.

"It was my job to protect her." Tad choked on the words.

One leg was twisted like a broken doll. Blood dripped from the abrasions on Megan's forehead into her hair and onto the pavement. Road-rash dotted with blood and pebbles covered her exposed flesh. Her eyes were closed. Megan's chest looked distended.

Oh wait, her backpack is still on her back. Keep it together, Regina.

"Peggy. Tad. I'm sorry, I'm so sorry," said a skinny teenage boy. His body shook and perspiration soaked through his sweatshirt. "I didn't see her, I swear. Peggy, I'd never hurt Meg . . ."

Looking up from her sister's crumpled body, Peggy's eyes held the young driver's for a moment. Recognition made her gasp. "Miles?"

Tad lunged for the driver who wasn't much bigger, although he had to be a good two years older. "She's my sister. You stupid jerk!" Tad's overflowing eyes were filled with rage.

Grabbing him around the waist, Regina locked her hands together, glaring daggers at the shook up young driver. "It was an accident, Tad. Beating him up won't help her, although it would probably make us both feel a little better."

Bowing his head, Tad's chest heaved. "I should've been here, maybe I could've . . ." Taking a deep breath he looked up once more, eyes focusing for the first time. "Miles? What the . . . ?"

The name Miles finally penetrated Regina's foggy brain. The driver was Peggy's boyfriend. Chills slipped down her spine while her palms began to sweat.

Oh, my, God. This is too surreal.

Swallowing with some difficulty, Regina said, "Tad, it's certainly not your fault. The bus driver said she called 911, so help will be here any second. We have to keep it together, okay?"

He nodded. Regina still felt his pounding heart, but loosened her grip. Her stomach flipped over and she thought she might vomit.

Crap. How can her little body survive being struck by a car?

The EMS vehicle pulled up beside the bus. A police cruiser with lights pulsing to the beat of Regina's heart stopped behind it, blocking the street.

"Stand back, please," said the bald police officer. He leaned down and put his big hand on Peggy's shoulder. "Young lady, let the paramedics have some room."

Staggering back, Peggy looked at Regina, tears streaming down her pale face. Her hands shook and her jaw quivered.

The two young paramedics checked Megan's vitals, assessing her condition. The snow-white gauze they applied to her bloody wounds soon blossomed red. They splinted her leg with care and placed a cloth neck brace beneath her lolling head. When they lifted her onto the gurney, her arms fell limp at her sides. The little girl's eyes didn't open.

A sob broke from Regina's throat, but she couldn't form any words. Tears fell from her chin. Sweat bathed her upper lip. She'd never felt so helpless in her life.

How do I fix this? The kids were my responsibility, and look what happened. What am I supposed to do now?

Tad stood rigid in Regina's arms, while Peggy clung to her. Time seemed to slow. Their neighbors stepped back, forming a horseshoe around Megan. The family stood in its curve.

"Is her mother here?" the blonde female paramedic asked, looking at the crowd.

"Her mother's dead. I'm her temporary guardian." Regina stepped forward.

"We have to take her to the hospital. She's unconscious, her leg is broken, but her vital signs are stable . . ."

"Can we . . . go . . . with her?" Peggy asked, gasping between syllables.

"No, I'm sorry, only an adult. If she wakes in the ambulance she'll want to see a familiar face." The paramedic covered the unconscious Megan with a blanket and began stowing her gear.

Straightening her shoulders, Peggy squeezed her brother's hand. "We'll be fine, Regina. We'll try to get a' hold of Gram, but she's probably on her way home by now."

"Don't worry," the officer said. "I'll be here for a while."

"Tad, run and get my purse," Regina said.

The boy dashed away, reappearing in a couple of minutes, his chest heaving and his face crimson.

Touching his cheek, Regina tried to smile her thanks. He nodded his understanding. She turned and followed the gurney into the back of the ambulance. Regina looked at the pale-faced teens holding hands. The female paramedic pulled the doors shut then knelt beside the unconscious child.

"Here's her backpack." She handed Regina the purple bag covered with pink flowers and *Hello Kitty*. "It protected her."

Taking the road-scarred bag, Regina clutched it to her chest. One side was torn and stained with blood, a flower ripped part way off, like a dying bloom.

I never believed in guardian angels, until now. The ones that made this bag deserve our thanks. Megan gets a new one in any color she wants. Even purple.

"Ready!" the paramedic shouted. The siren wailed as they raced away.

Regina yearned to touch Megan's soft face, but she didn't want to get in the way.

God, help our little girl.

Chapter 10

THE POLICEMAN stayed while Peggy called the hospital, but Annabelle had already left. Peggy felt the walls were too confining, the house hollow without Megan and Gram. Ms. Pickles sat at the top of the stairs watching the door.

"Gram's on her way home," Peggy told the officer. "We'll be fine until she gets here."

"Yeah, we're not little kids." Tad threw back his shoulders. "But thanks for hanging around." The officer shook Tad's offered hand and gave Peggy his card.

"You give me a call if you need anything. I patrol this area most days."

"Thanks." Peggy clutched the card with a trembling hand. He had already crossed the yard when Peggy called out. "Sir?"

He opened the car door and paused. "Yes."

"What happened to Mi . . . the driver who hit her?"

"He was taken downtown for questioning. He passed the field sobriety test."

"Will he be arrested?" She asked.

"I don't know yet, young lady. You just take care of yourselves, okay?"

"Okay."

The officer shut the door and started the car. Before backing out, Peggy could see him talk on his radio. Then he was gone.

"I'm going to go see if I can find Joe and Tillie's cell numbers." Tad went back inside. Peggy heard drawers bang and the sound of things hitting the floor. There would be a mess to clean up, but she didn't care. Sitting on the porch swing, Peggy took a deep breath. It hurt her chest.

Why did bad things have to happen? Dumb question. That's life, dork. And Miles? Why did it have to be Miles who hit my baby sister with his stupid car?

She rested her chin on her hand, her feelings about Miles a jumble.

The slamming screen door made Peggy jump.

"Can't find it. I'm going across the street to see if one of them stayed home instead of picking up Gram."

She reached for her brother's hand. "I'm sure they both went to get her." He sat down and started to rock the porch swing. He smelled of soap and sweat. Normal. The warmth of his solid form and the swinging motion soothed Peggy's frazzled nerves.

Joe's black SUV pulled into the drive. Tillie helped Annabelle up the walk as Joe retrieved her bag from the back. Peggy began to shake when Annabelle looked at her.

Seeing the alarm in Peggy and Tad's faces, Tillie clutched Annabelle's arm. "What's happened?"

"We couldn't find your cell number," Peggy said. "I'm sorry."

"Where's Megan?" Joe asked.

Annabelle's cheeks turned beet red, but Peggy didn't know if it was from anger or fear.

"I'm . . . I mean, she's . . ." Tears choked Peggy's throat so the words wouldn't come.

"They took her to Wesley," Tad said. "Peggy's a-hole of a boyfriend hit her with his car when she got off the bus."

Catching her as Annabelle swayed on her feet, Tillie and Joe leaned her against the car.

"How badly is she hurt?" Joe asked, concern etched on his brow.

Clutching the front of her dress, Annabelle swallowed hard. "Joseph, take me back."

"Wait, take us, too," Tad said.

"Don't leave us!" Peggy cried.

Turning away from the teens, Annabelle stepping toward the car door. She reached out to steady herself, leaving a sweaty palm print on the shiny black hood.

"Annabelle." Tillie held onto her arm. "I'm so sorry."

"Wait." Joe gave Annabelle's shoulder a squeeze. "Let's call Regina and find out what's going on, okay? You just got home and need your rest."

"Bullshit." Pulling her arm away from Tillie, Annabelle staggered. Her friends each grabbed an arm and helped her into the house. She sagged onto the couch, closing her eyes. Peggy slid in beside her grandmother, burying her face in her shoulder. Instead of rose scented lotion, Annabelle smelled like the soap in the nurse's office at school. Not normal.

Everything is totally weird. Nothing feels right or smells right or anything. My stomach hurts. Things are spinning totally out of control.

Dialing the hospital, Joe asked for the status of Megan Malone who had been brought in by ambulance an hour or so ago. They all hung on his words as he peppered them with questions.

"We'd like to come up and see her, but her grandmother just arrived home from the hospital," he said, then listened for a few moments. "A heart attack. Megan's adult cousin is there with her now. I see. Are you a nurse? Of course, my apologies."

He pulled a pen from his pocket and wrote a number on the palm of his hand. "Very well, thank you." Hanging up the phone, Joe turned to the anxious group.

"Megan's awake, but they've given her something for the pain that will knock her out for the night. They've set her leg and it's in a cast. They want to keep her for observation, and they'll allow only one family member to be with her, but she thinks Megan will be okay."

"Fine, then I'm going." Annabelle pushed herself up from the couch, but lost her balance, landing back down on the cushion.

"They don't recommend it, Belle. The nurse said we should all get some rest tonight, especially you. She'll have Regina call as soon as Megan gets to a room. Maybe we should let Regina and the nurses take care of her tonight."

"It's after five," Tillie said. "Peg, why don't you come help me rustle up dinner?"

Removing her arm from around her grandmother's shoulders, Peggy followed Tillie.

"I don't think anyone is hungry," Peggy said. She watched as Tillie wrote something on a piece of paper and put it on the refrigerator.

"Here are our cell numbers, in case you need them."

"Thanks, Tillie." Peggy turned in the kitchen doorway to look at her grandmother.

"We have to do something normal, honey. Fixing food helps me think."

"Okay." But Peggy didn't move.

Gram's not going to disappear, you dork. Tillie's right. We have to act normal for things to get back to normal. Megan is going to be okay. We need to take care of Gram.

Joe filled Peggy's vacated spot on the couch. Tad flanked their grandmother.

"Want me to get you something?" She heard Joe ask.

"No, just give me a minute." Annabelle took a deep breath. "She knew I was coming home today and probably wasn't paying attention when she got off the bus. Lord, help me, I feel like it's my fault."

Tad handed his grandmother a box of Kleenex.

I feel like it's my fault, too, Gram, and I don't know what to do.

"It's no one's fault," Tillie said to the distressed young woman.

Twisting a tissue between her fingers, Annabelle sighed. "Why can't I go back to the hospital to be with her? I'm her grandmother."

Leaning forward, Joe clasped their friend's cold hands. "Be sensible. You can't do anything for her right now. You've got to get well so you can be here when she comes home."

The shrill ring of the telephone startled them all. Tad reached it first. "Hello. Yes. How's Megan?"

48

Annabelle's chin shot up and her arms flailed, tearing her tissue. She reached out for the phone, letting the pieces drift to the floor.

Holding her breath, Peggy's heart pounded in her ears. She strained to hear the conversation from the kitchen doorway.

"Hang on, here's Gram." Tad carried Annabelle the receiver.

Tillie and Peggy listened in on the kitchen extension.

"Is she alright?" Annabelle's voice sounded constricted.

"Yes. She has a broken leg and a concussion," Regina said. "They're going to keep her overnight for observation. Her backpack cushioned her, preventing a more serious injury. She's going to be okay, Annabelle. I'll stay tonight to make sure."

"Thank God. Regina, I want to be there."

"Don't worry! I'll take care of her, I promise. Don't you dare let that heart of yours even skip a beat, do you hear me?"

"I hear you. Thanks. Did you call Sam?"

"That's next."

"Ask him to find out about Miles, okay?"

"I will. And Annabelle, don't worry. She's in good hands."

"I know." Annabelle handed the receiver back to Tad and bowed her head.

Tillie hung up the extension and hugged Peggy. "She's going to be A-Ok."

Wiping a tear from Peggy's cheek, Tillie went into the living room where she knelt in front of Annabelle.

"Honey, I told you Megan's going to be fine. Let's get you to bed. I'll stay until they get back home tomorrow, okay?"

The knot in Peggy's stomach began to ease as she heard those words.

Tad dropped down onto the sofa beside his grandmother. His stomach emitted an angry growl. "Uh, sorry, I guess I'm hungry."

Totally normal.

Annabelle smiled, "Tillie, would you mind feeding this bottomless pit?"

"I wouldn't mind a bit."

"Megan's a tough little girl," Joe said, patting her knee. "How about I escort you up the stairs?"

"Thanks." Annabelle leveraged off of the sofa. "I'm pooped."

He held out his arm so she slid her hand into its crook.

"Gram," Peggy said. "I know Miles would never hurt Megan on purpose."

Annabelle sighed, "I know. And that's a memory he'll never forget."

ANNABELLE STRETCHED out on the bed with a wet cloth over her eyes. Peggy sat on the floor holding her grandmother's hand. Ms. Pickles curled up at the foot of the bed, one eye open.

"I'm sorry," Peggy said, her head lowered so her hair covered her face.

"What about?"

"About Megan. Skipping school. Making you worry. Not helping around the house more." She pressed the pad of each finger into her grandmother's palm.

Annabelle studied her granddaughter's serious expression. She tucked Peggy's straight blonde hair behind her ear.

"What happened to Megan was an accident, but I'm not comfortable with you riding alone with Miles anymore. As for the other, no more skipping school, okay?"

Peggy made a big "X" across her chest with her finger. "Promise."

"Good. How was detention?"

The teenager sighed. "Boring."

There was a knock on the bedroom door. Tillie peeked inside.

"Hi there," she said. "Are you doing okay?"

"I'll live."

Tillie pulled up a chair. The clock chimed half-past eight. "You went to bed without eating. Are you hungry?"

"Not really. A cup of hot chocolate sounds pretty good though. Maybe it would help me sleep." Annabelle reached for her friend's small hand. "Did the kids eat?"

"I wasn't very hungry." Peggy shifted her position on the floor.

"Tad ate some, but not nearly as much as he usually packs away. I phoned your doctor to let him know about Megan. He said to take the muscle relaxant he prescribed when you were discharged. Joe picked it up at the pharmacy." Tillie held out a glass of water and a tablet.

Taking it in silence, Annabelle swallowed the pill.

"I know I need sleep, but I'd rather go up to see Megan."

"You can't do her any good if you're ill. Regina is with Megan. She's going to be fine. She'll be running around making us all nuts in a few short weeks. You need to take care of yourself and let others help you for a little while," Tillie said.

Climbing onto the edge of the bed, Peggy snuggled up to the cat. "I'll help."

"Where's Tad?"

"He's in his room. Possibly eavesdropping." Tillie grinned and tipped her head toward the wall.

"There's not much to hear," Annabelle said.

Tillie winked at Annabelle and whispered. "Maybe not, but I've used the glass to the wall trick myself over the years. It works."

"Good to know." Pushing up on her elbow, Peggy gave Tillie an exaggerated wink. "Tad can do the laundry and the dishes and vacuum while I sit in here with Gram."

A muffled laugh came from the next room.

Closing her eyes, Annabelle heard the door click and knew she was alone except for Ms. Pickles who snuggled against her feet.

"Be brave, Megan girl." Annabelle whispered before she succumbed to sleep.

Chapter 11

UNABLE TO REST, Regina sat vigil in the ugly vinyl recliner watching Megan's chest move up and down. The room was stark and gray with only blinds to cover the windows. The lone print on the wall had faded to gray as well. When the sun had risen above the downtown skyline, the phone in her lap rang. She jumped, grabbing it before it hit the tile floor. "Hello?"

"Regina? How's our girl doing?"

"Oh, Sam." Regina lowered her voice. She took the phone into the bathroom and started to cry. "She looks so tiny on that big bed." Regina took a deep breath. "But she's going to be okay."

"Good to hear. What about you?"

"Me? I'm fine."

"You don't sound fine." His soft voice soothed her sleep-deprived nerves.

"She has a purple cast."

"Colorful."

She heard the humor in his voice.

"The night nurses have already signed it. They'll probably discharge her about noon. Will you pick us up?" Leaning her warm forehead against the cool tile, Regina felt her worries subside.

"I'll be happy to. Have I told you lately that I love you?"

She produced a watery smile. "Thank you, sweetheart. I love you, too."

Wiping her eyes, Regina took the phone back to its cradle next to the hospital bed.

Megan opened her eyes. "Was that Sam? Why are you crying?"

"I never cry. I'm just allergic to questions."

"I'm hungry."

Giving the little girl a gentle hug, Regina pressed the nurse's call button.

"Can I watch cartoons?"

"Sure, honey." Regina grabbed the remote and searched until she found *Spy Girls*, leaving the volume down low.

A tall, voluptuous woman whose nametag read "Maris," came in and checked Megan's vitals, making notes in her chart. When the nurse smiled, her teeth shone against her chocolate colored skin.

"You're looking pretty good today, young lady," Maris said. "Doctor says you can go home at lunch time."

It felt good to have that confirmed. Regina quietly exhaled.

"Cool. My Gram just got out of the hospital yesterday. She had a stick put in her heart. I can't wait to see her. Will you sign my cast?"

"I'd be honored." Maris took out a black marker and wrote "Nurse Maris" putting a heart over the "I".

Regina slipped into the restroom and washed her face with cool water. It had been a long night, but Megan seemed to be fine. Glaring in the mirror, she sighed. Blue smudges swathed each eye and the whites were mostly red.

Worry and lack of sleep will no doubt show my age fairly soon. How could this happen and to such a sweet child?

She was thankful it was a clean break. The cast would come off in six or eight weeks. They'd fitted Megan for crutches, saying it would heal better if she didn't put weight on it. The physical therapist had shown her how to use the crutches and given instructions to take baths instead of showers, keeping her foot out of the water. Regina was sure Peggy would help Megan wash her hair. Hopefully, Annabelle would be up and around soon. Two months as caregiver to a child in a cast and a woman recovering from a heart attack seemed rather daunting, not to mention the amount of time away from Sam and Sugar.

Cooking has never been my strong suit. Thank God there's take out, delivery and frozen food. I'll manage.

Tucking an errant strand of gray hair behind her ear, Regina patted her messy braid and tugged on her wrinkled top. She might look like she'd been up all night sitting in a chair, but she didn't have to act like it. Straightening her shoulders, she went back to sit beside Megan.

"Can I practice my crutches?"

"Sure, sweetie."

The hospital gave Megan a pink sock with rubber nubs on the bottom so her good foot wouldn't slip on the shiny linoleum. The bed had been lowered far enough that she could almost touch the floor, but not quite. Regina helped her slide off of the mattress, handing her first one crutch then the other.

"Can we go out into the hall?"

"If you feel up to it."

Megan started off with two big steps but quickly modified it to a more natural stride matching Regina's.

"Slow down. This isn't a race."

"This is kind of fun, but my pits are a little sore."

"Your pits? That's not very lady like. We need to find a better word.

I'm afraid you'll be sore for some time. Just take it easy and don't go too far until your arms get used to the pressure."

"Okay. It's going to take me forever to go up and down stairs."

"You may need to stay on one floor most of the time or go up and down the stairs on your fanny."

"Can I get a new book to read?" Megan beamed at Regina.

"I don't see why not, but we ought to double check with your teacher to see what you've missed. You don't want to get behind in school."

"I get A's, Regina. I'll catch up easy. Besides, school's almost out."

They stopped at the nurse's station so Megan could rest. Her damp hair stuck to her forehead.

"Hi Maris." Megan's flushed cheeks were proof of her exertions.

"Howdy-do, young lady. You're getting around just fine with those walking sticks."

The little girl giggled.

"Take it easy for a day or so until your arms get used to them."

"That's what Regina said. Bye." She turned and headed to her room.

After Regina tucked her into bed, Megan closed her eyes and went instantly to sleep. In some ways she didn't act like a ten-year-old. Although book-smart, she seemed to hide behind her older siblings. They must've taken care of her and protected her from their mother's drunken rages before she died.

What do I know? I've really never been around children her age. My Beth died so young. Do some constructive thinking! What is that girl going to wear since they've cut off most of her clothes?

When Regina couldn't reach Sam by cell, she left him a message and called Tillie.

"Hello."

"Hey, girlfriend. How's it going?"

"Would you mind getting Megan a clean shirt, shorts and some flip-flops to wear home? I've left Sam a voice mail to pick them up." Closing her eyes, Regina sighed.

"No problem. You sound beat."

"I am a bit tired. It's only seven, so I'll rest my eyes for a few moments before the meal tray comes."

"Good idea. Don't forget to take care of yourself, too. I'll also be around this evening if you need anything."

"Thanks." Regina hung up the phone and drifted off.

The sounds of clanging dishes woke her. She looked over to see Megan playing with a new brown teddy bear with a big pink bow around its neck.

"I had cinnamon toast and oatmeal. It was good. No rubbery eggs this time. Thanks, Regina."

"I'm sorry. Thank you for what, sweetie?"

"My bear." Megan held it up and wiggled one arm at Regina.

"I'm afraid I slept right through your breakfast and whoever brought your present. Where did you find it?" Regina's shoulders began to tighten as she examined the room. The hairs stood up on the back of her neck.

"When I woke up it was tucked under my arm."

The clock read nine-thirty.

"It's a very nice bear." Regina went into the bathroom and splashed cold water on her face again.

Who left the teddy bear? Sam? No, he's at work. Joe? No, he probably would have stayed.

Dabbing the water with a paper towel, she wondered if the nurses had gifted Megan for being such a good patient.

No, I don't think so. Get a grip, Regina Louise, and ask the nurse.

Like a roller coaster, her feelings were barely attached to the track. Why didn't she wake up when someone came in the room? Thoughts of the nightly news ran through her head and all the bad things that happened every day in any town, at any time.

"I'll be right back."

"Okay." Megan hugged her bear and watched cartoons.

Regina took note of the few people in sight. She approached a young man and woman in colorful scrubs who were standing by the nurse's station.

"Excuse me, but did you see anyone going in or out of Room 304?" Her eyes kept scanning the halls and doorways.

"Just food service," the male nurse said. A dour expression covered his baby face; his shaved head reflected the overhead lights.

The tropical flowers on the red headed nurse's top were wild, but much more friendly than the old white uniforms Regina had associated with health care workers.

"I didn't see anyone. Is something wrong?"

"Someone came in while the child and I were napping and left a stuffed animal. Does the hospital do that for young patients?"

"Not on this floor. I think they do on pediatric oncology, though." He looked at her without smiling.

"Oh. Well. Thank you." Regina went back down the hall. As she entered Megan's room the male nurse's voice carried to her ears. "What's wrong with giving a sick kid a present?"

By the time they discharged Megan, it was almost one o'clock. Sam sat with them for an hour watching cartoons. Annabelle had called twice and they were both anxious to be back together. When the paperwork was finally completed, they wheeled Megan to his SUV and drove straight home.

Sam pulled into the drive, Megan chattering with excitement.

"I'm home! I can't wait to show Tad my cast. Peggy will love my new bear. Do you think Nurse Maris will remember me? I hope Tillie makes dinner. I didn't really like hospital food. Or maybe we can get Chinese? Will Gram be able to eat Chinese? Is it good for her heart?"

"Slow down, munchkin," Sam said. "How about I give you a ride up to the porch then you can show off your new crutches."

"Oh, yes. Hurry, Sam." Megan bounced on the car seat.

"I'll get the crutches," Regina said.

"Thank you, Regina, for staying with me and everything."

"You're welcome, sweetie."

Sam scooped Megan up in his arms and carried her up the stairs, setting her down in front of the door. She wiggled and giggled. Her enthusiasm was contagious. Regina handed her each crutch with a smile then held the door open so Megan could go ahead of them.

"Welcome Home!" shouted Tillie, Annabelle and her siblings, their arms in the air. Smiles split their faces as they met her in the entryway.

"Hi!" Megan hobbled in. Balloons of every primary color were tied from the first floor to the second with only inches in between. "What pretty balloons! Look at my purple cast. Isn't it cool? You all have to sign it."

Her brother and sister rushed to give her the first hug. Tillie and Annabelle stood back, grinning. Tad nabbed her first, giving Megan a big squeeze.

"Am I the first one to get crutches?"

"Nah, I sprained my ankle when you were a baby," Tad said.

"Oh. Well. I'm the first to have a purple cast, right?"

Peggy hugged her little sister. "Yes, you are."

The exuberant clan moved their reunion into the parlor where Annabelle and Megan took up most of the couch. They huddled together, Megan leaning against her grandmother's side.

"Do you remember what happened?" Tad plopped down on the floor with Ms. Pickles in his lap.

"Not really. I was anxious to get home, so I jumped off the bus without looking. Then I remember waking up in the hospital. Regina was there and Nurse Maris."

"That's not a very good story," Tad said. "At least you could make something up like you felt yourself flying and crashing on the street like a raw chicken."

Peggy punched him in the arm.

"Gross," Megan said. "I prefer stories with happy endings. Chicken guts on the street isn't my kind of story."

"I like your new bear. Did you give it to her, Regina?" Peggy asked.

"No. It just appeared when she was sleeping."

And I still haven't figured out who snuck into her room to deliver it.

Shifting in the rocker, Regina looked at Sam and shook her head.

"Kinda like Santa Claus," Megan said.

"Awesome." Tillie rubbed her hands together. "You can never have too many teddy bears."

Regina wasn't so sure. She took in her cousin's high color and hoped the strain hadn't been too much. "How are you feeling, Annabelle?"

"Much better now that we're all together again. But I am a little bit tired."

Megan slipped her fingers into her grandmother's. "Me, too. Could I take a nap in your room?"

"Sure, you can be my life sized teddy bear." Annabelle smiled at her granddaughter.

"How about I give you a ride up those stairs." Sam looked at the little girl but put his hand on Regina's shoulder to give her comfort. He scooped up Megan and turned toward the stairs.

"Thanks. You're my hero. My under arms are kinda sore." Megan put her arms around his strong neck.

They all laughed and followed them up the stairs, Peggy carrying the crutches.

"You might want to go up and down the stairs on your butt, like you did when you were learning to walk," Peggy said.

"Good idea, but won't my butt get sore?" She yawned.

Tad laughed. "Probably. You don't have a diaper for padding this time. Maybe I could tie a pillow on your seat?"

"That might work." Megan closed her eyes and leaned on Sam's broad chest, snuggling into his warm neck.

He laid her on Annabelle's bed, pulling an afghan over her legs.

The teens tucked their grandmother in beside her. Ms. Pickles crouched under the bed until the group moved away. Curling in a ball between the already snoozing forms, Ms. Pickles' green eyes kept watch over her two precious people.

Closing the door softly behind her, Regina followed Sam and Tillie downstairs into the kitchen.

"Why don't you take a nap, too," Tillie said. "You look wiped."

"I didn't get much sleep last night. Maybe I'll get a snack first."

"I'll get it, honey," Tillie said. "Have a seat."

Sam pulled out a chair, and Regina eased down. Now that she could relax, she felt every aching muscle, compliments of a lumpy vinyl recliner. No matter how many blankets she'd piled on, the cold vinyl still penetrated. Warm hands kneaded her tight shoulder muscles, and she sighed.

"You have great hands, Mister."

He kissed the top of her head.

"Here you go. I'm so proud of you." Tillie sat a glass of milk and a saucer of oatmeal cookies in front of her.

Sam stopped his ministrations so Regina could concentrate on the snack.

"Would you like me to carry you up the stairs, too?" he whispered into her ear.

She blushed. "I would not. I can still walk . . ."

"Oh stuff it, Regina Louise," Tillie said, waving her arm in dismissal. "Let the man get you into bed. I'll hang out down here. I've got some heart healthy recipes I want to make and freeze for you guys before I go home."

Giving her best friend an exhausted hug, Regina took Sam's hand and went upstairs.

"Do you want me to stay awhile?" he asked.

"Don't you need to get back to work?"

"It can wait."

"I'll be fine once I've had some sleep. You go on. After you take care of Sugar, would you call me?" She stroked his hand. "I'm hoping things will feel more normal after a little rest."

"Talk to you later." He pressed his warm lips on each of her closed eyes before leaving.

The last thing Regina heard was the click of the door shutting. Her thoughts returned to the teddy bear. Could Tom have been the one to deliver it? How would he know Megan was in the hospital unless he called or something.

Does he think a teddy bear makes up for being missing for ten years? Between that and their mother's abuse those kids have had enough heartache. Annabelle and I won't let them get hurt again . . .

Chapter 12

FRIDAY MORNING was like any other morning, with someone already occupying the upstairs bathroom. Regina took her towel and washed in the half bath just off the parlor. Neither the sounds nor smells were familiar anymore. This was no longer her home. She missed Sugar's cold nose and Sam's warm embrace. While Regina hadn't thought that she would be able to nap for long, she had slept the night through, waking marginally refreshed.

Smoothing her clothing, she decided to check on Annabelle before going to start the coffee. The bed was empty. She heard giggling behind the bathroom door. Happy sounds were a welcome start to the day, so Regina continued downstairs.

When she entered the kitchen, Peggy stood at the stove stirring eggs, a dishtowel wrapped around her narrow waist, while Tad made coffee. The table was already set for five.

"Something smells good," Regina said.

"That's the coffee. Peg's burning the eggs," Tad said with a smirk.

"They aren't burnt, you moron."

"Yet," Tad replied.

"No doubt Tad will eat the lion's portion." Regina grinned at the teenagers.

"He may not get any if he doesn't chill." Peggy shook the spatula at him, oblivious to the tiny pieces of yellow dropping on the floor.

The cat kindly disposed of the evidence.

"Are Gram and Megan up?" Tad asked.

"They were in the bathroom. I'm not sure who was helping whom."

"Maybe I should see if they're okay." Peggy untied her impromptu apron.

"They're fine."

Tad placed a pile of napkins on the scarred wooden table. "Why do girls always have to go to the bathroom in pairs? That's just gross."

Regina chuckled, pouring herself a cup of coffee. She could hear a soft thumping on the stairs and assumed the *girls* were descending with care.

Megan and Annabelle joined them at the table. They both had color in their cheeks again. Peggy served eggs to everyone while Regina sliced one of

Tillie's coffee cakes. She'd left it in the middle of the table with a note that read, "This is much better than donuts. Enjoy. We'll catch up later. Tillie." Tad poured coffee for Annabelle, and they all sat down.

"Can we say grace, please?" Annabelle said.

"Why?" Tad asked.

"Because we have a lot to be thankful for."

He poked at his breakfast with his fork, grimacing. "Prayer is probably a good idea from the look of these eggs."

Keeping her lips firmly shut, Peggy glared at her brother before bowing her head.

"Shhh." Annabelle closed her eyes. "Thank you, Lord, for bringing us all back together."

"And bless this food," Tad added. "It needs it."

Peggy stuck her nose in the air and proceeded to cut a piece of the cake.

Regina patted her hand. "Good girl. He doesn't deserve a response."

"Hey, Peg." Tad spoke around a mouthful of yellow eggs. "These aren't half-bad."

The young woman sat down at the table without looking at her brother while Megan giggled.

When the eggs were eaten and the coffee cake sufficiently devoured, Regina refilled her and Annabelle's coffee cups. She looked at Megan's angelic face and smiled.

"Do you think you're up for school today? I can take you." Regina turned to her cousin. "If you think you'll be all right alone for a short time."

Annabelle nodded. "I'll be fine. I have some reading I'd like to do."

"Well?" Regina turned to Megan. "Your doctor gave me a note so you can go back to school anytime."

"I don't know. School will be out soon, so I don't want to miss any more. But, I won't be able to keep up on crutches. Everyone will leave me behind."

Giving her little sister a hug, Peggy said, "Your friends will slow down for you, I promise. That's what friends do."

"I don't have many friends. Just Becky and Sherry."

"Two good friends is a lot. Most people only have one really good friend," Peggy said.

"Hey, I have an idea," Tad said. "I'll get a marker and you can have everyone in your class sign your cast." He rummaged around in the junk drawer. Holding a marker triumphantly above his head, Tad skidded across the floor to his little sister's chair. Bowing at the waist, he handed it to her.

"Okay."

Shaking her head, Regina smiled. His gallant antics surprised and charmed her.

"Come on, I'll fix your hair," Peggy said.

Standing awkwardly, Megan put one crutch under her arm and flinched.

"Want a ride?" Tad turned around, so she climbed onto his back.

Grabbing the crutches, Peggy followed, leaving her grandmother and Regina in the kitchen with their coffee.

"Looks like they're going to pitch in just fine. Want a hand getting upstairs, Cousin?"

Chuckling, Annabelle said, "No. I can manage, I'm just a little slow."

Chapter 13

REGINA SAT IN the long line of mothers picking up their children, her red Cadillac out of place amongst the mini vans and SUVs. Several of the women leaned out of their vehicles talking, but she couldn't hear them clearly through the half-open window. The exhaust fumes nearly cancelled out the smell of the white leather seats she loved. She'd gotten there early so Megan wouldn't have far to walk with her crutches. After reading a few pages of her paperback, Regina heard the bell and placed the dog-eared romance on the seat beside her. When the rush of kids slowed to a trickle, Megan made her way slowly across the sidewalk. Leaning over to open the door, Regina waved and smiled. Fatigue lined the ten-year-old face as she dropped into the passenger seat and buckled her seat belt.

"Hello. How are you feeling?"

"I'm tired, sore and thirsty," Megan said.

"Let's get you home then for a snack and a nap before dinner."

"Are there any more cookies?"

"Probably." With a laugh, she patted the little girl's leg. "If we run out, Tillie will make more."

When they got home, Annabelle was waiting at the kitchen table with Peggy and Tad, a chocolate sheet cake sat center stage.

"We left you some." Tad pointed at the uncut pan.

"Whose 'we,' you pig?" Peggy growled at her brother.

"Ice cold milk and chocolate cake. It doesn't get any better than that, does it, little sister?" The preteen dug into the gooey dessert, taking a huge portion for himself, then serving his little sister.

"Mmm," Megan replied, her mouth already full.

The phone rang.

"I'll get it." Regina crossed to the wall phone, picking it up on the second ring. "Hello."

"Hi Regina, this is Tom."

"Yes."

"How's my little girl?" he asked.

"How did you . . . ?" Regina stepped into the formal dining room pulling the cord on the relic as far as it would reach.

Annabelle really needs to get a cordless.

"What do you want?" She hissed.

"Did Megan like her bear?"

"That was from you? What do you think you're doing? What do you want?" Regina struggled to keep her voice from rising.

"I want to see my kids."

"Oh, really? That's all?"

"Yes."

"What about money? Isn't that really why you called after all this time?"

"I have a job at Jenny's Diner. I'm doing okay."

"Good. Why don't you leave the kids alone? They don't even know you."

"I'm their father."

Her eyes closed and her empty fist clenched.

"Then why haven't you acted like one the past ten years?" She jabbed the disconnect button. "*Merde*," she whispered.

Regina turned to find the rest of the family filling the doorway, watching her in grim silence.

"You heard?" She already knew the answer by the looks on their faces.

"Who was that?" Peggy asked.

"Your dad. Let's go back in the kitchen and sit down. Annabelle, I think it's time we had a family talk. Do you want to start this conversation or should I?"

"I will," Annabelle said. Once they were all seated, she began.

"What do you kids remember about your dad? Megan?"

"His picture and some stories. That's all," Megan said.

Tad looked at the ceiling. "I remember this tall guy with a big scary voice. He was always yelling. I was four when he left."

"Peg?" Annabelle asked.

Peggy sat with her eyes cast down. "I remember some good times and some not so good. I always sat by the window, waiting for him to come home. He used to give me rides on his shoulders and tickle me until I nearly wet myself from laughing so hard."

Refilling her coffee cup and Megan's milk, Regina's hands shook, but she kept silent. This was Annabelle's story to tell, not hers. A year or two ago she would have taken control, but not now. She no longer felt the need. Her cousin had grown.

Waiting until Regina resumed her seat, Annabelle continued. "Before Megan was born your mommy and daddy had problems."

Tad closed his eyes and Peggy nodded.

"Your daddy had a friend who didn't have a family but had lots of money. And he did bad things with his money."

Megan leaned forward and whispered, "You mean like drinking and drugs?"

"Yes, how did you know?"

"There was an assembly at the junior high, and we kids got to go. A lady came and talked about how bad alcohol and drugs were. I heard Peg talking to Tad about Daddy doing that kind of stuff."

"You've got some big ears," Tad said.

Annabelle glared. Tad closed his lips tight around whatever else he had been ready to say so Annabelle continued.

"He got involved in drugs and lost his job."

Peggy looked at her grandmother through her bangs.

"Your mother was really upset, so he left for a while. But I think he missed you kids and came back."

"I remember," Peggy said. "Things were good for a while when he came back."

Forcing a smile, Annabelle said, "He tried to straighten out . . . I think he was afraid."

"Afraid of me?" Megan asked in a tight voice.

"No, having a family is hard work. Your mom and dad started fighting again and couldn't stand living together. Being drunk was easier than learning to get along." Annabelle folded her napkin, smoothing the crease.

Megan sipped her milk and silence filled the room. Regina and Annabelle watched each child process the information. Megan's big brown eyes were glassy. Peggy hid her expression behind her long hair. Tad vibrated with anger over long ago hurts and fear.

"But Daddy left and Mommy started hitting us. I thought daddies were supposed to be strong and protect their children," Megan said.

Reaching out, Annabelle squeezed Megan's hand. "They usually are, but not always. Drugs and drinking can make a good parent into a bad one. Plus your parents were both very young."

"Kids having kids, right?"

Regina nodded her head. "You are a very smart girl, Megan Malone."

Crossing his arms over his chest, Tad slumped down further in the chair. "Why is he calling now?"

Annabelle looked at each of the children in turn before she spoke. "He wants to see you. The day of my heart attack I talked to him." The creases in her wrinkled forehead grew deeper.

Straightening in the chair, Tad slapped the scarred tabletop. "But what if I don't want to see him?"

"Then you don't have to." Annabelle said. "If you change your mind, we'll be there, too."

"Do you think he just wants money?" Tad said.

Regina responded. "He told me he has a job."

"Really? What else did he say?" Peggy asked.

"He wanted to know how Megan was and if she liked her new bear." Regina waited for the little girl's reaction.

A gasp escaped Annabelle, but she quickly cleared her throat, pretending to cough.

Careful, cousin, this is their truth. Let them find their way through it.

"He really gave it to me?"

"That's what he said."

She looked thoughtful then smiled. "That was nice of him, wasn't it?"

"Yes," Annabelle whispered. "But how did he know?"

"I told him," Peggy said. "He called when everyone was asleep but me."

The young man crossed his arms tighter over his chest like a shield. "I don't care. I don't remember anything good about him. I don't care if I ever see him again."

Exchanging worried glances, Regina kept silent. Annabelle clenched her fist then removed it from the table.

Looking from her big brother to her grandmother, Megan spoke, "I think I'd like to see him if you'll be there, too, Gram."

With a small lift to the corners of her thinning lips Annabelle nodded to the little girl.

All eyes turned to Peggy. When she lifted her head, Regina could tell she was trying not to cry, without much success.

"I don't know what I want!" Peggy blurted out then fled from the room, slamming out the back door.

Regina grimaced. "*Merde.*"

Chapter 14

THE SHEER CURTAINS wafted in the breeze coming through the bedroom window. Peggy watched as Tad pitched himself furiously onto the yellow bedspread.

When Tad's angry, he looks just like mom.

"I don't give a shit!" Tad said.

Peggy hissed. "Keep your voice down. You don't want Gram or Regina to hear."

"I won't see him no matter what you want. He never did anything nice to me. I don't need him." His fists bounced as he pounded the mattress.

Megan covered her ears. "Stop shouting." Ms. Pickles hopped off of the bed and crawled under it.

Their brother sat up, giving Megan a quick hug. "Sorry." He rubbed his knuckles on the top of her head making her squirm.

"We have to talk about this," Peggy said. "I want to understand why he left and why he stayed away so long. He's our Dad. You just don't remember him. We used to have peanut butter and jelly sandwich picnics on the living room rug, and he'd carry me on his shoulders when we went to the River festival. He'd buy me funnel cakes, and we'd get powdered sugar all over our faces. He'd tickle me and talk baby talk and laugh."

"I don't care," Tad said, moving away from his sisters to lean against the headboard. "He used to turn me upside down, but it made me want to throw up. He laughed when I told him to stop. He called me 'wussy boy.' I swear he used to push me down just to see me cry. He wanted to hurt me. Then the yelling started, and his breath always smelled like a dirty ashtray. He'd grab my arms and shake me until my teeth rattled."

"Dad never really hurt you, though, did he?" Peggy asked.

"Not physically, but I was scared all the time. I never knew when he'd scream at me or push me down. Mom would just laugh, too. They both made me sick."

Tad grabbed a pillow, squeezing it against his stomach.

If that was all I'd experienced, I'd be mad all the time, too. It's so unfair.

"I swear, Dad wasn't always like that. Megan, what do you recall?" Peggy asked.

"Just the pictures that I've seen him in. Nothing else, really."

Stroking her tattered stuffed dog, Megan sighed as Ms. Pickles rubbed against her ankles.

"So, what do we do now?" Peggy asked, looking from one sibling to the other.

Looks like I'm alone on this one and it sucks. I guess I get it, though. I have to know why and only Dad can tell me the answers.

"Do whatever you want." Tad threw the pillow against the wall. "I don't need him. Period."

"Megan?"

"I wouldn't mind getting to know him a little better, but not by myself. Would you stay with me Peg? Or do you think Gram would?"

Stroking her sister's brown hair, Peggy smiled. "Sure. Now that we each have decided what we want to do, we'll let Gram and Regina know together."

"Peg?" Megan's brown eyes were sad. "What if you don't like what he says?"

"What do you mean?"

"The reasons why he changed. Why he left."

"It doesn't matter to me." Turning toward the wall, Tad dismissed his sisters.

"I may not like the reasons, but at least I'll know the truth. I have to know. Let's go down and get a bite to eat." Peggy picked up Megan's crutches. The cat slipped under the bed, out of harm's way.

"Come on, squirt, I'll give you a ride." Getting up from the bed, Tad leaned down so Megan could climb onto his back.

"Thanks, big brother." She leaned her head on his neck.

I feel like a traitor, but I know there's a reason. There has to be some reason that makes sense. But Megan could be right, the little smarty pants. Maybe he didn't want to be our dad anymore. Why were our parents so screwed up? Did us kids do something that made things go wrong?

Peggy followed them down the stairs dragging her feet.

THE SMILE FADED from Regina's face as she watched the kids shuffle into the kitchen.

Annabelle went to get bowls and spoons. "Want some ice cream?"

"Sure." Megan said as Tad put her down by her chair.

"Can I try some coffee?" Peggy asked. "I think I need some."

"I suppose." Annabelle poured a bit in a cup, handing it to her granddaughter.

"Why do you think you need coffee?" Regina asked. She watched Peggy's face over the rim of her own cup.

"It smells good." She took a sip then scrunched up her face. "It's bitter!"

Annabelle handed her the sugar, struggling not to laugh. "You might like it better with milk and sugar until you get used to it."

Shoveling the ice cream in like it was his last meal, Tad ignored everyone else at the table.

"You'll get a headache eating ice cream that fast," Regina said.

With a sigh, Peggy pushed away her first cup of coffee.

"We've decided what we want to do about Dad."

Sliding into her chair, Annabelle took a fortifying gulp of her granddaughter's coffee.

"Tad doesn't want to see Dad at all. Megan would like to meet him with Gram, you or me . . ."

"And?" Regina scrutinized each of their faces.

I think I know what's coming and it looks like Peg's alone in her decision.

"And I want to talk to Dad. Alone. I want some answers."

Tugging on the hem of her blouse, Annabelle sat up straighter.

"I'll be glad to be there with you, Peg. You don't have to do this alone."

"I know, Gram. I want to. This is between me and Dad." She turned her face to Regina, her eyes pleading.

"It's her decision, Annabelle. We'll be close by if she needs us." Regina covered Peggy's hand with her own. "We'll always be there for you."

Peggy gave her a thin smile, punctuated by the doorbell.

"That's probably Sam," Regina said.

"Oh, dear, I look a fright." Annabelle patted her fuzzy hair and scurried out of the kitchen and up the stairs.

Drinking the last drop of melted ice cream, Tad smacked his lips.

"Time for me to practice dribbling with my left." He put his dirty dishes in the dishwasher before heading out the back door.

"I need a shower," Peggy said, following her grandmother's steps.

The doorbell sounded again.

"Guess it's just you and me kid." Regina smiled at Megan then got up and went to the front door. She could tell by the massive silhouette in the window that the caller was, indeed, Sam.

"Aren't you going to open it?" Sam asked from the other side of the door.

"I'm still deciding."

"Ah, come on, Reggie."

She turned the knob. It was past time to forgive him over Annabelle's guardianship designation. There were much more urgent issues in the family now.

Whatever happened to the peaceful days of reading heaving bosom books and painting? Families are a mess.

"Hi." Regina smiled at him through the screen.

"Hi, yourself."

She opened the door and opened her arms. They held each other for several moments until their hearts beat at the same time.

"I wasn't entirely sure yesterday when we brought Megan home from the hospital. You seemed so distracted."

"I was exhausted. There's really nothing for me to forgive, even though you didn't tell me my cousin signed my life away." She smiled and kissed him, happy to be in his arms.

"How's everyone doing?" He linked fingers with hers, scanned the foyer and walked to the stairs, his other hand caressing the finial.

Regina glided through the dining room to the kitchen, pulling him in her wake, then poured him a cup of coffee.

"Hey. Megan!"

Taking his cup, Sam gave Regina a quick kiss.

Just when I think he's good, he gets even better. I feel a purr coming on.

Megan giggled.

"My daddy called and talked to Regina," Megan said.

Sitting down between them, he reached for Regina's hand.

"What did he say?"

He focused on Regina's face. "He says he's got a job and wants to see the children."

Sam turned his attention to the little girl. "I see. What do you think about that, Megan?"

"I guess it's okay. Tad says no way. But Peggy really wants to talk to him."

Megan picked up her crutches. Ms. Pickles sat beside her chair, flicking her tail.

"Want a ride?" Sam leaned down and held out his hands.

Megan wrapped her arms around his neck and held him tight.

"I knew you'd come," she whispered.

He squeezed her and chuckled. Ms. Pickles meowed.

"I couldn't stay away from my girls. Especially when one of them is in trouble." He tickled her until she laughed.

In a flash, Megan's smile melted away.

"Why do things happen all at once? Gram's heart, my busted leg, and then Dad comes back. It's too much," Megan said.

"You're all going to be fine, sweetheart." He kissed her forehead.

"Especially now that you're here. Will you stay with us for a while? Please?" Megan asked, batting her eyelashes.

Where did she learn that? He doesn't have a chance.

He looked at Regina over the girl's silky brown hair. Regina gave him a weak smile and a nod.

"If you want me to."

"I do. And Regina does, too, don't you?" Megan looked at her for approval.

"Yes, I suppose I do."

Slipping her crutches under her arms, Megan smiled.

"How about that ride?"

"Nah, I'm cool." She hop-stepped toward the door.

Going to the sink to get the cat some water, Regina bent over and slid her hand down the skinny back that arched in response to her touch.

Pausing, Megan turned and looked at them. "Can Sugar come, too?"

"Ms. Pickles won't like having a big dog around very much." Regina sat back down at the table. The cat punctuated her remark with a timely sneeze then stepped over to her bowl for a sip.

"She won't mind. She's only playing when she hisses and bats at Sugar's nose. They're secret friends." The purring feline rubbed against the purple cast.

"Really? I didn't know that," Regina said.

"I need to get cleaned up and dressed while Peg's around to help me."

Megan really lights up when Sam's around. I guess girls do need a man in their lives just as much as boys do.

"Well? What do you think about all of that?" Sam asked.

"I think she's right. Annabelle's too fragile right now to handle the stress of Tom being back in their lives." Regina stirred her black coffee with a spoon. "But he *is* their father. Can he go to the court for custody?"

"He can try. The courts prefer that children be with their parents. Do you want me to do a little research? Find out where he's been and what he's been up to?"

Sitting back, Regina had doubts about how to proceed. "I don't know. It's really not my decision to make."

"It's never stopped you before, honey." He ducked his head just in time. Regina's playful slap only missed by a fraction.

"I'll ask Annabelle when she's feeling better," he said. "How long since Tom and Liddy divorced?" Sam held the cup in his hands, his eyes on Regina.

She stood and began pacing the length of the room.

"I'm not sure. He abandoned them right after Megan was born."

"And she's ten now?"

"Yes."

Taking a sip of the steaming brew, Sam said, "His parental rights should be terminated, but when Liddy died he became their sole parent. If he can prove he's in a stable job and has a home for them, he could contest the guardianship."

She sank into the chair opposite him.

I think better with a paintbrush in my hand. Right now I'm confused and worried.

"That would break Annabelle's heart. She and the kids are so close."

"Don't worry. We'll figure this out." Sam gave her hand a pat.

She could feel the heat moving all the way up her arm and into her chest.

Lord, I love this man.

Squeezing his fingers, she sighed.

"Want to go upstairs and get reacquainted?" Sam attempted to leer.

Can he read my mind?

Goose bumps popped all over Regina's arms. "While that is an offer I'm loathe to refuse, no. Let's wait until we get home."

He put his cup in the sink.

"You're right, of course. I was momentarily overcome. You do that to me, you know. When do you think you can come home?"

"I'm not sure. Tillie is still working at the Bistro part-time, so she can't come over much. Joe's keeping an eye on things, but he can't be here twenty-four-seven. I hate to leave them alone until Annabelle's stronger. She goes to see the cardiologist next week. I'm planning on tagging along. I'll stay while I'm needed."

He leaned back against the cabinet and crossed his legs at the ankle.

"So, at least another week?"

"Looks that way. We need to get Annabelle moving more." She felt sad at the prospect of being away from home so long, a temporary necessity.

"Since Sugar and I are moving in for the time being, I don't have to worry about you all being here alone with Tom at large."

"He's made no threats." Regina ran her finger around the edge of the coffee cup.

"Unfortunately, he has to commit a crime before the police can do anything, anyway."

Joining him at the sink, Regina leaned against his warm body. He put his arms around her. She heard the stairs creak.

"What do we do now?" Sam asked.

"Whatever is necessary." Regina disengaged herself with reluctance.

"Like cooking?"

The humor in his voice was evident, so Regina's spine straightened and her hands went immediately to her hips.

"Hey, Mister, you know I can make a mean peanut butter and jelly sandwich."

His hands came up to ward off any blows, then he grinned when she didn't wallop him.

"That you can."

What would be wrong with marrying this wonderful man? We've lived together for a year already. So I know it'll work. I could be Regina Louise Morgan-Smith-Duncan . . . uh . . . too many hyphens. Regina Louise Duncan has a nice ring to it. I've been hyphenated long enough.

"I'm glad you're here."

His eyes twinkled.

Annabelle walked into the kitchen looking less disheveled. Her hair had been combed and she wore a blue tunic top with slacks.

"Hello, Sam."

He held out a chair for Annabelle, patting her shoulder when she sat.

"Where are Tad and Peg?"

Regina's hands stopped at her hips. "Tad's tossing a few baskets and Peggy is helping Megan get dressed for school. You ought to go for a walk with Tillie, it'll help you to get stronger."

"Perhaps I'll do just that," Annabelle said with a lift of her chin.

Her cousin gave her a look that said exactly what she was thinking.

When? I want to go home.

Ms. Pickles wandered in and settled on Annabelle's slippered toes to take a nap.

"What are your plans?" Annabelle asked.

"Sam's going to stay with us for a while."

"Oh?" Annabelle stared at Regina. "Where is he going to sleep?"

"He can sleep in Tillie's old room, not that it matters." Regina held Annabelle's stare, hands resuming their position on her hips. "We're adults, Cousin. You can stuff your hanky in it if you don't like it."

Sam cleared his throat. "Ladies. Sugar and I are only going to stay for a few days, just until things settle down."

"Thank you, but I really don't know why. We're doing okay." Color bloomed in Annabelle's cheeks before she looked at the floor.

"Because I asked him to." They hadn't heard Megan appear in the doorway. "He's part of our family."

"Well, that's that then." Without looking at anyone Annabelle headed toward the parlor.

"So it is." Her cousin's abrupt departure stunned Regina.

I wonder what's really bothering her?

Her loving beau kissed Regina on the cheek.

"I'm going by the office, then out to the house to grab the dog and a few clean clothes. I'll see you before dinner, okay?"

The little girl reached up her arms toward Sam. He knelt so she could put them around his neck.

"Thank you." She kissed his ruddy cheek.

He closed his eyes and gave her a squeeze. "I'll be back soon. I promise."

Megan smiled.

Tomorrow would be Saturday. You never know what the weekend will bring around here. Not to mention another person to compete for the bathroom. This should be interesting.

"When are you going to marry Sam?" Megan's words slapped her out of her musings.

"I, um . . . we're not, I mean . . . I don't know the answer to that question." Feeling her cheeks warm, Regina placed her cool hands up to cover them.

"Grown-ups!" She slipped her crutches under her arms and left Regina there to molder in her embarrassment and indecision.

Chapter 15

THE NEXT MORNING, when Peggy pulled up with Malissa and Mrs. Monahan, Malissa's mom, she watched Tad wave at the driver who had dropped him off. He stayed near the drive, waiting for her.

He is so "in like" with Malissa. It's pathetic. But I can't rat him out, even to my best friend. It would break his little heart.

Peggy opened the door to the back seat and smiled at her best friend's reflection in the rear view mirror. "Thanks for the ride, Mrs. Monahan. I'll see you later, Malissa."

"You're most welcome. Tell your grandmother I said hello," said Mrs. Monahan.

"Later, gator," Malissa said with a wiggle of her fingers.

"Hey, brother o' mine." Peggy poked him in the ribs, the one place that still made him squirm. She dashed out of his reach and they raced up the steps to the door. Wrinkling her nose, she stopped. "You stink."

"I do not. Besides, that's the manly smell of sweat from exercise." Tad flexed the slender muscles in his arms.

"More like the smell of dirty underwear."

Girls never smell that rank. It has to be a guy thing. Hormones and bacteria all mixed together. Yuck.

He gave her arm a poke and laughed.

Damn. That hurt.

She turned away to rub the spot without him noticing.

"I won't pass any sniff tests, for sure." He opened the door for her, but squeezed in beside her as she entered. They nearly got stuck.

Her shoulder bag swung at her side as Peggy cupped her hands over the newel post. She leaned back. Tad threw his gym bag in the corner by the stairs.

"I smell food."

"You smell food even when there isn't any. How can you smell anything over your B.O.?"

He chased her into the kitchen where they found Regina, Annabelle and Megan sipping their liquid of choice. A jar of peanut butter and plum jelly sat on the counter.

"Hi. See, told you I smelled food. Any bread left?" Tad asked.

"I thought only dogs could smell peanut butter a block away," Peggy said.

"Hi." Regina pointed with her thumb. "There's another loaf in the bread box."

Peggy leaned down and hugged her grandmother while her younger brother made a sandwich.

"Hey there, baby sister." Tad ruffled Megan's brown locks.

"Hi, Tadpole. You smell funny."

"That's what I hear. I worked up a sweat on the court. Not too gross, right?"

"Whatever," Peggy said. "What's on the agenda for today? Since it's Saturday, we ought to go shopping."

I really need a new pair of flip-flops, but I'd rather look at cell phones.

"Actually, I was thinking of getting my hair done," Annabelle said. "I've had wool head long enough. I'll call Roxanne and see if she has any openings."

"Yeah, time to jazz it up again, Gram." Tad winked at his grandmother. "Peggy says you're too young to look so old."

"Gee, thanks," Peggy said.

Megan giggled.

Smoothing her little sister's thick locks, Peggy said, "Maybe I can French braid yours, since it doesn't look like we're going shopping."

"Okay."

"What are you going to do, Tad?" Regina asked.

"There's a game on TV this afternoon, so I'll just hang out and watch." He took a huge bite of his sandwich. "You're welcome to join me. B.Y.O.P."

"Excuse me?" Regina said.

"Bring your own popcorn."

"I'll have to pass, I'll probably be the designated driver, you know." She put finger quotes around her next phrase, "Regina's taxi service. Maybe you can con the girls into making you some popcorn."

"Dream on, little brother. Megan and I have better things to do than wait on you. I hope you take a shower before you stink down the house."

"Don't worry, I will, and I'll use lots of towels, since it's your weekend for laundry." The last bit of bread disappeared behind his teeth. He swallowed and licked the jelly off of the tips of his fingers.

Putting her hands on her hips, Peggy said, "Maybe I'll just burn your clothes and save the soap. That way your germs won't get on anything else."

Tad pointed a finger at his sister and growled. "You touch my basketball stuff and I'll . . ."

Peggy couldn't help but grin. "Gotcha."

He stormed from the room and stomped up the stairs.

"That wasn't very nice," Annabelle said.

Lifting her open palms in surrender, Peggy said, "No, but it was funny. After Tad finishes his shower, I'll wash and braid your hair, Meg."

"Okay." Megan twirled a lock around her finger. "I think I'll head upstairs. It takes me a while." She stood, slipped the crutches under her arms and hop-dragged out of the room, the rhythm very similar to the three-legged cat.

"It's terribly late. I hope they can squeeze me in." Annabelle headed toward the parlor with Ms. Pickles on her heels.

Peggy looked at Regina. "What do you think we should do?"

"Clean up the dishes, I suppose."

"That's not what I meant . . ."

"I know. We need to make things as normal as possible. Get back into a routine so both Megan and your grandmother will start to relax."

"That makes sense." The tension in Peggy's shoulders visibly eased.

"Maybe we'll go out and get them something new to read. You know, I think we need a better way to keep tabs on one another."

"Like maybe a cell phone?" Peggy held her breath.

Oh, please say yes. Please.

"Exactly."

The teenager rubbed her hands together. "Way cool."

"A little one you can put in your pocket and keep with you all the time. Perhaps then Annabelle wouldn't worry so much when you're out with your friends."

Oh, my, God. I can't sit still. I want to go now. Breathe. Be calm. You're almost an adult.

"That's a good idea. Malissa uses hers all the time."

Regina extended an index finger toward Peggy. "That's not why I'm getting it, young lady. It's for security, okay?"

Don't ruin it, dope, or you won't get your wish—a new neon cell phone!

"Do you really think she worries about me?" Thrusting out her chest, she put her hands back on her narrow hips. "I'm almost grown."

"You won't be sixteen for another month. Don't be in such a hurry to grow up. While Megan's on crutches, your grandmother is going to have her hands full. And it's summer, so you'll be off doing things without us. I'm hoping you'll use the cell phone responsibly like an adult."

I hate lectures. Don't roll your eyes, Peg. Keep your poop grouped.

"I just lost my head for a minute." She looked at Regina through her lashes and grinned.

Regina smiled and put her hand on Peggy's skinny arm. "You're entitled. Now, let's get your Grandmother to the stylist so we can go shopping."

Peggy wrapped her arms around her cousin's middle. "Thanks."

"For what?"

"For everything you're doing for us." Feeling a featherweight touch to her hair, Peggy sighed.

"You're very welcome. Oh, by the way, Megan asked Sam to stay with us for a few days. He'll be in Tillie's old room."

Releasing her hold, Peggy looked at her cousin. "Too bad."

"Why do you say that? I thought you liked Sam."

"I do. He's cool. I just figured you'd rather he stayed in *your* room, since you know, you and he are, well, living together." Peggy stifled a laugh.

"That would not be appropriate in front of you children." Regina turned and led the way up the stairs.

"Yeah, whatever you say Regina." Peggy pumped her fist behind Regina's back and headed upstairs to braid her sister's hair in record time.

SMILING, REGINA was happy that Sam would be home early. Regina felt needed right now, but hopefully not for long. It had been a month since Annabelle's heart attack and her strength was returning. She seemed more certain lately, albeit a bit touchy. Regina definitely liked the improvements in Annabelle's wardrobe.

Good grief, what kind of a statement have I been making all these years by wearing broomstick skirts and dangly earrings? Aged hippie? Nothing wrong with that. It had certainly pissed off mother, who thankfully, no longer haunts my every decision.

"Annabelle," Regina called down the hall. "What time is your appointment?"

"Three-thirty. Will you be able to drive me?"

"Not a problem. Peggy, could you come into my room please?"

Peggy headed her way. Megan veered off at Annabelle's room.

"How about we go now to get you that cell phone?" Regina slipped on her skirt.

"Okay, we're ready, except for shoes."

"Have you said anything to your sister?" After buckling her sandals, Regina looked in the mirror. Her braid had come loose so she pulled off the band at the bottom and started brushing it out.

"About what?" Peggy asked. "Wow, your hair is so long."

"The cell phone."

After wearing it this way for years she could braid her hair in a flash.

"She won't have a problem with it. She knows I've been dying to get one."

"But, it's not just for talking to your friends all the time, okay? It's for your protection and that of your siblings." Regina turned to inspect her work. She could see Peggy watching her reflection in the Cheval mirror.

"I know. But I can still call my friends, can't I?"

"Within reason." Regina laid the brush on the dresser, leaning closer to Peggy's image in the mirror.

Peggy shrank back from her scrutiny. "What about Tad?"

"What about him?" Regina turned to face the young woman.

"He's fourteen. I know he'll want one, too. Heck, we know kids who are ten who have cell phones."

Regina smiled at Peggy.

"Let's see how it goes. You'll be the guinea pig. If it works with you, we'll get one for Tad at Christmas."

"Okay, but you tell him, not me," Peggy held up a hand like a traffic cop.

"Whatever."

"Aren't you a little old to say things like that, Regina?"

"I think we'd better stop this conversation before I change my mind."

Scooting out of the room, Peggy went to get her little sister.

Regina smiled, donning her largest silver hoops and slim matching bracelets.

I'll show her who's old.

The four females gathered at the bottom of the stairs. After locking up the house they piled into the Caddy to head for the store. Tad opted to stay home with Ms. Pickles and the televised baseball game.

"I still don't see why you have to buy Peggy a cell phone," Annabelle said to Regina. "She doesn't need it."

"It's for safety. They're less expensive now. When she's out with her friends, you can reach her." Regina kept her eyes on the road, but cast the occasional glance at Peggy in the back seat.

"If it's an emergency, I could always call the police," Annabelle said.

"Gram! That would be mortifying. Come on, it'll be fine. I promise not to use it in school. The plan Cousin Regina is getting has limited talk time. I'll be very careful not to use it too much. Just to check in and stuff."

When they arrived at the phone store, Peggy couldn't wait for Megan and the ladies to get out of the car. She dashed inside, straight for the displays.

"Are you getting the red or the pink one?" Megan asked once she caught up with her sister.

"I think the lime green one. Pink is a little too . . . pink for me. Red seems more like a mom color."

"Oh." Megan leaned on her crutches, her forehead furrowed.

"Why do you have to sign up for a two year contract?" Annabelle asked.

"It's the most economical, and you get the phone free," Regina said.

"I think that's a bit more of a commitment than I'd be willing to take. This is just an experiment, right?" Annabelle fingered the tiny buttons on the phone in front of her.

"You'll like having one around. Sam uses his all the time." Regina walked up beside Peggy who had stopped to admire one of the bright colored phones.

"Why don't *you* have one, then?" Annabelle asked.

Regina ignored her and turned to the clerk. "How much would it cost to add other family members onto the plan?"

"We're having a nine ninety-nine special on these phones," the clerk said.

"Well, then sign me up. I want a red phone," Regina said.

And I'll never forgive Tom Malone for forcing this situation. I hate cell phones. They're irritating, and I won't be able to escape anyone, unless I turn it off, of course. Which defeats the whole purpose. Oh well, time to adapt.

Whispering into Megan's ear, Peggy smirked, "See? What did I tell you about red?"

Megan smiled up at her sister. "What number will you get, Cousin Regina?"

"The clerk said I could use the last four numbers of my home phone with a different prefix, so that's what I'm going to do. It'll be easier to remember."

"Peggy, could you do that, too, use part of our phone number?"

"Ah, Gram. I wanted my own number."

Looking over Megan's head, Regina stared into Peggy's eyes, willing her to read her mind.

"Well," Peggy stammered, her cheeks coloring. "Okay, Gram, I guess that's a good idea. It'll be easier for all of us to remember."

Annabelle squeezed her granddaughter's shoulder. "Thank you."

Regina nodded toward Peggy, who turned away in defeat. Her rounded shoulders soon straightened as the sale was being completed.

"Oh my," Annabelle said. "It's almost time for my appointment. We need to get going."

"Not a problem, I'll activate your numbers while you settle the bill," the clerk said.

Chapter 16

REGINA FELT STRANGE being alone back in her dim old room with Sam and Sugar just down the hall. Thinking of the dog, she wondered where Sugar had slept. Had she stayed all night with Tad, or left in the wee hours to patrol and finally bunk with Sam? When Regina couldn't sleep, Sugar would keep her company on the living room sofa, lying on her stocking feet or with her big head in Regina's lap.

Time to get up and get moving. Coffee is first, then getting the Sunday paper before anyone else.

Sam was an early riser, too. They often sat in companionable silence enjoying their first cup of the morning, content to appreciate the heady aroma.

I can't wait to get back to those mornings . . .

It wouldn't be long before the thundering children would interrupt. She felt she did better with the kids in small doses and had struggled to get used to the twenty-four-seven occupation. It won't be for long, she promised herself, just until Annabelle is back to one-hundred-percent or maybe ninety-nine-point-nine.

She wrapped her terry cloth robe around her nightshirt and smiled. Before she tied the belt, she looked at her form in the mirror. "Not bad for almost sixty."

Smiling, she shook her long hair sending it swinging at waist high.

All this hair just might have to go. It had been a quiet act of rebellion forty-three years ago.

Rather than a chignon at the base of her neck like her mother wore, Regina had chosen a braid to tame the long locks she'd refused to cut. Her mother hated it from the beginning, which was the main reason Regina had kept the style.

"Time for another change," she said, lifting it off her shoulders. She'd borne the weight long enough. "Too bad I didn't think of it yesterday at the beauty shop."

Maybe they could get her in for a cut on Monday. She could donate her hair to the wig makers for cancer patients. Natural waves colored salt and pepper were still attractive. When Tillie lost her hair last year, she'd chosen to wear skullcaps that Annabelle knitted for her instead of a wig. Tillie would like the idea of Regina recycling her hair. Sam might be surprised, but she didn't think he'd really mind.

It's only hair.

Regina grimaced at the thought of all of the changes she'd gone through since Annabelle showed up on her doorstep that fall day two years ago. Her surprise arrival after eight estranged years irritated Regina then saddened her. She had resigned herself to the fact that the cousins would probably never be close. But, they could help each other. Family was supposed to do that kind of thing. And now, two years later, they had both mellowed and matured, with a surprising intimacy having sprouted between them.

The cousins had made peace with past differences of wealth and status. They were family and had even become friends. On that note, Regina decided it was time to get a move on. She'd call for an appointment as soon as the shop opened Monday morning.

Sam opened his door just as Regina exited her bedroom.

"Dibs on the bathroom," he said.

She retrieved a towel and washcloth from the linen closet, handing them to him.

"Go ahead, I'll go make coffee. I can brush my teeth and wash my face downstairs."

"Thanks. By the way, do you know where Sugar spent the night?" He looked around the landing and peered over the handrail to the floor below.

"With Tad, I imagine. I doubt Ms. Pickles would let her near the girls' bed. That's cat territory."

"You're probably right. Sugar will let Tad know when she needs to go out."

"No doubt."

He stared at her a moment, his head cocked to one side. "You look different."

"How so?" She stood on her toes and gave him a quick kiss.

"You're clothed," he whispered in her ear.

Regina could feel the heat rising from her neck to her cheeks. Goose pimples climbed her arms.

"Good to see you can still blush." He winked.

"You'd better hustle or you'll have to share the bath."

He patted her behind as she passed. "Right."

Her step energized, Regina descended the stairs on her way to the kitchen and her morning java. She heard the alarm go off in the girls' room.

There goes the quiet.

Their door opened, and Regina called up. "Sam's got the bathroom first today."

"I'm next," Peggy said.

"He'll hurry. He knows he has to share."

The cat stepped into the kitchen while Regina finished making the coffee.

"Good morning, Ms. Pickles. I'll get your breakfast before Sugar comes down."

The three-legged cat crossed the room to her bowl. The huge dog bowls placed beside them were empty. The cat wandered over, sniffed then sneezed and walked back to her now-filled dish to start eating.

"My, aren't we the regal feline this morning? Eat up, dear. Sugar will give you a race for your meal."

Pulling cereal and granola bar boxes out of the cabinet, Regina set them in the center of the table. She took down bowls and spoons, adding them to the pile.

Footsteps thumped on the stairs. Regina smiled, recognizing Sam's heavy stride. A big man, considerably taller than her five-foot-nine, he had hands the size of dinner plates. She loved those gentle hands.

"Good morning again, my love." He kissed her before pouring himself a cup of coffee. "What's going on today?"

"It looks as though I need to buy groceries," she said.

"By the way, the cell phones were a brilliant idea. Peggy is so excited. She said you picked a red one. What's your number, honey?" He sat down at the table.

"Um."

Sam grabbed her around the waist and pulled her into his lap. Pinning her arms, he nuzzled her neck.

"Okay." She recited the number and made a token effort to struggle.

"Great idea, using the last four digits from our home number. I only have to remember the prefix. I like it."

"What do you like?" Regina asked leaning against his chest.

He kissed the base of her neck at the shoulder. "I like this spot right here."

She laughed. "You'd better let me go or someone will see."

"All right, but I think this crowd is old enough to understand love and affection, don't you think?" He released his hold on her and she turned in his lap.

"Maybe." She tweaked his nose.

"While you're at the grocers, Sugar and I will take Megan and Tad to the park."

"Good idea. Expend some physical energy. They've been cooped up too much lately. I'll fix sandwiches for a picnic lunch."

"You're getting quite domestic." His eyebrows rose.

"Don't get used to it." She slid off of his lap and dodged the swipe he took at her behind.

"The kids can learn to help out. I just hope Megan will be off of her crutches soon, so she can enjoy her summer break," he said.

Regina filled the napkin holder and added it to the center of the table.

"She'll be better in no time, big guy." Her blue eyes softened as she looked into his chocolate brown ones. "I think she feels more comfortable with you around." She squeezed his hand.

"Maybe I can be home to meet her bus after school Monday."

"She'd love that." She caressed his cheek.

"Who'd love what?" Megan asked from the doorway. She leaned a little to the left, her right toe balanced on the floor behind her.

"I thought you might like me to meet your bus tomorrow," Sam said.

"Would you?" The little girl beamed and hobbled over to the table.

"At your service, princess."

She gave him a quick hug. "That's great. Thanks." Megan poured herself some cereal.

"Where's your sister?" Regina asked.

Making painting gestures on her face, Megan closed her eyes and turned up her nose with an air of haughtiness. "She's putting her face on."

"Sounds scary." Sam winked at Megan, who giggled in response.

"Not as scary as she used to be. Probably 'cuz of Miles." Megan batted her eyelashes and cupped her hands over her heart. "At least, she used to. He hasn't been around since the accident."

Sam took a sip of coffee.

"Was your grandmother up?" Regina asked, changing the subject.

"She's waiting for Tad to finish in the bathroom."

"At least he doesn't have to shave yet," Sam said. "That takes a long time."

"He has a whisker now." Megan's finger pointed to her chin. "I saw it. But he won't shave it off because it's his first." Moving her thumb and pointing finger a quarter of an inch apart she continued, "It's like this big and blond."

"Really? I guess he wants to admire it for a while. I know I enjoyed my first whisker."

"He looks at it every time he passes a mirror." Megan informed the folks around the table.

"Can you really see it?" Regina asked.

Megan scrunched up her face like she was looking at a tiny bug and spoke around a mouthful of *Cheerios*. "If you look real close and there's lots of light you can."

"Good to know." Regina hid her smile behind her coffee cup.

Sam pointed across the room. "Look, Ms. Pickles is making a statement."

The cat was sound asleep in the dog's empty bowl.

Megan's giggle blended with Regina's laughter.

"Well done, cat," Regina said. "Let's just hope Sugar doesn't decide to eat her."

"Naw, they're friends." Megan finished her cereal.

Kissing both of them on the cheek in turn, Sam headed toward the door. "I'm going to wash my car. See you later." He did a backhand wave.

"Hurry up, Tad," Peggy yelled from the foyer.

"I'm coming. Don't get your panties in a twist."

"Woof." Sugar barked as they bounded down the stairs.

Clearing the table of crumbs, Regina smiled as an energetic Tad bounded into the room like his four-legged friend. His grandmother entered a few sedate steps behind with her hair flattened on one side.

Handing Tad a granola bar, Regina pointed to the back yard. "Take Sugar out. You can have cereal when you get back."

Peggy reached for the box. "If there's any left."

"Annabelle, do you feel up to going to the supermarket with me?"

"I think so. Peggy, would you like to come, too?"

"Sure. What about Tad and Megan?"

Regina shook her head.

"Sam's going to take the kids and the dog to the park this afternoon," Regina said.

"Sounds like fun. Can Ms. Pickles come, too?" Megan asked.

"I don't think she'll enjoy the park as much as Sugar. Why don't we let her guard the house while we're all gone?"

"She's not much of a guard cat." Megan watched Ms. Pickles step out of the bowl and curl up on the rag rug. She closed her green eyes.

Regina and Annabelle exchanged a look of relief. This would be the first real outing, besides school, that Megan had been on since she'd broken her leg. Evidently, she was feeling stronger.

"Why don't you take my digital camera along?" Peggy poured herself a half-cup of coffee. "That way you can take as many pictures as you want. I'll run up and get it after breakfast."

"Thanks, Peg."

Pouring equal parts milk and sugar into her coffee, Peggy stirred the concoction and took a sip.

Annabelle smiled at her eldest granddaughter. "That's very sweet."

"She'll be careful. I trust her with it more than Tad. He'd probably drop it out of a tree or into the river."

Annabelle chuckled.

IN THE EVENING, the children were lazing around the parlor with books and magazines while Annabelle mended. Sugar curled up on the floor beside Tad and the cat fell asleep in Megan's lap. Regina sat with Sam in the dining room drinking coffee and talking in hushed tones when the telephone rang.

"I'll get it." Regina crossed to the kitchen extension. "Hello."

"Hello, Regina, how are you?" Tom asked.

Before disappearing into the kitchen, Regina motioned her long fingers for Sam.

He followed and leaned in to listen.

"What do you want?" Grinding her teeth and making a fist, she felt her chest tightening.

"My kids."

"Are you sure about that?" Sam watched her mouth the words 'it's Tom.' His eyebrows climbed his forehead.

"They're my kids. I miss them. How's Megan doing?"

"What do you really want?" Regina twisted the phone cord around her finger.

"I'd like to come by and see them."

"When?"

"Today."

"You're out of your mind." Regina looked at Sam. "We need a little bit of notice."

"Could you put Peg on the phone?"

"Not right now."

Sam took the phone from Regina. "Tom, this is Sam Duncan. Maybe it would be better if you talked to me."

"Who are you?"

"I'm Regina's fiancé and the family lawyer." Sam's soothing voice made Regina sigh in relief.

"Great, that's all I need. You can't keep them from me forever."

"Where can we reach you?"

"I work at Jenny's Diner on Douglas and Hillside. I'm there most days and some evenings, too, but that's because I don't have anything else . . ."

"Okay, I'll give you a call back with a convenient time."

"Whatever," Tom said and disconnected.

Sam set the receiver back in the cradle.

"What should we do now?"

"You all will have to decide that as a family."

Regina sighed. "He is their father."

"Do you want me to talk with him?"

"Thanks, but I think I'll nab Peg and have a talk with her first."

"Honey, I don't think that's a good idea."

She ignored his advice and walked through the dining room to the stairs. Regina hoped to make it without disturbing anyone, but that wasn't meant to be.

"Who was on the phone?" Annabelle asked.

"Wrong number."

The look on Annabelle's face told Regina she wasn't fooling anyone.

"I think it's time I did a little sketching. Peg, there's something I want to show you." Regina waited until Peggy acknowledged her before leaving the room.

"You should draw a picture of Ms. Pickles," Megan said. "She looks sweet all curled up. Or maybe Sugar."

Rolling his eyes, Tad shook his head at his baby sister. "It's kinda hard to draw a ball of fur, squirt."

"I'll decide when I come back down." Regina headed up the stairs.

Peggy unfolded herself from the corner of the couch she'd commandeered and followed Regina.

"What's so . . ."

"Shhh, not here." Regina put her finger to her lips then gestured up.

The two entered the sanctuary of the attic studio and Regina shut the door.

"What's the big deal? Am I in trouble?"

Regina sat on the lone stool and faced Peggy. "That was your father on the phone."

"Just now?"

"Yes."

Peggy paced the small room, arms folded behind her back.

"Have you decided when you want to see him?"

"Not really. I'm curious and afraid at the same time." She wrung her hands and kept moving. "He never hit us kids, you know, only mom did that. But he used to get so mad at Tad."

Regina watched the antsy teen. "He was a kid with three kids. Young and stupid go hand in hand."

This whole situation isn't fair for the kids or Tom either, for that matter. I wish I knew what to do.

"Yeah. And he's a grown up now. Where has he been all these years? He never called. He never wrote." Peggy abruptly stopped and leaned toward her cousin. "What's up with that?"

Clearing her throat Regina decided not to censor the young woman's words.

Peggy has a right to her anger and she's out of earshot of her siblings or grandmother, so no harm, no foul.

"I don't know. Maybe you should ask him that question."

"I'm afraid of the answer. What if he really didn't want us? Could he have changed his mind?"

"I wish I could tell you. But having three kids before you're twenty-five is a hard way to grow up."

"Please, tell me what to do, Regina. I want to see him but I don't, you know?" Peggy's eyes glistened. "What would you do?"

Regina's heart softened, feeling glad she hadn't been in either Tom's or Peggy's positions, then or now.

Good question. What would she do indeed?

"I can't answer that, sweetie. But if you want to talk to him, either your Gram or I will gladly go with you."

Peggy straightened. "Really?"

"Of course, you're not in this alone."

"Okay, I might want to talk with Dad first, without the other kids, to get a feel for where his head is at."

"Whenever you decide is fine."

Although Regina felt nothing but turmoil, years of hiding her true feelings from her mother and her wayward husband had perfected a mask of cool detachment. It might be a good idea for her to go ahead and ask Sam to check into Tom Malone's whereabouts the past decade after all. She picked up an old drawing pad, flipping pages until she found a blank one she could use. She grabbed a pencil and an eraser, putting her arm around Peggy.

"Let's get back downstairs. Megan would love a drawing of that stupid cat."

Peggy opened the door as Regina doused the light.

So much for a peaceful and relaxing Sunday . . .

Sometime in the middle of the night the ringing of the phone woke Regina. Her heart clutched with fear. Her icy hands gripped the phone.

"Hello."

"You can't keep me from my kids." Tom's words were slurred. Regina wasn't sure she had understood.

"What? Are you going to start calling all hours of the day and night?"

"What else is there to do? Regina, I need my kids."

"What did you say?"

"Why can't I see my kids?" He sounded desperate.

"Why do you want to see your kids when for ten years you didn't care?"

"I never stopped caring. You don't understand." Tom hung up.

She replaced the receiver. Regina shook her head. He'd hung up before she could tell him that Peggy was ready to talk.

He's getting frustrated and angry. I can't really blame him. But he has some things to answer for, and it's past time he did.

Chapter 17

MONDAY AFTERNOON, the phone rang twice before Annabelle could pick it up. She half feared who might be on the other end.

"Hello."

"Mrs. Hubbard?" a man asked.

"Yes." Annabelle didn't recognize the voice.

"I'm calling about Tad Malone. Are you his grandmother?"

"Yes." She clenched the receiver. "Is he all right?"

"He's fine, just some trouble at school. Fighting."

"Who is this?"

"I'm sorry. I'm the assistant coach, Phillip Edwards."

"Is he hurt, Mr. Edwards?" She grabbed the front of her blouse in her fist.

"Nah. Just some bruises and not much blood. The other boy is going to be fine. Bloody nose is all. Tad may have a shiner by tonight."

She relaxed her grip and smoothed the fabric. "I'll come and get him as soon as the girls get home from school."

"No need. I can drop him off. You live in Riverside, right? South of the castle?"

"That's right. I remember you from the games. If it's not too much trouble, I'd appreciate it." Annabelle saw a blurry picture in her mind of a stocky man with no hair.

"No trouble. I live close by, over on Coolidge."

Detecting a slight southern accent, she smiled. "Well, thank you, Mr. Edwards."

"We'll be there in about twenty minutes."

"Thank you, again." Annabelle hung up the phone. She remembered he had a huge smile. The day she noticed him, the boys had lost the game by two points. He had been gruff but supportive with the boys. She'd liked what she'd seen and felt at the time, sort of "interested."

The girls came through the door giggling.

"Hi, Gram," Megan said. "Sam picked me up from school, but I wanted to walk home from the corner with Peg, so he dropped me off. He said something about an errand."

"How's it going?" Peggy asked before slinging her backpack over the chair.

"I'm not sure right now." Annabelle frowned.

"Isn't Tad at basketball?" Sitting down at the table, she faced her grandmother.

"He's on his way home."

"Why so soon? That was a short practice."

"Are there any cookies?" Megan hop-stepped her way toward the kitchen.

"Yes, but don't eat too many. Save room for supper."

Peggy and Annabelle watched the little girl reach down in the belly of the cookie jar.

"I don't know what's gotten into that boy lately." Annabelle tugged at her blouse hem.

"Sounds like he's in trouble. I wanted all of us to be good for you." Peggy's mouth was a thin line across her slender face.

"I know, honey, but he's been fighting."

"He can be a real hot head sometimes." Crossing to the refrigerator, Peggy retrieved a soda.

"I think he's still mad about Tom." Megan had to push two cookies in her mouth before she could use her crutches to get to the table and sit down.

Unconsciously, Annabelle tugged at her sleeve. "Whatever the reason, he can't hit people. It never solves anything."

Grabbing a cookie, Peggy poured milk for her little sister then sat back down. "He's just mixed up about Dad and everything."

Shaking her head, Annabelle said, "I know. Coach is bringing him home. When he gets here, would you all go upstairs? I'd like to speak with his coach alone."

"Sure."

The girls finished their snack. Peggy carried the backpacks to their room while Megan followed behind.

Annabelle paced the parlor until she heard the car pull into the drive. She waited with the front door open while Tad and Coach Edwards got out. The coach had a long stride and showed her a mouth full of white teeth when he smiled at her.

"Mrs. Hubbard? Phil Edwards." He saluted her and ascended the porch steps.

"It's nice to see you again, Mr. Edwards."

Tad hung back, chin on his chest.

"Go upstairs and take a shower, Tad. I'd like to have a talk with your coach."

"Okay." He didn't lift his head.

Intercepting Tad as he passed through the doorway, Annabelle lifted his chin. "Yes, it looks like you'll have a shiner."

Tad blushed. "Josh started it. I wasn't going to take any of his crap." His eyes darted to his grandmother, then quickly down. "I mean . . . yes, ma'am."

She scowled then kissed his cheek before he climbed the stairs without looking back.

"Excuse my manners. Won't you come in, Mr. Edwards?"

"Thank you kindly, ma'am."

Annabelle led him into the parlor, feeling the warmth of his gaze. "Have a seat. Would you like tea?"

Looking around the room, he scowled and waved his hand. "No, I'm fine. You know, you really need to take a firm hand with boys." He sat in the chair and stretched his long legs out in front of him.

"Excuse me?"

Puffing out his chest, he sat up straighter. "I've been working with boys for forty-some years, and I know how handle them. Women are just too soft."

What an arrogant man.

Fisting her hand in her skirt, Annabelle took a deep cleansing breath. "Do you know what started the fight?"

"Not really. Tad's had a short fuse lately. It doesn't seem to take much to set him off. He usually limits it to shoving, but today, it came to blows."

"Does Tad usually start it?"

"Sometimes, but he's a good kid. I think he's got something bothering him right now. Do you have any idea what that might be?"

It's none of his business, the nosey old—

Annabelle slipped a tissue into her palm to give herself something besides his thick neck to strangle. "The kids lost their mother last year."

"Where's their father?"

He didn't even extend the courtesy of saying he was sorry for our loss. The nerve—

Struggling not to grab him and shake him, Annabelle cleared her throat. "Are you sure you don't want some coffee or tea, maybe?" She half rose from her seat.

Mr. Edwards leaned toward Annabelle. "No, ma'am, I'm just fine, but I can see by the color in your cheeks that I've overstepped my bounds. I'm right sorry."

"There's a lot going on around here. I'm sure you read about Tad's little sister being hit by a car?"

"Why, of course. Margaret Malone is Tad's sister?"

Her nose rose as did the tone of her voice. "Megan Malone."

"Pardon me." His voice stilted.

The old goat. He didn't even ask how she's doing. He may sound like a southern gentleman but he obviously isn't one.

"Broke her leg, if I recall. I wouldn't worry. Kids mend pretty fast."

"Yes, luckily they do."

"That still doesn't explain Tad's anger."

Annabelle straightened her spine. "Tad acts like he's responsible, but he's not. And the rest is none of your business."

She flexed her fingers.

"My, well, I hear you all have had more than your share of troubles. Who'd you piss off in heaven?"

Of all the . . . I can't believe this stuffed bull.

Tears building along with her anger, Annabelle squeezed her eyes shut to keep them back. She didn't trust her voice or the color that must be continuing to rise in her overheated face.

Mr. Edwards leaned back in the chair. "I've seen a lot of boys with troubles in my sixty-nine years. Most of them turn out just fine."

Most . . . of them? Oh great.

Annabelle willed her body to calm. "We may need to pull him out of basketball until things settle down."

"No, don't do that. The exercise should help him work through things. I'll talk with Coach Barnes."

"I thought you were his coach." A new surge of anger infused her.

"I'm the assistant coach. I only work part-time. I'm technically retired and just help out at the school because they're short staffed. Keeps me busy and in shape."

He patted his flat stomach and Annabelle ground her teeth. The sunlight glared off the top of his domed head.

I need sunglasses. This man will make me blind as well as mad as a scorched calf.

"I'm sure the boys and the school are very grateful for your help."

How do I get him out of here?

"I'm sure they are. I taught history and coached before I retired. After my wife died, I had to do something with my time. No more honey-do lists." He flashed his bright smile at her, but Annabelle wasn't charmed at all. "Coaching's just what I needed."

"I'm sorry to hear about your wife." Annabelle stood. "I know what you mean about kids. My three are a handful."

He looked her up and down.

It is definitely time for you to go, mister.

She extended her hand for him to shake.

"I'm sure you do just fine with them." He gently shook her warm hand. A shock of electricity arched between their joined hands.

"Well. Thank you again for bringing Tad home. I'm sorry about all the trouble."

He made a slight bow. "Don't you worry your pretty head, ma'am."

Pretty head . . . condescending jerk. I'm getting a headache and my teeth hurt.

She escorted him to the front door and watched as he got into his car and drove away. Her body felt tired, like she'd run a marathon.

Anger's hard on you.

Pulling herself up the stairs by the banister to Tad's room, she wiped her face with her hands and knocked. When he didn't answer, she opened it, stepping across the threshold.

"Tad. We need to talk."

On top of the covers, Tad hugged a pillow against is chest. "About what? It's no big deal."

Her hands rested on her hips. "I'd say a black eye and a bloody nose are a pretty good-sized deal."

"Ah, sorry, Gram. I just got really pis . . . mad."

She crossed the room and sat on the edge of his bed. "Why?"

"Josh got carried away on the court, elbowing and bumping and stuff."

"Isn't that normal in basketball?" She watched his brown cheeks turn burnt orange.

"I suppose, but he . . ."

Her soft voice interrupted him. "Got carried away?"

"Yeah." He wouldn't look into her eyes.

"Sounds like you might've gotten a little carried away yourself." She laid her hand on his and noticed how much longer his fingers were than hers.

"Maybe I shouldn't be playing ball right now." He looked into her eyes for the first time since he'd come home.

She leaned back and crossed her arms. "Oh. Why is that?"

"I could meet Megan's bus and walk her and Peggy home from school. She'd be safe with me." He sat up straighter.

Good grief.

"I'm sure she would, but don't you think she needs to learn to be independent?"

"She's just a little girl, Gram. She shouldn't have to be scared of cars and stuff." He hit the pillow with his fist.

"You're right, but we can't be with her every minute. She has to learn to be on her own once in a while. Walking home from the bus is a big thing for a ten-year-old. I've started watching from the porch and I think Joe watches from his house, too. We've got it covered, honey. Honestly." She gave his hand a squeeze. They were growing as fast as his feet. She thought he might be as tall as their friend Joe when Tad reached adulthood.

The boy sat silent, looking at their entwined hands.

"If she wants me to walk her home, I'll quit basketball tomorrow."

"She knows that, honey. But I'm thinking that you're trying to avoid going back and facing your friends."

"You think?" He looked into her eyes then began fidgeting once more.

"But you are going back to finish the season, or whatever they call it. And no more fighting." She let go of his hand.

"Okay. Hey, what did you think of Coach Edwards?"

"He's . . ." She didn't want to use the words that best described what she thought. "He's very fit for a man his age."

"He's pretty cool for an old guy." Tad ducked his head.

"He's not much older than me."

"You are kinda old, but kinda cool, too. And well preserved." He tossed his pillow at the headboard and grinned at her.

Laughing, Annabelle said, "Thank you, I think. Let's go put ice on that eye before it swells any more."

"Is there any cake left?"

"I think so."

He grabbed her shoulders and gave her a hard squeeze.

"I love you, Tad," Annabelle whispered in his ear.

His cheeks and the tops of his ears turned red, but he smiled.

When they opened the door, they found a sniffling Megan and Ms. Pickles leaning against the jamb.

"Hey, squirt. Were you listening?" Tad ruffled her hair.

"Yes." Megan's big brown eyes looked sad. "Please don't quit basketball because of me."

"Oh, dear." Annabelle removed the tissue from her pocket and wiped the tears from Megan's cheeks.

"Now don't start blubbering," Tad said. "I'm not quitting, but . . ."

"No buts, Tadpole." Megan sniffed.

He grinned. "If you ever need me, you know I'll be there, don't you?"

"You're the best big brother I could ever have." Megan took his hand. He pulled her into a one-armed embrace, dumping a crutch next to Ms. Pickles.

"Meow."

"Sorry, cat." Tad turned to his little sister. "Did you eat all the cake?"

"No. I saved you some, but I think I'll change my mind since you called me squirt."

He scooped her up and tossed her over his shoulder, starting down the stairs.

"We'll see about that." Her body bounced against his back.

"Whoa." Megan giggled. "I'm gonna throw up!"

"Tad. Slow down, please." Annabelle picked up the discarded crutches.

He turned and smiled at his grandmother then proceeded at a slightly more normal pace.

Annabelle's heart melted. "We are truly blessed." She followed in their wake; calling to them, "Don't spoil your dinner!"

She heard the key in the lock before she noticed the tall silhouette in the glass.

I wonder who that could be?

The door opened and a tall woman with chin length, salt-and-pepper colored hair stepped into the entryway.

"Regina?" Annabelle's hand covered her gaping mouth. "Where's your hair?"

Her cousin smiled. "Hello to you, too. Close your mouth, Annabelle. You'll catch flies."

"Oh, my." Annabelle sat down on the stairs.

I've had enough surprises . . .

"Thanks, I like it, too." Regina fluffed it with her hand. "I'm amazed at how light it feels. Are there any snacks? I skipped breakfast." She glided across the foyer and out of sight before Annabelle could respond.

"Well, I'll be damned," Annabelle spoke to the now-empty space.

Chapter 18

REGINA'S THOUGHTS wandered as she put the Sunday dinner dishes into the dishwasher. Another week had gone by and the household had re-established a routine.

"Why do you think Dad hasn't called this week?" Peggy wiped the crumbs from the table. "I'd like to talk to him first, before Tad and Megan. Okay?"

"Sure, honey. Your grandmother will support whatever you want to do regarding your father." Holding the cabinet door open, Peggy wiped her hands over the trashcan.

"You know, I think Gram's doing much better. She's not sleeping so much. Not even naps."

"That's a good sign." Rinsing the sauce from the plates before putting them in the dishwasher seemed stupid to Regina, but she knew if she didn't there would be food stuck on them.

Rubbing her arched back, Regina smiled at the cat. "I think Sugar and Ms. Pickles have reached an understanding about who eats out of what bowl. It seems the cat wins all contests."

"I think I'll go upstairs and listen to some music." Peggy examined her fingers and frowned. "It's time to do my nails, too."

When Regina scanned the tidy kitchen, she decided to have a talk with Sam, joining him outside on the front steps, enjoying the summer evening. Ms. Pickles followed then curled up between Megan and Annabelle on the porch swing.

Regina sat down beside Sam. "How about we go home?"

"Things do seem to be settling down around here. It's almost boring." Sam winked at Megan and Annabelle.

"Thank you both for all you've done." Annabelle paused, her crochet needle above the afghan she had started.

"Thanks for staying with us." Megan absently stroked the cat.

Nodding, Sam smiled. "You're most welcome."

The chains on the porch swing creaked as Annabelle and her youngest grandchild moved back and forth. Tad had come around the side of the house and joined the family.

"Can Sugar stay?" Tad asked. "She's a lot more fun than a silly cat."

Sam smiled and watched to see how Megan would react.

Megan giggled. "Sugar can stay, but you've got to go."

"Yes, things are pretty much back to normal around here." Sam slapped his thigh and cleared his throat to hide a laugh. "Who will round out the household if Tad comes home with us?"

Annabelle stopped her crochet hook once again. "I think I'd like for him to stick around a little longer. Wouldn't you, Megan?"

"I suppose, but don't call me squirt anymore. I don't like it." Megan threw a broken twig at her brother. "If my legs were longer, and I didn't have this cast, I'd be able to run just as fast as you."

"In your dreams, little sister."

Regina felt grateful for their banter.

"By the way," The swing paused again as Annabelle spoke. "I've been meaning to ask you, Regina, why did you cut your hair?"

"I felt compelled to do it and I'm glad. It feels better with that weight off my shoulders." Regina shook her head for emphasis.

"I like the way it swings," Megan said.

"It is very flattering." Annabelle resumed her crocheting. "I think it makes you look younger."

Sam ran his hand through Regina's loose waves. "I have to admit it's growing on me."

"I don't like it." Tad crossed his arms over his chest. "I can't tell when you're mad anymore."

Regina turned a puzzled frown toward the young man. "What?"

"You can't do that flip thing with your braid anymore. So I don't have any warning."

Sam started laughing. "You know what? You're right! I hadn't thought of that."

Stroking the purring cat, Megan smiled at Regina. "Peggy tosses her hair like you used to. I think it's nice."

"I think it's funny." Tad mimed taking his hair and throwing it over his shoulder.

"I guess I didn't realize . . . it was purely reflex." Feeling her cheeks warm, Regina looked down the quiet street.

"Well, it was a sure sign that you were going after someone." Gesturing with his hands, Tad continued. "Like when you stood up to Mom under the bridge. I knew you were ready for anything when that braid went flying."

Sugar's low growl interrupted their laughter. Ms. Pickles' head came up. Regina watched a beat-up silver sedan crawling down the street. It practically stopped in front of the walk then continued on when all eyes turned to see what had the animal's attention. Megan sucked in her breath.

The driver wore a black baseball cap, his face in shadow.

"Who's that?" she asked.

Sam stood and walked toward Tad and the Labrador Retriever standing at the bottom of the steps.

"Do you know who that was?" He rested a hand on Tad's shoulder.

"I didn't get a good look at his face, but Sugar didn't like him much."

"What do you think? Should Regina and I stick around a while longer?" Removing his hand, he stood beside the growing young man. "We can if we need to."

Tad looked up at Sam, steel in his eyes. "We'll be fine. Honest."

Sam gave his shoulder a squeeze. "Then we'll leave in the morning."

Straining to see where to car went, Regina sighed. "I couldn't see his face. Could you, Annabelle?"

"Not really."

Megan sat very still.

"The mosquitoes will be hungry as soon as the sun goes down. Let's go inside." Annabelle stood, the back of her legs stopping the swing.

"We have packing to do if we're going to go home tomorrow. I can take Sugar and our bags home while you're at work."

"Thanks, love." Kissing Regina's cheek, Sam gave her a hand up.

"How do you feel about having a dog around here, Annabelle?" Regina asked.

"I have to admit, I like it."

"Maybe Sam and I can come up with a substitute for Sugar."

"I don't want a puppy. They're just like having babies."

"True. Maybe Tad and I can go to the Humane Society and rescue an adult dog." Sam watched the grinning boy bound up the stairs.

"That would be way cool."

"I'd like that," Megan said.

"Then it's settled. We'll go dog hunting this coming weekend."

Folding the yarn project, Annabelle stood and stretched her back then tugged at her blouse. "He has to get along with the other animals."

"We'll make sure of that," Sam said.

"And make sure it's a breed that will guard and protect."

Tad turned his back to her and bent his knees so Megan could climb on. "Let's see if Joe will let us research dogs on their computer and see what breeds are good for that. Come on, kiddo, you can help."

Annabelle handed Megan her crutches, which she held in the crook of her arm.

"Okay, but I like all dogs, even the really big ones."

"Keep it under a hundred pounds," Sam said. "No bigger than Sugar."

"How much does she weigh?" Tad asked.

"She used to weigh seventy-five pounds, but I think you guys have made her fatter since we've been here."

Tad looked at Megan and they said in unison, "She likes Gram's oatmeal cookies."

Sam rolled his eyes. "As if she wasn't spoiled enough."

Chapter 19

PUSHING A POT of swollen beans to the back burner of the stove, Annabelle spoke over her shoulder. "Tillie and Joe are coming for dinner. I'm making ham, beans and cornbread."

"Not very gourmet, Gram." Peggy picked up her cereal bowl and put it in the sink.

"Tillie's the gourmet, honey, not me."

"I know. Just teasing. I like your beans and cornbread. Especially with a little honey and butter on the cornbread."

Tad wrinkled his nose. "Don't forget the bean stuff."

"We don't need 'gas be gone.' The secret is soaking the beans overnight. It helps with the gas."

"I'm a guy. Soak or not, beans plus guys equals gas." He drank the remaining milk from his cereal bowl.

Annabelle's eyes widened. "Hurry up, now. Finish your breakfast and get, so you don't miss your buses."

"I'm going to Malissa's after school, but I'll be home by six." Peggy put the strap of her backpack over her narrow shoulder and smoothed her ponytail.

Tad grabbed his gym bag. "I've got basketball. See you around five-thirty or six."

"Will you meet me at the bus stop, Gram?" Megan tucked her crutches under her arms.

"I'll be happy to, honey."

"Will Tillie bring dessert tonight?" Tad's sweet tooth surpassed even Annabelle's and Megan's.

"As a matter of fact, she said she had a new recipe to try out on us."

"Guinea pigs, huh?" Tad didn't appear concerned.

"What's wrong with that?" Peggy asked.

"Nothing. Even her flops are fantastic." The young man licked his lips.

"Tillie doesn't make flops," Peggy reminded him.

"Good point."

Annabelle put her hand on his shoulder. "Be good today. No fighting."

"Promise." He crossed his heart with his finger.

"Hurry up now, or you'll miss the bus." Annabelle poured another cup of coffee and listened to the kids' voices grow softer as they proceeded down the block. The house creaked, settling after the chaos the kids created on their way out the door. Ms. Pickles had re-emerged and was enjoying her own breakfast in peace.

Regina and Sam had been gone for a couple of days. Annabelle was happy to have the house to the four of them again. It would've been nice if Sugar stayed, but she could tell the dog missed being able to run outdoors. Chasing a three-legged cat created no challenge.

The morning passed quickly. Annabelle took a short nap after lunch and woke when the alarm went off.

"There's something to be said for a twenty minute nap."

She waited on the porch at three, crocheting and watching every car that drove down the street. She studied the drivers, afraid one might be Tom.

What if he comes? What should I do?

"Offer him some tea, I suppose." She laughed at herself and checked the street corner again. No sign of the bus, but she knew it would be there any minute. She decided to walk down to meet it. Annabelle needed the exercise, and it was a beautiful day.

Ms. Pickles meowed from behind the screen.

"Sorry, girl. No walk for you. Maybe Peggy can take you later."

Whoever heard of walking a cat?

Annabelle went down the steps to the sidewalk.

The days were warming up quickly. School would be out soon, and the Kansas summer heat would kick in full force. There'd be no official basketball, but she knew Tad would practice all summer. Annabelle hated the really hot days. Her body looked much better covered in layers.

The girls looked cute in their shorts and flip-flops. When she and Regina were children, they wore cotton dresses. Annabelle loved going barefoot, but she couldn't remember a single time when Regina hadn't worn shoes. The poor thing never knew the joy of cool mud between her toes or wading in the pond. Regina wasn't even allowed to get dirty.

In some ways, I had it better than Regina growing up. No money, but few rules.

The squeaking brakes brought her back as the school bus pulled up to the corner where she stood. Peggy and Megan got off together, laughing.

"Hey, there. Malissa's grounded, so I just came home on the bus with Megan."

"Hi, Gram." Megan gave her grandmother a one-armed hug, balancing on her crutches. "You should've seen Bradley today at school. He got his hair shaved off and looked weird. He let me touch it. I thought it would be scratchy, but it's soft."

"Probably his summer do." Peggy tightened her ponytail.

"I guess. Only two and a half more days. I'm going to miss my teacher. Mrs. Rose is so nice."

"I'll have three months to work on my tan and drivers education." Peggy swung her purse by her side.

"Oh." Annabelle put her hand over her heart.

"Come on, Gram. I'm almost sixteen. I can get a learner's permit and drive with you."

Annabelle stumbled. "That's what I'm afraid of."

Megan giggled. "Maybe we should have Tillie or Joe teach you to drive. They have bigger cars."

Patting her chest with her hand, Annabelle took a deep breath. "It's not the car that's the problem. It's the thought of my grandchild driving it that makes my heart skip a beat."

Peggy put her hands on her narrow hips. "I'm growing up, and there's nothing anyone can do about it."

"True, but if you don't mind, I'd like to relish these last few moments before you're racing down Amidon or dragging Douglas."

"Gram, they don't drag Douglas anymore. That was at least a hundred years ago." Peggy paused to wait for Megan. "We talked about old timey stuff like that in American History. You know, drive-in movies, ice cube trays, eight-track tapes, skates with keys, stuff like that."

"There's still a drive-in theater left in town. We'll have to go there. You can't really understand what it's like if you haven't seen a movie from your car." Annabelle smiled remembering her teen days, the steamy windows and the heavy kissing going on in the front seat.

"I really like stadium seating, surround sound and 3D. I can't imagine sitting in the car with a giant hot dog dancing on the screen."

Megan paused, her nose wrinkled in confusion. "What are you talking about?"

Peggy and Annabelle laughed. "We'll show you this summer."

When they got to the house they went single file up the walk to the porch, Peggy in the lead and Annabelle bringing up the rear.

When Peggy got to the top step, she froze to the spot. "Gram."

"Yes, dear." Annabelle's smile fell when she followed Peggy up the steps. "What is it?"

"Dad?" Peggy said.

On the porch sat Tom Malone. He rose from the swing, a tentative smile on his face.

"Oh, my." Annabelle felt a major power surge through her body. Her son-in-law hadn't changed much, still lanky, but his hair was thinner and as she studied him she realized he seemed softer somehow.

Peggy's tears choked her voice. "What are you doing here?"

Megan stood mute beside her grandmother.

"I wanted to see you. Looks like you're getting along good, Meg."

"Her name is Megan. Why didn't you call first?" The teenager's face was red with anger.

"Megan, go on in the house." Annabelle gave her a careful nudge toward the door.

"But . . . Gram . . ."

"Now."

"Bye." She wiggled a couple of fingers at Tom before she turned and went inside.

"Bye, Megan." Tom called to his youngest daughter.

Annabelle watched her hobble inside then turned her attention to the unexpected visitor. Peggy took deep uneven breaths but seemed to be gaining some control over her emotions.

Okay, no door mats today. Make sure he understands they're just kids and to go easy.

"Tom, you have no right to just show up." With him seated on the swing, Annabelle towered above his head.

"I tried calling, but no one would listen."

Still struggling to breathe normally, Peggy's cheeks were flushed. Was it fear? Annabelle wanted the kids to feel safe and her eldest granddaughter was obviously in distress.

Straightening to her full five-foot-six inches, Annabelle said, "For how long, Tom? A week? A month? And will you leave again, taking another ten-year vacation from fatherhood?"

Putting her hand on her grandmother's arm, Peggy stood up straighter. "I'll be okay out here with the door open. I have some questions that need answers. Just keep Megan inside. Please, Gram."

Annabelle's face burned while sweat began to trickle down her back. "I'll be right inside." She turned daggers toward Tom. "You'd better not hurt these children, inside or outside."

"I won't." The old Tom Malone smirk was thankfully absent, so Annabelle nodded.

The phone rang several times before Annabelle could get inside to answer it.

"Hello."

"Belle, this is Joe. I see you have a visitor. Is everyone okay?"

"We're fine. I'll call you when he's left."

"Is that the kids' dad? Are you sure you're all right?"

She sighed. "We'll be fine, but could you just watch . . . to make sure he doesn't try to take her somewhere?"

"No problem. I'll go one better. I'll sit on the porch and make sure he sees that he has an audience."

"Thanks, Joe." She hung up the receiver and wiped her damp upper lip with her index finger, but just as Annabelle turned to leave the parlor, the phone rang again.

"Hello."

"Annabelle, this is Regina."

"What is it Regina? My hands are kind of full right now."

"I'll make it quick. Tom's been in jail the past five years."

"What? How do you know that?" She pulled the phone cord as far as it could reach so she could see out front. Her heart thudded in her ears.

"Sam made the discovery."

Looking over her shoulder, Annabelle covered her mouth and the receiver with her cupped hand. "Why was he in jail?"

"Vehicular manslaughter and driving while under the influence."

Sinking into the rocker, Annabelle expelled her breath.

"Oh, my."

He killed someone when he was driving drunk. What do I say to him? How am I going to tell the kids?

Ms. Pickles hopped up onto the seat beside her. She ran her hand over the cat's back then stroked it under the chin. The action served to calm her shaking hands.

"He's here now, talking to Peggy on the porch."

"Do you want us to come over?"

"No. I'll talk to you later." She hung up even though Regina hadn't finished speaking. Annabelle closed her eyes, breathing deep.

There's been too much loss in this family. I failed Liddy by being her father's punching bag, but I won't fail this time. A doormat doesn't make a good mom, and my grandchildren need me.

She straightened her spine. Annabelle could hear Peggy and Tom speaking in low tones. The words weren't clear, but they sounded relaxed. Slipping up to the screen, Annabelle stood beside the open door.

"Where have you been, Dad?"

"In jail."

Peggy gasped. "Why?"

"I was driving drunk and hit someone."

"Did they die?" Peggy's voice quivered.

"Yes."

"Oh my God, Dad. You killed somebody? But, still, why didn't you call, or write, or something?"

"I did."

"I don't believe you. Mom would've said . . ."

"I hurt your mother pretty bad, Peg. I let her down. I let you all down."
The swing creaked.

Leaning against the door jam, Annabelle listened to the mournful rhythm of the swing.

"I think you'd better leave now." Peggy whispered.

"I'm sorry, kiddo. I was messed up. I had to hit bottom before I could climb back up. Unfortunately, that meant dragging my family down with me."

Tom's bitter laugh made Annabelle's heart constrict.

"It seems clear now, but back then, I had no clue what was going on or what I was doing."

Peggy made no comment.

"Here's my number if you want to call me. I'm cooking at Jenny's Diner. Come by and I'll make you the best cheeseburger and fries in town."

"I'll think about it."

"Annabelle?" Tom called.

Smoothing her skirt, Annabelle stepped into the doorway. "What is it Tom?"

"I need to get to work pretty quickly. Could I see Megan for a minute?"

Turning toward the stairs, Annabelle called. Megan came out of the kitchen with chocolate and a smile on her cherub cheeks. She stopped next to their grandmother behind the screen door.

The porch swing squealed as he stood. "I, uh, just wanted to say hi and I hope you'll let me come by sometime so we can talk."

"Sure. Thanks for the bear," Megan said.

"Okay, good," he wiped his hands on his jeans. "Well, you all look great. You're doing a great job with them, Annabelle. Tell Tad I said 'hi.' I've got to get to work now. Love you kids." With a half wave, he dashed down the steps.

"Bye," Megan called and went back to the kitchen.

Listening to Tom's receding steps, Annabelle turned to Peggy who held her arms against her stomach, her head bowed so her hair covered her face. A sharp pain of anxiety filled Annabelle's chest. She went onto the porch and wrapped her arms around her granddaughter. They stood in each other's embrace until Peggy's tears stopped flowing and only the hiccoughs remained.

Stroking Peggy's sweaty brow, Annabelle kissed her head. "I'm sorry that was so hard."

"Me, too," Peggy whispered. Giving her grandmother a squeeze, she went into the house and up to her room.

Annabelle watched until she closed the door then went in search of

Megan. As she suspected, the little one had raided the cookie jar. An empty milk glass and cookie crumbs sprinkled the table before her.

"Hi there. Did you save any cookies or should I mix up some more dough real fast before Tad comes home?"

Megan's smile was still smudged with chocolate. "I left some, but fresh ones would be good."

"Maybe later. I think I'll grab a glass of milk, too." Annabelle poured some for herself then dialed Joe. "Hi. We're fine. Thanks for keeping an eye on us. I'll talk to you later, okay? Bye now."

Peggy came into the kitchen, retrieved a soda from the refrigerator. She sat down beside her little sister, sipping in silence.

A car door slammed out front.

A few moments later, Tad banged through the front door and yelled, "Come on in, Coach. We always have plenty of cookies around here."

"Tad." Annabelle whispered.

"Hey, Gram." He took one look at her face and stopped. "What happened?"

Peggy leaned against the ladder chair back and sighed. "Not in front of . . ."

The smiling face of Coach Edwards fell.

"I'm sorry, Mr. Edwards, we need a minute. Could you take a seat in the parlor?" Annabelle slipped her arm in his, escorting the bewildered man to the sofa. "Thank you for bringing Tad home."

"You're very welcome."

"Excuse me." Annabelle approached the kitchen in time to hear Peggy say their father had come by.

Tad stood rooted to the floor. "Shit."

You took that word right out of my thoughts . . .

Chapter 20

THE KIDS WENT up to their rooms. Annabelle felt shy and uncertain after the last uncomfortable exchange she had with Tad's coach. Today was not the day to have more company. His timing stunk. She sighed, remembering her grandmother's advice to 'always be hospitable.'

"Would you like coffee?"

"That would be nice, thanks." Coach Edwards smiled at Annabelle, warming the cold dread that had filled her body. She led him to the kitchen table and started a fresh pot. Doing something ordinary would help her cope with her churning emotions.

"Don't make a new pot on account of me." His southern vowels were soft. His hands rested on the back of the chair.

"It's no bother. I need a cup." Annabelle kept her thoughts on the coffee pot in her hand.

"Do you want to talk about it? Maybe I can help." She heard the chair scoot on the linoleum as he sat down. The scraping sound made the hairs on the back of her arms rise.

"I doubt that."

"Why don't you give it a try?" The arrogance was absent, but she didn't trust him. She didn't know him at all, but a crazy part of her wanted to, very much.

"I'm not sure." Sliding the pot from under the spigot, the coffee sizzled when it hit the burner. "Blast." A charred copper smell filled the room.

He handed her a paper towel and took the cup she held in the air.

"Annabelle."

Mopping the spreading brown puddle with her head down, she felt the heat rise in her face. "The kids' dad is back after ten years, and he wants the kids."

"Where has he been?"

Annabelle turned to face him, her shoulders set, hands at her sides.

"Let's just say he's been a guest of the state for a while."

Tad's going to be furious with me for telling all this to his coach. Oh, well, it's done.

"No wonder you're upset." He leaned back, scowling.

"I don't know what to think. He was such a mess before he left.

Drinking, staying out all hours, using drugs . . ." She crossed her arms over her ample bosom.

"And now?" Concern etched his face.

"I just don't know. He seemed sober, but maybe today's a good day. He does seem different." She poured a half-cup. He sat back down and pulled out a chair for her.

"What do the kids want to do?" He took a sip of his coffee, failing to hide a grimace.

"Sorry. I should've warned you. I make a poor cup of coffee."

"No worries." He set the cup on the table and wrapped his hands around it.

"You heard Tad, he's angry. Peggy's confused. And Megan doesn't remember him."

"Do you want to know what I think?" He fingered the lip of his cup.

"I don't think so—" Feeling exhausted, Annabelle rested her elbows on the table, her shoulders rounded to prepare for the blow his words might cause.

"Do you know why Tad is so angry?" He stared into Annabelle's face. Her frustration had to show.

"While I'm driving him home, he's told me damn little. But I get the feeling he's really mad at his dad."

She felt a mixture of disbelief and anger. "How would you know?"

"Years of experience with boys Tad's age. And I'm a father of two boys. Hell, woman, I was a teenager once myself." He waved his youth away like it was nothing.

They drank in silence for a moment before Annabelle quietly spoke.

"I'd appreciate it if you didn't tell anyone else." She cringed to think what Regina would say if she knew about this conversation.

"His dad probably dried out while in jail. You ought to encourage Tad to see him."

"Maybe, but I can't agree, Mr. Edwards." She stared into space.

"Have you talked to him, the father?"

"Not really. Every time he calls I just get angry and scared."

"Scared of what? You're a full-grown woman. It's time you stood up and acted like it."

Struck speechless, Annabelle's mind boiled.

How dare this bald know-it-all tell me what to do?

He finished his coffee and took the cup to the sink then turned to face her. "He is their father. People can change. I'll make sure Tad gets to practice and back home. At some point, though, you'll have to talk to the man."

He offered her his hand, and she took it reluctantly. She felt the heat in her cheeks, but rose from the chair with grace and determination.

"I'll see you to the door."

"Thank you, ma'am." He bowed over her hand, giving it a squeeze. She nodded.

They walked side by side. His arm brushed hers. Annabelle felt warmth spread to her belly from the contact.

It's just nerves. He makes me so angry. Am I doing it again? Attracted to the wrong kind of man? No, Coach is nothing like David. Tillie would tell me to get my poop grouped, I'm sure.

"I'll see you tomorrow when I bring Tad home from practice. Think about what I've said. As a teacher, I've met all kinds of people. You can trust your instincts most times. You'll know when you talk to him what he really wants."

Annabelle stood in the doorway, lifting a hand in a half-hearted wave. *He's probably right and that makes me mad enough to spit. Men!*

He walked down the steps to his car, looked over his shoulder and waved back. He sat in the car until she shut the door. She clicked the lock, letting out the breath she had been holding.

"Damn." Annabelle's emotions were raging right along beside her hormones. She would give his words some serious thought with reluctance.

Admit it, Phil makes me feel like I haven't felt in years. My dearly departed David squashed my heart like a June bug. No. I won't allow myself to be hurt like that again.

"Kids!" Annabelle called up the stairs.

"Yeah."

"Get washed up for dinner, please."

"I'm clean." Tad zipped down the stairs.

The girls stood in the bedroom doorway; their eyes followed their brother. Annabelle sighed before turning down the hall to the back of the house.

"This whole dad thing is creeping me out," she heard Peggy say.

"Let's get dinner on the table. Joe and Tillie will be here soon."

Tad zipped back up the stairs before Annabelle could stop him.

"We'll help, won't we, Megan?" Peggy said.

"Sure." Megan joined Annabelle and Peggy and headed into the dining room.

FOR TWO DAYS, things were quiet, the kids subdued. None of the usual yelling and teasing occurred. Peggy could tell her grandmother worried but didn't know what to do to make her feel better. Yesterday was the last day of school and they couldn't stay cooped up all summer. Saturday, Sam planned to look for a dog at the pound, but it would take a while for the animal to feel at home or be protective. Peggy would just have to keep an eye on everybody. And hope that Gram's heart wouldn't give out again.

"Why don't you go with Tillie for a walk this morning," Peggy said. "We'll be okay while you're gone. Promise." She laid her hand over her heart.

"I do feel like I need to move. I'll see if Tillie will bring her cell. Then you can call us if you need anything. We won't go too far."

"Quit worrying. I've got mine right here in the pocket of my shorts." Peggy gave it a pat. "We'll be fine."

Ten minutes later, Annabelle came downstairs in her walking shoes, just as the doorbell rang.

"I've got it!" Annabelle yelled and pulled open the door.

Peggy slid into the entry just as Tillie stepped into the foyer.

"Hi there, ladies. Ready to do some hoofing, Annabelle?" Tillie wore her favorite wild woman tee, khaki slacks and well-worn tennis shoes.

"Yes. Did you bring your phone?"

"Wouldn't leave home without it." Tillie flashed her turquoise cellular before putting it back in her pocket. "All charged and ready to go."

"We'll be back in thirty minutes, tops." Annabelle kissed Peggy on the cheek. "Love you."

"Love you, too."

Tad and Megan yelled their good-byes from the top of the staircase. Putting her crutches in one hand, Megan bumped down the stairs on her fanny.

"I'm going to see if I can find a good movie to watch." Megan stepped into the parlor and turned on the television.

Tad came down the stairs two at a time. "If there's a game on, I'm watching it."

"Too late!" Megan yelled, "I got first dibs."

Peggy eyed her brother's back as he stood in the doorway to the parlor with his hands on his narrow hips.

He's getting so tall! Only a year and a half between us, yet he spurted up a head taller than me. What happened to my "little" brother?

"You better not be watching some sappy chick flick. It'll rot your brain."

"Right, and car chases and gun fights are so grown up." Megan threw a pillow at him.

In the doorway, Peggy chuckled. The first day with no school had been too long and too quiet. They definitely needed to establish a new routine, and she wondered if Miles would be a part of it again. She'd avoided him the last week even though he rode the same bus. His friend Mark said his dad took away his car and he had to do community service.

There was a tentative knock at the door. Tad jumped off the couch and stood just inside the door jam, out of sight.

"Who is it?" Peggy said. The curtain obscured the male silhouette that was the wrong shape or size to be either Joe or Miles.

He knocked again. "Peg."

"Who is it, please?" Peggy asked.

"It's me, Peggy, open up."

Recognizing her father's voice, she put the chain on the door and opened it a crack.

"Dad? What do you want?"

"Can I come in?" His quiet voice sounded nervous, unsure.

"No. You can't. We're not supposed to let anyone in when we're . . ."

His face flushed and Peggy felt the hairs on her neck stand up. "I saw your grandmother walking around the corner. I want to talk. Now open this door."

She felt the heat of anger emanating from her brother. Peggy put her hand on his.

"Leave us alone!" Tad yelled.

"Tad? What's the matter with you? I just want to talk."

Her father's voice sounded strained. Peggy stuck her right hand in her pocket and felt the phone. He shoved on the door, bouncing it on the hinges. She used the edge to block the right side of her body, using her left hand to hold the door in front of her.

"Go away," Tad said from beside her.

"I just came to see you. I want to know you're all right." Tom kicked the door. The bracket that held the chain twisted away from the doorframe.

Peggy used her body to keep the door between them while she took her phone out of her pocket and Tad slid it from her hand.

"Go away, Dad. I can't let you in. Call Gram and we'll set something up . . ." She turned to her brother and whispered. "Call 911."

"Why should I? You're *my* kids, not hers."

"She's our guardian." Peggy held the edge of the door so tightly it hurt her hand.

"Don't give me that crap." Tom leaned his body against the wood.

Tad slipped back into the parlor. Peggy could hear her sibling whisper, then silence.

"Why won't you let me in? I've missed you kids. Come on, Peg . . ."

"You can't be here without Gram." She struggled to prevent him from shoving the door back any further.

Impatience twisted his features. "I'm your father, dammit."

"Please, don't get mad. We're not allowed to have people over when we're alone."

The door exploded back. Peggy fell on the tile. Pain streaked from her butt to her head.

"Why shouldn't I be mad? I'm family and I'm being treated like dirt." He stood over her, chest heaving.

Peggy used her feet to scoot backwards, away from his towering form. She slid a few feet, stopping at the door jam.

"Where are your brother and sister?"

"They aren't here. They went out the back."

"Why are you lying? I heard Tad yelling." He reached down and grabbed her arm, pulling her onto her feet.

Tears fill her eyes. She bit her cheek to prevent them from falling. "Stop it. That hurts!"

Tom let go, causing Peggy to stumble.

"I'm sorry. I lost my temper." He ran his hands through his thinning hair. "I didn't mean to hurt you."

"What kind of a father are you?" Peggy rubbed her sore arm.

"I'm out of practice. I guess I never was a good dad. But I want to try." She flinched when his arms reached for her.

"Just leave, Dad. The neighbors will call the cops. Please."

He staggered back, his arms outstretched. "I'm sorry . . ." Sirens wailed. "Let me explain. I'm . . . I'll call and talk to your grandmother." He turned and jumped over the porch rail, running around the side then behind the house. The sirens were very close which meant help wasn't far away. Peggy kicked the door shut. Hunkering down with her back against it, she slid to the floor. Tad peeked around the corner.

"You okay?" he asked.

She nodded. "Where's Megan?"

"Behind the china cabinet in the dining room."

"Good spot. She can come out though, he's gone." Peggy's behind hurt, and her head ached. A lone tear slipped down her cheek.

"Hey, Megan, coast is clear. You can come out," he said. "See, he is scary isn't he?"

"Yeah. He was really mad. Better call Joe and ask him to go pick up Gram and Tillie. They're probably running this way, and we don't want Gram to have another heart attack."

"Yeah." Tad made the call.

Slipping into the entryway, Megan sat on the floor beside her older sister. "Don't cry." She put her hand over Peggy's larger one and squeezed.

"I'm okay. I just fell and hurt my butt." Peggy leaned over on the cheek, rubbing the sore flesh.

With a giggle, Megan smiled at her sister. "You were very brave."

She wrapped her arm around Megan's shoulder and gave her a quick hug. "I love you."

"I love you, too."

Chapter 21

THE LIGHT FROM the western windows in the top floor studio illuminated the canvas Regina had nearly finished painting. The oil colors were luminous, capturing the early summer wildflowers in the field of bluestem behind the home she and Sam shared. Sugar curled up on the rug in the middle of the floor beside her master's unoccupied recliner.

The need to paint woke Regina that morning and still gripped tight. She'd jumped out of the bed, grabbed a banana and a cup of coffee then went up the stairs to get to work, still in the old tee shirt she'd slept in. The day passed quickly. She moved the easel to follow the shafts of light. When her stomach growled earlier she grabbed a peanut butter sandwich. By the time the sun had moved directly overhead, her now-shorn locks were tucked behind her ears.

"Hey there, love." Sam materialized in the doorway.

She didn't take her eyes from the canvas. "Hi."

"Looks like you've been painting for hours. Wow, that's beautiful. Are you about finished?"

She stuck the paintbrush behind her ear and stepped back. "Close. What time is it?"

"Almost two. I decided to leave early to see if you wanted to roll in the hay."

Her eyes never left the painting. "Hum."

"Guess not."

She turned to look at him, momentarily distracted. "I'm sorry. What did you say?"

"Never mind. I wouldn't think of getting between an artist and her muse. I might get hurt."

"Ahuh." She nodded and turned her attention back to her work.

"When do you plan to take a break?"

Looking up from the painting, Regina saw the twinkle in his eyes. "I think now would be a good time." She cleaned her brush then covered the easel with a cloth. Regina looked down at her bare legs and paint-stained tee, feeling heat rise in her cheeks.

"I have an idea. Come downstairs and talk with me while I fix a snack. Being in court all morning made me miss lunch."

"Okay." Shaking her head at her disheveled appearance, Regina wiped her hands on the ruined shirt and followed him down the stairs.

He glanced over his shoulder at her. "I talked with Annabelle today."

"Has something happened?"

"Tom came by the house after Tillie and Annabelle left for a walk. Peggy answered the door and he pushed his way in. Tad sneaked off with Megan and called 911 while their sister kept him busy. Sounds like he got pretty pissed off."

"Did he hurt her?"

"Nope. She's tough like her Cousin Regina."

He grabbed the bread and peanut butter, continuing the narration. "He's obviously losing his patience. Annabelle is going to have to do something before he blows."

He took a huge bite of his sandwich, washing it down with a gulp of milk. "I want to ask you something." He paused to swallow. "Do you want Annabelle to change her Will so you're not responsible for the kids anymore?"

Regina pulled a diet soda from the refrigerator and sat by the bar. "No. I think it's the right thing to do. They're my family."

Sam let out a long breath. "Good. Will you let her know that it's okay to leave it as it is? I think she'd appreciate hearing it from you." He slathered peanut butter and jelly on more bread, slapping the two pieces together with a pat.

"I can, and I will. But I think I need to get a shower and dress first." She gave him what she hoped was a seductive smile.

"I kinda like the view like it is, disheveled, colorful and lovely. Especially the little smudge of purple on your cheek."

He laughed as she grabbed a napkin and wiped the wrong cheek in an attempt to clean the paint from her skin. He took it from her and gently wiped the spot, kissing it when he finished.

"I'd like them to keep the house, too. When Annabelle's gone, Peggy can have it." She felt the heat suffuse her neck and flow up to her hairline.

"Okay, I'll draw up the papers. Did you know they're getting a dog from the Humane Society?" He ate his second sandwich with just as much gusto as the first.

"Really? A year ago I would've been furious, but now I'm glad. They could use the protection along with the companionship. Although, I don't know what Ms. Pickles will think of a permanent canine in residence. She tolerates Sugar's periodic visits, but full time—"

"The cat will adjust."

"She'll probably choke on a hairball." Regina deposited the pop can on the counter.

Looking pleased, Sam said, "I get to help them choose."

"Really? I just figured Tillie or Joe would do it." Regina started pacing.

"The kids and Annabelle like Sugar so much I think they're hoping we'll find a dog that's her equal." His eyes followed her back and forth.

"That's a good idea. Then Megan can take the dog and Ms. Pickles for walks."

Sam chuckled. "Carrying the cat once her cast comes off, no doubt."

"No doubt. Three legs just aren't enough to keep up with that youngster."

Regina took another sip of her soda in silence. Sam finished his snack, placing the plate in the dishwasher and rinsing out his glass.

"I have another question for you."

"Alright. Go ahead." She leaned back against the counter.

He wrapped himself around her, nuzzling her neck. "Why did you really cut your hair?"

"Time for a change." She fingered the wavy locks, flipping it back with her hand.

"I think you look freer with it short. What did you do with all your hair?" His warm breath left a train of goose bumps on her bare skin.

"I donated it to make wigs for cancer patients." Her voice quivered.

He touched a curl. "It's sexy."

"Nice of you to notice." She batted her eyelashes at him, but he didn't smile.

"If something happened to me, Reggie, where would you live?"

"Here. It's my home. The Queen Anne is for Annabelle and the kids. I thought I made that clear. Unless you were thinking of leaving your house to someone else?" She stuck her nose in the air.

"No. You want to know something?" He stroked her shining hair, burying his fingers deep in the waves.

"What?" She closed her eyes.

"I'm impressed."

"With what?"

"How much you've changed." He gave her a quick squeeze.

"Do you mind that the spit polished Regal Regina no longer exists?" She stroked his jaw with her paint-spattered fingers.

"I love it. You're just showing the woman I knew was there all the time." He kissed her palm.

"I've been thinking a lot about my Aunt Rose, Annabelle's mother. I think she'd be especially proud. My mother, on the other hand, is probably moldering in her grave." Regina leaned her cheek against the back of his hand. "She doesn't haunt me anymore, though."

"Good deal. And your dad?"

"He didn't care about me. He was too busy making the family fortune." She tucked her hair behind her ear.

"There's something to be said for financial security." His voice was serious.

"Not really. It never made me feel loved or even safe. I'm learning you really can't purchase happiness."

"What about freedom?"

"Yes. There is that. I was free to paint and not work, because I lived frugally. And the house was paid for. It just required upkeep. I was luckier than Annabelle. Although a womanizer, my husband was a good companion, not like her husband, David. At least he never beat their daughter. Not that it mattered. Lydia still grew up hating Annabelle."

"What about your daughter?"

"Beth? I imagine she'd be tall like me. Peg reminds me of her." She leaned her face on his chest, sighing.

"The hope of her?"

"Very astute counselor." She straightened her painted tee shirt and looked him in the eye.

"Peggy took a couple of hard knocks both physically and emotionally from Tom's visit yesterday. She's probably feeling pretty raw right now. She could use a woman's ear."

Regina paused to consider his words. "I wonder . . . maybe I'll go by and see if she wants to go shopping."

"You? Shop?" He laughed.

"Darling, I didn't get my lovely wardrobe by osmosis. There's a fabulous shop in Old Town I haven't been to in a while. I may have to see what Lucinda's has in stock. If nothing else, I'll buy new earrings." She stood, her open arms punctuating her words.

"Why? You have hundreds." He was smiling, laughing at her.

She pointed at him and winked. "You can never have too many earrings, love."

"If you say so. I guess I may as well go back to work. I'm not wanted around here."

She took his hand. A smile slowly spread across her face. "I need someone to wash my back. Care to volunteer?"

"I am at your disposal." He rose to follow her.

"I'm counting on it." Regina tugged him toward the stairs.

Chapter 22

THE KNOCK ON the bedroom door woke Peggy. Bright sunshine filled the room, and the tall bedposts cast shadows across the sheets.

"Time to get up!" Annabelle called before opening the door. "Who's going with Sam to find us a dog?"

"Me!" Megan rolled to the edge of the bed and hobbled into the bathroom.

"What about you, Peg? Are you going?"

Peggy lay still a moment then stretched her long sleepy limbs. She smiled at her grandmother.

"You know, I think I will. Is Tad up yet?"

"Yes. He was up while it was still dark. He's cleaned out the cookie jar and he's eaten half a loaf of bread."

The teen threw off the sheet. "Then I guess I'd better get dressed and supervise this adventure. Are you coming?"

"I wish I could, but I have things to get done around here. Remember, no small puppies, but no really old dogs either. Make sure it gets along with other animals, too. This is Ms. Pickles' home and Sugar needs to be able to visit."

Pulling on her jean shorts, Peggy laughed. "Gee, Gram. You sound as excited as Megan."

"We always had dogs and cats on the farm. I enjoyed all the animals. It was my job to feed and water them, just like it'll be you kids' job to care for any pets around here. They'll love you all the more for it."

"Okay, Gram, I get it." Peggy ran a brush through her hair as her sister wobbled around, wiggling into her clothes.

With a smile Annabelle turned to leave. "Off with you, then. Sam's out front. Grab a granola bar for you and your sister."

"Thanks." After giving Megan a hand, Peggy made a run for the door with their breakfast bar. "Tad, Megan, come on, Sam's here!"

"Coming." Megan flip-flopped down the steps in her one sandal.

"Out of my way, small fry." Tad pushed past her so he could take the stairs down two at a time.

"No you don't, Tadpole." Megan thumped down only a few steps behind him.

"Ha! Give it up." He stopped near Peggy in the entry.

The three of them went out the door, slamming the screen in their wake.

"Hi!" Megan leaned into a crutch and waved at Sam.

"Hey, Man," Tad said. "Shotgun!"

"Hi, Sam." Peggy helped her sister into the back seat.

"Hello all and buckle up, please." Sam backed the car out and drove through the neighborhood of mature trees and turn of the century homes, before turning onto Thirteenth Street. "What kind of dog do you plan to get? Did you do your homework? Do you want a big dog? A smart dog?"

"That's a lot of questions," Megan said. "Yes. We did all of those things, and yes, we want a *big smart dog*."

"Not too big," Peggy said. "We don't want all our money to go for dog food. And a really big dog might knock Gram over."

Geez, I sound like Regina. Peggy sighed.

"I want a Rottweiler." Tad put his arm over the seat back to look at his sisters.

Peggy shook her head. "Too big and too mean."

"Good guard dog, though." Tad turned back around with a shrug. "Besides, who died and made you boss?"

"I'm the oldest. Get over it." She crossed her arms over her chest. "You're such a dweeb."

"What about a Labrador Retriever?" Sam asked.

"Like Sugar Bear? Cool!" Megan said.

"That'd be okay. She's smart. All Labs must be smart. They're on TV all the time." Tad smiled at Sam.

"What about you, Peg? What would you like to get?" Sam asked.

Shrugging, Peggy said, "I don't care. A mutt is fine with me. Or a German Shepherd."

"Or a Doberman," Tad added. "Shepherds and Dobies were good war dogs."

"They're neat looking, but I don't want a war dog. We're not in a war." Megan stuck her tongue out at her brother.

Sam smiled at Megan in the rear view mirror. "Well. That gives me an idea about what to help you look for. We'll have to wait and see what they have, though." Sam signaled the turn.

Megan leaned close to her sister. "Do you think we could get a kitten, too?"

"I don't think so, honey." Peggy whispered back to her now pouting sister.

"Ms. Pickles will be outnumbered when Sugar visits."

Peggy patted her little sister's hand. "Ms. Pickles can hold her own."

The group pulled into the Humane Society lot and parked in front of the new building. Made of brick and concrete, the smoke stack was discreetly situated at the back. The empty fenced-in play area had lots of shade trees. Sam held open the glass door for the kids to precede him. The shiny floors were gray concrete. Muffled barking penetrated the closed doors on the east side of the room. The disinfectant in the air didn't quite cover the animal smells.

A young volunteer in green scrubs sat behind the counter and smiled. "Hello, can I help you?"

Sam held up his hand and ticked each requirement off his fingers. "We're looking for a young dog, about a year old, but not too large, that gets along with other animals and children."

"Most of what we have right now are puppies and kittens, but - there might be one. Turbo gets along with other dogs and cats. He's not more than two. He's a pretty big boy, but he's very well mannered. He's a Labrador Rottweiler mix," said the attendant.

Tad's face split in a huge grin. "Perfect."

"May we see him?" Peggy asked.

"Sure. Join me in room one. If you're interested, we'll bring him out to the common area."

Peggy nodded then watched the clerk walk away thinking that she couldn't be more than twenty. "I hope this dog isn't too big."

The meeting area was about the same size as the kitchen back home with a bench on one wall and a chair on wheels in the corner. A modern structure designed with sparse furniture and easy maintenance. The bright colored laminated cabinets and wall of windows allowed the sunlight into the entire building.

Sam and Tad stood next to the built-in bench, while Peggy and Megan sat down. They all watched the door, anticipating what would be appearing any moment. No one spoke.

The clerk opened the door and allowed the black dog to walk in a couple steps ahead of her. He didn't pull on the lead, but stood waiting for her to close the door. He wagged his tail then turned to the crowd watching him from across the room. He slurped his nose, his tongue lolling into a pant.

"Look, he's smiling." Megan grinned and reached out her hand.

Blue-black with small flopping ears, he had two brown spots above his eyes like round eyebrows, a white blaze on his chest, and four brown socks on his feet.

"His coloring is like a Rottweiler, but he's almost the same size as Sugar." Tad called to the dog. "Hey, boy, you're a good-looking dog. Come here."

The dog's whole back end wagged with excitement. He tugged on the leash, crossing the room to the boy's waiting arms.

Tad rubbed his head, scratched him down his back and under his chin. "You're a good boy, aren't you?" The dog leaned against his legs, his body vibrating with joy.

Standing up, Megan showed the dog her open palm. "Hi, Turbo."

He gave her hand a lick and she giggled. He wagged a couple of steps forward so she could pet his big black head. "He's soft," Megan said.

"Sit." Peggy snapped her fingers.

The dog stopped wagging and plopped his bottom down on the tile facing her. "May I give him a treat?" Peggy asked the attendant.

"Sure." She handed Peggy two dog biscuits.

"Good boy." Peggy held the treat out to the dog. He took it in between his teeth, never touching her fingers.

"Do you know if he is house-broken?"

"Yes, he is. We run our dogs through a series of tests, and Turbo rates very well. He's good with kids and shows no aggression to other animals. He's been obedience trained and doesn't like to go to the bathroom indoors," she said. "Because of the mix of breeds he is, he'll be a good watch dog. Most Rottweilers bond to their families and are very protective."

Sam stood by and watched as Peggy and her siblings took turns petting the friendly animal. "Why did the owners get rid of him?"

Good question, Sam, I'm glad you're here.

"They had to move out of state and couldn't take him along."

"Lab puppies are usually very destructive," Sam said, his arms crossed. "I had to replace the arm of my chair and the feet on one of my table legs."

"That usually stops once they are past a year. Turbo is nearly two and shows no signs of such behavior in his room."

"I like him." Megan leaned her head on his neck.

Tad sat on the floor scratching the dog's chest. "He's cool."

"I think so, too. Do you think Gram will like him?" Peggy thought Turbo liked them all and looked really happy to have all the attention.

"She'll love him." Sam turned to the clerk. "We'll take him."

The young woman smiled and stroked the dog's head. "He's been neutered, had all his shots and been wormed. Let's go start the paperwork."

"Great, I'll go with you." Sam held the door open for the young lady to precede him.

Megan looked confused. "What did she mean he'd been tutored?"

"Neutered." Peggy laughed. "It means he can't make puppies anymore."

Tad frowned. "That's just wrong."

Peggy shook her head at her little brother and sat back up on the bench. They stayed in the room with Turbo, waiting for Sam. The dog's tail hadn't stopped wagging since he came in.

"Look at that tail," Tad said. "It doesn't go back and forth, it goes round and round."

Peggy smacked her forehead with her palm. "Duh. I'll bet that's why they call him Turbo."

They all laughed, and Turbo seemed to smile.

"Can we look at the kittens, too?" Megan's eyes pleaded with Peggy to say yes.

Tad looked at Peggy, raised his brows and shrugged.

"I don't know. Gram didn't say anything about getting a cat, too."

"But you heard the clerk say they had kittens, and Turbo gets along with them. Please!" Megan vibrated with excitement. "Ms. Pickles is Gram's cat. I want one of my own."

Studying the pattern in the tile, Peggy said, "I don't know if that would be fair to Turbo. He should get all of our attention since he's new to our family, don't you think?"

Tad touched his little sister's sleeve.

"I guess." Megan's eyes glistened. "But she could be friends with Ms. Pickles. I like orange kittens."

"I'll ask Sam what he thinks." Peggy left Tad and Megan with the dog and crossed the foyer to where Sam stood going over the adoption papers. "Sam?"

"Hi, kiddo, what's up? Did you change your mind?"

"No, we love Turbo. He's a great dog. But Megan would really like an orange kitten. Do you think Gram would mind?"

"Do you have any orange kittens?" Sam asked the girl behind the counter.

"As a matter of fact, we do. There's a litter of two-month-old kittens. One of them is orange with yellow eyes. It's the cutest little thing."

"Why don't you call your Grandmother and ask her?"

Peggy pulled out her cell and punched in the number. "Gram? Hi. We found a dog. He's perfect. He's two years old and trained and everything. He's mostly black with brown eyebrows and feet."

"Does he have a name?"

"Turbo, because of the way his tail spins around. It's really funny." Peggy leaned from one foot to the other.

"He sounds fine."

"Would it be all right if we brought home a kitten for Megan? They have one like she wants."

"I don't know, Peggy . . ."

"They said he isn't aggressive with other animals at all."

"Well, Ms. Pickles will probably have a fit, but okay. I don't know how I'm going to pay Sam back for two animals," Annabelle wondered aloud. "We'll figure something out. Don't forget, taking care of them is you kids' responsibility."

"Okay, thanks, bye." Peggy snapped the cell phone shut, her eyes shining. "She said yes. Could you get the orange kitten? We need to see how it gets along with Turbo."

"Sure." The girl in green went through a different set of double doors and emerged with a tiny kitten in her arms a few moments later.

"She's precious." Peggy took the kitten and stroked the tiny head. The kitten rubbed its nose under Peggy's chin and purred. "Oh my, she's soft and so tiny. I hope Turbo doesn't sit on her."

"I'll take her." Sam scooped the kitten into his palm cradling it against his chest.

They walked back into the meeting area and found Megan and Tad sitting on the floor with Turbo lying on his back getting his tummy rubbed. They stopped and watched as Turbo rolled onto his feet. Sam knelt down. "Come, Turbo. Here, boy."

The dog's nails clicked as he walked over to Sam and sniffed the kitten. He pushed it with his nose and the kitten batted away the big black nostril. Turbo licked the kitten's head. The kitten mewed and purred in Sam's arms.

"Good boy, Turbo." Tad grinned at his little sister.

Putting her hands on her hips, Megan stared. "What's going on?"

"Gram said we could have a kitten, too," Peggy responded.

"Really?" Megan took the tiny kitten in her arms. "Hello, little one. We're your new family." The kitten's motor thrummed as she snuggled into Megan's neck. "I'll call you Tang."

Her brother rolled his eyes. "What kind of a name is Tang?"

The little girl stood tall, her chin high. "She's the color of Tang orange drink."

"You know, I think you're right," he said, rolling his eyes again. "Come on Turbo. Tang. Let's go home."

Chapter 23

THE NEXT SATURDAY, Regina pulled up in the drive of the Riverside house and honked, watching for signs of life behind the curtains. Megan peeked out with an orange fur ball under her chin and waved. Waving back, Regina smiled. "Such a cutie," she said aloud.

The front door opened and Peggy came out wearing white shorts and a red tank top, her flowered bag over her shoulder. "Bye," she called before she closed the door. Peggy skipped down the porch steps and crossed to the passenger door, opened it and plopped into the seat.

"Hi, how are you?" She put on her seat belt and smiled.

"Hello, young lady. I'm just fine, thank you. I was thinking we might head to Old Town?"

"I'd love to go to Lucinda's. She has the coolest stuff."

"Good. I can always find a pair of earrings I like there." Regina turned the car towards the middle of town.

"They have a sale on shirts, skirts, summer dresses and shoes—well, everything. Plus they have silly stuff we could get for Tad and Megan."

They crossed over the bridge at North High School, passing by an area that had seen better days. Some of these houses had been built near the same time as her family's home near the Arkansas River, though most had smaller yards and had been turned into multi-family dwellings.

"We'll see what they have and then decide. How do you feel about gelato?"

"I love the stuff, but it is way too expensive." Peggy dug in her bag and found a zipper coin purse, opened it and fingered the contents. "I don't think I have enough."

"My treat."

The kids have learned to watch every penny. That's good, but a little sad.

"In that case, I want chocolate." Peggy zipped her bag closed with a content look on her face.

"Don't you want to try something unusual like Pumpkin Pie or Cotton Candy?"

Peggy shook her head. "Nope. Chocolate."

"You're a young woman of impeccable taste. Chocolate is my favorite, too."

"Can we shop first? You know, work up an appetite?"

"Sure."

The radio was set to an oldies station so Peggy punched in the numbers for a station that played more modern music. The thumping bass filled the air around them.

No parking was available in front of the store, so they opted for the parking garage.

"Do we have a budget today? I don't want to overspend. Just tell me what you're willing to pay and I'll make sure I don't go over."

"As a matter of fact, no. We're open to whatever possibilities present themselves."

The young woman's eyes widened. "Really? I like that. But I also like a sale. You get more for your money."

They found a place to park on the first level, locked the Caddy up tight and headed into the square. The bell above Lucinda's door jingled as they entered.

Regina gestured to the lovely brunette behind the counter. "Hello, Ellie."

Returning Regina's smile, Ellie walked around the counter and extended her hand. "We haven't seen you in a long time. Wait until you see the summer things we have on sale."

"I'm here for earrings. It's past time for a new pair."

"Of course." Ellie led them to the glass case.

Peggy walked past the jewelry counter, through the archway to the part of the shop filled with clothing, shoes and handbags. Racks and displays crowded the aisles. Accessories draped over hangers and wire mannequins adding color and glitz to the scene. Regina watched Peggy finger through the rack of eclectic colored summer dresses, pulling out one after the other. She held a sundress up against her body and swung around smiling.

"Look at this one, Regina. Isn't it fabulous?" Peggy held a turquoise dress, patterns of pink and purple swirling along the bias.

"Those are great colors on you. Go try it on."

Peggy didn't waste a heartbeat before going into the dressing room and pulling the curtain.

"Show me what earrings you have in those colors," Regina said to Ellie. "Nothing too large or flashy, but they have to be fun."

"I have just the thing." Ellie went to the earring display and returned with a pair of earrings sporting a short dangle, and a bead for each color in the dress.

"Excellent." Regina took the earrings to the dressing room door as Peggy emerged swirling around in the crinkly cotton dress.

"What do you think?"

"Hum. I think you need these to go with it." Regina held the earrings up against the fabric and smiled at the shine in Peggy's eyes.

"The colors are perfect." Peggy hugged Regina and returned to the dressing room to change back into her shorts.

"Now Ellie, let's find something equally fun for me." Regina scanned the beautiful displays, her eyes drawn by the sparkle and color.

After choosing a pair of Vintage Swarovski Crystal earrings that flashed blue, gold, or red depending on the light, Regina joined Peggy where the most unusual and funny gift items were displayed. Peggy had already picked out bacon-flavored toothpicks and skull and cross bones bandages for Tad. She held a small beaded heart-shaped box and a decorative hanging with butterfly wings on a half-moon for Megan. Across the moon there was a saying about dreams by Eleanor Roosevelt.

"Good choices." Regina felt warmed by the pleasure in Peggy's eyes. "Now what about your Gram?"

"They used to have some great lotion that has bees in the name."

"And here it is." Ellie handed Peggy a bottle with yellow bees on the label.

"That's it!" Peggy grinned and turned her loaded arms towards Regina. "Is it too much?"

"No, it's just right." Regina took a few items and handed them to Ellie.

Taking the rest of their purchases to the cash register, they laughed at the funny magnet display while Ellie rang them up.

"One twenty-five, thirty-two, today."

Peggy gasped and froze in place, her eyes watching for a reaction, but none came.

Regina handed over her credit card. "I think it's time for gelato."

It feels good to surprise them once in a while.

"Thank you, Regina, this is so cool," Peggy whispered. She shook herself and gave Regina a quick hug. "I'm having a great time."

"Good. Thanks, Ellie." Regina stowed her wallet in her purse and took the bag Ellie handed over the counter. To Peggy she said, "I thought we needed a bit of girl-time."

They crossed the cobblestoned square and went into the café that advertised gelato on the sign. In the entry area there was a large glass top freezer with compartments that held different flavors. It was circular and twirled around like a carousel.

"We'd both like chocolate and I think we'll eat it outside under an umbrella." The handsome middle-aged woman motioned for the waitress nearest the doorway and smiled.

"Cherie will seat you while I fill your order. What size would you like?"

"Medium for both of us, please." Regina and Peggy followed the waitress to the door.

"Very good. Chocolate is the best," the waitress said. The young woman's stark black hair matched the studded collar she wore around her neck.

At least her face didn't look pierced like a pincushion.

She smiled and took them to the fenced off patio. "Would this be all right?"

"This is fine, thank you," Regina said.

It was a calm day, a pleasant surprise for Kansas in late June, which had often been known to reach nearly a hundred degrees with thirty-mile-per-hour wind gusts. In the shade, it felt cool and comfortable.

The waitress brought out their gelato and glasses of iced water. "Here you go. Enjoy."

"Oh, we will." Peggy took a bite and closed her eyes with pleasure.

Regina chuckled. They ate the first few bites in silence, savoring the creamy chocolate flavor and the cold smoothness sliding across the tongue.

"How are you doing?"

"What do you mean? I'm doing great. Mmm." Peggy took another bite.

"That's good. Have things been okay around the house since . . . ?"

The young woman's eyes grew large. "Oh, you mean since Dad came by?"

"Yes."

"It's kind of spooky. We're all super-conscious of noises and constantly checking the windows when a car drives by."

Taking another luscious bite, Regina waited for it to melt down her throat. "How do you think Tad and your grandmother are doing?"

"I don't think Gram sleeps much. Tad is trying to be all manly and bossy."

"What can I do to help?"

The teenager took another nibble before speaking. "I don't know. We've got Turbo now, and he seems to be settling in okay. I think he senses our fear 'cuz he growls whenever he hears something outside."

"That's good. Do you think Sam and I should move back in for a while?"

Peggy shook her head. "No. There's too many people around for the bathroom now."

"I see." Regina laughed.

"That's not really it. I just wish . . . I dunno. I guess I wish Dad was like he used to be when I was little. Do you think that's silly?"

"No. We all want to relive the good times. Did Tom answer some of your questions?"

The teen put her spoon down on the napkin and looked at her cousin. "He said he'd been in jail for running over a guy when he was drunk. Do you think that's true?"

"Yes."

"But why wouldn't he call or write or something? Mom would've said so, right?"

Possibly not. Your mother had some serious problems, too. Merde, this is so hard.

Peggy's troubled face softened Regina's heart.

"I don't know, honey."

"He said he wrote to us. If that's true, where are the letters? We would've found them in Mom's stuff if she hadn't told us, right? Am I right?" Peggy's fisted hands lay on the tabletop.

"I don't know, sweetie."

She sighed and picked up her spoon. "I wish . . ."

"That things had been different?"

"Yeah, something like that." Peggy took a spoonful of gelato into her mouth and closed her eyes again. "This tastes so good, it kinda makes all the other stuff go down easier. Do you know what I mean?"

"Yes, I do. You know, people can't always be the way we want them to be. For whatever reason, Tom couldn't be a good dad to you kids. He was just a kid himself. But I'm thinking he wanted to be, or why would he marry your mother and have you kids?"

Peggy shrugged and finished the last of her frozen dessert, signaling an end to the discussion.

"Have you heard anything from or about Miles?" Regina asked.

Playing with her spoon, Peggy looked sad. "I was so mad, I didn't want to talk to him the last few days of school. His dad took his car and he has to do a bunch of work for his dad until the court decides what they'll do. We know it was an accident but I just wish it never happened. I miss him."

Watching the young woman twirl her spoon on the tabletop didn't conjure any words of wisdom for either of them.

"Is there any place else you'd like to go?" Regina asked.

"No. I think I'm ready to go home." Peggy wiped her mouth with the napkin. "Thank you for everything. The clothes. The cell phone. For being there, both you and Sam."

"We're family, honey. I'll always be there for you." Regina reached over and squeezed Peggy's slender hand. "Try not to worry too much, okay."

"But I am. I'm worried about the kids and Gram. Megan's quiet again, and Tad gets mad so easy. Plus Gram's heart . . . and Miles and me . . ."

"With a little more exercise and a healthy diet, your grandmother will be fine. We Morgans are made of tough material. You're all Morgans, too."

"Yeah, but us kids are also Malones," Peggy said with a sigh.

Sad, but . . .

"True, but you have to know the Morgan side is very strong."

"More stubborn, you mean?" Peggy smiled.

"That, too." Regina placed cash under the empty glass and included a generous tip.

Walking out of the café side-by-side, both women were tall and slender. With shoulders straight and chins high, they resembled artfully mismatched bookends.

Chapter 24

ANNABELLE ENJOYED the new summer routine. Every morning while she walked with Tillie, Tad took Turbo out to do his business. Megan and Peggy took care of the animals' food and water. After breakfast, they all pitched in to clean one room each day, with laundry on Monday and Friday. Afternoons were free time to read, watch television, shop, rest or go to the neighborhood pool. The older kids walked Turbo before dinner so he'd take a nap and let them eat in peace, at least in theory.

Megan was counting the days until her cast came off and she could join them on their walks, with Ms. Pickles in tow, of course.

The little girl was more than ready for July second, cast removal day and a Friday. Her leg was hot and itchy and smelled rotten if your nose got too close. The dog loved it, snuffling at it every chance he got and tickling her with his whiskers. The whole family planned on a ceremony with balloons and ice cream after the procedure. Megan couldn't sit still in the doctor's office until the saw came out. Then she and Annabelle barely breathed.

The doctor removed the grayish purple cast with care and palpated her leg. "There you go, Megan. As good as new."

"It's all skinny and white!" Megan started crying, scraping her nails up and down the offending limb. "It's ugly and it itches."

He took out a cotton ball and soaked it with disinfectant, gently wiping her leg. "You'll have it tanned and stronger in no time. Do you like to swim?"

"No." She carefully stood up, then staggered. Annabelle reached out to grab her, but the doctor was quicker. "It feels like it won't hold me anymore."

"It'll hold you. It's healed just fine. Start walking a little bit at a time and I promise by the end of the summer it'll be like new." He patted her shoulder with a smile.

She sniffed and hobbled out of the room. "The scar looks kinda cool where they went in to fix it."

Tad and Peggy sat waiting in the lobby.

"Think of the stories you can tell." Tad grinned at her. "You were shark bit, or you jumped out of an airplane without a parachute or . . ."

"Tad!" Annabelle couldn't believe her ears.

Megan giggled. "I like reading stories better than making them up, remember? But you may have given me some ideas to think about, in case I take up writing."

"Looks like you won't be running any races for a while."

She crossed her arms over her chest, her chin jutted out. "No, but I'll be just fine by the end of summer. Doc said so."

"That's for sure." Peggy tucked her arm under her little sister's and mimicked her stance. "Back off, Tadpole."

"Hey." He raised his hands in surrender. "I know when I'm out-numbered." Annabelle grinned. Nothing more needed to be said.

On Saturday, summer hit full force and the temperatures climbed into the high nineties. The July 4th holiday weekend had arrived, and they planned to watch the fireworks by the river.

"Do you think Turbo and Tang will be scared of the noise?" Megan asked Annabelle.

"We'll just have to wait and see. He and the cats can stay at home and guard the house while we're gone. They'll be fine. If they get scared, they can curl up together under the sofa." Annabelle tucked another sandwich into a plastic zip lock bag.

Megan giggled. "I don't think Turbo will fit under the sofa."

"You could be right."

Tad waltzed into the room and ruffled Megan's hair. "Hey, squirt, what did you do with the flashlight?"

She batted his hand away. "It's on my night stand, and don't call me squirt."

"Been reading under the covers again, eh?" He winked at her.

"So what? I don't want to disturb anybody."

"Except maybe Peg?"

"Nuh uh. I always turn my back to her so it doesn't shine in her eyes."

"What fun is that? Are you putting that mangy kitten under the covers, too?"

"Tang is not mangy. You're the mangy one. Besides, she sleeps on top of my pillow, not under the covers, boy-breath."

Tad pushed her playfully. "That's man-breath to you."

Turbo nudged his big black head between them, wagging his tail.

Megan ran her hands over his soft fur. "Ha! Even Turbo thinks you need to back off."

Ruffling the dog's ears, Tad said, "Hey, dog-breath, what do you think?"

The dog rolled onto his back and offered up his tummy for a scratch. Both kids bent down to oblige him.

Annabelle chuckled, shaking her head. "He's so smart. You're an important part of this family, now, Turbo. Yes, you are."

"What did the big fella do now?" Peggy asked as she entered the kitchen with Ms. Pickles close behind her.

"Turbo just separated your brother and sister who were picking on each other."

"Really?" Peggy knelt down and scratched his tummy. "You're a good boy."

Putting the pile on the table, Annabelle surveyed what they had gathered. "I've got an old quilt for us to sit on. And I've made ham and cheese sandwiches. There are strawberries and a thermos of iced tea."

"Are there any cookies?" Megan and Tad asked at the same time.

Rolling her eyes, Peggy snorted. "Kids."

Annabelle spread her arms and smiled. "Of course, and deviled eggs and potato salad, too."

"Oh, man. I better go dig out the cooler and red wagon." Tad slammed out the back screen door, heading for the carriage house.

"I'll get the flashlight and the bug wipes." Megan scurried out of the room as fast as her mismatched legs would carry her.

Holding up her contributions, Peggy smiled. "I've got a charge on my cell phone and the sunscreen."

Annabelle set the sunscreen on the pile. "You kids stay close. It gets pretty dark by the river at night."

Peggy stuck the cell phone in the front pocket of her shorts. "Don't worry, Gram. We won't stray far. Promise." She crossed her heart and held up her palm.

"I'm not taking my pocketbook. Just keys and cash." Annabelle ran a hand over each pocket to double check the contents.

The pile on the kitchen table grew monstrous from their contributions.

"Malissa's folks should be dropping her off any time now." The doorbell rang and Peggy broke into a smile. "I'll bet that's her now." She ran to answer it, Turbo on her heels.

"She must be psychic." Annabelle whispered and followed.

Peggy opened the door to find her best friend chewing gum, one iPod earphone plugged in and one dangling. Malissa's short black hair framed her heart shaped face and freckles sprinkled her nose. Shorter than Peggy by a good three inches, they were both lanky as colts, their bodies just beginning to curve in all the usual places.

"Woof." Turbo joined them in the foyer doing his famous tailspin.

"Whoa, nice dog." Malissa stuck out both hands to halt the eager canine. "Hey Chicky. Are you ready for some major sparks?"

"Oh, yeah. We just need to put everything on the wagon and go."

Annabelle liked her granddaughter's best friend. "Hello, Malissa."

"Hi, Mrs. H. Wow, have you lost weight? You look really nice."

Annabelle felt her cheeks heat up. "Yes, um. Thank you."

Leaning close to her friend, Peggy teased, "She's been walking a lot and there's this guy hanging around."

Turbo leaned against Malissa's legs; his head swiveled up to allow her better access to scratch his velvety throat.

"No way! Good for you, Mrs. H." Malissa staggered then reached down and scratched the monstrous head between the ears.

"Don't you start telling stories, Miss Peggy. Mr. Edwards is your brother's coach and a nice man, that's all."

With a wink, Peggy and Malissa walked arm-in-arm to the kitchen while Annabelle closed the front door, turning the bolt. Turbo was right behind the girls, panting and bouncing to get their attention.

Shaking her head, Annabelle couldn't help but smile at the dog's obvious enthusiasm.

I could see myself having dinner with Phil, maybe even a movie sometime. But, he'd have to clean up his domineering act first. I'd enjoy the attention, and when he moves on I'll wave goodbye. There's no way Annabelle Hubbard's falling in love again. No way at all.

Megan had the orange kitten tucked under her arm. "Are Regina and Sam coming?"

"Yes, they are."

"What about Joe and Tillie?" She stroked the tiny head. Ms. Pickles rubbed against her newly healed leg and purred. Megan reached down and scooped her up in the other arm, rubbing her chin across both of their furry heads.

"Yes, Tillie and Joe are coming, but not the cats. We'll have the whole group down by the river tonight. It should be great fun."

"Almost like a family reunion," Peggy said. "All our favorite people will be there."

No one said a word about Tom.

"They certainly will. Just like when I was a kid on the farm . . ."

Tad slammed in the back door. "I've got the wagon. I even washed all the dust off."

"Then let's load up." Annabelle grabbed the food from the refrigerator.

After dumping ice in the bottom of the cooler, the girls helped Annabelle arrange the food and drinks. Megan still had the orange kitten in her embrace, but Ms. Pickles was absent. She started toward the door.

"Megan, the animals have to stay here."

The little girl sighed and set the cat on the floor.

Everyone grabbed an armload and carried it down the back steps to load the wagon. When they were done, it was piled so high they started to laugh.

Annabelle draped the quilt over the cooler. "We should be prepared for anything."

"I'll get a couple of bungee cords," Tad said. "We can tie everything down so it won't topple."

"It looks like we're moving out," Peggy said. "And we probably forgot something, what do ya bet?"

"I can't imagine what." Her grandmother patted the pile. "If we don't have it, we must not need it."

With a smile on his face, Tad returned, red and green cords in hand. Hooking two together he was able to go from the lip of the wagon over the cooler and quilt to the other side.

He surveyed his handiwork. "That should hold it."

"I'm impressed," Malissa said.

Pink rose in Tad's cheeks as he looked at his sister's friend and gave her a lopsided smile.

He's growing up fast. They all are. Too bad my daughter didn't live to see this. Poor Liddy never realized she had so much to be thankful for.

"Good job." Annabelle patted her grandson on the back. "You kids take turns pulling it. Tad, you want to go first?"

"Sure." He flexed his muscles.

They walked behind the wagon, around the house to the drive and across the street to Tillie and Joe's. Their friends sat waiting on the porch steps.

"Hey there everybody!" Tillie stood, brushing off the seat of her Capri's. "You moving out?"

Peggy laughed. "That's what I said."

"How's it going, Malissa?" Tillie asked.

"Goin' good. You look cute in your *Life is Good* tee shirt. Jake is the bomb." Malissa gave her thumbs up.

"That has always been my philosophy." Tillie tugged her shirt down, smoothing the wrinkles.

"What's your philosophy? Chocolate rules or is it coffee?" Tad asked Tillie.

"That life is good, silly boy!"

"Heck, yeah. That's no lie." Tad did a shortened fist pump.

"And I agree wholeheartedly." Joe kissed the top of Tillie's head, a very easy task with his six feet to her five.

The females giggled, including Annabelle.

Tillie frowned. "Where's Regina?"

Annabelle held her gaze. "On her way, I hope."

"Ever since she moved in with Sam, she's late everywhere," Peggy said.

"She's in love." Tad dismissed the words with a flip of his arm even though he blushed.

"Cool," Malissa said.

The red Cadillac convertible pulled in front of the house and honked. Sam was behind the wheel, a sight Annabelle had never seen before.

No one drives Regina's car but Regina. A lot has certainly changed.

"Hey, there." Peggy walked toward the Caddy. "You're late!"

Sam got out and walked around to open the door for Regina.

Malissa whispered in her friend's ear. "Oh man, that's cool."

"So is he," Peggy whispered back.

Grinning, Annabelle walked across the grass toward her cousin.

"I love your hair cut. Every time I see you without your braid, I'm stunned."

"I had it most of my life. Don't you think it was time for a change?"

"I guess so." Annabelle smiled up at her. "Are you ready?"

"Let me put the top up and lock the car," Sam said.

"I'll help you unload your stuff." Joe walked over to Regina who had opened the trunk.

"No worries. We're traveling light these days." She pulled out a quilt and a soft-sided cooler then shut the lid.

"Let's get this crowd moving before all of the good places are taken."

Joe took the cooler from Regina, slinging it over his shoulder.

The clan walked through the neighborhood, crossing over the bridge to the park and the Arkansas River. The night was warm and still, thankfully. They paired up or walked in threes and talked the half-mile, taking their time for Megan's slow gait and Tad's oversized load.

About a half-mile west of the Indian Center they stopped. It was a fairly open, quiet spot, so they laid out their blankets side by side. They would be able to see the fireworks at Cowtown as well as downtown from this vantage point, since the river wound around both places.

Tad tossed a stone up in the air and caught it. "I've got a pocket full of stones, Megan. Want to try skipping them on the river?"

"Sure."

Annabelle watched the children run toward the water.

"Be careful, Megan." She let out a sigh.

"I will." Megan called over her shoulder.

"Tad will look out for her, Grandma Worry Wart," Tillie said. "Besides, they won't go far."

"Oh, I know. It just made my heart skip a little, that's all."

"How is that old ticker of yours? Has it been behaving itself?" Tillie turned her dark eyes toward her friend, concern creasing the corners.

"Seems to be."

"Good."

"And you're feeling okay these days?" Annabelle watched the lines smooth out as her friend smiled in response.

"Yup. Our walks help keep me strong and flexible." Tillie sank into a ballet pose, flourishing her arms.

The two friends turned to watch Sam and Regina smooth out the quilt next to them.

They're sweet together. It's amazing that Regina fell so hard so late in life. She'd been alone for a very long time. Sam is a wonderful man and fits right in with the family.

"Annabelle?" Regina startled her. "What are you day dreaming about?"

"Just wool gathering." She hoped the heat of her embarrassment wouldn't show on her face. They might think she was nuts, wandering off into La-La land.

"Peggy tells me you have a beau."

"Where does she come up with this stuff?" Annabelle tugged at her shirt. "Just because I've seen Coach Edwards a couple of times. He's okay, I guess, but I'm not ..."

Regina smiled at her. Annabelle felt her cheeks warm again.

"Whatever you say, Cousin."

"Oh, leave her alone, Regina Louise." Tillie poked her best friend. "It's not like you don't know what it's like to have a favorite fella."

"I've tried to get her to make an honest man of me," Sam said. "But she won't have it."

Tillie leaned against Joe's shoulder. "I highly recommend marriage. We're enjoying every minute."

"I don't need a piece of paper to say I'm married." Regina sat up straighter. "Sam knows he has my heart."

"Now if I were to say that, you'd have Gram ground me for life," Peggy said.

"That's because you're only sixteen. I'm an adult."

There was no real censor in her voice because Annabelle knew Sam and Regina were soul mates. "And setting quite an example, too."

Regina didn't have to remind her.

Malissa leaned toward Peggy and whispered. "Your family is cool, all this talk about love and stuff. My folks sure don't talk that way. And my grandparents ... well, they just talk about where they hurt and what operation someone just had."

"I think your grandparents are older by like twenty years." Peggy kept her voice down and her mouth close to Malissa's ear. "Besides, some people are just born old."

Annabelle overheard and agreed with the girls, but didn't voice her opinion. *I like to let them think they can't be heard, I learn more that way.*

"Let's go see if any of our friends are around." Malissa popped up off the ground.

"Okay." Peggy turned to her grandmother. "We're going to walk along the river and see if anyone we know is here. Okay with you, Gram? I've got my cell."

"Sure, if Regina and Tillie have their cell phones, then it's fine. Just be back before it's completely dark, okay?"

"Mine's here." Tillie patted her pocket.

"Mine, too," Regina chimed in.

The girls strolled off, giggling and talking, their voices fading as they distanced themselves from the crowd of family and friends. Annabelle shook her head, realizing how much Peggy resembled her slender mother. And what tiny little Malissa lacked in height, she made up for in personality. Peggy was lucky to have such a good friend.

Although she sat alone on her quilt, Annabelle didn't feel lonely. She watched the two youngest skip rocks across the water and smiled with simple enjoyment. When she turned and looked at Joe and Tillie lounging on their blanket, then Sam and Regina whispering to each other, she felt a peaceful warm.

Just being together is enough. But it might be time for me to get a cell phone, too. Past time to join the global village they're always talking about on TV.

As the darkness grew, the expanse of grass became dotted with blankets and lawn chairs filled with families gathering for the fireworks. Fireflies blinked in the bushes, like tiny stars twinkling off and on between the patches of darkening color. The cicada serenade tuned up in the trees, their song a lullaby to the night. A slight breeze picked up and coolness caressed Annabelle's skin from the direction of the water. She dug out a windbreaker from the piled up wagon.

Megan and Tad walked up the bank toward her.

Tad flopped down beside her and grabbed his stomach. "We're hungry."

"You're always hungry," Annabelle said. "The food is in the cooler. Help yourselves."

The kids dug out a handful of sandwiches.

Annabelle handed them each a paper plate and plastic fork. They piled on deviled eggs and globs of potato salad.

"Want lemonade to wash it down?" she asked.

"That sounds great," Megan said around a mouth full of egg.

Annabelle got out cups and the thermos and passed out paper towels.

Tad tucked a towel under his chin. "Rolled napkins are the best kind. More absorbent."

Megan giggled.

"Got a couple extra deviled eggs in there?" Joe asked.

"Sure." Annabelle laid out what they had on her quilt then Joe and Tillie added to the spread.

"We've got brownies and chicken salad," Tillie announced.

Megan took a chocolate square from Tillie's outstretched hand. "I love brownies."

Smiling, Tillie handed one to Tad. "They're my favorite picnic dessert."

"Personally, I prefer watermelon," Joe said. "But the ants like it too much."

"I like spitting the seeds." Tad puckered his lips to show he knew the method well.

"You like spitting them at people," Megan said.

"Yeah. I do. Especially squishy little sisters."

"I'm not squishy!" Megan threw a plastic spoon at her brother.

Snatching it out of the air, Joe handed it back to Megan. "My sisters and I used to have contests to see who could spit the seeds the farthest. I always won by a mile."

"I'll bet they got even, though." Tillie wrapped her arm around her husband's broad shoulders. "With mud pies and chocolate laxatives."

"Yes, they did. They were mean. You gotta watch out for sisters, Tad. They'll get you back when you least expect it."

Nodding her head, Megan grinned. "That's right!"

It was nearly dark when Peggy and Malissa strolled up and sat down beside Annabelle.

"Hi," Peggy said.

"Did you have a nice walk?" Annabelle asked.

"Sure did."

Megan moved closer to the girls. "Did you see any cute guys?"

"A few." Peggy looked at Malissa who burst out laughing.

"What's so funny?" Megan asked.

"We saw Miles Asher. He is so in 'like' with Peg." Malissa made quotes with her fingers around the word 'like.'

"Shhhh."

Malissa leaned back on her elbows. "Well, he is."

Joining her best friend in the relaxed pose, Peggy said, "Whatever."

Megan made a dreamy face. "I think Miles is cute."

Tad tossed an ice cube on his older sister's stomach. "So does Peg, but he's a lousy driver."

She flicked it off. "Shut up, Tadpole."

Annabelle could see Tad's short temper starting to flair. She interrupted the conversation before someone erupted.

"Aren't you girls hungry? We've got ham and chicken salad sandwiches."

"Are there any deviled eggs left?" Peggy asked.

"I think so. And Tillie made brownies, but you two had better hurry before they're all gone."

"I love chocolate." Malissa helped herself to two, handing one to her friend. "I don't think I could live without it."

"Me either." Megan snatched another from the almost empty plate. "Or cookies."

"Yes. Cookies. And Cheetos," Malissa said.

Megan giggled. "You like cheesy feet?"

"Yes, and gelato," Peggy added.

"I second that." Regina turned on the radio when it was time for the festivities to start.

It was full dark. They packed up the remains of their snacks. Everyone but the girls lay on their blankets, looking at the sky in anticipation. Peggy and Malissa were huddled together on the edge of the quilt talking, giggling and watching the people walk by.

Startled by a loud explosion, the sky rained gold and silver sparks in time with the music broadcast. Great arches of purple and green sprinkled down and disappeared before hitting the ground. A chorus of 'oh' and 'ah' joined the night sounds. All eyes were on the sky, watching as color and light exploded in the heavens.

Tad had his hands under his head. "Now that's what I call a Fourth of July celebration."

Putting her head on Sam's shoulder, Regina turned her eyes back to the sky. "Indeed."

Everyone responded to the whistles and spinning lights with mouths open or squeals of delight. It was a colorful celebration and they all enjoyed the spectacle.

The fireworks continued for almost thirty minutes. When the sky stilled, they gathered their belongings to head home.

"Happy Independence Day," Annabelle said to one and all. "What a wonderful way to end the day."

"Whose idea was it to walk, anyway?" Tad stretched his back. "I'm pooped."

Peggy took the wagon handle. "I'll pull it."

"Cool, thanks."

"We were supposed to take turns and we forgot," she said.

He shrugged his shoulders. "No biggie."

The walk back was more leisurely with little conversation. The cars along the river were bumper-to-bumper, crawling then stopping for the foot traffic.

Gesturing toward the automobile congestion, Regina sighed. "This is why we walked. We'll be home long before any of the people who drove."

The number of cars thinned the closer they approached home. When they arrived, they parted in the middle of the dark street. Sam and Regina got into the Cadillac and pulled away, arms waving out the windows.

"Good night, Annabelle, kids." Tillie readjusted the quilt on her arm. "See you later."

"Night all." Joe pulled the keys from his shorts pocket.

"G'Night." Annabelle walked behind the children to the porch. The porch light was on and the bugs were doing Kamikaze dives into the bulb. She heard Turbo barking.

Running ahead, Tad fumbled for the key he kept on a chain around his neck. "I'll get the door."

The girls were giggling and hadn't reached the steps. Annabelle looked over their heads to Tad who stood perfectly still.

"Tad? What is it?" Then she noticed that the broken window beside the door was stained with . . .

"Blood," he said.

Chapter 25

WHILE TAD QUIETED the frantic dog he'd let out the front door, Annabelle called the police on the cell phone. Peggy and Malissa had to hold Megan to prevent her from going inside to find the kittens.

"Gram," Tad said. "Turbo has a cut on his nose and on his paws, probably from all the broken glass. There's blood around his muzzle. Do you think that's his or someone else's?"

"I'm guessing Turbo took a piece out of the person who tried to break in tonight." Annabelle bent down and examined the dog's snout. "It's all right. You're a good boy." She stroked his broad head. "It's not too deep. I don't think he'll need stitches, but we'll clean it up and take him to see the vet tomorrow to be sure."

"He doesn't seem to favor his feet. I don't think there's any glass in his pads," Tad said.

Two police cars pulled up, lights flashing. They asked Annabelle and the kids to stay outside while they made sure the house was safe and secured any evidence. Joe crossed the street and joined them on the porch while they waited.

"I called my mom to come and get me, Mrs. H." Malissa said. She and Peggy still had their arms around Megan. "You don't need an extra kid around tonight."

"Thank you, sweetie. I'm sorry this happened."

"Heck, it's much more exciting here than at my house, but I wouldn't want anyone's house to get broken into and their dog hurt. That's so wrong."

It wasn't long before Malissa's mom showed up.

"Everyone okay?" Mrs. Monahan called.

Annabelle waved. "We're fine."

Malissa got in the car. "I'll talk to you later, Peg."

They all waved back, looking sad.

"Mrs. Hubbard," the officer said. "We've done what we can. Everything's secure. Do you have a board that I can nail over the broken window for you?"

"Tad, go out to the carriage house and bring back some wood. Don't forget the hammer and nails, honey."

141

"Yes, ma'am." He handed Turbo's leash to Peggy.

"I'll go with you." The youngest officer flicked on his flashlight.

"Awesome light. I need one of those," Tad said.

The policeman chuckled as they rounded the corner of the house toward the garage.

It didn't take Peggy and Megan long to locate the cats hiding under the girls' bed. Peggy held Ms. Pickles close and stroked her back.

Megan cradled Tang against her throat and rubbed the furry head with her chin. She sang softly, "I love you a bushel and a peck, a bushel and a peck and a hug around the neck."

Annabelle marveled that the little girl still remembered the song she had sung to her when she was a baby. It was a loving time and Annabelle would never forget how her granddaughter would hug her neck and wouldn't let go, just like she held the kitten now.

"We're really tired, Gram," Megan said, stroking the kitten's orange fur.

"I'll bet you are. It's already morning."

"Thirty minutes after midnight. This is the third house broken into tonight in this neighborhood alone," Officer Johnson said. "We checked on every floor, closet, under the beds, as well as the windows and other doors."

"So, it's safe now for us to call it a night?"

"Yes, ma'am. And you can go on home, Mr. Linden," the officer said to Joe.

"I think I'll wait until everything is buttoned up tight before I call it a night."

Annabelle laid a hand on his arm. "Thank you, Joe. I'm glad you convinced Tillie to go on to bed. We don't want her getting sick again."

He leaned down and lowered his voice. "I've checked and our curtains have moved a time or two. I'm guessing she's been watching and waiting."

"Oh my," Annabelle said. "That stinker."

"She is that. Looks like the other curious neighbors have gone to bed, too."

"It won't be much longer," the officer said. "It's a wonder no one called 911 earlier."

"The whole neighborhood enjoys the fireworks on the river," Annabelle said. "I doubt anyone was home."

Tad came around the corner shining the officer's light on the ground in front of them. He carried a hammer in the other hand.

"This should work nicely," the policeman said.

The young officer and Tad nailed up the board over the broken window in short order.

"This should keep the weather and mosquitoes out until you get it fixed tomorrow," the officer said.

Annabelle stood and offered her hand. "Thank you. We appreciate it."

He shook her hand. "I'll give you a call as soon as we have something, Mrs. Hubbard. In the meantime, a car will patrol the area to keep watch," the officer said.

"Thanks. Come on, kids. It's way past time for bed."

"Good night," Joe said. "I think I'll go put Tillie to bed although she'll probably run up the stairs and fake sleep once I turn around."

"Thanks again. I'm ready to call it a night." Annabelle led them inside and locked the bolt on the door. "Bed, guys. The sun will be up before we know it."

"You know, my heart was really pumping at first, but I'm pooped now," Tad said.

Peggy nodded. "It's called adrenalin. Fight or flight."

"I was ready to fight, but now I'm ready to sleep," he said.

"Me, too." Annabelle gave her grandson's shoulders a squeeze. "You go on while I double check the back door. Turbo, you can keep me company."

The big dog's tongue lolled to the side as he trotted along with Annabelle. His lack of concern gave Annabelle added confidence. She went to the kitchen, wiped his wounds and gave him a small drink of water.

"You were a brave boy tonight. I'm glad you're here."

The dog's tail spun with joy, and he made a *woof*.

She put her extended finger across her lips. "Shhhh. Whisper."

The dog cocked his head to one side. *Woof*, he quietly barked again.

She stroked his big head and smiled. "Good boy."

As she flipped off the light in the kitchen, the phone rang.

"Hello," she said.

"You okay?" Tillie asked.

"Yes, we're fine."

"Okay. Goodnight then."

"Goodnight, Tillie."

There was a click, and the line went dead. Annabelle hung up the phone and walked through the darkened dining room. Peggy's silhouette filled the living room doorway.

"Gram?" she said. "Who was on the phone?"

"Tillie."

"She's supposed to be asleep."

Annabelle crossed to the living room. "Yes, come on, time to rest."

"As if." Peggy fisted her hands. She followed her grandmother and the dog up the stairs, stopping in the entry to her room. "Goodnight."

Turning around, Annabelle kissed her granddaughter's head and stroked her cheek. "I love you. Sleep tight."

Peggy kissed her grandmother and went into the darkened room, slipping between the covers. Her little sister was already asleep, the orange kitten curled around the top of her head.

The dog turned in circles at the top of the stairs, round and round before flopping down. He laid his huge head on his paws facing the front door.

Patting his back, Annabelle smiled. "Good boy." She went to her room to get ready for bed.

She could hear Tad's snoring, but didn't close her door. Annabelle didn't think she'd sleep the last few hours of the night; she was too keyed up. They had been through so much already. Why couldn't they find any peace? Regina would probably blow a gasket when she heard about the broken window.

Pulling the covers back, she stripped down to her under things and pulled a cotton gown over her head. It was the coolest thing she had to wear. The air conditioner was struggling to cool the house since the front door had been open for the last hour. She wondered who the culprit was, but she didn't know what to do about it if she did.

Maybe we should get an alarm. No, they cost too much. Turbo will be our alarm. I'll think about it tomorrow. Not tomorrow; it's already tomorrow.

Her eyes closed and she slowed her breathing, exhausted.

The mantel clock struck two and she sighed. She had to get to sleep, to gather her strength for whatever lay ahead. Her thoughts wandered to Phil. She didn't know how she felt about him. She couldn't really afford a handyman and Tad didn't have the experience needed to glaze a window. Maybe she'd ask Phil to help fix it. He seemed handy. If not, Joe would surely help out. Of course he would, that was what friends did.

Annabelle rolled out of bed and went to her knees. She said the Lord's Prayer and gave thanks that everyone was safe. She said it every night before she went to sleep, but tonight what she really meant to say was, *thanks.* Saying amen and crossing herself, she crawled back into the bed and fell instantly to sleep.

Chapter 26

"JOE, WHAT IS IT?" Peggy asked. She turned the small canister around in her fingers, inspecting the spray nozzle.

Covering the sprayer with his hand, Joe pushed her arm down. "Don't point it toward your face," Joe said. "It's mace."

"Mace? Why on earth would Peggy need mace?" Annabelle asked.

"I've got one for you, too, Annabelle."

"No way I'm carrying that." Peggy tried to hand it back to Joe, but he wouldn't take it.

"Tillie carries her cell in one pocket and mace in the other when she walks."

"Why do I need one? No one would want anything from a middle aged lady like me, surely?"

"For safety. It'll help protect you against dogs or whatever," Joe said.

"But why do I need one?" Peggy held the small spray canister with two fingers.

Joe threw up his hands. "Because you're dating and you and your friend are out alone sometimes. It pays to be protected."

Turning it around, Peggy held it up by the key ring. "How does it work?"

"You point it at the face of the person you want to stop, push the button then run as fast as you can in the opposite direction."

"Won't it just piss them off?" Peggy asked.

"Yes, but it burns like crazy. It's just to be safe. That's why I got you the little half-ounce bottles. They're pocket sized."

"I don't think Malissa has one of these. Maybe it'll be good to have protection from muggers in the park," Peggy said. "It kinda creeps me out, though, you know?"

Annabelle's hand flew to her heart. "There are muggers in the park?"

Tipping her head to the side, Peggy looked at her grandmother. "You know what I mean, Gram."

"Actually, I hope I don't." She relaxed a bit.

"I want all my girls safe," Joe said.

Oh, Lord, I don't want to think about this. With the break-ins on the block, though, everyone should be more careful.

She felt the tension in her chest building again. "You didn't get one for Megan, did you?"

"No, she's too small to carry one around," he said.

"I'll talk to her about it so she'll know it can be dangerous. I'll warn Tad, too." Annabelle fingered the ring that held the canister. "We don't want any accidents."

"Agreed," he said.

"Gram?" Peggy clipped the ring on her purse strap.

"What, honey?"

"A bunch of us are planning on going to a movie at the mall tonight. Can I go?"

Studying her granddaughter's face, Annabelle asked, "Who all is going?"

Peggy hid behind her bangs. "Malissa, me, Beau and Miles."

Ahuh. That's what I thought. I wondered when or if she'd start dating Miles again. He meant so much to her before the accident.

"Like a double date?"

"Malissa's mom said she'd drive us there and pick us up after."

Forcing her face from betraying her concern, Annabelle realized she couldn't protect the kids from everything. They had to live and learn. "That's fine, then."

"Good opportunity to carry your new little bottle of protection," Joe said.

The young woman's eyes narrowed. "I'd never mace Miles."

The soldier in Joe showed through, in his straight back and firm jaw. "I would hope not, but you can't be too safe."

Peggy looked from Joe to Annabelle and back again. "You guys are so old!"

Joe's cheeks turned red, making his shiny gray hair stand out even more.

He really is handsome.

"Never you mind. You know what he means, young lady."

Peggy smiled. "Thanks. I appreciate it."

"I just hope you never need it," he said.

"Me, either. I have to get ready. See you later." Dashing up the stairs to her bedroom, Peggy shut the door.

"She'll be fine, Annabelle."

"I think so, too—most of the time. Thank you, Joe, for caring so much about us."

Joe chuckled and left Annabelle gazing after his retreating figure.

What a lovely man. Tillie's a lucky lady and so are we. I'm a bit nervous about Miles. He's avoided us since the accident. Maybe things will be easier now that Megan is out of the cast.

They fixed frozen pizzas for dinner. Before Peggy dashed out the door she grabbed a quick piece of Tad's and laughed. "You don't need to hog the whole thing."

"I'm a growing boy," he said with his mouth full.

"Gross." A car horn honked and Peggy waved goodbye.

The last piece of Annabelle and Megan's pizza lingered on the counter a little too long, so Tad made it disappear. The two younger siblings put their plates in the dishwasher and ran upstairs leaving their grandmother behind. She wiped down the table and counters, started the dishwater and checked the lock on the back door before turning off the lights.

The lamp in the parlor cast a soft inviting glow. Annabelle sat down in the rocking chair and picked up her crocheting, feeling content.

An hour passed by before she realized it. The silence had gone on long enough. She replaced her yarn project in the basket that sat beside the chair and got up.

As Annabelle turned toward the stairs, she saw an orange flash cross the floor to the banister. The kitten peeked around the spindle and mewed.

"Well, what have we here?" She scooped her hand under the kitten's fuzzy belly and tucked her against her chest. "What do you say we go upstairs and see what Tad, Megan and Ms. Pickles are up to? They've been quiet a long time."

The kitty purred and pawed at her chin.

"We'd better check on Turbo, too."

"Mew."

The familiar creak was a comfort as she climbed the old stairs. Age wasn't such a bad situation. After all, things improved with age like wine and cheese and people, too, mostly. People grew softer, inside and out. Living made a person feel things deeper and overreact less.

"Don't go getting philosophical. You don't have enough education to pull that one off, even if you've done some living in your sixty-seven years. Good grief, I'm talking to myself, again." Annabelle shook her head with a sigh.

She approached Tad's bedroom and heard the murmur of voices. With a tap she waited a moment before opening the door. The dog's big black nose filled the crack before she could enter.

"You kids want to watch a movie with me?"

The two youngest were seated cross-legged on the bed, a Scrabble board between them. Ms. Pickles curled up beside Megan's weak leg.

"I suppose," Tad said. "What do you want to see?"

Megan poked her brother. "You can't quit now, I'm winning."

"Are not."

"Think you could stand to watch an old timey film?"

"What? Like John Wayne?" Tad asked.

"I like old movies. Sure, Gram, let's watch *The Quiet Man* again." Megan bounced and the wooden disks slid off the board.

Tad gave his little sister a gentle poke. "No, thanks. How about one of his westerns? Nothing black and white, though, they're *too* old."

Always the peacekeeper, Annabelle smiled. "Let's go see which DVD is handy and watch that one. Anyone want popcorn?"

Woof. Turbo added his vote.

"I'll take that as a yes." Annabelle handed the kitten to Megan and scooped up Ms. Pickles. "Clean up your game and meet me in the parlor as soon as you're done."

"Dibs on the couch," Tad said.

THE KIDS SLID the wooden squares into the box and folded the board, setting it on top.

"Do you think she heard anything?" Megan cuddled her kitten close.

"No, I don't think so. But you need to tell her."

"I can't. Gram's been so worried since the house got broken into."

Crossing his arms over his chest, Tad said, "If you don't tell her, I will."

The little girl's brown eyes filled with tears. She stared at her brother.

He relaxed his arms and put the lid on the box. "Don't worry. I'll stay with you when you tell her."

She gave her older brother a grateful smile. "Okay. Thanks."

WHEN PEGGY GOT home at ten-thirty that night, Megan and Annabelle were asleep on the sofa. Tad sat in the rocking chair, eating the old maids from the popcorn bowl while watching the television with the sound off. Turbo watched her move into the room while his tail thumped the floor.

"Whatcha watching?" Peg dropped her purse on the floor beside the couch.

"*Hellfighters.*" Tad tossed the last piece of popcorn to Turbo, who caught it in the air.

"How come the sound is off?"

He tipped his head toward the sofa. "Didn't want to disturb the ladies."

"May as well wake them up and send them to bed, don't you think?"

"I guess." He set the now empty bowl on the coffee table.

"Is this what you did all night, watch movies and eat popcorn?"

"Pretty much." Her brother scowled at her. "From the looks of your face I'd say you've been making out all night. Was it Miles?"

Peggy's hand covered the lower portion of her face, but she could feel the heat flow all the way up to her hairline.

He stared at her then shrugged. "Take Megan up, and I'll wake Gram."

"Thanks." Peggy crossed the room and slid her sister's arms around her neck, then braced her own arms under the little girl's bottom. "Come on, sweetie, let's get you to bed."

"Huh. Peggy? I'm sleepy."

Staggering under Megan's weight, Peggy paused. "I know. Why don't you see if you can walk up the stairs? You're getting too big for me to carry."

"Okay." Megan slid her feet to the floor. "You smell good, like perfume and popcorn."

"You're half asleep." Peggy kissed her sister's cheek.

"What about Gram?"

"Tad will help her." The girls stumbled to the stairs.

"H'okay. Got to tell, but don' want to."

Scowling, Peggy asked, "Tell what?"

"Can't find Gram's pearls. Lost 'em. She'll be mad."

Peggy helped her little sister into their room and over to the bed. She pulled the covers back and watched Megan curl up in a ball on the clean sheets, pulling her stuffed dog under her chin. The orange kitten hopped up on the bed and circled behind the crook of Megan's knees before settling to sleep.

What did she mean about Gram's pearls? Megan never played with Gram's jewelry. All Gram has is cheap costume stuff and those pearls Grandmother Morgan gave her when she died. I have more jewelry than Gram. I'll ask Megan about it tomorrow when she's awake. She must be dreaming.

Chapter 27

"HELLO! ANYBODY home?" Bright as the morning sunshine, Regina called from the back door. "Annabelle?"

She listened to the silence. Everyone must still be asleep or already gone.

The clock struck eight. Regina smiled at the tidy kitchen. Things had improved. Maybe the kids were helping out around the house after all. As she walked through the formal dining room she saw the parlor was more in keeping with her expectations. Pillows, empty bowls and glasses were strewn all over the room, every flat surface covered in clutter of one form or another. There were no signs of dust, however, so maybe there's hope for her cousin's family yet.

"Hello?" Regina called out again.

A door upstairs slammed and footsteps thudded on the floor above.

She heard a distinctive *woof* and what could only have been a curse. When Regina stepped from the parlor into the entryway she came face to face with a spike-haired Annabelle whose pink chenille robe hung half off of one shoulder, while she struggled to tie the belt.

"Regina? What on earth? Is everything all right?"

"Good morning, slug-a-bed." Regina fought a smile. "I didn't honestly believe you were still asleep at this hour. You've always been such an early riser."

Obviously flustered, Annabelle finally succeeded in tying the belt around her middle and puffed out a big breath. "We had a late night and didn't expect company."

"So I see." Her cousin inclined her head toward the parlor. "And what happened to the front window?"

"We had a break-in. I was going to call you this morning. Don't worry, the leaded glass is on order and I'll take care of it."

Regina did a quick scan of the room. "I thought maybe the kids got a little rowdy . . . is everyone okay? Was anything stolen?"

"We're fine. Nothing was taken." Annabelle's bare feet slapped across the wooden floor as she started righting the parlor. "You usually call before you come by." She folded the throw and laid it on the back of the sofa and tossed the pillows at each armrest. Setting the dirty glasses into the two large bowls Annabelle turned to her cousin.

"Would you like a cup of coffee? I could use some."

"Thank you, I would." Following her into the kitchen, Regina took a seat at the table and watched her cousin put the dishes in the dishwasher then fill the carafe with water.

"How are you feeling?"

Her older cousin's reply was clipped. "Fine."

"And the kids?"

"Doing well." Turning toward her cousin, she threw out her arms. "Why are you here?"

"My, aren't you blunt in the morning?"

She's obviously half asleep. I ought not to bait her this way, just because things are a mess in my house and hers.

"I guess I'm still a little tired. Is everything all right?"

Smoothing her skirt, Regina shook her head. "Actually, no. Sam and I had an argument."

Annabelle leaned her hip against the counter and watched the coffee fill the pot. "I'm sorry to hear that."

"There's nothing for you to be sorry about. I was wide-awake and restless. The car just drove itself here."

Annabelle pulled two cups out of the cabinet and filled them with the aromatic liquid.

"This should help us both, then." Setting the cups on the table, Annabelle sat down.

"If you must know . . ."

Taking a sip from her coffee, Annabelle tried to smooth her messy hair. "I don't have to know."

"We fought about this house."

"Really? Then I am sorry." Her back became ram rod straight. "When do you want us to leave?"

"No, no. You misunderstand." Regina reached across the table for her cousin's hand, which was quickly withdrawn. She leaned back.

This isn't going well at all.

"All right, then. Can you afford the upkeep on this house? The taxes?"

"Minor things we can manage, but I'm not sure about the taxes." Annabelle blew in her cup. "They're due now aren't they?"

"Yes, and unless you have a couple of thousand dollars stuffed in your brassier I'm thinking you can't afford it on Social Security."

Annabelle clenched her jaw. "Two thousand? No. I can't."

Sipping the heady brew, Regina watched the discomfort pass across her cousin's face before she continued. Regina gazed into her cup and seeing no answers in the dark surface, she sighed.

"Sam thinks I should deed the house over to you, but then you'd be stuck with the tax burden if I do. He wants to marry me and says he's worried that if I'm not shed of this house I'll always feel I have an out."

Frowning, Annabelle cradled her cup in both hands. "Do you need an out?"

"I don't think so." Regina looked into her cousin's eyes.

Will she think my offer is charity and refuse? All I can do is toss the idea out there and watch her reaction.

"I could put enough money in trust to cover the taxes for the next ten years. By then, the kids will be old enough to care for it if something happens to one of us."

Conflicting emotions crossed Annabelle's face. "Is that what you want to do?"

"I think it is . . ."

They sipped in silence for a few moments, collecting their thoughts.

Setting down the cup, Annabelle leaned forward. "Is that the only reason you don't want to marry Sam?"

Regina's cup hit the table with a thud, coffee sloshing over the edge. "I don't know."

"This is quite a switch. I'm used to *you* having all the answers and me all the questions."

She stared at Annabelle for a moment then lowered her head. "Me, too."

"Want a muffin?" Annabelle got up and placed a square plastic container in the center of the table.

"Yours or Tillie's?" Not waiting for an answer, Regina took a big bite of one.

"Mine."

"Okay. Mmm. Good."

Why is food always such a comfort? We should all be as big as the park by now with all the sweets we consume around here. Oh, well. You can't live without food.

"You *must* be upset if you're willing to take a chance on my baking skills. Don't worry, they're banana walnut and almost healthy."

Smiling, Regina accepted another one.

"The only thing better than muffins for breakfast is . . . cake." Annabelle gave her a wide grin in return.

Leaning back in her chair, Regina relaxed. "You know, I was never allowed to eat anything but eggs or oatmeal for breakfast. Mother had to die before I could buy a box of Raisin Bran."

Shaking her head, Annabelle took a muffin. "When did you start expanding your menu for breakfast?"

"After mother and father died. When Devlin and I got married, he corrupted me. His favorite food was a mixing bowl full of Frosted Flakes during the ten o'clock news." Regina saluted the air with a laugh.

"My mom's favorite breakfast food was oatmeal raisin cookies. She'd make the dough the night before, roll it up in a long round cylinder, wrap it in wax paper. Then before I got up, she'd bake a dozen for us to eat, still warm from the oven." Closing her eyes on the memory, Annabelle sighed.

"That sounds nice. Aunt Rose was very sweet."

Not like my mother, the Wicked Witch of Wichita.

With an animation Regina hadn't seen in some time, Annabelle continued, "We learned to grow vegetables and harvest them together, too. I loved to sit on the porch with her, snapping beans. We'd talk about music and books and she'd tell me stories about fairies and magical kingdoms."

What a delightful experience.

"My mom used to call her 'fey.'" Feeling her smile fall from her face, sadness enveloped Regina. "Did you know when you were little that your dad beat your mother?"

Annabelle struggled to swallow, her former enthusiasm now gone.

"Not for a long time. She'd tell me the bruises were from clumsiness. But she was so graceful."

"How did you find out?" Regina sipped her coffee, watching her cousin over the rim.

"I heard them shouting one night. I woke up and wanted a drink, but even though I couldn't hear the words they said, I heard a slap and then she cried out. I hid under the covers and eventually fell asleep. The next morning, she had a bruise on her cheek. I knew then, my daddy hit her." Both of Annabelle's hands gripped the cup.

Afraid of the answer, Regina asked in a whisper. "Did he ever hurt you?"

"Only with his words. He called me fat and lazy. He said I'd grow up to be just like my mama, which I thought would be wonderful, but he didn't mean it that way."

Regina reached over and squeezed her cousin's quivering hands. "No, I don't suppose he did."

Finding starch in her spine, Annabelle sat back. "I don't imagine your dad ever hit Aunt Victoria. He wouldn't dare."

Regina stared at the bottom of her cup. "No. There was never that much emotion in our house. At least you knew your mother loved you."

"Yes, she did." Annabelle looked at her cousin and smiled. "She let me get dirty, too."

Laughing, Regina leaned forward, but checked over her shoulder before she spoke. "Growing up, I envied your dirty bare feet and ratty hair."

Annabelle's eyes widened. "Really? I wanted to be like you. I thought you were beautiful, like your china dolls." She tried to smooth her pillow-smashed hair again without success.

"It's difficult to enjoy a porcelain doll. They're fragile and never allowed to get mussed. I used to dream about running through the rain until drenched then splashing in the mud puddles. I even painted it once."

The painting had hung in a gallery in Kansas City until Sam purchased it several years ago. It now hung on the wall in front of his recliner.

"And you never ran through the puddles, ever?" Surprise etched Annabelle's soft features.

"With my mother around? Not a chance. It was not done. Only poor ragamuffins could find entertainment in the filth of the gutter." To punctuate her sentence, Regina lifted her nose in the air just like her mother used to do.

Annabelle cocked her head. "Is that a quote?"

"Word for word."

"If you couldn't go outside and play, what did you do all day?"

"I studied piano, read and when I got older, I painted. She allowed me one old shirt of my father's to paint in so I wouldn't smudge my clothes. I painted in my stockings for fear of ruining my Mary Jane's."

"It would've been easier to take the socks off, too."

"I know that now, but back then I felt almost undressed—decadent, in fact."

"Lord, that's sad." Annabelle helped herself to another muffin.

"I only had to burn a couple of pairs of stockings. Mother never knew."

Annabelle laughed, covering her mouth with her hand.

"Have you heard any more from the children's father?"

"Not lately." Annabelle traced her finger along the rim of her empty cup. "Could he get them back?"

"Good grief. I would hope not, but I'm not the one to ask. Give Sam a call. If he doesn't know, he'll find out for you."

Fisting her hand on the worn tabletop, Annabelle said, "I don't have anything I love more than those kids and Grandma Morgan's pearls. I'll never part with either if I can help it."

"Enough sweets. It's making you all feisty." Regina put the lid on the container and placed it back on the counter top. "Have you ever had a yard sale, Annabelle?"

"Of course. Why?"

"We never had them when I was growing up. Perhaps we should check the cellar and clean out the brick-a-bract to raise the tax money?"

As she said the words, her heart felt lighter.

Shaking her head, Annabelle said, "Your mother would turn over in her grave."

"She would, but we could have it on the drive instead of the lawn. I can help you sort it all out and you can price it."

"You'd do that for me? For us?"

She looks shocked, but I think it's a brilliant idea.

"We're family, patchwork though it may be. We'll call it the house fund."

Transfixed, Annabelle's eyes shone. "That's a great idea. Thanks."

Splashing an inch of dark liquid in both their cups, Regina gulped hers down and faced her cousin.

"Now, do you think I should marry Sam or not?"

Placing her hand on Regina's shoulder, Annabelle smiled. "Yes, I think you should. True love is hard to come by."

"You're right about that. It took me almost sixty years to find it."

"You never loved Devlin?"

I don't know why she looks so surprised.

"We were friends. He married me when I needed a husband. Then he slept around and embarrassed us both. No, Sam is the one. What about you? You've been dressing nice lately and your hair isn't quite as . . . frizzy. Do you have your eye on someone?"

Annabelle crossed her arms over her chest. "I do not, Miss Nosey."

Although I couldn't laugh, I had to smile.

"It's about time. Are you being discreet?"

"Excuse me?" Annabelle coughed. "You'd better wash your mind out with soap, Regina Louise."

Tucking her dirty cup in the dishwasher, Regina gave her cousin a sly grin. "I'll ask Tillie, she knows everything that goes on around here."

Annabelle shook her index finger in her cousin's face. "You will not! It's none of anyone's business."

Regina turned her back with a smile and dumped the cool contents from Annabelle's cup before placing it beside her own. "Perhaps not, but you can't stop me from wondering."

"You've been reading too many romances. I don't have time for love."

In response to Annabelle's sigh of exasperation, Regina lightly touched her cousin's hand. "Oh, honey, I highly recommend you make time. It's well worth it."

"Hi, Regina," Megan said from the doorway, the kitten cuddled in the crook of her arm. "Did you have muffins for breakfast, Gram? Can I?"

"Yes and yes. They're banana walnut."

"Good, that means they're healthy."

The two women laughed.

The little girl put the kitten down on her way to wash her hands. Megan filled a glass with milk then put two muffins on a napkin before she sat down at the table. She took a bite and closed her eyes. "I don't remember the last time we had homemade muffins for breakfast. How are you, Regina?"

"I'm fine, sweetheart." She ruffled the girl's tangled brown locks. "How are you?"

"Better now."

"From breakfast?"

"Ahuh. I . . . I have something I have to tell Gram, and I don't know how." Megan cast her eyes down, oblivious to the milk mustache on her upper lip.

Regina and Annabelle exchanged a subtle smile.

"Do you want to talk with your Gram alone?"

"No. I don't want to talk about it at all, but I have to." Taking another swallow of her milk, Megan straightened her shoulders and looked her grandmother in the face.

"I lost something."

"What is it, sweetheart? Maybe we can help you find it." Regina sat down across from the little girl.

Echoing her cousin's concern, Annabelle touched Megan's hand. "What did you lose?"

"Can I tell you why first?"

"If you want to," her grandmother said.

"After the window got broken and Turbo got cut I got scared . . ."

"Oh, honey." Annabelle put her hand on the small shoulder and gave it a quick squeeze.

"I thought someone was trying to take our things, so I hid your pearl necklace."

"Oh." Annabelle's face fell.

"I put it in a very good hiding place, but now I can't remember . . ."

Feeling the heat rise inside her, Regina struggled to keep it down. "You forgot where you put it?"

"Ahuh."

Fat tears fell from Megan's big brown eyes.

"I . . . I hid Gram's pearls, but now I can't remember where . . ."

"Oh." Annabelle stared at Regina. "We'll find them, don't worry. We'll go over the whole house until we do."

With an eruption, Regina slammed her hand on the tabletop making them all jump. "You're damn right we will." Displeasure froze the grim set of her mouth. "Don't you know better than to touch things that don't belong to you?"

"I do, but . . ."

"Annabelle, how could you be so careless? And with Grandmere's pearls? I don't know what I was thinking when I left this house to you. The place is a mess, and now Grandmere's pearls are gone . . ." Ms. Pickles scurried under the table to join Tang between Megan's feet.

Annabelle stood. "Stop it. You're out of line. She's trying to protect them, Regina. She didn't mean any harm."

Megan burst into tears and ran from the room, the cats on her heels. But Regina couldn't control the unreasonable anger she felt.

"You may not value the things you've been given, but I do. I can't stand by and watch . . ." Grabbing her purse off of the back of the chair, she headed for the door, Annabelle shouting after her, "Those were my pearls, not yours. What are you so mad about?"

Turning, Regina spat. "She gave them to you, but I wanted them. She gave the house to me and now you have it. The kids . . . our daughters . . . it just doesn't seem right . . ." Regina grabbed the back door handle.

"Well." Annabelle said before Regina reached the bottom of the back steps.

Chapter 28

"UNGRATEFUL . . ." Regina muttered and jerked the car door open. Her shallow breathing made her head ache.

Why am I so angry? Megan would never do anything mean, she's the sweetest kid alive. And it wasn't Annabelle's fault either. What in the world am I really pissed about? Sam? Why? He loves me and wants to marry me. He's made a home for me. Is it Tom's interference with the kids? The house? Oh, nothing makes any sense. I'm not jealous, surely. I have a man who loves me, enough money and the time to paint, so basically everything I've ever wanted. I even have a dog. What is my problem?

She backed out of the drive and headed toward Riverside Park. Maybe she could sit by the water and sort things out. It had been a long time since she'd been alone with her thoughts. Maybe she needed a vacation from everything? A weekend to herself or with friends in Chicago or Sun City might do her good. Regina pulled over to the curb and locked her purse in the trunk. Walking along the edge of the river would soothe her, especially when the only sounds were the water, squirrel chatter and the occasional car driving by.

A Salerno wood sculpture depicting a girl reading atop a tree stump used to keep sentinel on this particular patch of green grass. She missed it. Sighing, Regina continued walking to the bridge and stopped. Grabbing gravel off of the road, she dropped one stone at a time into the water and watched the ripples flow out, one after another, just like life. A jumble.

Her best friend's voice came from behind her. "What are you up to?"

"Just looking at the water."

Tillie stepped beside her and leaned on the railing.

"You look like a lost puppy. What's on your mind, Regina Louise?"

"I do not. What are you doing here, anyway?"

"I was walking and saw you drive by. I could tell by the set of your jaw you were mad. Want to talk about it?"

She tossed in another stone. "Not particularly."

"Okay, have it your way." Tillie stood beside her in silence.

A row of baby ducklings followed their mother near the shoreline.

"Are you ever sorry?" Regina asked.

"About what?"

"About getting married?"

"Nope." Tillie picked up some gravel and dropped a pebble near Regina's last plop, the circles intersecting.

"Do you ever wish you'd had kids?"

The ducks waddled onto the grass, still in formation behind their mother.

"Nope. I've got Annabelle's grandkids whenever I get the urge."

"Do you miss living with me?"

"Sometimes." Touching her friend's arm, Regina turned toward her. "What's got your knickers in a twist?"

"Sam wants to marry me. He wants me to sign the house over to Annabelle, but she can't afford it. Tom wants to be in the kids' life again. And, the straw that snapped this particular camel's serenity . . . Megan lost Grandmere's pearls."

"Wow. That's quite a load you're carrying around. Let's take it one thing at a time, okay? I think it's been too long since we had one of our therapy sessions over coffee." Tillie linked their arms and pulled. Regina reluctantly followed her. "Let's start with Sam and marriage. Why aren't you comfortable with him asking to marry you? It's not like you're too young."

"Gee, thanks." Regina stomped her well shod foot. "You're only six months younger than I am!"

Tillie rolled her eyes. "That is beside the point. Answer the question."

"I've already been married, look how it turned out. Devlin screwed around then he died." Anger had Regina stretching out her steps so Tillie had to double-time it to keep up.

"Bad news, we all die." She touched her friends arm, giving it a slight squeeze. "You didn't really love Devlin anyway, not like you do Sam. It's not the same thing."

"I know. I don't understand why I'm hesitating," Regina wrung her hands. "Maybe I just don't want to share."

"But you are sharing. A helluva lot more than you ever have. Is that it?"

"No. I love Sam to distraction. I can't imagine living one single day without him." Sunlight glistened off the tears that filled her eyes.

"Okay, then there really isn't a good reason not to marry that cuddly bear. You're living with him, so it's not like you're strangers. You know you're compatible in every way that counts." Tillie laughed and bumped her friend with her hip.

"Very funny. I imagine you and Joe enjoyed some sheet time before you two got married."

Tillie smiled and swung her arms wide. "Wouldn't you like to know?"

Regina chuckled. "I guess I just needed you to put it all into perspective. And maybe kick my butt a bit."

"Now, what's the problem with the house? I thought you gave it to Annabelle and the kids."

The two friends walked side-by-side, oblivious to anything around them.

"I did, but on paper it's still mine. I'm paying the taxes because she can't afford them, but I think I've figured out how to handle that. I'll put money in a trust to manage the house."

Reaching over their linked arms, Tillie gave Regina's hand a squeeze.

"That's brilliant. Then it can belong to her and the kids, and you can't run home whenever you feel boxed in." Tillie grabbed her friend by the arms.

Looking down into her diminutive friend's dark eyes, Regina sighed. "Damn, but you are harsh, Matilda Jean."

"Sorry, but you and I have never tip-toed around things much. It doesn't work." Tillie dropped her hands.

"True." Regina chuckled. "I think I've missed you."

"Back at you. Now what's this about Grandmere's pearls?"

They stopped in the shade of an old oak tree.

"Well. After the house was broken into, Megan hid them and forgot where. It just rubbed my hair on end. I lost my temper." She looked at her feet.

"You?" Tillie winked at her friend. "Never. Listen. We all do or say unreasonable things once in a while. That's part of being human. We're flawed, but we do the best we can."

They started walking back in the direction Regina had parked. She couldn't see her car but knew it was just around the bend. The wind whispered through the leaves.

"And Tom?" Tillie asked.

"It's not my decision, but I feel like he deserves a second chance. He was a partier, but he never hurt the kids and he only returned blows with Liddy, who probably hit first."

"Wow. You really have grown up."

"And I know what I need to do. I'm just struggling against it."

"It's hard to do the right thing sometimes, but I know you will." Tillie gave Regina a quick one-armed hug.

Regina stopped in mid-stride. "Will you be my matron of honor?"

"I'd love to. I'll even help Megan find Annabelle's pearls if she wants me to."

"Oh, dear. I made poor Megan cry." Regina sprinted toward her car.

"Hey, slow down will you? My legs are half as long as yours."

Regina stopped and Tillie collided with her. "Sorry. Want to come back to the house with me?"

"You need brake lights, woman. Which house? Annabelle's or yours?"

Regina smiled at her friend's obvious reminder. "Annabelle's."

"I think you got yourself into this mess, so you need to get yourself out."

"You're a big help."

"And you are a big girl."

"Thanks, Tillie."

"You're most welcome, my dear friend."

They walked in companionable silence until they reached Regina's red Cadillac.

"Want a ride?"

"No thanks, it's not that far. I love these unseasonably cool August days. I'll see you around."

"No doubt. You're just like a pixie popping up, Matilda Jean."

Tillie beamed. "Don't be an ogre to the kids. Go apologize. Grovel if you have to. Megan loves you and will forgive you."

"Thanks." Regina got in the car and drove by her friend. She waved and watched Tillie wave back before she followed the curve and her friend was out of sight.

"Now to face the music." Regina pulled up the drive. Annabelle and Megan were on the front porch swing, talking. Megan wiped her eyes as Regina approached.

Annabelle stood, patted the little girl on the shoulder and went back into the house alone.

"Hi. Can I join you?" Regina asked.

Megan nodded her head, but scooted as far over as the armrest would allow.

Regina sat down. "I'm sorry I got mad."

The little girl looked at her with those big brown eyes and Regina felt her heart constrict.

"I know you wouldn't do anything like this without a good reason. I was wrong."

"Okay," Megan whispered.

They sat still in the swing until Megan started to move her legs. She could just touch the porch with her toes. Regina used her longer legs to give it an extra boost. From the corner of her eye she saw the little girl's smile and felt better.

"Do you want some help finding the pearls? I know a lot of good hiding places."

"No thank you. I can do it."

"Okay. Megan, would you mind being a flower girl sometime soon?"

She gave Regina a toothy grin. "Sure. But I think the dress I wore last year at Tillie's wedding is too small."

"That's all right. We'll all get new dresses. It's a special occasion after all. Would you like that?"

Her little head bobbed. "Ahuh."

"Good, but don't tell anyone yet, okay?" Regina put her hand on the child's knee.

"Why?"

"Because I haven't told Sam, and he probably should be next to know, don't you think?"

"Ahuh. I do." Megan smiled and slid closer to Regina on the swing. "I won't tell."

"I know you won't."

Regina gave her a hug. They sat together enjoying the slow swaying, friends again, dreaming about the future.

Chapter 29

WHEN ANNABELLE awoke, she lay beneath the sheet counting the bongs of the mantel clock and realized it was only six in the morning. The chirping of the birds outside her window interrupted the quiet of the house. Her mind wandered. She hadn't seen Phil since school let out. Basketball practice would start before long and she almost looked forward to the possibility of seeing him again.

She slipped out of bed and dressed in navy Capris, which were getting baggy, and a white button down cotton shirt. She found her sneakers under the chair. Annabelle finished getting ready and slipped down the stairs to go for a sunrise walk. She and Tillie had started walking early before the thermometer hit its crescendo. Turbo scratched at Tad's door. She opened it just enough for him to escape.

Annabelle patted Turbo's big head. "Hey there, handsome."

The black dog wagged his whole body and nuzzled her hand.

"Ready for a walk?"

He pranced to the staircase and back to her then sped down the stairs to the front door.

"Hold on a minute, boy. Let's get a water bottle. Tillie won't be out until 6:30. We've got time." They went into the kitchen and Annabelle pulled an empty plastic bottle from the cabinet and filled it with cool tap water. She popped two pieces of bread into the toaster and retrieved the margarine from the refrigerator. When the toast popped, she skimmed on the butter and gave one piece to Turbo while eating the other. She still had half of her piece when he finished his. He focused on every bite that went from her hand to her mouth.

"This one is mine. You had yours." She chewed the last bite and grabbed the leash off of the nail and hooked it on his collar. "Come on. Let's go.

He hopped into the air, but didn't place a paw on her as they proceeded to the front porch and down the steps to the sidewalk where Tillie stretched.

"Hi, there. Hey Turbo, how's my handsome lad?" Tillie stooped down and ruffled the fur behind his ears. He licked her chin. "Nice shot."

The ladies headed down the sidewalk toward the river, the big dog walking between them and the street, his nose snuffling the ground with every step.

"Must be a kaleidoscope of smells," Tillie said.

Annabelle nodded. "I expect."

"How's it going?"

"It's going. I suppose you heard from Regina that my pearls are missing?"

"Yes. But she and Megan are friends again, aren't they?"

They matched their stride to each other and began pumping their arms in rhythm.

"Yes, we'll find the pearls eventually. She was just trying to hide them in case of another break-in."

"Of course she was. She knows how much they mean to you. I wouldn't worry."

"No, no. I'm not."

They walked around the corner and crossed the quiet street.

"Tillie?"

"Hum?"

"Do you remember when you started being . . . you know . . . sexually active . . .?"

"Sure. Why do you ask? I don't mind telling if you really want to hear the story."

Kicking a stone from her path, Annabelle hesitated. "No, that's okay . . . it's just that . . . I think Peggy might be . . . thinking about it. She is sixteen and really likes that boy, Miles."

"I see. And she's not talking?"

"Not to me." Stumbling on a crack in the sidewalk, Annabelle slowed her pace.

"What makes you think she might be interested in sex?"

"They're seeing each other again, you know, after the accident. I thought it might be over, but she's come home with her lips all swollen and red several times. I didn't say anything, but I'm worried how far she'll go . . . to find love. I remember how glorious first love can be."

"Do you trust her?"

"Yes . . . No . . . I don't know." Annabelle threw up her right hand, while the other white knuckled the leash. "I don't know what Liddy might have said to her before she died. With television and movies like they are, she probably knows more about sex and boys than I did at her age."

Tillie chuckled. "You might be right. Are you going to ask her?"

"I want to, but I just can't. I might not say the right thing."

Putting her hand on her friend's arm, Tillie slowed them to a stroll. "Well, then you'll have to wait until she comes to you. You could speak to

Regina. She and Peggy seem to be pretty close, maybe she can bring it up in conversation."

"I'm not ready for Peg to be . . . grown up," Annabelle felt her shoulders sag.

"You don't have a choice about that. She's going to do it, regardless."

"I know." Annabelle wiped perspiration from her lip. "How's Joe?"

"He's fit and full of sass, just like me. Let's finish up our walk so I can get home to his gourmet coffee. Did I tell you he started roasting the beans in the garage? He's even grinding them himself."

"My goodness." Annabelle looked at her friend and tripped on the uneven sidewalk, again. Tillie gave her a hand to steady her.

"It beats the high dollar coffee shop for flavor. Talk about fresh, yum. Want to come over for a cup?"

"Yes, but I'd better not. The kids were still asleep when I left. I'll suffer through my own coffee. I can't really taste the difference anyway."

"Honey, you don't know what you're missing." Tillie's arms punctuated her enthusiasm. "But I understand. Has Tom been around lately?"

"Not since the blow up with Peggy. I don't understand why he would stay away when he talks about wanting to see the kids so bad."

"It'll all work out. Don't worry. Did he ever hit the kids like Liddy did?"

"No. He was too busy partying. Liddy was the one who lashed out with her fists, just like her father."

"Those poor kids. They are so lucky they have you."

"I hope you're right, Tillie."

They rounded another corner and headed back down the street to their end of the block. Annabelle checked her watch. "Twenty-five minutes today. Not too bad for two mature ladies. I seem to get a little further each day, which is good for both of us."

Now, if she could just stop the heavy feeling in her chest. Probably indigestion, she had eaten that toast pretty fast. They stopped in front of the house. Turbo accepted the parting scratch that Tillie gave his back, his tail churning the air.

"See you later."

"See you." Annabelle unlocked the front door and unhooked the leash. The dog bounded up the stairs and hit Tad's door, bouncing it open.

"Ack. Down, Turbo, down!"

Humming, Annabelle went into the kitchen to make fresh coffee and set out the breakfast cereal. The kids would be up and wanting to be fed. Turbo dashed into the kitchen and stood panting by his empty bowl.

"You're pretty proud of yourself, aren't you? I suppose waking the kids up deserves a little something." Annabelle filled the dog bowls with kibble and water.

"Now mind your manners, no walking around chewing, it makes a mess." She shook a finger at him. "And no sloshing water on the floor."

Tad entered the kitchen laughing. "Good luck with that, Gram. He's the original bucket mouth dog."

"True, but it can't hurt to try." She put her hands on her hips.

He shook his head. "You're a strange lady."

Making an abbreviated curtsey, she smiled. "Thank you."

Megan entered the kitchen carrying the orange kitten in her arms.

"Put that poor creature down, Megan. She has legs you know. She needs to learn how to use them," Annabelle said.

"But, Gram, Turbo will step on her." Megan put the kitten down on the tile in front of her feet.

Scampering across the floor, Tang started rubbing against the huge dog's back legs. He ignored her and continued to gulp down his food.

"I'll feed her," Megan said. She filled the kitty bowls and set them across the room from the dog.

Annabelle put her hands in the pockets of her Capris. If the cat didn't eat something before the dog finished, he'd clean them out, too. Ms. Pickles had the bluff in on Turbo, but not the kitten.

"I've got it." Snapping her fingers, Annabelle took Tang's food and water into the mudroom by the back door. Placing them on the top of the washer she called the kitten.

"Here Tang. Here kitty, kitty."

The orange ball of fur streaked through the door, leaping onto the washer. She meowed her appreciation before starting to eat. The three-legged Ms. Pickles hopped over to her own bowl and gave her full attention to its contents.

"Cool idea," Megan said.

"Morning," Peggy stood in the doorway, her hair pulled up in a messy ponytail. Her face looked freshly washed.

"You're looking chipper this morning. What's on the schedule for today, kids?"

"I'm painting," Tad said. "Regina gave me a new canvas."

"I'm only halfway through a new book, so I thought I'd sit on the porch to read and get some sun on by leg."

"And how about you, Peg?" Annabelle asked.

"I'm meeting Malissa at the mall. We're going window-shopping. What about you?"

"Making cookies. We're getting kind of low."

Megan giggled. "That's because Tad eats so much."

Her brother patted his thin stomach. "No, that's because I've got a man-sized hunger."

"And from the look of it, man-sized feet," Gram said. "You look like you need another new pair of shoes."

"It's cool. Holey tennis shoes are fine for summer. I can wait until school starts, unless you're feeling flush . . ."

"You sure?"

Teens and the grunge look. Things always seemed to come around again. I loved the look of a white tee shirt and crisp jeans on a young man when I was a teen.

"Yeah. It's no big thing."

They all sat down to eat their cereal. Annabelle read the newspaper headlines but nothing caught her eye.

"Gram?" Megan said.

"What honey?"

"Do you want me to start looking for your pearls today, instead of reading?"

"I could help," Peggy added. "We're not going to the mall until this afternoon."

"That's a good idea," Annabelle said. "We can spend a couple of hours checking all the likely hiding places. If those don't pan out we'll try to think of the unlikely ones."

"I can help if you want." Tad shifted in his seat like he had a burr in his shorts. "But I have a really good idea for a painting and want to draw it out first."

"You go ahead. We'll holler if we need help," Annabelle said.

"Thanks."

Chapter 30

THERE WAS NO sign of the pearls in any of the main floor rooms. They checked behind every book and inside every dish, vase and drawer. Nothing.

"Don't worry, Megan." Peggy patted her little sister on the shoulder. "We'll find them. We've only just begun to look."

"I wish I could remember, but I can't. It's like I forgot on purpose." Megan fisted her hands. "That way no one can torture the information out of me."

"Let's hope that never happens," Annabelle said.

Peggy rolled her eyes. "You've been reading too many books. There's not a lot of torturing going on in this neighborhood."

Annabelle smiled. Peggy and Tad's imagination was even more vivid than Megan's.

"Gram," Megan said.

"Yes, honey."

"Can we stop for a while? Maybe if I get my mind completely off of them, I'll picture where I put them."

"It's worth a try."

Peggy poked her sister. "I think she just wants to finish her book."

"Do not!"

"Sure you do, and I want to get cleaned up to meet Malissa."

"Go ahead, girls, we'll search more later." Annabelle wiped her dusty hands on her pants.

The phone rang. "I'll get it," Peggy said.

"Hello."

"Oh, hi. Ahuh, she's right here. Gram, it's Mr. Edwards." Peggy handed the receiver to her grandmother.

"Hello."

"Annabelle? Phillip Edwards here. How are you?"

The warmth in his voice made Annabelle smile. She couldn't recall when he had transformed into someone she was happy to hear from. "Hello there. I'm doing fine, thanks. And you?"

"Fit as a man half my age. If you don't have any plans tonight, would you like to go to dinner? I hate eating alone, and I have a craving for a meal made by hands other than my own."

Her heart skipped a beat. "How nice, but it's kind of short notice. Can I call you back in a few minutes to let you know?"

"Sure thing." He gave her his phone number.

Annabelle hung up, realizing she had wound the phone cord around her hand several times. As she unwound it, she started laughing. It felt good to have a man interested in spending time with her. She dialed Tillie's number. After three rings, Tillie answered.

"If you can watch the kids, I have a chance for a free dinner."

"You do? With who?"

"Tad's basketball coach. I know it's last minute, but . . ." Her wistful tone wouldn't be easy to miss, especially when Tillie's internal radar could sense when the weather and other things were about to change.

"Then we'd be happy to watch the kids. We can make homemade pizzas."

"Thank you! Oh," Annabelle gasped. "What should I wear?"

"You sound almost giddy."

"I feel light headed all of a sudden. Isn't that silly? I'm not a kid anymore. It's probably what my grandmother called the vapors."

Tillie laughed. "I don't think it's the same thing, but I understand. You need to get out more often. Wear that denim skirt we bought at the thrift store with your pink button-up blouse. You look great in that."

"That's a good idea. Oh. My hair's a mess." Spreading her fingers, Annabelle patted her hair.

"Call the shop and see if they can get you in. No more frizz, okay? It's just too, out of control."

"Could you come with me?" Annabelle closed her eyes. Tillie always looked sharp with her naturally wavy locks.

"Honey, I can't, but I'll watch the kids while you're at the beauty salon. You'll do fine, just tell them you want something more modern."

"I'll try. Will you stay with them over here tonight? They should be okay for a couple of hours this afternoon."

"Sure, that way we can watch the critters, too."

"Thanks, Tillie, you're a life saver."

"I think I'm beginning to look like a jelly bean. I'm getting fat," Tillie said.

"You are not. I've got to go. See you about six."

"See you."

Grabbing the phone book, Annabelle dialed the beauty shop and begged the receptionist to get her in for a cut, style and color and found that Tammy would be available in thirty minutes. Annabelle called Phil back to confirm dinner at 6:30. He sounded as pleased as she felt.

She dashed up the stairs to brush her teeth and grab her purse, hollering for the kids. They came running into the hallway outside her bedroom door.

"What's up?" Peggy asked. "You okay?"

"Where's the fire?" Tad sniffed the air.

"No fire, I'm just going to get my hair done. I'm having dinner out tonight. You'll be eating pizza with Tillie and Joe."

"Chill out, Gram. Who's making the pizza?"

"What? Oh, sorry Tad, Tillie's making it."

Peggy winked at her grandmother and crossed her arms over her chest. "Dinner with who? Where are you going?"

"I'm going out to dinner with Mr. Edwards, Miss Nosey."

"Ah, Gram, not cool." Tad threw his arms into the air. "He's my assistant coach. That's just gross."

Halfway to the door, Annabelle turned and stared at her grandson.

Am I doing the right thing? I have no intention of getting serious; it's just a meal. Then why are you so excited? You thought Phil was a bossy creep when you first met him. Go figure.

"You behave yourself, young man. Gross? Where do you come up with this stuff?"

"Television."

"I don't doubt that. Megan, you stay inside and read so Turbo and Tad can keep an eye on you while Peggy and I are gone. Do not answer the door. If anyone calls, just say I can't come to the phone right now and I'll call them back."

Tad threw his arm around Megan's neck. "Come on munchkin, you can watch me paint."

"I'd rather read."

"Okay, but come upstairs so I can keep my eye on you." Tad gave her a google eyed stare.

"Come on, Peggy. I'll take you to the mall on my way." Annabelle opened the door, but didn't wait for her granddaughter.

"Thanks, Gram." Peggy grabbed her purse off of the newel post.

They raced out the door leaving the two youngest to fend for themselves.

Annabelle picked up Malissa then dropped her and Peggy outside the mall by Dillard's. She made it to the beauty shop right on time.

Tammy, a tall, skinny blonde in her late twenties had recently graduated from cosmetology school. She took all the walk-ins. Her own hair was a curly style that looked like all she did was run her fingers through it.

"Tammy, can you do something with this mop of mine? It's fuzzy and the color isn't doing a thing for me. I want it to look more styled, but natural. What do you think?"

The young woman wrinkled her brow, picked up a brush, lifting chunks of Annabelle's hair. She inspected the ends and rubbed a few strands between her fingers.

"Mrs. Hubbard, I think you just need a good cut and some conditioning. You've got some natural waves in your hair. How about we go with a warm gray all over color and layer it to give it more texture?"

"If it'll help, do it!"

"Your hair is healthy and thick, but dry on the ends. Let me see what I can do."

She wrapped a pink camouflage cape around Annabelle and pumped up the chair. Handing her a magazine, Tammy smiled at Annabelle's reflection in the mirror. "I'll go mix the color and be right back."

For two hours, Tammy worked on Annabelle's hair. She colored it, washed and conditioned it, then massaged her scalp. Annabelle listened to the constant talking in the shop. Having her hair done always made her drowsy. Tammy focused on her subject, not requiring much talk. Annabelle was content to let the stylist work her magic. She watched as the young woman picked up locks of her hair, angling them this way and that, snipping the ends. When Tammy was done with the scissors, she took out the blow dryer and a round brush and started styling.

When Tammy stepped from in front of her, Annabelle didn't recognize the woman in the mirror. The face was right, but the hair looked like a magazine photograph. It hung in soft waves around her face and positively shone.

"Is that me?"

With a huge smile on her face, Tammy nodded. "You're a very attractive lady, Mrs. Hubbard."

"How can I possibly do all this?"

"Did you watch me? Just use the round brush, a blow dryer and your hair will do the rest. It just needed a little TLC and some spray to hold it in place."

Reaching up, Annabelle tested her hair and watched it spring back. "It doesn't feel stiff."

"These new sprays are really nice for a natural hold, not like when you and my Mom were young and wore helmet hair."

"Are they expensive?" She didn't want to spend the whole amount she'd managed to save, a quarter and a dollar a time over the last year.

"As a matter of fact, they're on sale. Let's get you fixed up with a round brush, some conditioner and hair spray."

When they were done, Annabelle was poorer, but her reflection in the car window, and again in the rear view mirror, showed her it was worth it. She knew that Tammy had given her the products for practically nothing. That sweet girl had a new regular customer.

Driving home on autopilot, Annabelle bobbed her head to the radio. There was plenty of time to get dressed and put on makeup. She knew that she looked better than she had in years. Maybe even better than she ever had when she and David were married. He'd never complimented her on how she looked. He didn't act as if it mattered. After a while she had stopped caring. When he started drinking, she couldn't make him stop. Once he'd hit her that first time, it became easier to hit her again.

It's all bull. It was never my fault.

Annabelle exited the car in a fog of memories. Had he ever really been happy? Had she?

Ascending the stairs and through the front door, she didn't notice Megan until she spoke.

"Gram? Is that you? You look beautiful." Turning she yelled, "Tadpole, come here quick!"

"What do you want, dork?" Tad yelled from his room. When he came out, he stopped mid-staircase, his mouth gaping.

"Wow, Gram. You look nice, for an old . . . I mean . . . you look really nice."

Feeling the warmth fill her cheeks, Annabelle smiled at the off-handed compliment. "Thank you both."

Megan gave Annabelle a big hug. "Wait until Peg sees. She'll be proud of you."

"Thanks, honey. Now, what have you been doing while I was being beautified?"

"Tad's been painting. Turbo's been panting. Tang and Ms. Pickles have been sleeping. And I've finished my book." She counted them off on the pudgy fingers of one hand.

Annabelle looked at her grandson. "May I see what you're painting?"

He shook his head. "Not yet, it's not finished. You know artists don't like to have our work seen before it's ready."

I'd better not roll my eyes or he'll be crushed.

"Oh, right. Guess I forgot. I have to finish getting ready. Want to come talk with me, Megan?"

"Sure. Are you going to wear makeup, too?" The little girl took her grandmother's hand and matched her stride on the steps.

"Why not?"

"Awesome!"

The girl followed Annabelle into the bathroom where she stored the new products she'd purchased. They rummaged around in the vanity drawer looking for makeup.

"I don't seem to have much anymore, just blush and a very old lipstick."

"Use Peggy's, she'll never know." Digging in a small drawer, Megan held up sticks, brushes, compacts and all manner of cosmetics. "Besides, she has more than she can use in a hundred years."

"I won't use very much. I hope she won't mind."

Hopping on the counter, Megan's head moved back and forth, looking first at her grandmother's face then the reflection in the mirror.

"Gram, when can I wear makeup? Some of my friends already do."

"At ten? Oh my. Things are different now, I know, but I don't think you need makeup. Your cheeks are already rosy. Your eyes sparkle. Let's wait until you're at least thirteen, okay?"

"I guess. I think that's when Mom let Peggy wear makeup, but she kind of painted it on. She's much better at it now."

Concentrating on the brush and color she applied to her eyes, Annabelle released the breath she'd been holding.

"I'm a little out of practice. I'll just go easy and see what you think."

The little girl watched her grandmother brushing color on her cheeks and mascara on one eye. "Does it look like too much?"

Megan studied one eye and then the other. "No, that eye looks bigger. Do it on both sides."

She followed directions by adding the mascara and soft pink lipstick.

"Well, I'm too early for Halloween."

With a smile, the little girl hugged her grandmother. "You look pretty. He's going to love looking at you."

"Do you think so?"

"Ahuh. And I think cousin Regina will be jealous."

I don't look half bad. A little color takes years off my face and gives me a little pizazz.

"That'll be the day . . ."

The clock struck six and the doorbell rang.

"Oh, no. He's early. I'm not finished dressing."

"I'll get it." Megan hopped off the counter and ran down the stairs.

Tillie and Joe were at the door with a bag full of groceries.

"Hello, sweet pea." Joe gave Megan a quick hug.

"I'll put this stuff in the kitchen," Tillie said, without waiting for a reply. "Where's your grandmother?"

"She's getting ready. Wait until you see her." A grin stretched from ear-to-ear.

"I'm right here." Annabelle stood at the top of the stairs while Tad stood grinning beside her.

"Have I got a nice looking Gram, or what?" He puffed out his chest.

Joe stood at the bottom of the stairs with a startled expression he couldn't quite hide. Tillie poked him in the ribs. "Down boy! Sweetie, you look like a zillion bucks."

"Thanks." Annabelle felt thrilled and embarrassed at the same time.

Joe whipped out his cell phone and took Annabelle's photograph. "For posterity."

"Annabelle, get down here before he slobbers on the floor," Tillie said. "Behave yourself, Joseph."

With grace that she never felt she had, Annabelle descended the stairs. All eyes were on her. She felt her face warm. As she reached the bottom of the stairs, the bell rang again.

"He's early." Tillie said.

Megan opened the door for Mr. Edwards, who walked into the cluster of people in the foyer.

"Is there a party?"

Tillie and Joe pushed the kids into the hallway toward the kitchen. "We're making pizza," Tillie called over her shoulder.

Phil smiled at Annabelle. "Wow. Ready to celebrate?"

"Celebrate what?" Annabelle asked.

"Whatever we want. You look smashing, by the way." He took her arm, and they headed out the door to his car.

Goose bumps rose on her arm from where his warm hand held her. She knew without turning around that all eyes watched them from behind the parlor curtains.

Chapter 31

REGINA STOOD back and admired her handiwork. A table set for two, complete with candles and wine glasses. She'd tossed a salad and soaked the chicken breasts in marinade while the potatoes boiled. Rice was too unpredictable, if she remembered correctly. She decided mashed potatoes were an easy substitute. Sam's wonderful homemade vinaigrette graced the middle of the table with a stick of real butter. The vintner had recommended a nice blush wine, chilling in the refrigerator. All the evening lacked was soft music, easily remedied, and the object of her affections.

Sugar curled up on the rug by the back door, watching every move Regina made. Sam was a tidy chef who seldom spilled, but often shared little nibbles here and there. Being less comfortable in the kitchen, Regina spilled lots more but shared less, so the dog cleaned up every crumb before going to sleep.

"A lot of help you are," Regina said to the snoring Labrador Retriever.

The dog's big yellow head snapped up as a car pulled into the drive.

"Woof." The dog barked, then dashed off to the front door, tail wagging and nails tapping on the terracotta tile.

She fluffed her hair, straightened her shoulders and glided into the front room just as Sam opened the door. His broad face split in a grin at the sight of her. She couldn't help but return his smile.

"Hello, gorgeous."

He planted a kiss on her lips. Warming to her toes in seconds, Regina swayed when he let her go to ruffle the dog's ears. "I didn't forget you, Sugar Bear. You are both my favorite females."

"Dinner will be ready in about twenty minutes."

Sam froze, brows raised. "You cooked?"

"Now that's not a very nice way to say it. Yes, I cooked. Are you alarmed or surprised?"

"A little of both, to be honest." Grabbing her around the waist he picked her up and nuzzled her neck. "What's the occasion?"

"I felt like it, that's all."

"No. I'm not buying that. You never feel like cooking."

"Careful. You'll spoil the surprise."

"Ah, there is an ulterior motive."

She looked at him through her lashes. "Perhaps."

"Did you sell a painting?"

"No."

"Did Megan find Annabelle's pearls?"

"Uh, no." Regina furrowed her brow.

He laid his huge hand on her stomach. "You're pregnant?"

She slapped it away. "I am not!"

"Well, then I give up. What's the surprise?"

Regina narrowed her icy blue eyes at him. "You are just going to have to wait and see, my very handsome man. Put on some music, would you?" She turned and walked back toward the kitchen knowing he would comply.

A moment later cool jazz played throughout the house.

"Nice choice." Regina muttered to herself, smiling, as Sam and Sugar pounded up the stairs to the bedroom. Her hips swayed to the rhythm of Coltrane. A test of the potatoes revealed that they were done and ready for mashing. She poured off the steaming water, added butter, milk, salt and pepper then looked all over for the masher.

"Damn. Sam! Where's the potato masher?"

Coming down in stocking feet prevented her from hearing his approach.

"I don't have one."

"*Merde.*" Her hand flew to her heart. "You scared me."

"Use the hand mixer, it's in the cabinet by the fridge. The beaters are in the drawer with the other serving utensils." He went out to start the grill.

She dug around until she located them, right where he said they'd be. She proceeded to beat the vegetables into submission. Concentration and noise prevented her from hearing Sam's return. He slipped his arms around her waist and gave her an easy squeeze.

"You smell good," he said.

Leaning her head against his cheek, she clicked off the appliance and turned in his arms.

"So do you." She kissed him soundly. "I have a favor to ask."

"Name it."

"Would you mind grilling the chicken? I'm afraid I'll burn the place down."

"I don't mind a bit." He kissed her neck. The dog followed him back onto the deck. "Sorry, girl, no time to play tonight, I'm grilling. Maybe after we eat." He patted the dog's furry head and accepted a "woof" in return.

Regina followed them out with the chicken and his favorite grilling tongs.

"Here you go. I'll cover the potatoes so they don't get cold."

"Sounds good. And we'll just nuke 'em if they need a little warming up."

"Good point." She sat on the railing and watched him arrange the meat on the grill. The sizzling sound and potential snack had the dog's undivided attention.

"How long will it take?"

"Just a few minutes. Is there any wine, I need the fortification?"

"Absolutely." She went back inside and returned a few moments later, a half-filled wine glass in each hand. "Here you go."

He took a sip. "I like it."

"It's Portuguese." She gave it a try. "Mmm. I like it, too."

He joined her at the railing, leaning one hip beside hers.

"Are you going to tell me what you're up to?"

"Not yet. I'll put the rest of dinner on the table." She pecked him on the cheek before she left him alone to finish the meat.

After consuming the meal and wine, Regina reached across the table and held Sam's warm hand. She marveled once again how large they were.

"Would you be willing to help me set up a trust to cover the taxes and insurance on the Riverside house for the next eight years?"

"Of course, we can draw up a draft here and email it to the office for Marvel to finish up. What brought this on?"

"Annabelle and the kids can't afford to pay the taxes. I can."

"Why not just continue to pay them?"

"I want to put the house in their names. That way they'll have a place to live until the kids come of age and decide what they want to do in life."

"But what about you?"

"What about me?"

"That's your inheritance."

"Now it's theirs. I don't need it anymore."

He took her hands in his and squeezed.

"Does this mean what I think it means?"

"It means you're stuck with me." Regina lifted his hand and kissed it.

"Forever?"

"At least that long."

"But . . ."

"But, I was wondering if you might make an honest woman of me?"

"I'd be honored." Sam leaned across the edge of the table and kissed her lips. "I have a question, though."

"All right."

"Will you also take my name?"

"You can't expect me to be Regina Louise Morgan-Smith-Duncan, can you?"

"Well, no, I was hoping . . ."

"How does Regina Louise Duncan sound?"

"Heavenly." He kissed her again, stood and pulled her from the chair for a bear hug. Lifting her feet from the floor, they spun around in a circle. "Rags, you've made me so happy!"

"Mother will probably kick her way out of her grave. The women of my family have kept the Morgan name for three generations. Long before it was fashionable. But I'm thinking that it's time to break with tradition and start a new one."

He ran his fingers through her silky hair. "First your hair and now your name. You're full of surprises."

"Perhaps, I've only just begun."

He smiled. "I can't wait to see what'll happen next."

"How do you feel about having the wedding here? Say about Christmas time?"

"Sure, unless you'd rather run off to Vegas and get married by an Elvis impersonator?" Regina shuddered. "God forbid. No, I think I'd like to get married here. In *our* house."

"Then that's the way it'll be, but let's do it a little before Christmas. I want the kids to have Christmas Day. I'm assuming you want Tillie to stand up with you."

"Actually, yes, and Peggy, too. Annabelle can give me away."

"They'll love that. Joe and Tad can be my best man and groomsman."

"I love it. I love you."

His hand stroked her cheek. "And I love you."

The phone rang, but it didn't break the spell. Regina watched as Sam crossed to the phone, his eyes never leaving her.

"Hello."

"We'll be right there. Don't worry."

"What is it?"

"Annabelle said the police just dropped Peggy off at the house."

"Is Peggy all right?"

"Shook up, but fine. Let's put the food away and go."

Chapter 32

SITTING ON THE sofa staring into space, Peggy knew she was in serious trouble. Her skin felt cold and her bones tired. Megan and Tad were upstairs supposedly doing their homework.

Yeah, right. Why did Gram have to call Regina and Sam? What were they going to do?

Peggy's hands began to sweat. First Miles gives her the "you don't love me" speech, then the cops pick them up with their clothes half-off. Gram looked ready to strangle her. Maybe she needed Regina here to keep her from doing it?

Oh crap.

She stroked the orange kitten asleep beside her thigh. Ms. Pickles had deserted her when Annabelle slammed the door. Thank God Tang was more curious than afraid. The little feline motor started up, vibrating against her. It felt good to touch the tiny creature's silky hair and to feel its warmth. Peggy's heartbeat slowed, but she could still feel the pulsing in her ears. Her hand shook like she'd been overdoing caffeine.

"Thanks for sticking close, Tang. I could use a friend right now. Even a little furry one."

The doorbell rang, and she stood up to answer it. She heard the dog bark, but didn't wait for him to bound down the stairs.

"Hello, sweetheart." Regina gave Peggy a hug.

She must really be worried. Regina doesn't go around hugging people.

"Hi."

Turbo joined them, snuffling and woofing, making sure they smelled right. Ms. Pickles was nowhere in sight.

Sam shut the door and led them into the parlor.

"Where's your grandmother?"

"She's upstairs."

"Peg, are you okay?"

"I guess so."

Sam put his warm hand on her cold ones.

"Want to tell me what happened?" Regina asked as she sat down beside Peggy.

"Not really. But I guess I have to." Peggy absently patted the dog's big black head. He nuzzled her hand then lay down on her feet. She wiggled her toes in his hair and stroked his ear.

"Hello," Annabelle said from the doorway.

Peggy bowed her head and looked at her grandmother through her bangs.

She's still pissed. I am so dead.

"Did you tell them what happened?" Annabelle asked, her back straight, her chin and her ample breasts thrust forward. The muscle in Annabelle's jaw jerked like she was grinding up nails.

"Not yet," Peggy whispered, staring at Turbo's chocolate syrup eyes.

Crossing to the rocking chair, Annabelle eased down, and began the seesaw motion.

Peggy could see she wasn't going to get off easy, so she swallowed the rising bile, lifted her chin, and looked into Regina's silver blue eyes. No way was she going to look into Gram's wild ones right now.

"Miles and I went out this evening. We got bored at the mall and went to the park to watch the sunset and ducks and . . . stuff." She rubbed her hands but couldn't wash away the feelings of dread.

My ass is grass.

Annabelle savagely kicked the carpet with her feet. "Humph." The chair nearly tossed her from its cushioned seat.

"It got cold by the water, so we got into his car."

Neither Peggy nor Regina looked away. An invisible string tied them together. Sam and Annabelle were blurs on the edge of Peggy's vision.

"We started kissing . . ."

Clearing his throat first, Sam stood. "Excuse me." Out of her peripheral vision she saw him leave and heard his footsteps on the stairs. She could not look at her grandmother.

Regina didn't move, listening to Peggy's story without comment.

Taking a cleansing breath, Peggy continued. "Things got a little carried away. The windows were steaming up. We didn't see the policeman until he shined his light in the car window. I was so scared." She wiped her damp palms on her jean-clad thighs.

The vicious rocking slowed.

Regina held Peggy's gaze. "What happened then?"

Her voice choked with tears. "He took Miles to the back seat of the cop car. Then he asked me if I was all right and if Miles had done anything I didn't want him to do."

A flood rushed down Peggy's hot cheeks. She gulped for air. "I was so embarrassed, I thought I'd die."

"Did you? Did he?" Annabelle's eyes glistened with unshed tears.

"No, God, no. We didn't go all the way, I swear." Peggy gripped the front of her shirt, twisting the hem. "We just, we were kissing and touching . . ."

The rocker stopped.

"I'm sorry, Gram. I just love Miles so much. He makes me feel . . . loved, too."

"That's not love," Annabelle whispered. "You're too young . . ."

"What happened next?" Regina prompted.

"I said I was okay. Then he talked to Miles. I stayed in the car. I think Miles must've said something bad, because the policeman made me get in the front of the cop car. He locked Miles' Mustang then drove me home with Miles in the back behind the cage. I hope they didn't put him in jail. We didn't do anything, really!"

Cold sweat trickled down Peggy's back while tears scalded her cheeks.

"Why don't you go wash your face?" Regina said, giving her hand a pat.

Glancing at her grandmother, Peggy noticed her eyebrows merge over narrowed eyes.

She did as she was told, but didn't close the door all of the way. She took a washcloth and quickly soaked it with cold water, wrung it out and held it to her flaming cheeks.

"Annabelle, settle down before you have another coronary."

"I can't. I don't know what to do. I'm so mad, scared and frustrated."

Peggy had never heard her grandmother sound so angry before.

"Is that why you called? Were you afraid you'd strike out in your anger?"

Listening very hard for the answer, Peggy heard her grandmother hiss, "Yes."

"Okay. What do you want me to do?"

"Talk to her, please. Explain what a mistake it would be to go so far so young. And certainly not with Miles, he was the idiot that mowed down her sister with his car."

"It was an accident, Annabelle. Miles would never hurt Megan or anyone on purpose. And I don't recall listening to my mother when she warned me about infatuation and the physical effects of hormones."

Twisting the washrag into submission, Peggy could feel the heat in her cheeks.

Oh, my God. This is so gross.

But the next thing that Peggy heard was a chuckle from her grandmother. She held her breath then exhaled very quietly.

"I can't talk to her about sex. It's too hard. She'll always be a little girl to me."

"She's not a small child any more, Annabelle."

"Oh, Lord. I know, but . . ."

"No buts. I'll talk to her. However, you really should be the one, you know."

"I didn't say anything about the hickey or the swollen lips, but I'm worried how far she'll go. Surely she knows she's loved." Annabelle's voice sounded more desperate than angry now.

"It's been a long time since we were teenagers, but don't you remember the hormones stirring, Belle? Nothing about it is logical. Young love feels wonderful."

"Do you think Peggy is really in love?"

"I don't know, Belle, but I've gotten pretty good at reading Peggy's face. If she isn't, she's very close to it. Your blowing up will only hurt and confuse her more."

The wet rag was warm now. Peggy's cheeks weren't quite so cherry red. She'd have to go back in there and face the music. Being brought home in a police car wasn't good and she had to find out what had happened to Miles.

Slipping out of the bathroom and into the kitchen, Peggy dialed Miles' cell.

"I'm not around. Leave your stuff. I'll call ya back later."

Crap.

"Miles, it's me. You okay? What happened? Please call and let me know."

Peggy hung up. Turning to go into the dining room, Sam filled the doorway like a huge grizzly bear.

"Hey."

"Hey." Peggy looked down at her feet.

"Want me to find out if Miles is okay?"

"Could you?" Peggy's face split with a smile. Her heart began to race.

"Sure. But you'd better get back in there. Go take your medicine."

She wrinkled her nose then sighed. "It'll be awful, I'm sure."

"Probably. Be brave if you want them to know you really are growing up." He reached out and squeezed her shoulder. "Go on."

"Okay." Peggy wiped her eyes on the back of her hands.

Let them do their worst.

When she walked into the parlor all eyes turned to her. Speaking stopped.

Annabelle stood, straightened her top and took a deep breath. "Peggy, you're going to be grounded from that boy for the next three weeks. No using your cell unless it's an emergency and someone is bleeding."

Peggy's arms punctuating her next words as she looked into her grandmother's stern face. "Three weeks! Why? We didn't do anything wrong. Honest."

"Coming home in a police car is wrong, young lady." Her forefinger pointed at her granddaughter's chest. "You shouldn't have been necking half undressed."

Her hands on her hips, Peggy scoffed. "I'm sixteen, Gram. I'm not a baby anymore, I can take care of myself."

"A baby is more predictable than a teenager, that's for sure." Annabelle sank back into the rocking chair, but held it still. "You're grounded from dating anyone for three weeks, period."

"What a crock. You're just being mean because it was Miles and because I want to see my Dad." Peggy's hair swung around as she pivoted toward the door. Regina's face looked sad, but she didn't say anything as Peggy passed her and took the stairs two at a time. She slammed the bedroom door as hard as possible then slid down to the floor.

Gram can't treat me like a kid. Time to talk to Dad, again. Maybe he'll understand what I'm going through.

Her breath caught in her throat as she realized she had no idea how her father would react to her being alone with a boy or being brought home by the police.

He might be even worse than Gram. Would he go looking for Miles? Crap. Now what am I going to do? She reached for her cell phone. Malissa had called. I wonder if Sam found out anything? What a mess . . .

Chapter 33

THE RINGING PHONE was real, not a dream, Annabelle realized.

"Hello."

"Annabelle?" said a familiar southern drawl.

"I'm sorry, who is this?"

"Did I wake you? My apologies. This is Phil."

"Phil? What time is it?" Annabelle rubbed her eyes with the back of her hand, rolled her head on her neck and flexed her toes.

"It's seven-thirty. I thought for sure you'd be back from walking and wide awake."

"Usually I am, but we were up late last night. It's so quiet, I imagine the kids are still sleeping, too. What can I do for you?" She ran a hand over her sleep-mussed hair.

"I'm hoping I can take you to dinner tonight. Maybe a movie? Casablanca is playing at the Orpheum. I thought you might want to go since it is Saturday night."

"We did have a nice dinner last weekend . . ."

"I was hoping you'd be interested."

"Could I get back with you in a little bit? I'm really not awake. I'm not sure what we're doing today."

"Surely. I doubt they'll sell out. Just let me know. If I don't answer the home phone, call my cell."

"All right. I'll call you back."

"Sorry I woke you."

"It's fine, really." She hung up the phone and leaned back against the pillows.

Two weekends in a row. What had gotten into him? Should I impose on Tillie and Joe again? With Peggy's misbehavior, should I leave the kids alone together? Was there anything on the calendar? Get up and find out.

Poor Turbo, he was probably full to bursting by now. She took care of her own business then went down the hall, stopping at Tad's door. She opened it a crack, snores poured out. Turbo's big black nose quickly filled the space. She pushed the door open far enough for him to escape. Annabelle followed him down the stairs to let him out back before she fixed a half pot of coffee. The calendar tacked to the refrigerator had most days filled with some school event, but this evening looked open. She smiled, picking up the phone to call Tillie.

"Good morning. Why didn't you wake me up to go for a walk?"

"I knocked on the front door, but there didn't appear to be anyone up, not even the dog. I went on by myself this morning. I hope you don't mind. Were you up?"

Annabelle took a quick sip of wake up juice.

"No, we all slept in. Phil called and woke me up or I'd still be snoring like Tad."

"No one snores like Tad." Tillie chuckled. "I've heard you. You snore like a girl."

"Thanks, I think." She lifted the lid off of the cookie jar only to find it filled with nothing but crumbs. Annabelle dug around in the cabinet for a granola bar. Her teeth hurt just thinking about the sugary cereals the kids liked to eat.

"What did Phil want, as if I couldn't guess?"

"He wants to go out tonight."

"Again?" Tillie laughed. "Why it's only been a week since the last time? Does this mean you've changed your mind and you kind of . . . like him?"

Feeling her cheeks warm, Annabelle cleared her throat.

"I wouldn't go that far. He's fun when he's not bossing everyone around." Breaking off a piece of the crunchy oat bar, she popped it into her mouth. Chewing it would be too loud on the phone so she let it soften on her tongue.

"Yes. I've seen him at your house a few times, too."

"Dropping Tad off doesn't count as seeing someone unless you're a teenager and never been kissed. I haven't been kissed for a very long while and I'm no teenager."

Why did I say that? Time to wake up before you say something really stupid.

"All the more reason to have a good time. We'll watch the kids. I'll make tacos, or Joe can grill burgers. We'll figure it out."

"The kids could probably stay by themselves if Peggy wasn't grounded."

"I saw her come home in the police car. I figured you'd tell me what happened as soon as you cooled down. I was really looking forward to our walk this morning."

"Sorry."

"No problem. You can tell me later. But for tonight, don't worry. I can be very entertaining. This way they can torment us grown-ups instead of each other. Plus, I think they kind of like my cooking."

"Tillie, everyone likes your cooking." Annabelle smiled.

"Hey, let's have Phil over for dinner instead."

"No. I don't think that's a good idea at all. I kind of like going *out* to dinner once in a while. He wants to take me to the Orpheum to see an old movie." She slid her free hand slowly down the coiled cord and back up again.

"Are you going to neck in the balcony?"

It sounded like Tillie had put her hand over the receiver, but Annabelle still heard her snickering.

"Shame on you. Of course not."

"Then why go at all?"

Annabelle laughed at her mischievous friend before changing the subject. "Do you think I should call Tom?"

"Why?" Tillie genuinely sounded puzzled.

"He is the kids' father. He wants to see them. Maybe Peggy is acting out or something."

"Do you really think that's what's going on?"

"Not really. I don't trust him. He was never there when Liddy or the kids needed him, always off partying. And now he's been in jail. I don't think my heart could handle the stress." She put her hand on her chest, feeling the slow thump through her palm.

"I don't know what to tell you, Belle. I've never had kids, but if I had I'd probably feel about the same as you. What does Regina think?"

"Believe it or not, she just says she'll support any decision me or the kids make." She added hot coffee to her cooling cup.

"Wow, that's a switch. He is their father, so maybe you or Regina can be there, too."

"I suppose. I just feel so confused. I don't know the right thing to do."

"Just be there for them. You'll know what to do when the time comes, I'm sure."

"Thanks. I'll call Coach, I mean Phil. I don't know what to call him."

"Honey bunny?" Tillie snickered.

"I think I'll call him Phil. Coach brings out the bossy side of him." She inspected the half-eaten breakfast bar. "My husband David insisted I call him nothing but David. Not Dave or Davey or hey you. I kind of like having a choice."

"You've always had choices. These are just better ones."

"True. Thanks, Matilda Jean."

They both laughed, hanging up the phone.

After confirming her date with Phil for 5:30, Annabelle decided to make pancakes. She got down the largest ceramic bowl to mix the batter from scratch.

Turbo liked being in the kitchen where food things happened on a regular basis. Ready for kibble, his nose sampled the air indicating he liked the smell of pancakes even better.

"If there's any left after everyone is done, I'll put it in your bowl." Annabelle smiled down at the tail-churning dog.

"Woof." Turbo sounded in acknowledgement.

Just how much he understood, Annabelle didn't know, but he sure seemed to know a lot of English for a canine. How could anyone get rid of such a smart animal? She rubbed his ear then washed her hands to resume breakfast preparations. She personally liked warmed syrup and bacon with her pancakes. The aroma of cooked bacon reminded her of Sunday mornings with Grandma Morgan. No doubt Tad would wake up when the smell reached the second floor.

Before she'd completed the thought she heard feet pounding on the stairs. She smiled when the bed-headed boy entered the doorway.

"What smells so good? Pancakes? Bacon? What's up, Gram? What are we celebrating? Is it someone's birthday?" He helped himself to a glass of orange juice.

"I just felt like making breakfast, that's all."

"Man, it's late. Don't worry, the girls were getting up when I came down."

Looking over her shoulder, she smiled. "That's good. Now set the table."

"I get the first batch, don't I?"

"I think that's fair. And let's save some of the last batch for Turbo."

Laying out the silverware in haphazard fashion, Tad grabbed the plates, glasses and set them all around.

"Don't forget the peanut butter, Tadpole." Megan said, as she walked into the kitchen.

"I won't." He set the jar of creamy peanut butter down in front of her plate, grabbing the crunchy for himself.

"Don't all those nuts make your pancakes taste weird?" She wrinkled her nose in disgust.

"Nah. I like the different textures. Tillie taught me that."

"Oh." Megan reached across the table. She used her clean fork to dollop a little crunchy onto her plate. "Maybe I'll give it a try then."

Sliding into her chair, Peggy sipped her juice, but didn't say a word.

Tad dug into his cakes. His eyes closed with bliss.

Annabelle grinned and flipped another pancake onto each of their plates.

"Good morning, sunshines."

"You're weird, Gram." Tad said with his mouth full.

"Thank you."

"Isn't that in a movie?" Megan asked. "The mother always says rise and shine and the son says he'll rise but he won't shine."

Pausing with her spatula in the air, Annabelle tipped her head. "I don't know."

"It's a story about a girl and her glass animals. We're reading it in English class." Peggy grabbed a piece of bacon before her brother could nab them all.

Annabelle enjoyed the homey sounds of forks clanking on plates. She started to hum while she cooked another batch of pancakes.

"What's that song?" Megan asked.

"It's a record my mother used to play years ago. I don't think I ever knew the name, but it makes me think of her."

"What's a record?" Megan asked.

"Oh my." Annabelle turned to her grandchildren and shook her head. "It's like a big CD that's played on a turntable with a needle. I think I read somewhere that they are making a comeback."

Tad nodded. "That's right. They're reissuing old records, but I'm not sure it will catch on. They're much bigger than a CD, and you need the right kind of equipment and stuff."

Peggy ate in silence, pouting between bites.

"Do they scratch as easy as CD's?" Megan asked.

"I don't know," Tad said. "I like CD's. But when I get my own iPhone, I'll just download the music I buy."

"An eye what?" Annabelle asked.

Tad cupped his hands over his ears, bobbing his head. "You know, you listen to music with ear buds attached to your cellphone."

"Oh, yes. I've seen the commercials. Maybe Santa will bring one for Christmas. We could all share it."

Crossing her arms over her chest, Peggy scowled.

Tad laughed and poked his older sister. "Peggy probably won't use ear buds that have other people's ear wax on them, Gram. That's gross!"

Megan rolled her eyes. "There's no such thing as Santa Claus."

Tad and Peggy looked at Annabelle, but didn't say a word.

"Don't you believe in magic?" Annabelle watched her youngest granddaughter.

"You mean like *Harry Potter* magic?"

Annabelle nodded. "Sure. Like when special things happen that no one can explain?"

Megan shrugged her shoulders. "I guess."

"Personally, I believe in magic. Santa is magic. You don't want to chance it and have him not show up because you don't believe, do you?"

"Well, no, but Gram, he's fat. He can't fit in all those chimneys . . . ."

"There are a lot of things in this world that we can't explain." Annabelle resumed eating.

The children watched her for a moment then finished eating as well. There was one pancake left. Turbo got all but the little bit that Megan pinched off for each cat, which were curled up on the rag rug together.

"Tad, you clear the table. Girls, you load the dishwasher." Annabelle sipped the last of the coffee.

Peggy sighed.

"By the way, I've got a date tonight. Tillie has offered to make tacos or burgers. You kids get to choose."

"Ah, come on, Gram. Not Coach Edwards, again!" Tad slammed the cabinet door.

Peggy poked her brother. "We don't need a sitter."

Annabelle ignored Peggy's remark.

Dropping into the chair beside his grandmother, Tad stretched out his long legs. "If I'm going to continue to be humiliated by my grandmother, then I want tacos."

"I want burgers," Megan said.

"Then I want burgers, too." Peggy stuck her tongue out at her brother.

"I'll let Tillie and Joe know." Annabelle called her friends across the street.

ANNABELLE DIDN'T mind the crowded restaurant. She enjoyed the quiet voices accompanied by the tinkling of glassware. Especially when someone else was doing the cooking and the cleaning.

Phil touched her hand. "Hello, where are you?"

"Oh, sorry. I was thinking how nice it is to be waited on." She felt her cheeks warm.

"Me, too. I'm not much of a cook, and you're a very nice dinner companion."

"I haven't bored you with all my stories about the kids and animals, yet?"

"Not at all. It's like being there when you tell me stories about your family. I like it. It's way too quiet at my house." He watched Annabelle as he spoke, ignoring the bustle around them.

"Maybe you should get a dog." Annabelle sipped her water.

I need to keep my wits about me. One minute he sets my teeth on edge, the next, my knees melt.

"Oh, I don't know. Martha always had little dogs. I never felt like they were mine to enjoy."

"Turbo certainly isn't small. Why don't you come over for dinner sometime and see what you think of having a big dog around? Of course, you have to be willing to put up with the shedding, paw prints and slobbers all day and night. We also have two cats that hide when people come to visit. Perhaps a kitten would better."

They gave their orders to the waiter and sipped their iced tea. Annabelle glanced around the room but doubted she'd see anyone she knew. Phil touched her hand.

"I've never had a cat, even growing up. My dad didn't like them. Martha was allergic." *He keeps staring at me. I wonder if I have lipstick on my teeth.*

"We always had critters on the farm. I can't imagine a home without pets. We had an indoor cat, several barn cats and a couple of dogs that herded our few cows around. My mother loved animals. She didn't even mind when I brought home a turtle or horned toad. It was more like a menagerie than a working farm. She drew the line at snakes, though. Frankly, they just aren't what I'd call a pet."

Their salads were placed in front of them, so they paused to put napkins on their laps and taste the food. The mildly spiced vinaigrette was a delightful addition.

"I have to agree. One of the boys on the basketball team had a pet boa constrictor once, but he told me it got lost. They never found it before they moved."

"Oh, my." Putting down her fork, Annabelle frowned. "Can you imagine moving into a new house and finding a snake already lives there?" She patted her heart. "I don't think I could live in a house with a snake."

"Neither could I."

Damn, but he can be charming sometimes.

When their steaks came, they ate the first bite in silence.

"This is the most tender steak I think I've ever eaten. We don't eat much steak at our house. With a growing boy around, we go more for quantity than quality." Annabelle dabbed the corners of her mouth with her napkin.

"I'm happy you're enjoying it. I like a good piece of beef, but they're so pricy these days. I'll give you a tip. Always check the meat markdowns first. That's where you'll find a decent priced steak."

Phil sat back in his seat and smiled at her.

"Shall we head to the theater?"

"Yes. Thank you for dinner."

He squeezed her hand. "My pleasure."

WHEN THE MOVIE was over, Phil and Annabelle walked to the car, hand in hand. It was a cool night. The starlit Kansas sky was clear of clouds.

The occasional car that passed them on Broadway ignored. Annabelle enjoyed the quietness of the night and her companion.

"What's your favorite part of the movie?"

"I like it all, but when he says, "Here's looking at you, kid." I get goose bumps. I've heard it a thousand times, but I love it."

"Here's looking at you, kid." Phil kissed her hand.

Oh no. What's happening here? I'm too old for this romantic stuff, but it feels so nice.

She let him open the car door. She couldn't say a word. David had never been affectionate let alone chivalrous. She couldn't recall them ever going out for dinner and a movie, there'd never been any time or money for that sort of thing. It felt good to be close to a man. He had an infectious smile, nice manners, once you got past the whole know-it-all routine. He even smelled good, like Old Spice. Annabelle enjoyed having an adult companion. Being with the opposite sex was nice, too.

They drove through the park on the way home. Moonlight danced like huge fireflies on the black water. Trees masked the streetlights, hiding them in darkness. She felt like they were the only two people around. The night air smelled sweet like new mown grass. The breeze cooled her warm skin. Phil pulled the car up into the drive. The lights were on in the house. She could see the blue glow of the television behind the curtains.

"Thanks again for a wonderful evening, Phil."

"I'll walk you to the door."

He got out then gave her his hand to help her out. He escorted her up the walk to the porch.

"I love this old house." He smiled, looking around. "And the roses."

"Me, too. It's been in our family a hundred years."

"It suits you." He opened the screen door. They stood facing one another.

Her heartbeats filled her ears and her chest.

I hope I'm not having another heart attack.

"It's old fashioned. Like me, I guess."

"It's beautiful, warm, and comfortable, like you."

At least he didn't imply I am as big as a house, like David would've done.

"Goodness, thank you." Annabelle could feel warmth climb from her throat to the top of her head.

Phil kissed her cheek then released her. "Good night, Belle."

"Good night."

Uh, oh. Now I'm in trouble, but Lord it feels good all over. I'd better nip it. No lovie stuff for me. I'm too old, with too many bad memories. He'll have to understand I just want to be friends. That's it. That's all. The end? I hope not. I'm a mess.

Chapter 34

PEGGY CLOSED THE door to her bedroom and flipped the lock. Her little sister was busy watching a movie with Tad. Hopefully, they wouldn't even notice her absence. Tillie and Joe were in the kitchen with Gram. She pulled out her cell phone and dialed Malissa.

"Hey, girl."

"Hey."

"I need you to help me with something next week."

"Sure. What's up?"

Her hands were sweaty, but Peggy had made up her mind.

"I need you to cover for me so I can go downtown and see my father."

"What?" Malissa's voice had gone up an octave.

That's not exactly the response I thought she'd give, but I'll go with it.

"Yeah. He's working at Jenny's Diner and I want to talk with him."

"No way. You'll get caught and you're already grounded. How are you going to get there?"

"Bus. I checked the schedules. If I go right after school I can get a bus home by dinner time."

"You're grounded, remember?"

"Not from school. I'll just say you and I have a project to work on in the library."

Her best friend sighed loud enough for her to hear. That meant she would help.

"I hate riding the bus. All those weird people . . . but . . . I'll go with you."

"You don't have to. Just cover for me if Gram calls."

"She'll call *your* cell phone, stupid, not mine. It's for emergencies, remember."

"I thought of that. I'll just say the battery died."

Flopping down on the bed, Peggy kicked her shoes onto the floor.

"Why do you have to talk to him now?"

Staring at the crack in the ceiling, she paused.

"I want to ask him some things, you know?"

"I guess, but I think you're nuts. I'm coming with you, that way we won't be lying about being together. I really hate lying."

She put her feet on the bed, crossing one knee over the other.

"Yeah, me, too. If anyone asks, we took the wrong bus to the central library. Thanks, by the way. I really do appreciate it."

"What are friends for?"

She thought she heard the stairs creak.

"Gotta go."

"Later . . ."

Turning off the phone Peggy sat up on the edge of the bed. *What will I say? Or more importantly, what will he say?*

ON MONDAY, PEGGY and Malissa met in the commons after the last bell. They'd stowed their backpacks in their lockers. Neither had homework that couldn't wait. Slinging their purses over their shoulders, they headed to the city bus stop. A car honk got their attention.

"Hey, Peg, Malissa, wait!"

"Hi, Miles." Peggy leaned into the window of the old blue four-door Mustang he was driving again. "Where you headed?"

"Work."

"Where are you working?" Malissa asked. "And when did you get your car back?"

"I'm restricted, so I can drive to school and work. I'm working at the mall, want a lift?"

The girls exchanged a look then Peggy leaned in. "Can you take a little detour?"

"It depends on how far, my dad checks the mileage."

"Douglas and Hillside," Peggy said.

"There's a lot of cool stuff there, where are you going?"

"Does it matter?"

"Nah, I guess not. But, how will you get home?"

"We can catch the bus." Malissa stood next to her friend.

"Okay, hop in, but you can't tell anyone."

"We won't tell if you won't." Peggy gave him a quick kiss on the cheek.

"Sounds fair. Hop in."

"Are your folks still mad about the other night?"

"Just Mom. She thinks you're a bad influence on me." Miles winked at Peggy.

"Yeah. Well, Gram thinks you're a bad influence on me. We ought to get them together."

"Oh, boy. That would be a shit storm," Malissa said. "I wouldn't want to be anywhere near it."

Miles dropped the girls on the corner, waving as he drove off. The girls approached the concrete building. A pink neon DINER sign blinked in the front window, but it was too dark inside for them to see much.

"I can't believe you dragged me to a diner. If there are any old men with no teeth I'm outta here," Malissa said.

"Get a grip. We're not here to see the locals. I hear they have pretty good burgers and fries."

"What if you can't see him?"

"He's the cook and it's too late for lunch and too early for dinner. But, if he's not there then I guess I'll have to figure something else out."

"Why doesn't that fill me with confidence?" Malissa straightened her shoulder bag.

"Probably the same reason I don't feel confident myself. Let's get this over with."

The girls walked in and waited for their eyes to adjust.

"What can we do for you girls?" A short woman with frizzy platinum hair and big breasts wiped down a table with a wet rag, the front of her tee shirt soaked where she'd leaned over the wet surface.

Lifting her chin, Peggy approached her. "We heard you had a good cook."

Grabbing a couple of menus she walked to a table by the window, swinging her big hips in her low rise jeans, a muffin top hanging well over. "Schools out, I see."

Nervous and fidgety, Peggy didn't open her menu. "I'd like a diet coke and crispy French fries, please."

The waitress' lips were cracked from age or too many cigarettes. Her skin looked like old leather, her voice gravely. "How about you?"

"A coke, please, no ice," Malissa said.

Platinum scribbled down their orders then sauntered over to the cook's window.

"Tom, we need a fry, extra crispy, for two little gals from school."

As Peggy watched, the empty space filled with the face of her father. Their eyes connected. She squirmed in her seat.

"Got it, Maudie." Tom nodded.

"Is that your dad?"

"Ahuh."

"I hope he doesn't burn your fries, I'm hungry."

Grabbing her friend's hand, Peggy could feel fear crawling up her spine. She crossed the fingers of her other hand and said a little prayer.

Lord, help me not screw this up. And I pray . . . well . . . I don't know what I want, but I hope whatever it is doesn't hurt.

The girls waited in silence. Platinum Maudie sat two drinks and a bottle of ketchup in front of them. She rested her hands on her ample hips.

"Which one of you is Tom's girl?"

"What?" Malissa asked.

"Me." Peggy sat up straighter, attempting a smile. It felt more like a zipper pulled across her face.

"How old are you?"

"Fifteen."

"I'll be damned. Tom said he had kids, but I never thought they'd be almost grown." Maudie turned to Malissa. "Who are you?"

Malissa swallowed hard. "Her friend."

With a sniff, Platinum Maudie turned and walked away.

Leaning toward each other, the girls giggled.

"Holy cow. She's scary." Peggy let go of her friend's hand, wiping the damp palm on her jeans.

This is way intense.

They sprang back as a platter of fries appeared on the table.

"Hi, Peg. Who's your friend?" Tom asked, taking a seat next to her.

She straightened her spine and motioned toward Malissa.

"Dad. Tom, this is my best friend, Malissa. This is Tom Malone. My dad."

"Hi. Nice to meet you." He smiled, his chipped front tooth shining.

Malissa offered her hand, giving him a hesitant shake.

"What brings you girls by on this nice afternoon?"

Eating a French fry, Peggy didn't register the crunchy texture or salty flavor.

"We came . . ." She cleared the frog from her throat. "I came to ask you a few questions."

The smell of greasy onions wafted from his soiled white apron. His brown hair was slicked back, shorter than Peggy remembered, the hairline receding. His eyes looked kind and seemed to see no one but her.

"Interesting. Shoot."

"These are great," Malissa said, with her mouth full. She squirted ketchup on the corner of the plate and grabbed two more.

"You have to promise to tell me the truth," Peggy said.

"Sure, whatever you say, kiddo." Tom nabbed a fry and munched.

"Why did you come back after all these years?"

He stared at her for a long minute before answering.

"'Cuz your mom died. I knew you'd need me."

"After ten years, we were used to not having you around." Peggy watched his face fall. "Why did you really come back?"

"Peggy, I . . ." He looked at Malissa who kept her eyes on the fries. The platter was already half empty. "You know I was in jail. I wrote to you kids, maybe not a lot, but I wrote a few times. When no one wrote back, I gave up."

Crossing her thin arms over her chest, Peggy scowled. "Mom would've told us if you had written."

"Maybe not. She was really mad at me. I screwed up big time."

"You mean about the car accident?"

"Yeah. That, too, but I was a stupid kid, and I couldn't handle things." He wiped the sweat from his forehead on a bandanna he pulled from his back pocket. "I was too young and overwhelmed. I couldn't settle down to be a good dad or husband."

"So, you left us." Grinding her teeth, Peggy's eyes narrowed.

"That's about the size of it." Even though his words were flippant, Peggy could hear the resignation in his voice. It must've taken a lot to admit he'd been dumb, but it didn't make it all right. Not by a long way.

"I'm sorry, honey." He reached out a shaking hand to touch hers. She struggled not to pull it back. He must have seen the confusion on her face, because the touch was as brief as a breath.

"Mr. Malone." Malissa wiped her face on her napkin, and placed it in the middle of the empty plate.

Peggy and Tom turned their attention to the dark haired girl.

"Yes, young lady?"

"I really liked your fries. How'd you make them so crispy?"

He smiled. "Deep-fat-fried until dark golden brown."

"My mom needs a deep fat fryer."

It finally sunk into Peggy's distracted brain that her best friend had eaten all the French fries. She'd gotten only two of them. "You piglet!"

Tom's snaggle-toothed smile was a happy one. "They're best hot. I'll make you some more, honey."

Looking at the *Felix the Cat* clock on the wall, Peggy gasped. "We've got to go."

Putting his hand on her arm, Tom grew solemn. "Thanks for coming. I'm sorry about the other day. I didn't mean to scare you. I really just want to be a part of you kids' lives, honey. You know, find out what's been happening the last ten years. Honestly. I just want to see you sometimes, to talk and stuff."

"Okay. I can't today, I'm gr . . . I have to get back, but could you call so we can plan something?"

"Sure. I wish you didn't have to leave so soon." His smile looked sad.

"I'm sorry, too . . . Dad." Peggy gave his cheek a quick peck. She and Malissa hustled to the bus stop. When they were out of hearing range, Malissa touched Peggy's arm.

"You okay?"

"Yeah, I am." Peggy's stomach had finally stopped flipping. She wished she'd eaten some French fries.

"The fries were good, huh?" She winked at Malissa.

Her friend's cheeks pinked. "Really good. You should've . . . next time you get the whole platter, promise. Did you find out what you wanted to know?"

"Maybe not everything, but it's a good start."

"Your dad's not so bad. I watched him. I think he's really sorry."

"I hope so. Now I just have to explain to Gram and Regina that I went to see him behind their back."

"Sucks to be you."

She gave Malissa a playful punch in the arm, and they laughed.

"Gee, thanks."

The girls didn't have to wait long for the bus going northwest to Riverside. They climbed on, sitting near the front. The old driver had a kind face. He smiled at them in the rear view mirror. Peggy smiled back. She closed her eyes and leaned her head against the seat. She replayed their conversation over and over.

She had a lot to think about before she could share this with anyone. She only had a few minutes to get her feelings under control. At this rate, she'd be grounded until she turned eighteen.

"If you want to talk, just let me know." Malissa's whisper comforted her even more than the warmth from her presence in the seat beside her.

"Thanks." Peggy didn't open her eyes until they got to her stop.

Chapter 35

SEPTEMBER SWEPT past and then the last day of October was upon them. Annabelle grinned at her grandchildren. Tad dressed as a zombie even though he wouldn't be asking for candy, to take Megan the Magnificent Sorceress Trick-or-Treating through the neighborhood. Peggy stayed home to dole out candy.

"No one likes peanut butter taffy, Gram. I don't know why you bought them." Peggy's nose wrinkled in distaste.

"I like them. If the kids don't eat them then I will."

Digging through the Wallie World bag, she flopped a sack of candy on the table with a thunk.

"There's another one here that's never even been opened."

"That's all right. They were only ninety-nine cents. They freeze."

Rolling her eyes, Peggy walked into the kitchen to deposit the extra bag in the freezer.

"At least you let me pick out the good kind."

"I don't know how you kids eat that sour stuff. It makes my teeth hurt."

Peggy laughed. "I picked out chocolate, too."

"Smart girl, you can never have too much chocolate. There's enough candy here for an invading army."

The doorbell rang. Turbo's nails tapped on the hard wood floor in the entry. He stood between Annabelle and the open doorway.

"Trick or treat!" Behind the door stood a ghost, princess and clown.

"My, you look great." Annabelle said, holding out the bowl. You can each take two."

The greedy ghost took three then hopped off of the porch and ran. The clown unwrapped his candy right then, popping it into his mouth. A chorus of "Thank you's" came from the remaining two.

She shut the door, joining Peggy in the parlor. They were watching an old black-and-white vampire movie. Peggy wouldn't stop laughing.

"This is the hokiest thing I've ever seen. How could you be scared? It's so silly."

"It was very scary when I was young." Annabelle popped in another taffy, savoring the peanut buttery burst in the middle. "It isn't compared to the gory movies now. I can't bear to watch anything made after 1965, too gory. They give me nightmares."

"I don't think any movie has ever given me nightmares." Peggy shook her head. "No wait, when Tad was little, I saw *Alice in Wonderland*. The Jabberwocky gave me the creeps. I just knew he hid in the closet or under my bed. I was afraid to go to sleep. If I had to go to the bathroom, I'd jump into the middle of the room so nothing could grab my foot from under the bed."

"When did the bad dreams stop?"

"When I got more scared of being awake." Peggy's eyes never left the TV screen.

Muting the sound, Annabelle leaned forward. "Do you want to tell me what happened?"

"I don't remember why, but I do remember—Mom and Dad were drinking and yelling at each other. Mom told me to stay in my room. I peeked out of the door and saw stuff flying across the living room. A lamp first, then a big green ashtray exploded somewhere I couldn't see. A table we used to put our feet on flew by the doorway. There was crashing, screaming, cursing. I closed the door and hid under my bed. I guess I figured the Jabberwocky wasn't nearly as scary as my parents."

Those poor kids.

"Was your mother hurt?"

"They both had red marks on their faces and arms. There wasn't as much furniture in the house the next day. They acted like nothing happened at all."

"Did your dad or mom ever hit you kids when they were drinking?"

Peggy sat for a moment in silence. "Not Dad. Mom broke a ruler over Tad's boney butt once. What a screamer. She'd make you want to crawl under the floor and pull it over your head. When Dad left, she changed."

"Words can hurt just as bad as fists." Annabelle had felt their sting more times than she wanted to remember. "But when someone you love does both . . ."

"Yeah. That's the really scary stuff. I don't know if I'll have kids, but I don't want to ever make them feel afraid."

"That's why you won't, honey." Annabelle put her arms around her granddaughter.

The doorbell rang. Peggy took her turn, meeting Turbo at the door. Annabelle watched from the sofa. She wondered how they had survived the pain and anger. Stronger now, they had patched the family back together, and the pieces fit. An image came to mind of the crazy quilt she'd made as a newlywed. David said it looked like a bunch of scraps, hardly worthy of being called a quilt. But she knew better. Sometimes beautiful things came from odd pieces of fabric and it didn't matter if the edges were a little tattered, it still kept you warm. Just like family.

At nine o'clock, they turned off the porch light and sat in the dark watching a John Wayne western, eating popcorn and drinking juice. Tad and Megan would probably be home in the next thirty minutes as other folks closed up their houses for the night.

"I love John Wayne," Annabelle said.

"I know." Peggy smiled.

"We used to go to the theater to see his movies. I always thought my grandpa looked like the Duke."

"Yeah. I can sorta see that. Now we just watch him on DVD, over and over and over . . ." She rolled her eyes for her grandmother.

"They're comforting. They make me laugh when I'm worried. His old westerns help me remember being young. He's my hero."

"He's dead, Gram. Besides, you're not *that* old. I meant to tell you I love the way you're wearing your hair now. It makes you look even younger. Does Mr. Edwards like it?"

"I suppose."

"Do you like him a lot?"

"He can be a very nice man." Filling her mouth with popcorn, Annabelle returned her attention to the movie.

"But do you LIKE him?"

She looked at her granddaughter's earnest face.

"I enjoy his company. We're friends. Besides, it's none of your business. I don't ask you about Miles or the hickey."

Red colored Peggy from neck to hairline in mere seconds.

"Oh my God, Gram. Let's not even go there, okay?"

"No, we haven't been intimate, if that's what you're hinting at." Annabelle smiled, taking another hand full of popcorn.

"Gross. I told you I didn't want to go there. Jeez. There are some things I don't even want to imagine." Peggy covered her face with a pillow, making groaning noises into the fabric.

Cradling the bowl in her lap, Annabelle studied her granddaughter. "While we're on the subject, have you had sex yet?"

The pillow flopped into Peggy's lap. Her mouth hung open.

"What? Me? I'm not even sixteen." To Annabelle's surprise, Peggy's cheeks darkened even more.

"I read the papers. I watch television. I know that girls your age are having babies."

Hugging the pillow against her stomach, Peggy moaned. "I can't talk to you about this, it's too . . ."

"Too what?"

"Embarrassing."

"You know about AIDS? Venereal diseases, right?"

"Yes, I know about STD's. They taught us about them in health class. I also know what a condom looks like, but I have to say they make lousy water balloons—you can ask Tad about that."

"STD?" Annabelle asked.

"Sexually transmitted disease." Peggy hugged the pillow so tight Annabelle wondered if it would pop all the stuffing out. "I can't believe I'm having this conversation with my grandmother."

"It's not very easy for me, either, young lady."

"How could you just blurt it out like that?"

"I couldn't think of a better way. Can you?" Taking another bite of popcorn, Annabelle concentrated on the screen again.

"No, I guess not."

I don't know which one of us will curl up and die from embarrassment first. What was I thinking?

They sat and watched John Wayne and Dean Martin walking down the dirt street looking for bad guys around every corner.

"Gram." Peggy put the pillow back into the corner of the sofa.

"Ahuh."

"I haven't."

Placing her hand on her granddaughter's knee, Annabelle smiled. "I'm glad. It's special when you're fully grown, with a man you love."

"It's not like in the old movies though, is it?"

"No. It's not like the movies at all. It's very . . ."

"Very what?"

"Messy."

Peggy wrinkled her nose.

"Woof," Turbo barked, running to the door just as Tad opened it.

"We're home. You should see the haul we made," he said.

"Gram?" The sorceress pulled off her star covered conical hat.

"In here, kids. Let's take a look at this *haul* on the dining room table."

Peggy stayed in front of the television while Annabelle, Tad and Megan went in to the other room.

"Totally weird," Peggy said under her breath.

Annabelle heard her last words and chuckled. What a strange conversation that ended on a very unusual note. But it was only the truth. Sometimes things came with very messy consequences.

Chapter 36

LYING ON TOP OF the bed next to her sister, Peggy tried very hard to concentrate, without much luck. She'd read this page three times, still not sure what it said.

"Peggy?" Megan interrupted her sister, again.

"Ahuh." Peggy didn't look over the top of the teen magazine, just kept staring at the page.

"What am I going to do?" Megan flopped back on the pillows.

"About what?" Peggy finally laid the magazine aside to concentrate on her baby sister.

"I have to find Gram's pearls before Regina's and Sam's wedding."

"Then I guess we'd better get busy looking. Don't you remember anything about where you put them?"

"No. Usually I see things in pictures, but it's all black when I try to think about the pearls. I remember I put them in something, but . . ."

"That's a start. What do you say we spend today going through the upstairs bedrooms? We'll check all the cubby holes and stuff."

"You'll help me?"

"Sure." Putting her arm around her little sister's shoulders, Peggy gave her a squeeze. "What are big sisters for?"

"Thanks." Megan laid her head against her sister for a moment then stood up. "Let's start in our room. That seems like a good place, don't you think?"

"Sure."

The girls went through the nightstand, chest of drawers, looked under the bed, in the window seat and the cubby in the closet. They checked every box on the top shelf, including the pockets of the coats hanging in the back. Nothing. They felt all of the cushions, pillow cases and even under the mattress, but didn't find the missing necklace.

Together they inspected each of the other bedrooms, checking every corner thoroughly, but no pearls. It took them from breakfast to lunch to search the second floor, including the bathroom. In the hidey-hole behind the bathroom door, all they found there were cleaning supplies, old crocheted tissue covers and ragged towels.

"Kids, lunch!" Annabelle called.

Tad came down from the attic, his shirt covered with paint, just as the girls emerged from the bathroom, sweating and dusty.

"Whatcha doing?" he asked.

"Trying to find Gram's pearls," Peggy said.

Megan sniffed. "We're not having any luck."

"Do you ever go up in the attic studio?"

"Yes, but I didn't peek at your painting. I learned not to do that from Regina."

Peggy remembered the night Tad had hidden behind the bed from Regina's wrath after he had desecrated her precious art by putting orange mustaches on the portraits. He'd been angry, confused and did the one thing that might get them kicked out of the house. Sort of like a test, to see if there was love inside this family. He'd almost failed, but Gram stood up to Regina for the first time. Tillie showed Regina they could easily repair the damage with a swipe of a linseed oil soaked cloth.

They thumped down the stairs single file, stopping in the foyer.

"Thanks, but do you know about the other half of the attic? The walled off part?"

"Sure. You showed us that before you tried to ruin Regina's paintings, remember?" Megan said.

"Yeah, what a tough night. I'm wondering is if you could've put them up there. No one goes in there much. There's an old trunk and tons of boxes to hide stuff in."

"Maybe." Megan walked toward the kitchen. "All I remember is dark. That could be right."

"Let's go eat. I'll help you look after lunch. If you leave me some extra cookies."

Megan nodded at her brother.

"That room's creepy." Peggy hung back. "It's filled floor to ceiling with stuff. There's even an old dressmaker dummy from a hundred years ago. Not to mention cobwebs and spiders."

"It's a cozy room, filled with secrets, like in a story." Megan looked dreamy eyed. "You know what, Tadpole, you might be right."

They joined their grandmother in the kitchen and wolfed down their sandwiches.

"My, you're all in a hurry today. Want to help me with the cleaning?"

"We think we might have an idea where the pearls are," Peggy said.

"We're going to check as soon as we're done feeding our faces. After I've wiped out the cookie jar." Tad scooped out a handful of cookies, scattering crumbs everywhere.

"Oh, well, I appreciate you helping Megan. I'm sure they'll turn up, maybe even while I'm cleaning."

"I hope we find them soon." Megan picked up her dirty dishes, stacking them in the dishwasher.

Her siblings joined her on the stairs.

"Wait a second." Tad slipped into his bedroom, coming back with a flashlight. "It's pretty dark up there."

"Good idea," Peggy said.

They mounted the creaky stairs to the attic in single file. Tad led with the light. He pulled the string on the bulb that hung in the painter's studio and crossed the room to a narrow door that opened into the storage area of the cupola. This side of the room didn't have any windows, even the flashlight cast deep, dark shadows. Tad pulled another string. A single bulb struggled to brighten the center of the cluttered room.

"Take a look around. Is there anywhere in here you haven't been?" Tad roamed the narrow aisles of leaning boxes.

"I don't think so." Megan wandered the other direction, meeting him in the middle. "I've looked in almost every box, the old trunks, everywhere. There are lots of cool old clothes and papers. I hoped I might find Regina's old china doll, but I didn't."

"Let's start from the back and work our way forward," Peggy said. "You probably wouldn't hide any stuff close to the door. That would be too easy for a burglar to find."

"Brilliant deduction, my dear Peggy." Tad bowed in her direction.

Peggy slipped around the boxes on the right, Tad walked toward the left, and Megan decided to go straight down the middle. The boxes and trunks were stacked along the walls in rows; a few had been placed in the center.

Blowing dust off the top of a box, Tad coughed. "I doubt it's in here, too much . . . dust."

"Look anyway." Peggy coughed, pointing a finger at her little brother. "Try not to fill the air with dust. We're trying to breathe here."

"Okay, okay. There's mostly papers in this one."

The trunk lid squeaked as Megan lifted it open. "This is full of old clothes." She pulled out a hat with a crushed feather and slipped it on top of her head.

Laughing, Peggy turned to the box in front of her, peeling back the flaps. She could hear the rustle of cloth or paper behind her, hoping no multi-legged creatures were anywhere close by.

This old stuff is weird, like forgotten memories hidden in shadows.

She discovered a batch of envelopes tied with a brown string, addressed to L. Malone & kids. "Oh, crap." Flopping on her bottom on the dusty floor Peggy gasped. "Tad, Megan, come here."

Her siblings knelt beside her, reading over her shoulder.

"They're letters from Dad." She gave an envelope to her brother, continuing to read the note she clutched in her trembling hands.

Tad turned, walking a few feet away to stand under the light bulb. Holding up the letter to read, he said, "I can't believe it."

Peggy looked at her brother then turned to Megan. "Do you want to read one?"

"Okay." Megan took the offered envelope, pulling the contents out with care.

There were ten in all, the first two written close together, the last ones much later. Letting the tears fall, Peggy read one right after the other then passed them to Tad, who was conspicuously quiet. The dust filled room muffled the sound of breathing and the rustle of paper.

Tad handed the last letter to Megan, watching Peggy neatly stack the rest. "Man, I can't believe it. Mom really must've been pissed at him if she wouldn't share these with us."

"You were wrong about him, Tad." Megan put the letter on the stack. "He missed us."

"Maybe. Let's keep looking for the pearls. I gotta think about this." He opened another box in the far corner. He muffled a sniff, but Peggy heard, understanding his sadness.

Megan put her finger in the middle of the string so Peggy tied it tight. Setting the packet aside, the sisters resumed looking in the box.

Beside where the letters had been, there was a cigar box filled with sepia photographs of men and women in long dresses with button shoes, tight fitting shirts and bustles. She didn't recognize anyone.

I should show these to Gram, she probably knows who these people are.

Underneath the letters, a fabric covered heart box caught her eye.

"Megan, do you remember being in this box?"

"Sure, that's a cool one. It's got jewels in it."

Opening the heart shaped box Peggy found an assortment of brooches, marbles, earrings with clips, but no pearls.

"Where's the marble bag?" Megan asked.

"Marbles?" The young man's head snapped up. He peered over his sisters' shoulder. "Old marbles are really cool."

Hopping up onto her knees, Megan began to bounce. "The pearls should be in *that* box. They've got to be." She squirmed in closer. "I think . . ." She pulled out the items on top, and there in the corner was an old bag made of leather and faded blue fabric. It was held together with a leather thong. The uneven stitches were coming loose near the rounded bottom. Megan pulled open the drawstring, holding it over her cupped palm. Out fell her grandmother's string of pearls.

Her smile lit up the room. "I remembered, just then. I could see them in my head!"

"Where are the marbles?" Tad asked.

"I'm so glad you found the pearls." Peggy gave her sister a hug. "Let's go give them back to Gram."

Megan held them close to her chest, tears making tracks down her dusty face.

"Thanks for helping, guys."

"No problem. It helped us solve another mystery, too," Peggy said.

"About Dad?" Megan asked.

"Yeah."

"But where are the marbles?" Tad shook Megan's shoulder.

Extending her finger, Megan pointed at the heart box. "In there."

He opened the heart to find them nestled in amongst the jewelry. "Gross. Now they're covered with girl germs. You don't put marbles in a jewelry box. They're guy things, ya know."

"Whatever. You're strange, little brother." Peggy led her siblings out of the dusty room.

Chapter 37

ANNABELLE AND THE kids were cleaning the house from top to bottom in preparation for the holiday gatherings. Thanksgiving dinner would be at the Riverside house this year. Tillie would cook the meal, while Annabelle provided pies and rolls.

We have truly been blessed. And Lord, I promise to do better this year on my pies.

Last year when Tillie returned from the hospital, Annabelle had made a beautiful cherry pie, but she'd gotten the bulk containers of sugar and salt mixed up. It hadn't been edible. She promptly bought a normal salt dispenser like her mother had used, so she'd never get them confused again.

Two of the pumpkins from Halloween had remained untouched, hidden on the back porch where it was cool and dry. Megan volunteered to help scrape out the seeds. They were baked with salt, to snack on all day. Annabelle cooked down the raw pumpkin to make four pies. There were only eight people coming, but this way there might be some left over. Pumpkin pie with a big glop of whipped crème was one of her other favorite breakfast foods.

"Whatcha doing, Gram?" Megan asked.

"Hi, honey, I'm getting ready to make pies for Thanksgiving. Want to help?"

"Sure, what do you want me to do?"

Annabelle had the crust mixed up in the largest ceramic bowl they had. She extracted one of the four balls, putting it on the flour sprinkled counter. A rolling pin sat beside it.

"Wash your hands. Then roll out this dough pretty thin." Annabelle measured with thumb and forefinger. "Just about an inch bigger than the pie pan edge."

"Okay." Megan went to the sink, cleaned up, and approached the waiting dough.

"Here." Annabelle tied a big kitchen towel around her granddaughter's waist. "Put a little flour on your fingers so the dough won't stick."

Megan dipped her fingers into the canister of flour and patted the ball of dough. She flattened it out with the palm of her hand then picked up the rolling pin.

"Where did you learn how to do that?"

"From watching you."

Smiling, Annabelle continued gathering the spices from the rack to mix into the filling. She preheated the oven before she started measuring then mixing.

What a great memory this will make.

"Is this thin enough?" Megan asked.

"Let's see." Annabelle wiped her hands on her apron. She laid the pie pan upside down on the now flattened dough. "It's perfect. Have you been taking cooking lessons from Tillie?"

"No. I just remember. You make the best pumpkin pies."

"Thank you, honey." Annabelle cut the ragged edge of the crust then squeezed the scraps of dough into a tiny ball. "If there's enough left, maybe I can make you a personal pie of your own, for helping out."

This is why I was given the kids to raise, to make a happier family.

"That would be cool. Could you flip the dough into the pan? I'm afraid I'll tear it."

"Sure." Once she finished crimping the edge of the crust, Annabelle sprinkled more flour onto the counter and handed Megan another ball of dough. They worked in companionable silence until there were four pies ready for the oven. Annabelle had a little bit of everything left. She pulled out a small baking dish and prepared the crust. "You want to pour in the rest of the filling?"

"You bet." Megan tipped the bowl over the dish and it filled it nearly to the edge. "Wow, there was just enough."

Annabelle put two of the large pies and the small one into the oven. She set the timer.

"What do you want to do while we wait?"

"I just finished my latest book. Could we just talk?"

"Of course we can. Do you want some tea?"

"May I have a soda?"

"No sugar, okay?"

"Deal," the little girl said.

They sat down at the kitchen table with their beverages and sipped.

"Gram?"

"Ahuh."

"When can I see my dad?"

Sitting back in her chair, Annabelle studied her granddaughter. "Do you want to?"

"Ahuh. I think I'd like to get to know him. He sounded sorry in his letters to us."

"I'm so glad you found the letters. He and your mother were very young when they got married. I always wondered if things would've been better if they had waited." Annabelle looked toward the window.

"Why didn't they wait?"

"They were in love. When your mother made up her mind, nothing would change it."

The little girl touched her grandmother's wrinkled hand. "Was Mom always mean to you?"

"No. When she was little, Liddy used to follow me around the house, doing what I did, always helping. But when she got older, she liked being outside with her father best. She said that sometimes, when the watermelons were ripe, David would accidentally drop one on his toe and it would break. They'd eat the heart of it with their hands, coming back to the house with sticky red faces and fingers."

Megan looked at her own hands, still sprinkled with flour, although she'd washed. "I don't remember her smiling all that much."

"It was very hard on your mother when your daddy left. She had to work long hours, and that job wore her out. I tried to make it easier when you were born by coming to live with you, but she really missed your grandpa. Then, when Tom left . . .'"

"She was really sad." Megan squirmed in her chair.

"Yes, it turned into frustration then anger."

"I was afraid of her. One time Tad and I were fighting in the back seat of the car. She turned around and slapped me over and over again. My whole head hurt."

"I'm sorry, honey. She never learned to control her anger."

"Tad's like her that way."

Annabelle nodded. "Yes, he has a temper, too."

"I don't think I do, Gram. I don't like to get mad. It makes my stomach hurt."

"Me, too." Reaching across the table, Annabelle patted Megan's hand.

"Do you think she's happier now?"

"I like to think she's rested and will always be young. Maybe she's with your grandfather. Maybe they're both happy."

"I like that." Megan smiled with her entire face. "I'll think of that when I think of her. It's much nicer than my memories."

Annabelle sipped her soda.

Liddy could never cope with the tough things life threw her. She had become as abusive as her father. What a legacy to pass along.

Her own grandmother's wise words echoed in her mind.

"Don't look back, sweetheart. You're not going that way."

"What are you thankful for, Megan?"

"I'm thankful I found your pearls."

Annabelle gave her granddaughter's hand a squeeze. "Me too, honey.

Thank you. But surely you're thankful for other things."

"Well. I'm thankful for pumpkin pies." She giggled, extending one finger for each item mentioned. "I'm thankful that you're better and that Regina is marrying Sam."

"Oh, yes. I love weddings."

"I'm thankful that I don't have to be afraid of Mom anymore."

"I am, too. No one likes being afraid."

"Were you afraid of my mom?"

"Not really." She slowly shook her head.

"Even though she beat you up?"

Straightening her shoulders, she faced her granddaughter. This question she had to address head on.

"Megan, I want to believe that your mother didn't mean to hurt me. But she had problems, honey. She just couldn't control herself. She needed help."

"I heard Regina say that Grandpa used to hurt you, too. That's just not right. Why did they do those things?" A tear slid down the little girl's cheek.

"He had trouble with anger, too. We didn't do very well on the farm. We owed the bank a lot of money. We had to auction everything off to pay the bills. I think it hurt him so bad that his anger just made him want to explode. He took it out on me. I shouldn't have let him."

"Is it herditory?" Megan's eyebrows were drawn together.

"Do you mean hereditary?"

The little girl nodded.

"I think it's learned. We make choices every day. Some people make bad ones."

"You can choose to hit or not to hit?"

"Absolutely. It's a matter of self-control."

"I don't think mom had any of that. We might need to get some for Tad, too. He gets really angry sometimes." Megan looked over her shoulder, finding no one behind her.

"Yes, he does. But he has to learn it on his own. It's not something I can teach him, except by example. That's why I don't let anyone hurt me anymore."

"Is that why you've never spanked us?"

Annabelle looked at her granddaughter's solemn face. "Yes. I don't spank unless it's real serious, life or death kind of stuff."

"Like what?"

"Hmm. Things that would injure you or someone else."

"Oh, like throwing knives at each other if we play circus?"

"Yes. I'd have to spank you guys for that one." Annabelle laughed.

"There are some things you just shouldn't do, no matter what someone else does."

"I get it."

"Yes, I think you do. But it's not always easy. You have to keep trying every day, no matter what."

The timer dinged. They removed the delicious smelling pies and set the last two on the rack to bake.

"Oh, look at my little pie. It's so cute! Can I eat it now?"

"It needs to cool first, maybe by the time the other two are done you can have it. It'll melt the whipped crème when it's hot."

"I don't care, it looks yummy. If you want, I'll share."

"No, this was made for one hungry little girl. I'll wait until Thursday to eat mine. The trick is going to be keeping your brother from getting into the pies while they cool."

"I'll make a sign."

"Good idea."

Megan went upstairs to retrieve a marker and index cards. She proceeded to write *DO NOT TOUCH* on one, *HANDS OFF* on another, *SAVE FOR THANKSGIVING* on the last one.

"That ought to do it," Annabelle said. "Let's put these on the dining room table. Move the chairs back so the cats don't jump up to taste them, okay?"

"I hadn't thought of that, maybe we should put them someplace else. Turbo will smell them. He could stand up to eat one. His manners aren't any better than Tad's, plus he can't read."

"I'll make room on the shelf in the pantry. It's nice and cool in there. We'll put a cover over each one, just in case a mouse comes in from outside."

"Good thinking, Gram."

"We make quite a team." Annabelle gave her granddaughter a hug.

"We always have."

The phone rang. Megan answered it while Annabelle rearranged the pantry, humming off key. "Who is it, Megan?"

"It's Regina."

"Tell her I'll be right there." Annabelle cleared a spot for at least two pies. She had a good idea what to move to make room for the other two, so she hurried to the phone.

"Hello."

"Hello to you, too. What are you doing? You sound out of breath."

"I'm making room in the pantry for the pies to cool so the animals won't be tempted."

"Two-legged, three-legged, or four-legged animals?"

Annabelle chuckled. "All of them."

"As long as there are no mice in the pantry, I'd say that's an excellent idea, Cousin."

"Thanks." Annabelle rolled her eyes. Megan giggled.

"I called to ask you a favor. Would you give me away?"

"What? Isn't that a man's job? Why don't you ask Joe? I thought I'd be your bridesmaid."

"Whoa, girl. Slow down. I asked you because you're my family. I think the line between men's and women's jobs are gone these days."

"And I'm the oldest, right?"

"Yes, you are, but that isn't why I'm asking you."

"I figured Tillie would be your matron of honor, but give you away? That just doesn't seem right."

I wanted to be the bridesmaid. I've never been one.

"I'd like Tillie and Peggy to stand up with me. Sam has asked Joe and Tad."

"I see, once again I'm the odd one out."

"You're being ridiculous. Okay, how about this? Megan can give me away and you can be the flower girl. Better?"

Wiping her brow, Annabelle sighed. "I'm sorry. It just hit me wrong. I'll do it if that's what you want."

"Thank you. Now go take a chill pill." Regina hung up.

"What's wrong?" Megan asked.

"I just over reacted. Good grief. She's right, I may need a nap."

"I'll go grab a new book and read until the pies come out if you want to go lay down."

"No. Well, okay. I'll lie down in the parlor, just in case you need anything."

Megan patted her grandmother's shoulder then dashed up the stairs.

What is wrong with me? Lord, I'm losing any sense I had.

Chapter 38

REGINA HUNG UP the phone in the kitchen and sank down at the table with her lukewarm coffee. "I had the most unusual conversation with Annabelle."

"Really?" Sam asked.

"She got very upset when I asked her to give me away. She implied some nonsense about it being inappropriate."

"That doesn't seem right. You and she gave Tillie away which is non-traditional. Something else must be bothering her, don't you think?"

"I can't imagine what."

"It's the end of the year, maybe it's the taxes. People often react badly to something innocuous when they're upset about something they don't know how to deal with."

Picking up her cup, Sam dumped the coffee in the drain and poured her a new one. She smiled when he handed it to her.

"Thanks. I suppose I should tell her what I plan to do before she has another attack over it."

"Honey, we don't know what's on her mind. She has three kids at home, a recently returned son-in-law, maybe a new boyfriend. And the taxes are due. She just might be a bit stressed."

"Oh, I know all that." She took a sip of her coffee, frowned, pushing it away.

"She's never been comfortable financially, has she?" He finished the coffee in his cup, took it to the dishwasher and reached for Regina's, which had barely been touched.

"No. I think farming was never as lucrative as her family hoped. Still, I never got the feeling they struggled to eat. I mean, she's always been plump."

"Woman, you're a snob! Sometimes it's not how much you eat, but what you eat."

"I am *not* a snob, not really." She slapped her open palm on the scarred tabletop. "I'm just stating a fact."

"You've been thin as long as I've known you and that's a very long time." His grin was infectious. "Wasn't her father a big man?"

"Yes. With a barrel chest and ham-size fists. I never understood what my Aunt Rose saw in him, neither could my mother." Regina began moving her spoon around in the cup.

"Now you sound like her. I'm a big man, what do you think of me?"

Regina slipped out of her chair, glided over to him and wrapped her arms around his waist.

For a lawyer, he's amazingly fit, and I love every bit of him. Good genes. Too bad I'm too old to have children . . .

"You, my delicious hunk of man, are perfect."

The top of Sam's ears turned red. He touched her face with his hand then hugged her.

"You're forgiven."

"For what?"

"You know I love you, my adorable snob."

She punched him, storming from the room. Her back turned so he couldn't see her grin.

"Insufferable man."

She heard him chuckle.

Sugar joined Regina on the stairs to her artists' studio. The three walls of windows gave her light most any time of the day. She loved it. To thank Sam, Regina created a special painting, a Christmas/wedding gift. She'd been very careful to keep it turned to the wall and covered. It appeared that the shroud had never been disturbed. He wasn't as curious as she, or maybe just better at respecting boundaries.

Even as a child she'd peeked into the closets and drawers until she found her gifts. Her mother would wrap them, but that didn't stop Regina. She knew how to carefully peel away the edge of the tape and slide off the ribbon. No one would be able to tell. Regina remembered finding a cashmere scarf and mittens, her china doll and her first box of paints. She had them still, sealed away in a trunk in the attic at the old house. Perhaps she'd see what kind of condition they were in. She'd always taken pristine care of her things, so other than age, they should be perfect gifts for the kids.

Yes, I'll go to the house and retrieve them for Christmas. Will they appreciate them? Will they feel cheated because they aren't new? Crap. I just don't know. They're valuable. Hopefully they'll accept them in the spirit they are given.

As for Annabelle, perhaps a Thanksgiving gift was in order. The trust, so she wouldn't have to worry over the house or taxes any more. Time to put things in order, before the taxes were due and she was officially married, and before Annabelle worked herself into a tizzy.

THURSDAY AT NOON, Regina and Sam picked up the wine and cider on their way to Annabelle's house. Strange to think of it really belonging to Annabelle, but the papers in Regina's bag confirmed that fact.

"I'm going to slip upstairs to the attic before dinner," Regina said.

"You don't think you'll be needed in the kitchen?"

Regina laughed. "Not likely. Just keep the kids from following me up. I want to get a few things without everyone asking questions."

"What?"

"It's a surprise for the kids."

"Ah. And what do you intend to do, Rags?"

"Oh stop. I have some things I've been keeping. I think it's time they were enjoyed."

His eyes left the road for just a moment to gaze at her, smiling.

"Pay attention to your driving, mister."

"Yes, ma'am. Thank you, ma'am. Anything you say, ma'am." His grin spread across his face like a white flag.

She slapped his arm and chuckled. Regina had brought along a large hobo bag that should hold her treasures. She'd fill it up then put it in the trunk of the car. No one would be the wiser, she hoped.

They pulled into the drive just as Tad, Megan and Turbo bounded out the front door.

"Hey there," Tad said.

"Hey yourself." Regina waved.

Megan ran up and gave them both a hug before running after her brother and the dog. "I'm glad you're here," she yelled over her shoulder.

Regina and Sam smiled at each other, grabbed their contributions to the feast, and headed into the house.

"Hello!" Sam called out.

"In the kitchen." Annabelle's voice carried all through the house.

"I'll take this stuff while you go do your thing," Sam said.

"Thanks." Regina kissed him on the cheek then dashed up the stairs, bag in hand.

Their voices faded as she ascended higher into the house. It smelled of dust and the stairs still creaked. She marveled at the mahogany railing, shiny and slick from all the hands that had slid along its surface over the years. It felt familiar.

No, I'm not going back, only forward. Just like Grandmere always said, which is quite prophetic. Yesterday is history, tomorrow is a mystery, and today is the day. That's what life is all about.

Opening the attic studio door, Regina noticed the easel sitting in the center of the room. Tad's unfinished canvas sat covered with an old cotton shirt. Regina peeked under it, awed at the young man's talent.

Good with color. I admire the raw emotion in every stroke. I'd love to watch him paint sometime.

Passing through the room to the storage area, she pulled the door open. Expecting everything to be undisturbed was obviously a mistake. Footprints marked the dust and boxes teetered precariously. Regina hoped the kids hadn't already found what she'd kept hidden all these years. She closed the door. Behind it sat a small flat-topped trunk with brass hinges and several other boxes stacked on top. They didn't look as though they had been touched.

Careful not to get dirty, Regina moved the boxes aside, kneeling down. She used the key from the pocket of her skirt to open the trunk. Inside, she found the ivory cashmere scarf and mittens, still wrapped in yellowing tissue paper. The wooden box of paints were untouched. And satin cloth, the pink graying with age, swaddled the china doll. Ignoring the other objects, Regina quickly put these three into her bag and zipped it up. She closed the trunk, turned the key then restacked the boxes on top.

As she descended the stairs, she listened for voices. It sounded like the adults were still in the kitchen. Regina slipped out the front door. On the porch, she looked for the children. Seeing them romping with the dog two front yards away, she rushed down the steps and locked the bag in the trunk of the car.

"Hey, Regina," Tad said, out of breath. "What'cha doing?"

She started, laughing to cover her discomfort. "Stealing the family jewels, of course."

"Good luck with that. I'm thinking Gram won't be taking off her pearls for the rest of her life. I wouldn't be surprised if she sleeps in them."

Walking back to the porch, Regina smiled at him. "I'm glad they're found."

"We found them together."

"But I remembered, too." Megan caught up with them and her big brother ruffled her hair.

"Woof," Turbo added. Regina reached down and gave him a scratch.

"Where were they?" She asked, walking up the steps.

"In a box in the attic," Tad said.

Regina stumbled and Tad caught her arm.

"Getting clumsy in your old age?"

"I'm fine, thank you. These are new shoes, that's all."

"I put the pearls in an old marble bag I found," Megan said.

Stopping in front of the door, Regina turned. "You found Grandfather's marble bag? It's been lost for years."

"I found it in a box, and I put the pearls in there, to keep them safe."

Chuckling, Regina said, "I'll be damned. He made that bag you know;

sewed it himself. Those old marbles are probably worth money, too."

"They're really cool," Tad said. "There's even a couple that look like they're made of wood."

"They were. Those were his father's and they're really old."

"Awesome."

"You take good care of them, young man. They're heirlooms."

Crossing his heart with his index finger, Tad held open the door. "I promise I will. I think it's cool to have one of my great, great-grandfather's things."

"I think so, too." Regina led them into the house.

Good to know that he's interested in special family objects. Maybe my gifts will be appreciated after all.

Chapter 39

AFTER THE GLORIOUS dinner had been devoured, the adults sat around the table drinking coffee. The kids were in the parlor watching a movie.

"Have you set a date?" Tillie asked.

"Yes, we have," Regina said. "December twenty-first."

"The winter solstice. How perfect!" Tillie said.

Annabelle nodded. "And the shortest day of the year."

"I know. It was Sam's idea." Leaning toward her fiancé, Regina gave Sam's arm a tender squeeze.

"Why, Sam, you old romantic," Tillie said.

"That's me!" Sam winked at her.

"Oh, there is one more thing," Regina said.

She and Sam exchanged a smile. Regina got up from the table, taking the envelope from the inside pocket of his jacket. She handed it to Annabelle then sat back down, pulling her chair closer to her cousin.

"Open it."

The plain brown envelope gave nothing away. Annabelle slowly pulled open the flap, taking out the stack of papers from inside. As she began to read, her eyebrows rose up her forehead. The color drained from her face. She looked at her cousin as tears slipped down her cheeks.

"Don't sit there blubbering. Tell me what it says," Tillie said.

"It says . . ." Annabelle pulled the tissue from her pocket and blew her nose.

"Elegant," Regina said.

"Oh, shut up," Tillie responded. "Did she give you walking papers? If she did, I'll kick her butt."

"Calm down, Little Bit," Joe said. "Those look like tears of joy."

"The taxes . . ." Annabelle couldn't finish.

"Do you want me to tell them?" Regina asked.

Annabelle nodded, wiping her eyes. "Please."

"It's just a little trust to cover the taxes and insurance on this house so she won't have to worry about it anymore."

"Way cool!" Peggy said from the doorway.

"For how long?" Tillie asked.

"Until Megan is eighteen. That way, the kids will have a home until they're old enough to make one for themselves." Regina smoothed her skirt.

"Well, I'll be damned. Regina Louise, I'm proud of you." Tillie hugged Annabelle.

"Congratulations. No more worries, eh?"

You've still got some years of teen angst to get through, my dear cousin, but you'll be able to do it with a roof over your heads.

"At least, no more worries about the house." Regina gave Annabelle a wink.

Taking Tillie's hand, Annabelle tugged her toward Regina's chair. They stood before her, smiling.

"Group hug!" The two ladies engulfed Regina in their arms.

The kids joined in.

"I'm a human blanket," Tad said, lying on top of Regina.

"You're crushing me." Regina gave a theatrical gasp for effect.

"That's the idea," Tad said.

With deliberate slowness, each of them extracted themselves from Regina's embrace. When she was clear of all the bodies, she smoothed her skirt and tugged her sleeves.

The kids went back into the parlor to continue watching the movie, while Joe and Sam stacked the dirty dishes and took them into the kitchen.

Tillie and Annabelle joined them, leaving Regina sitting alone at the table, a goofy grin on her face.

"Well, Grandmere," she whispered. "I'm very thankful, today. This family is going to be fine."

Regina stood and followed after her family, dirty dishes in hand.

HAPPY THAT THE kitchen was clean and the leftover food stored away, Annabelle followed as they all gathered in the parlor to watch *It's A Wonderful Life* for the umpteenth time. The kids were sprawled on the floor with the animals. Tillie and Joe had gone home, taking half of a pumpkin pie with them. Sam and Regina sat on the couch while Annabelle crocheted in her favorite chair.

"What are you making, Gram?" Megan asked.

"Hanger covers just like my mother used to make." Annabelle held up the long rope of yarn that didn't look like much of anything yet.

"We need more of those." Peggy poked her little sister. "Now that Megan is wearing nicer clothes, she's stealing all of them."

"Am not!"

"Are, too."

"Grandmere used to make those. They're perfect for silk blouses," Regina said. "Might Santa bring me some this year?"

"You have been very good. He just might," Annabelle said. She dropped her hands into her lap then scanned the room.

Sam gave Regina's hand a squeeze, whispering in her ear. "I love you."

Feeling a blush coming, Annabelle dropped her eyes, but only for a moment.

Regina kissed Sam's cheek and returned the squeeze. "Ditto."

"I know what that means." Peggy addressed the couple on the sofa. "I've seen *Ghost* ten times."

"Shhhh. The movie's back on," Tad said. "I love it when they fall in the pool."

"You would." Peggy slouched back against the couch, rubbing the cats flanking her on either side. Her little sister sprawled on the sleeping dog, her head moving slowly up and down with his breathing.

For a while they watched the movie in silence, allowing the food to settle. Tad hadn't even asked for popcorn. Annabelle wanted to absorb the love and closeness she felt into every pore of her body. When the phone rang she set aside her yarn project and went into the kitchen to answer it.

"Hello."

"Happy Thanksgiving, Belle," Phil said.

"Happy Thanksgiving to you. Did you have a nice holiday?"

"I did. My sister and her clan had enough food for an army. The boys and I watched football. They'll always be boys to me even though they're both in college and a foot taller than their uncle."

"What more could a man ask for?"

"The only thing missing was you."

Stunned into silence, Annabelle wasn't sure how to proceed, so she ignored his comment.

"We had a house full here, but there's always room for one more. You know you're welcome."

Where did that come from? I better get myself together or I'll have an unwanted man on my hands.

"Since Sis had already asked, I didn't have the heart to back out."

"I'm sure she appreciated you being there to keep the boys out from under foot."

"I enjoy them. They're a great bunch of guys. With any luck, they'll grow up to be as nice as their father. My baby sister did all right with Matt. He's a good one."

"I'm glad. What are you doing for dinner tomorrow night? Want to come over for leftovers?"

Lord. Am I crazy or what? Maybe he'll say no.

"Warmed over turkey, potatoes and gravy? Or sandwiches?"

"Are you choosey?"

"Not really, just curious. I love them both."

Don't friends feed friends? We do that with Tillie and Joe all the time. As Grandma Morgan used to say, in for a penny, in for a pound.

"Warm stuff, then sandwiches for Saturday lunch. By then I'd say most everything would be gone."

"Any pie left?"

"Of course, we made plenty."

"Done. What time?"

"About six?"

"Is there anything else I can bring? Like bread? I plan on making a couple of loaves in the bread-maker."

"You make bread? We love fresh bread. Thanks for the offer. See you tomorrow?"

"Until then."

Annabelle hung up the phone smiling.

He really could be charming.

She went back into the living room to resume her seat. All eyes were on the television. She picked up her yarn and needle.

"Who was that?" Peggy asked.

"Yeah, you were gone a long time," Tad said.

"Your boyfriend?" Megan asked, wagging her eyebrows.

The girls giggled. Annabelle could feel a flush coming on. "That was Phil."

"Oh, no. Not coach, again!" Tad held his stomach, rolling on the floor.

Regina laughed. "Why, Annabelle, are you dating Tad's basketball coach? He's a little old for you, isn't he?"

"Assistant coach, actually." Tad sat back up, since his little antics went unnoticed. "Coach Edwards is retired and helps out. Everyone's called him Coach, like forever. I didn't know his name was Phil until he started being friends with Gram. It's way weird."

"Get over it," Peggy said.

"Yeah, let Gram have a little fun, why don't you?" Megan said.

"I think you're out-numbered, Tad." Sam smiled at the boy.

"Better get used to it." Regina leaned back against Sam's broad shoulder.

"I give up!" The young man lifted his hands in surrender. "Can we make popcorn?"

"The movie is almost over. Why don't we skip it tonight?" Annabelle said.

"But I'm hungry."

"How can you be hungry after the feast we had this afternoon?" Sam asked. "Even I'm still full."

"That was hours ago. Come on, Gram, please!" Walking on his knees, Tad leaned on his grandmother's lap and gave her a doe-eyed look.

"I think it's time you learned how to make it yourself." Annabelle put aside her crocheting once again, heading into the kitchen to assist.

Regina followed her. "Need a hand?"

"No, we'll be fine." Annabelle got out the *Pop Master* popcorn popper. She watched Tad pour in the oil and added the kernels. Regina got a glass from the cabinet.

When it started to pop vigorously, she leaned over and whispered to Annabelle.

"Have you heard anything from Tom?"

"Not lately, and Peg's quit asking when she can see him. I think something is up."

"Interesting. Any idea what?"

"No, but I'm curious what'll happen next." Annabelle turned her back on Tad. "A little worried, too, about how his being back will affect our lives."

"The kids will be fine. They're tough. You've been good for them. You've all been good for each other. I don't think you have anything to worry about."

"I suppose. It's just, well, he is their father. They must have mixed feelings, but they've clammed up on me."

"Take a deep breath. Wait and see."

"I agree. Kids love their parents, no matter what kind of parents they are. They may be afraid of them, not even like them much, but they still love them."

"True," Regina said. "Whatever they feel is okay. They need to know that."

The snack finished popping. Annabelle unplugged the popper, showing Tad how to turn it over, the top making a bowl. She sprinkled on salt then handed several cold cans of soda to her cousin.

"This smells too good to waste." Annabelle scooped a small bowl for herself.

"I thought you'd see it my way." Tad grinned, eating a handful.

Regina laughed, following them out of the kitchen.

Chapter 40

WITH ONLY A MONTH until Christmas, Peggy had planning to do if she and her siblings were going to be prepared. She and Megan lay on top of the sunny yellow quilt covering their queen-sized bed. Peggy stared at the ceiling while Megan read another mystery.

"What do you want for Christmas, Megan?" Peggy asked.

"I dunno. It really doesn't matter. I know I'll like whatever I get."

"You are so different from most ten year olds. Did you know that?" She watched her sister frown.

"I am not."

"Sure you are. Most girls your age have lists of things they want. Disney stuff, or pink sneakers, or the latest boy band music."

"I'm just not into that stuff. I like books and baking with Gram and playing with Tang and Ms. Pickles. I guess I'm really boring." Megan closed her book with a sigh.

Peggy leaned across the bed, pulling her little sister close for a moment, then laid back to study the ceiling again.

"No, just different. But that's okay. Different is cool."

Laying her head on her big sister's shoulder, Peggy could hear the smile in Megan's voice.

"Thanks. I just don't want to be like everyone else. Do you?"

"Not really, but sometimes I wish I were invisible." Peggy closed her eyes to imagine what it would be like.

"Really? Why?"

"Then I could go anywhere I want to. No one would see me. I could visit other classes, or listen in on the girls who are always talking in the bathroom."

Megan rolled back on her side to face her sister. Her finger trailed along the quilt stitches.

"Like the Invisible Girl in *Fantastic Four*?"

"Exactly. Have you ever heard Gram say she wished she were a fly on the wall?"

Wrinkling her forehead, Megan asked, "No, why?"

"Well, that's like being invisible, too. No one notices you."

"Why don't you want to be noticed?"

"I don't know. I guess I get tired of watching the popular girls and guys hang on each other. Everyone knows who they are, and they have to act out all the time. They aren't even real. Everything is so fake, you know?"

Rolling onto her back, Peggy joined her sister who began to study the ceiling, too.

"There's a girl in my class who acts one way in front of the teacher and another way on the play ground. It's like she's two different people."

"That's what I'm talking about. I'd rather just be me and not have to pretend to be anything else, even if that means being invisible." Peggy punctuated her words with a swing of her hand.

"Me, too. But, what about boys? If you're invisible, they won't know you're there."

"Miles knows I'm there." Peggy smiled. "Does it bother you that I still like him, even after the accident?"

"No. He didn't mean to hurt me. But I don't have a Miles. None of the boys seem to like me at all. Jimmy says I'm a chunky monkey."

Taking her little sister's hand, she gave it a gentle squeeze.

"You're very pretty. You've got big beautiful eyes and thick shiny brown hair. I'd love to have your hair. Mine's all thin and straight. You're smart and funny."

"Thanks, but I'm not sure the boys in my class care about my hair or if I'm smart."

Peggy felt Megan's sigh as well as heard it.

"They will, I promise. Guys always look at your hair and your eyes. And if you're funny, too, you'll probably be one of the popular girls."

"Really?" Megan grabbed a stuffed animal off the pillow and straightened the bow around its neck.

"I don't know, Megan. I just know you're special. Someday you'll find a boy who knows it and appreciates it, too."

"Like Miles."

"Yeah, only better, because he'll be yours."

"Do you and Miles kiss?"

"Boy, you really are full of questions. Yeah, we've kissed." Peggy could feel the warmth flooding her cheeks.

"What did it make you feel like?"

Feeling Megan's stare, she rolled onto her side, propping her head on her hand.

"Warm. It made me feel kind of light-headed."

"Is that love?" Megan squeezed the fuzzy creature to her chest.

"I don't know. Why do you ask?"

"Cameron kissed me at recess. He sort of pushed on me with his lips. I think the other boys dared him. It felt weird. I hoped kissing was better than that."

Peggy laughed. "It gets better, I promise."

"How old were you the first time you got kissed?"

"About twelve, I guess. It was sort of dorky, but sweet, too. We were both surprised."

"Maybe that's why Cameron did the 'push away' kiss. Maybe he couldn't make up his mind whether to kiss me or not. I wouldn't mind if he did it nice like you said. At least, I don't think I would."

"You're a little young to be thinking about boys. I thought you were all about books and stuff."

"Just curious."

"Don't let Gram know. She'd have you home schooled. You're her baby, and I don't think she'd like the idea of you being kissed just yet. You're only ten. Give it a few years, okay?"

"I guess. I wouldn't want to hurt Gram. I'll wait a while. Do you think Regina and Sam kiss?"

"I don't know. I'm not sure I want to picture that in my head."

"They are getting married, so they probably do."

Giggling, Peggy squeezed her sister. "You really are funny."

"Let's go see what Tadpole is up to."

The girls went down the hall to their brother's room and knocked on the door.

"Tad? You in there?" Peggy said.

"Yeah, come on in."

They found their brother sprawled on his bed with a book. Turbo and Tang snuggled on either side of him. Ms. Pickles supervised from the top of the bed.

"That's where you were." Megan scooped up the kitten then reached for Ms. Pickles who lifted her nose in the air.

Turbo nudged the little orange fur ball and made a quiet "woof." The older cat would have none of it, batting his big black nose away.

Peggy scratched the dog's ear. "Don't worry, Ms. Pickles is just playing hard to get. She loves you, too."

"We were chilling out with a graphic novel. What's up?" Tad folded the corner of the page down, closing the book.

"Just talking," Megan said.

"About what?"

"Stuff." Megan shrugged her shoulders.

Tad looked at his older sister, his eyebrows rose in question.

Peggy shook her head in response.

"Do you ever wonder what it would've been like if Tom hadn't left us?"

Tad just can't call him dad, yet. That's so weird.

"No. But I do wonder what it would be like to have him around now."

"Me, too" Megan said.

"I went to see him," Peggy said.

Tad sat up on the bed then grabbed his older sister by the shoulders. "Are you crazy? When did you do that?"

"Malissa and I went after school." Her brother dropped his hands, frowning.

"What was he like?" Megan asked.

"Uncomfortable at first, but then he was alright. I saw him before we found the letters. I feel bad now that I didn't believe him."

"What else?" Megan asked.

"He seemed nervous. He's a cook at Jenny's Diner. Malissa says he makes the best crispy fries she's ever eaten. I didn't really taste them. I was too . . . distracted."

"Did he ask about us?" Megan's curiosity had no end.

"Yeah. He wants to be a part of our lives."

"Did he seem scary at all?" Tad asked. He moved a short distance away from them.

"Not really. It was almost like he was scared of me."

"He brought me a teddy bear in the hospital. That was nice," Megan said.

"Yeah. It was. Tad, do you think we could get to know him some? Maybe he's changed."

"How old was he when he left?" Megan asked.

"He *was* a grown up." Tad leaned back on the bed, putting his arm over his eyes.

"Only twenty-five or so. That's pretty young." Peggy watched as her little sister's eyes glistened.

"It's all my fault. He left after I was born."

Tad sat up, facing his baby sister. "You didn't do anything wrong."

"It's not your fault." Peggy stroked her sister's head.

"He's not so young now," Megan said. "Shouldn't we give him a chance?"

Peggy looked at Tad. "What do you say we ask Gram if he can come Christmas night, you know, after we've had presents with the rest of the family?" Her brother flinched.

"But I don't have a present for him," Megan said.

"We'll figure out something." Peggy met her brother's eyes. "Tad, will you try?"

"Yeah, whatever. My head says I should be a grown up about this, but my gut hurts just thinking about him. I'm not giving him any presents." Scrubbing his hair out of his eyes, Tad firmed his jaw and straightened his shoulders. "I'll keep an eye on him. I'm not a baby he can shove around anymore."

"I'll ask Gram." Leaving her siblings, Peggy walked out, Ms. Pickles at her heels.

Chapter 41

BETWEEN THANKSGIVING and the twenty-first of December, Annabelle completed the dresses for Megan and Peggy. She had some finishing touches on her own before it, too, would be ready for the big wedding day.

Regina decided on pale blue for her gown. Annabelle coordinated Peggy's bridesmaid dress and Megan's flower girl dress in a darker hue. The dresses were knee length.

Maybe they could wear them again. No, I doubt Megan will. She's growing way too fast.

They chose a simple style that worked no matter what time of year, with three quarter sleeves and a minimum of lace and absolutely no flounces. Regina wasn't a "flounce" sort of woman. Annabelle selected an elegant navy suit dress. Grandmother's pearls would set it off perfectly. She was anxious for Phil to see her in it. The flattering cut made her look taller, not that she really needed to be. Phil was only about 5 foot 10, and her 5 foot 6 fit well. They looked nice together.

Stop dreaming, you old goof. Keep stitching.

The kids took care of straightening the house while she was deep into the dress making business.

Although it won't meet with any white glove test, I'm relieved we aren't hosting the wedding. I've got my hands full with the sewing.

And now Tom was coming for Christmas. Good Lord, I'd better pay attention before I stick myself.

Tad complained this morning, refusing to eat any more sandwiches and canned soup. Could they please order a pizza? Annabelle agreed to celebrate since she finished sewing with a day to spare.

Had she not started her Christmas planning in the summer, she would've been frantic that there had been no time to shop. But she'd seen lovely earrings that Peggy would enjoy and a set of books by Megan's favorite author back in August. Those two had been taken care of in short order. Tad's feet had grown another inch or three, so he was due for new tennis shoes, but she didn't have the heart to buy him shoes for Christmas. It seemed so necessary, and Christmas wasn't about "necessary," it was about fun and surprises.

I'll ask Joe or Sam for ideas. Tad loves sports and art, so there must be something out there that I can afford, but not until after the wedding.

"Gram?" Peggy called through the bedroom door.

"Come in."

"How's it going?"

"Just a snip of this thread, and I'll be done with my dress." Annabelle bit the thread then put the needle into the spool.

"I love that color, such a deep blue. You're going to look awesome. Try it on. I want to see it."

"All right." Annabelle laid the garment on the bed.

Peggy sank down beside it, running her finger along the soft material. She studied her grandmother for a moment, her head cocked like a puppy.

"You've really lost a lot of weight, haven't you?"

"Oh, not really. I've just trimmed down from walking."

Slipping the dress over her head, Annabelle turned around to face her granddaughter. Even in her bare feet, she felt pretty.

"Oh, Gram. You look beautiful."

Facing her image in the full-length mirror, she turned from side to side. "Do you think I'll even pass Regina muster?"

"I don't know what muster means, but if you mean will Regina be impressed, I'd say yes, ma'am. Gram?"

"Yes, honey."

"I'll be ungrounded this Saturday. Can I go to the mall with Malissa? I need to do some Christmas shopping." Three weeks had turned to six due to Peggy's back talk, but she had taken it fairly well.

Annabelle turned, studied her granddaughter's face long enough for Peggy's cheeks to turn red. Her hands migrated to her hips, her feet braced apart. "Will Miles be there?"

Digging her sock clad toe into the carpet, Peggy lifted her chin. "No. I don't know. I haven't talked to him much. He's been grounded, too."

Dropping her arms, she relaxed. "Do you need me to drive you?"

"No, Malissa's mom will take us. I'm sorry, Gram. Honest." She crossed her arms over her chest then quickly dropped them against her sides.

"You're sixteen now. Old enough to drive. Old enough to make good choices."

"I will, I promise."

Nodding, Annabelle turned back to the mirror.

"Hey, Gram." Tad called from behind the door. "Are you done yet? I'm hungry."

"Oh, shut up," Peggy snapped.

He opened the door and froze. "What the . . . ? Wow, Gram, you look . . . awesome."

"All it needs are pearls, stockings and shoes." Annabelle gave him a glowing smile.

"You're pretty damn good with a needle and thread."

"Thank you for the compliments, but careful with the language."

"Sorry. Can we order that pizza? I'm starved." He grabbed his stomach for emphasis.

"Where's your little sister?"

"Right here." Megan poked her head around the door jam and stared at her grandmother. "I wish I could whistle."

"Enough, enough. All of you shoo. I need to change clothes. You decide what kind of pizza you want. I'll be down in a minute."

The kids left, casting backward glances as they shut the door.

That was fun. Now, if I can get the same reaction out of Regina. The black slip on shoes I wore last Christmas would work just fine.

She'd picked up a pair of pearl earrings at the same sale she'd gotten Peggy's Christmas gift. All set for the big day.

"I wonder how Regina is doing? I'd be a nervous wreck."

I'm never getting married again—period.

Chapter 42

REGINA HAD AN audience as she dressed for the wedding. Sugar hadn't left her side all morning. The dog had even helped supervise the set up downstairs. Now it was Regina's time to prepare. A profusion of red, yellow and white roses graced the mantle in the living room, on the end tables and bookcases. An explosion of color and sweet perfume filled the house. J.R. had done his usual magic with the floral arrangements. His assistant made sure everything was in the right place. The ceremony would start at eleven o'clock.

We're starting this marriage right, as the sun is rising, not evening, when the sun is going down. It's all superstitious nonsense, but why take a chance?

Sam dressed in the spare bedroom. He promised to stay downstairs. She didn't want him to see her before the wedding march played on the stereo. Meanwhile, the warmth of her favorite canine kept her company.

Her dress came to mid-calf, the bell shaped skirt swaying when she walked. Happy that she had chosen a pale blue, she thought even her mother would approve, this being her second marriage at a mature age. She fluffed her salt and pepper hair and smiled as it bounced. "Not bad for an old gal, eh, Sugar?"

Woof. The dog's head lifted, and she could swear she smiled.

"Good girl, even if you are on the bed."

Woof, woof. Sugar laid her head on her paws, giving Regina a doggy grin.

Regina wore an iceberg blue diamond teardrop on a platinum chain around her neck. She'd bought it for herself from the proceeds of her first successful art show. Her career had started slowly, but she'd persevered and eventually made a name for herself. She'd even taught a few painting classes at Wichita State University, Friends and Newman universities over the years. It had been fun to see the light in her students' eyes when their visions became reality on the canvas. She'd visited Paris and London, had paintings displayed at their major universities, where she'd studied. She'd been gone for months each time, while Devlin worked toward tenure. Little wonder Devlin strayed.

She'd never really been lonely when she painted. Her creative muse kept her company, urging her on. Time had no meaning then. Hours became days when she only stopped to nap and eat. Not many people had the opportunity to retreat into their art as she had. Once again, she counted herself among the lucky. Although her parents had died before she was twenty-one and Devlin before she was forty, she'd had a lot of good memories.

Devlin and she had married for convenience . . .

Now I'll marry for love. I wish my daughter Beth had lived to be a part of my life with Sam. If only, or what if . . . those words are not always happy ones.

Peggy had become almost a surrogate daughter during the past year. Regina hoped Peggy knew how much she meant to her. They didn't talk about things like that, though everything else was on the menu. It was fun to be together. Annabelle had done a good job these past couple of years. The kids were growing up well. She stepped into her shoes.

"I'll have to tell her."

"Tell who what?" asked Annabelle from the doorway. She pulled her tissue from her sleeve and dabbed her eyes. "You look beautiful."

"Thank you." Regina spun around then stopped before her cousin, mouth agape. "So, do you."

"Do I what?" Extending her arms from her hips, Annabelle turned around slowly.

"You look beautiful. Where did you get that lovely outfit?" Reaching out, Regina stroked the fabric.

"I made it." Annabelle turned around again, for her to get the full effect.

"I'd say you haven't lost your touch, very impressive. I wanted to tell you that I'm so proud of how you've handled the kids."

Annabelle stared at her cousin, uncertainty crossing her face. Slowly, a glowing smile filled it.

"Thank you."

"Speaking of the kids—where are Peggy and Megan?"

"They're downstairs."

"I didn't hear the doorbell."

"Sam must've heard us pull up. He had the door open. It's cold but sunny out. A wonderful day for a winter wedding."

Woof. Sugar bounded out the door.

Regina heard Megan giggle and Peggy say, "Down girl."

The two girls stepped into the doorway. Regina sank onto the bed with a sigh. Tears filled her eyes. "Oh, my. You two look lovely."

"Thanks, Regina," Peggy said. "Gram made our dresses, hers, too. Don't we look awesome?"

"Yes, you do. I'm afraid you three will outshine me. Where's Tillie? There's no doubt the bride will not be the most beautiful woman in this house today."

"Piffle," Annabelle said. "You look so pretty. All you need is this . . ." Annabelle handed her a small white box that contained a huge white rose, fully opened, with a lavender blue center. She walked toward her cousin and smiled. "This is for your beautiful hair."

Sitting very still, Regina waited to see how it would look in the mirror when Annabelle moved aside.

Will it look ridiculous? It has to look wonderful, because the smell is intoxicating. It's the most gorgeous rose I have ever seen.

"The florist fastened it to a clip for your hair. It has a tiny little vial of water on the stem. There." Annabelle stepped to the side.

Regina slowly stood. She walked to the full-length mirror, a smile blossoming on her face.

"Thank you, Belle. It's perfect."

"I'm father and mother today, so it seemed appropriate."

"Yes, you chose well." She wanted to hug her cousin, but a press of cheeks would have to do.

I'm turning mushy. God, forbid.

Peggy and Megan stepped into the hall as the music sounded below. Megan clutched a tiny basket, tied with a blue silk bow, filled to the brim with fragrant rose petals. Peggy stepped up behind her then turned around. "Where's Tillie?"

"Late as usual," Regina said.

"I am not." Tillie stood on the stairs below. "I'm just waiting for you to get a move on."

"You come behind me," Megan said.

"Okay, but give me one minute alone with the bride." Tillie winked at Megan as she stepped past her.

Annabelle softly closed the door so Regina and Tillie would have some privacy.

The two friends embraced. "You look fabulous, Regina Louise."

"Ditto, Matilda Jean." Regina sniffed, dabbing her eyes with a tissue.

"I'm glad you finally came to your senses about marriage. Cut it out, before your makeup starts to run."

Tillie opened the door, crossing the landing to the stairs and stepped in between the girls. She gave Regina a watery smile over her shoulder.

Pausing to take in the spectacle around her, Regina felt amazed at the beauty of her family and best friend. The three dresses were a darker shade of blue, but went well with Regina's. She was still in awe at the quality of the workmanship. Tillie's deep sky-blue dress was calf-length with a poof at the top of the three-quarter length sleeves. Peggy wore an elegant sheath that fit perfectly. Megan's had a bell shaped skirt similar to her bride ensemble, but with a blue sash. Regina was glad she'd hired a professional photographer, though no film could capture all this adequately.

Annabelle took Regina's arm and they followed the others down the staircase. They walked in time with the music, the only traditional touch. Pastor Posie stood centered in front of the fireplace. To the right, Sam stood with Joe and Tad, all three looking scrumptious in their black tuxedos. Tad agreed to wear the patent leather rental shoes instead of his Nikes like he did last year at Tillie's wedding—a sure sign of his maturing. The men wore pristine white shirts, ascots and cummerbunds, sporting matching roses in their lapels.

"Wow," Tillie whispered.

"I know," Peggy said. "Even Tad looks handsome."

Megan giggled.

Regina and Sam's eyes locked as she glided across the hardwood floor where he waited for her hand.

Pastor Pete Posie's curly red hair and beard were close cropped and tame compared to his usual mountain man appearance.

The continuous whir of the camera captured nearly every step of the procession. Regina couldn't help but smile. The beauty and warmth of this day filled her to bursting.

Sam took her hand as her attendants moved to the left. Tillie took the single white long stemmed rose that Regina carried while Annabelle stood behind and waited.

A dozen people were in attendance. Close friends from the galleries, Annabelle's Phillip, the vet and his nurse and Marvel, Sam's assistant. A very small, intimate ceremony—just like Regina and Sam wanted.

Pastor Posie began. "Who gives this woman to this man in holy matrimony?"

"I do," Annabelle said before stepping back. She took a seat on the front row beside Phil.

The pastor smiled at her, and the ceremony proceeded.

I can't believe it's really happening. It's never too late for love. That's all there is to it. Reality is much better than fiction.

The ceremony sped by, just like the goose bumps running along Regina's spine.

"I now pronounce you husband and wife. You may kiss the bride."

Over much too quickly, Regina felt as though she had dreamed the entire ceremony. The kiss that Sam gave her and the ring on her finger told her otherwise. She felt the warmth of his love fill her from the top of her head to the tip of her toes and back again.

"Happy Birthday, Mrs. Duncan," Sam said.

"Happy Birthday?"

"It's the first day of your being Mrs. Regina Duncan. I'd call that a rebirth, wouldn't you?"

She kissed his lips and smiled. "Yes, I do. Happy wedding day, Sam. Thank you for making my dreams come true."

"Ditto."

He winked at her, before they turned, facing the room. Everyone stood and cheered. Sugar added her own canine voice to the merriment. Someone had tied a blue ribbon around Sugar's neck. She seemed to preen, front feet hopping off of the floor in excitement.

Regina, Sam, Pastor Posie and their respective attendants stood before the fireplace for photos and stayed to receive the good wishes of their guests.

"There's a buffet in the dining room," Tillie announced.

"What did you make?" Tad asked.

"Oh, just a few goodies for the celebration. There are strawberries, chocolate, cream puffs, quiche, cheese and crackers, etc. The bistro bunch kicked in and helped put it all together. A thank you for all the times you've patronized their establishment," Tillie said.

"That's very sweet. I'll be sure to send them a thank you note."

"Do. They'd love to hear how much you enjoyed their contribution."

Sam poured champagne for all, including a little bit for the kids. Raising his glass for a toast, he said, "To many years of happiness."

"Hear, hear," they said and drank.

Megan giggled. "It tickles my nose, but it tastes good."

"Just one for you guys." Annabelle pointed at the children.

"Yes, ma'am," Tad said, saluting her with his champagne flute.

"I'm the designated driver." Phil handed Annabelle another full glass.

"Good idea," Annabelle said.

"Very. I'm happy Sam and I aren't going anywhere until tomorrow," Regina said. Her eyes were filled and sparkling, a perfect start to her new life.

"Ah, so the plan is to really celebrate?" Tillie asked.

"Something like that." Regina clinked her glass against her best friend's, and a soft tone resonated.

The guests filled their small china plates and wandered around the house. Everyone visited in small groups for a few minutes here and there.

Much later, Regina hung back, standing next to Sam. Tillie took over the serving, and Peggy walked around picking up empty dishes as soon as they were laid down. The dishwasher would get a good workout by the time it was all over.

"What are you thinking about?" Sam asked.

"Nothing in particular. I'm just watching, really."

"How do you feel?"

"Warm, contented, happy."

He kissed her cheek and smiled. "Me, too."

"Everything is beautiful."

"Yes. Thank you, by the way."

"For what?"

"For taking my name."

"I like the sound of it much better than Regina Louise Morgan-Smith Duncan. What a mouthful. Besides Morgan Duncan sounds like a line from a Dr. Seuss book. Regina Louise Duncan is solid and simple, something I've never been but always admired." She looked at her cousin.

"Regina Louise Morgan Smith Duncan does have sort of a rhythmic quality to it."

"Not for me. Regina Louise Duncan is perfect."

"Yes, you are." He kissed the palm of her hand, sending tiny tickles up her arm and neck.

Chapter 43

"GRAM," MEGAN SAID. "Get up, it's Christmas!" The little girl bounced into her grandmother's room and onto the bed. "Rise and shine."

"Merry Christmas to you, too, honey." Annabelle gave her granddaughter a hug and quick kiss on the head. "Let me go brush my teeth then we'll see what Santa brought."

"Hurry!" Megan followed her across the hall.

"Where are your brother and sister?"

"They're already downstairs. I lost the draw. They sent me to wake you up."

"I see. Afraid they'd get into trouble?"

"Probably, but it's Christmas. I knew you'd be happy."

They walked down the stairs and into the parlor, Megan chattering the whole way. The kitten curled up on the window seat. Turbo lay in the middle of the rug. Tad and Peggy sat under the tree shaking boxes.

"We've found our stuff," Tad said. "And here's one for Megan and you, too, Gram." He handed his grandmother and little sister their gifts.

"Well, then I guess we'd better start opening. We'll take turns so we can see what each of us got. You go first."

"Thanks." Tad ripped the paper from the box. "Awesome! These are the shoes I've always wanted. How did you know? They're great, Gram, thanks." He hopped up from the floor and gave her a kiss, then sat back down and loosened the strings on the shoes.

"I worried shoes were too practical, but Sam and Joe assured me these were the 'bomb' and that was good."

"They were right!" Tad slipped them on his bare feet.

Peggy opened her present next. She held up a knobby red cowl neck sweater, rubbing it against her cheek. "Oh, Gram, this is soft and cool and . . . did you make it?"

"Yes."

"When did you have the time? How did you do it without me knowing?"

"Here and there. When you were off gallivanting with Malissa." Annabelle was pleased.

You never know what kids will like.

Megan went next. She found wrapped in the tissue paper a pair of gloves, tasseled cap and matching scarf in variegated pastel colors.

She slipped on the gloves and hat then wrapped the scarf around her neck. "Oh, they're so pretty, soft like kitten fur. They fit perfect." Wiggling her fingers, she held up her hands and admired the colorful array. "They'll go with anything!"

"You look cute," Peggy said. "Well done, Gram. It's your turn."

"No, you kids finish, then I'll open mine."

The kids each had one more present to open. Tad started again. "Wow, look at this," he said, holding up a diver's watch. "I've never seen so many buttons and stuff. It has a stopwatch and a compass. Thanks!" He nearly knocked his grandmother over with his hug.

Peggy opened her tiny box and exclaimed. "I love them, Gram. Thank you." She put the silver earrings on and pulled her hair behind her ears to show them off, before giving her grandmother a big hug.

Megan pulled the paper off of her gift and found a boxed set of the *Harry Potter* books, which she had wanted for a very long time. "Oh, Gram. Thank you." She gave her grandmother a kiss on the cheek.

"Open yours, Gram," Megan said.

Annabelle heard rustling inside the box she shook.

"It's smaller than an accordion, but bigger than a hair clip," she said.

Megan giggled.

Annabelle slowly peeled the taped paper away from the package then slipped her finger under the lid of the box.

"What could it be?"

All three children watched her, anticipation painted on their faces.

Inside the box, wrapped in tissue, Annabelle discovered a scrapbook. She opened the cover to find photographs and keepsakes from things she and the children had done together. There were movie ticket stubs, pictures of each of them laughing together and smiling separately. One page had the pizza menu with drawings of pizza slices and a picture of them eating at the kitchen table.

The animal page had a picture of Ms. Pickles, Tang and Turbo in various acts of silliness. More pictures showed them baking cookies, reading and watching television. These were patches and pieces of their lives, going as far back as Megan's birth, when Annabelle still had blue hair. On the last page, Annabelle found a photo of her and Lydia together. While neither smiled, they looked peaceful, surrounded by crayon blue clouds and a yellow sun, no doubt Tad's artistic hand.

Tears coursed down Annabelle's face.

"This is special. How did you find all these photos?"

"We had a box of things from the old house. I also used the digital camera, and Tillie printed off the pictures," Peggy said.

"Do you like it?" Megan asked. "I drew the pizza."

"I love it. What a wonderful gift."

"There's pumpkin pie for breakfast," Tad said.

"All right. Let's eat now so we're finished and dressed when Sam and Regina get here."

They laughed over their pie and milk while Annabelle thumbed through the pages of the scrapbook again. All three kids had put a lot of time and thought into every page. So many wonderful memories were captured there. She felt her heart swell with pride that there had been happy times to record. The dark cloud of abuse no longer followed them.

The girls took their showers first.

Flexing his muscles, Tad said, "I don't mind a cold shower. Makes me more of a man."

"Whatever." Peggy rolled her eyes. "We took fast ones, so it shouldn't be too bad."

Annabelle had cleaned up the night before. All she had to do was fix her hair and dress. Cold baths weren't her favorite. She'd had way too many of them on the farm. She slipped on her clogs as the doorbell rang.

In the bathroom, Tad sang off-key. The girls raced down the stairs.

Peggy and Megan flung open the door. "Merry Christmas," they said in unison.

A police officer stood where they had expected to see Sam and Regina. The girls stepped back, allowing Annabelle to walk up to the open portal.

"Merry Christmas, Officer. What can we do for you?" Annabelle said.

"Merry Christmas, ma'am. Are you Annabelle Hubbard?"

He was tall, thin and fidgety.

"Yes, won't you come in?"

"I'm sorry to disturb you on a holiday, ma'am, but do the children of Tom Malone live here?" He stayed on the welcome mat just beyond the threshold.

Peggy and Megan scooted up to link arms with their grandmother. "Yes."

"There's been an incident involving their father. I'm sorry to report that he was injured."

"What?" Annabelle said. "How?"

Megan began to cry. Peggy stiffened at Annabelle's side.

"I'm sorry, there was a hold up at the diner where he works, and he . . ."

Car doors slammed in the drive. Sam and Regina approached the porch.

"Officer, is there a problem?"

"No, I mean, yes, sir. There's been an incident involving Tom Malone. He's in the hospital, sir."

"Why don't we go inside where it's warm," Sam said.

"But, sir."

"I insist."

"Let's go into the parlor." Regina hustled them into the room, not bothering to suggest they remove their coats and scarves.

They followed her in silence. Regina sat on the couch, and Annabelle joined her. Megan scooped up the kitten sitting in the window seat. Peggy sat rigid in the rocker with Ms. Pickles on her lap.

"Don't say anything until Tad comes down," Peggy said. "There's no use in talking about it over and over again."

"All right," Regina said, unbuttoning her coat. She pulled each finger of her gloves to remove them then reached over to squeeze Annabelle's inert hand.

The officer stood at attention by the fireplace, Sam at his side.

Tad came bounding down the stairs.

"Hey, what's going on?" Tad asked.

"Merry Christmas," Regina said.

Tad looked around the parlor and frowned. "What's going on?"

"Have a seat, son," Sam said. "Proceed, Officer."

Tad sank down on the floor by his grandmother and stroked Turbo's ears.

"There was a robbery at Jenny's diner last night. Your father was shot trying to stop the thieves."

"Is he going to be all right?" Megan asked, her voice filled with concern. She scooped up Tang from the seat for comfort.

"He was shot in the arm. I imagine he'll be okay."

"What hospital did you take him to?" Peggy asked.

"St. Francis."

Sam stood. "Is there anything more you can tell us?"

"No, sir. I'm sorry. Merry . . . Christmas." The officer bowed stiffly, letting himself out the front door.

Annabelle watched as Peggy put Ms. Pickles on the floor, stood and picked up one of the gifts under the tree. She put it into her lap and played with the bow in silence.

Scanning the brightly colored wrappings, boxes and gifts that littered the floor, Annabelle felt the beautiful morning dissolve.

Tom's nothing but trouble, but he's still their father. There's been so much pain in their short lives. It just isn't fair.

"What should we do now?" Tad asked.

"Maybe we should have *our* Christmas tomorrow," Sam said.

"Do you want us to stay, Belle?" Regina asked.

"It's okay. I think Sam is right. Maybe we could get together for dinner tomorrow. We need to find out if Tom is okay."

Regina squeezed Annabelle's hand and Sam kissed her on the cheek before they left.

The kids went upstairs, no doubt to discuss what to do about their father.

Annabelle slipped to the floor and put the lid on the boxes, folding the tissue and wrapping paper that could be used again. She made a pile of scraps and went to the kitchen for a trash bag.

Now is the time to admit it. I'm afraid. Things will never be the same with Tom around. I may have lost my chance to make things right.

When she came back, the kids were in the doorway. They stepped into the parlor and retrieved their gifts, kissed their grandmother on the cheek and went back to their rooms.

I'd better do something.

Annabelle didn't know what to say, but knew it would come to her. She straightened her clothing, walking up the stairs to the girl's room. Finding it empty, she heard their voices behind Tad's door. She knocked and opened it.

"We need to talk," she said. The kids were in the center of the bed, so she sat on the edge. "Do you want to go to the hospital to see your father?"

Being the oldest, Peggy spoke for the group. "Yes. If he's awake, we'd like to give him his present. Nobody should be alone on Christmas. Being in the hospital has to be even worse."

"I agree. You kids are pretty smart. Let's go."

The children nodded then followed her down to get their coats.

A SIX-FOOT CHRISTMAS wreath with blinking colored lights hung on the façade of the hospital building. They saw it a block before they reached it. Everything else looked bleak and gray. They parked in the half-empty garage. When they entered the corridor, the heater blasted their faces. Peeling off their gloves, scarves and coats they marched to the reception desk.

"Tom Malone is in room three-oh-nine," said the middle-aged man with black-rimmed glasses and a mustache. He pointed to the elevators. "Merry Christmas," he said with a look of sympathy.

There were fewer hospital personnel as well as visitors, but enough to know that it was business as usual in this health care facility. A tiny decorated Christmas tree sat at the nurse's station, the smell of spiced

Apple cider mixed with antiseptic and boiled potatoes filled Annabelle's nostrils.

Hospital food is so bland. I should've brought some pumpkin pie or something for Tom.

The kids entered his room in silence. The television was turned on, but not the sound. Tom lay in the mechanical bed partially upright, with extra pillows behind his shoulder and under his left arm. He was right-handed, if she recalled correctly. His eyes were closed, his hair a mess, his skin the color of bread dough, but his breathing sounded normal. The kids surrounded the bed with worried frowns.

"Merry Christmas, Dad," Peggy whispered.

His eyes fluttered open. He stared at his daughter for a moment before a smile formed on his thin face.

"Merry Christmas, kiddo." His voice was raspy and low, but strong. His eyes went from Peggy to Megan to Tad then Annabelle.

"How ya doing?" Tad asked. He rocked back and forth, from heel to toe, hands shoved deep in his pockets.

"I'm better after seeing all of you." Tom's eyes filled, tears sliding out of the corners.

"We brought your Christmas present," Megan said.

Laying the colorful box on his lap, Peggy stepped back.

He touched the ribbon with his unencumbered hand and tugged at the tape, nearly knocking the box off the bed.

"Want some help?" Megan asked.

"Sure. I'm not very good at this."

"That's okay. I'm a great present-opener." Megan scooted closer to the bed and pulled the bow off, then tore the paper from the box. Sticking her finger between the lid and the bottom, she yanked through the tape that held it closed. "There you go!"

"Thanks." He lifted the box lid and frowned. He folded back the cover of the large album. The kids had made their father a scrapbook, too, but this one was different, more a history of chronological events.

"We thought you might like to see what we've been doing all the time you've been gone," Peggy said.

Megan leaned over the bed rail. "This is where I was little. Right after you left."

With no accusation in her voice, she explained page after page of events.

"We don't have pictures from every year, but this'll give you a clue what all went on." Tad explained. "You missed a lot, Dad."

Tom looked up at his children, more tears slid down his face. "I know and I'm so sorry. This is the best gift I've ever gotten."

"Really?" Megan asked. She slid his hand into hers.

"We did okay, Dad. That's what the pictures should tell you." Peggy handed him a tissue. "We aren't mad anymore. We found the letters you wrote. We know you weren't lying about them."

"I didn't mean to hurt . . ." Tom choked on the tears.

"We know you didn't mean to hurt us," Megan said.

He wiped his face with the back of his hand and tried to blow his nose. It was awkward, but he got it done. "This all means so much . . . Annabelle?"

"Yes, Tom?" She stepped closer to the end of the bed.

"Thank you for bringing my kids. It's worth getting shot just to see them, even though it hurts like the devil."

Tad and Peggy chuckled. Megan smiled. "I'm sorry you're hurt. It seems weird to say it, but Merry Christmas."

He tugged at her index finger. "I understand. Merry Christmas to you, pumpkin."

A white-haired nurse in red and green scrubs with reindeer flying all over them stepped into the room. "Merry Christmas, family. How are you doing Mr. Malone?"

"Much better now."

"So, I see." She took his arm in hers and checked his pulse. "Seems you may have had enough excitement for a while. How about if the family comes back tomorrow? You'll be here a couple days more, until we know you can manage without popping a stitch." She left as quickly as she came.

"We'd better go, Dad," Peggy said. She gave him a quick peck on the cheek.

Megan couldn't reach him in that big bed, so she squeezed his free hand.

Giving his father's hand a shake, Tad left to follow his sisters into the hall.

Annabelle slipped to the side of the bed.

"Thanks, Annabelle. You don't know how much this means to me."

"Merry Christmas, Tom."

Chapter 44

NEW YEAR'S DAY dawned cold and sunny. The Kansas wind had calmed and the remnants of snow glistened on the grass. Regina and Sam would celebrate Christmas with the kids before the football games were in full swing. The guys planned to go over to Joe and Tillie's to watch their new flat screen TV and snack on junk food. The ladies rented a couple of romantic comedies and would camp out in the parlor with their own popcorn and drinks.

The kids opened their gifts from Tillie and Joe and gave out hugs and thanks. Regina's gifts were sitting by her feet and would be opened last. She handed them out and said, "Open them one at a time so we can all see what you received."

"I'll go first," Tad said, tearing into the paper around the large box he held in his lap. His eyes lit up as he realized what the wooden box might hold. It had a brass handle and clasp like a brief case and the wood was dark and stained with age. He lifted the lid. His mouth fell open. Inside were a multitude of compartments holding oil paints of every hue and brushes of various sizes. He fingered them smiling. "These are sable, aren't they?"

"You know quality brushes when you see them," Regina said.

"Were these yours?"

"My first set. I replaced the tubes of paint, but the brushes were my own."

He smiled at his cousin. "Thank you. I'll take really good care of them."

"I'm next," Peggy said, tearing off the paper that surrounded the white garment-sized box. She pulled off the tape, opened the lid and folded back the tissue. Her fingers glided along the creamy cashmere. "They're beautiful." She picked up the scarf and mittens, sliding them across her chin. "Thank you, they're wonderful."

"You're welcome," Regina said. "Those were my first cashmere items. I was your age when I received them. I hoped you would enjoy them."

"Oh, I will." Tears sparkled in Peggy's eyes.

"Now me!" Megan carefully peeled away the paper. She lifted the lid, then the fabric wrapped object onto her lap, putting the box on the floor by her feet. She uncovered Regina's china doll. "She's so pretty." Her finger traced the tiny features, her other hand cradling the painted head. "Does she have a name?"

"When she was mine, I called her Elizabeth. Now that she's yours, I think you should give her a new name."

"I'll call her Audrey."

"That's lovely," Annabelle said.

Regina agreed.

Megan cradled the doll carefully in her arms and stepped over to her cousin.

"Thank you so much. I'll take good care of her." Megan gave Regina a kiss on the cheek.

Heat rose in Regina's face, and her heart filled with love.

"It's going to be a very happy New Year!" Megan smiled at everyone.

"Happy New Year!" they said in unison.

Megan and Annabelle began stuffing the torn paper into a garbage bag when the phone rang.

"I'll get it," Megan said. She grabbed the phone only seconds before her sister.

"Hello. Oh, hi. Yes, she's here. Happy New Year to you, too." Megan put her hand over the receiver and whispered, "Gram, it's for you."

"Really? Who could that be?"

"It's Mr. Edwards."

"Okay, I'll take it in the kitchen," Annabelle said, grinning as Tad rolled his eyes.

"Happy New Year, Phil. How are you?"

"I'm just grand, Belle. Do you have big plans today?"

"We're just watching movies and eating popcorn. What did you have in mind?"

"Well, if you're busy with your family . . ."

"Would you like to join us?"

"If you wouldn't mind. I know it's a little cold, but the sun is shining and the river is beautiful. Would you take a walk in the park with me this afternoon?"

"I think a short one would be very nice. What time?"

"How about I pick you up at two o'clock?"

"That sounds fine. See you then." She hung up the phone and smiled. "What a nice way to bring in the New Year."

"I suppose you've got another date," Tad said when Annabelle joined them in the living room.

"Not exactly. We're going for a walk this afternoon. We won't be gone long. You can come with us if you want to."

"Joe, can we go to your house now? I don't think I want to be here when Coach picks up Gram. It's too embarrassing."

"Better get over it, son," Joe said. "I think they like each other."

Tad groaned.

"We're just good friends. You're the only man in my life now." Annabelle hugged her grandson.

Megan giggled.

"Okay, guys, let's resume this party across the street where there's a man-sized television," Joe said.

"Hear, hear." Sam stood and kissed Regina's cheek before following the guys to the door.

Hopping up, Tad waved at the women. "Wait for me, I'm with you guys."

Joe gave Tillie a kiss on the head. "Guess I'd better get going.

"All this lovie stuff is making me sick." Tad went out on the front porch.

"I take it he doesn't have a girlfriend," Joe said.

"Not yet," Peggy said. "Nobody I know is that dumb."

"Stop. He's only fourteen. He doesn't need a girlfriend at his age," Annabelle said.

"Whatever you say, Gram." Peggy waved at her brother. "What time is Mr. Edwards picking you up?"

"Two."

"Then we have time for one movie. What'll it be, *Sleepless in Seattle* or *You've Got Mail?*"

"Sleepless," Regina said.

"Done."

THE DOORBELL RANG at the stroke of two. The movie ended, and Annabelle stuffed a tissue in her sleeve.

Heading to the door, Megan called over her shoulder, "I'll get it."

Annabelle put her hand on the little girl's shoulder. "I've got it. Thank you, sweetie." She opened the door to Phil's smiling face. "Hello." His bald head was covered with the brown watchman's cap Annabelle had crocheted for his Christmas gift.

"I like your hat."

"Me, too. Get your coat and we'll be off."

"Come in while I get my things."

Phil stepped into the entry and waved at the rest of the ladies in the parlor. "Hello and Happy New Year."

"Thank you. Happy New Year to you," Regina said.

Annabelle donned her coat, added a bright red scarf, gloves and a gray wool cap.

"See you all later." She followed Phil out the door to his car.

They drove the few blocks into central Riverside and parked. Phil offered her his arm. "Shall we, my lady?"

Smiling, Annabelle nodded and stepped onto the curb. They strolled along the river in the sunshine.

"Did you have a nice holiday?"

"Yes, with the exception of Tom's injury."

"I'm sure that was hard. But he's going to be okay, right?"

"Yes. The kids want to see more of him. Sometimes I feel jealous and don't want to share them, but he's their father. He's changed. I just hope he doesn't hurt them again."

"Annabelle, it's part of living."

"I know that in my head, but my heart . . . isn't quite that smart."

Tucking her hand under his arm, they glided along, leaving footprints in the snow. "When I lost Martha it hurt. Even now, I get lonely sometimes. Spending time with you has made that go away. I want to thank you for that."

Stopping them in midstride, Annabelle held tight to his arm.

"Would you think I'm a terrible person if I told you I don't miss my husband at all?"

"How long has it been?"

"Oh my, years and years. Liddy was a teen when he died. She worshipped David."

"I've heard little girls are often closer to their fathers when they're young. Is that why you don't miss him?"

"No. He had a problem holding his liquor, his temper . . . and his fists."

Phil stopped. He looked at Annabelle's face.

"Did he beat you and your daughter?"

"No, not Liddy. Just me."

He wrapped his arms around her, giving her an awkward hug. "I'm so sorry."

A tear escaped her eye. She quickly wiped it away. "It was a long time ago. The bruises have long since healed."

"Maybe on the outside." Phil took her hand. They walked toward several benches along the edge of the lane. "Would you like to sit for a moment?"

"That would be nice." Annabelle pulled her collar higher.

Sitting with their shoulders touching, they looked out across the water. A flock of snow geese glided in for a landing on the opposite bank.

"It's peaceful here. I'm glad you brought me, Phil."

"I've done a lot of walking along this river over the years. The water is very soothing, and the birds are good company. But I like it even better with you."

He pulled a small red bag tied with a silver ribbon from his pocket. "I hope you don't mind. I wanted to get you a little something."

"Oh, Phil. No."

"Please, Annabelle. Open it."

She struggled with the knot in the bow, finally tugging it free. Inside the bag was a small wad of white tissue paper. Pulling it out she unfolded it to find a silver charm pin. On it were three figures, two girls and a boy.

"It's so sweet. Thank you, Phil." She leaned in to kiss his cheek, holding his chin with her gloved hand. "I love it."

He pinned it on the lapel of her coat. She rested her hand on it, tears filling her eyes.

His brow furrowed. "Is everything all right?"

I'm turning into a blubbering idiot in my old age.

"I think so."

"You seem troubled."

"I'm sorry. I guess I don't have anything to worry about now. My heart seems to be getting stronger. The kids will have a father around again, and Regina is taking care of the rest. I should be happy."

"But you're not." He covered her hand with his. "What is Regina taking care of that's bothering you?"

"The house." A wind gust blew snow around their feet.

"What do you mean?"

"I can't afford the taxes and insurance on the house, so Regina has set up a trust. Don't get me wrong, I'm grateful. I really am. It's just that I've always dreamed of taking care of things myself. This time . . . it feels like charity."

"But you're family. It's not charity to help family."

"But it feels that way."

"I see. You want to be independent?"

She looked into his face. His nose and cheeks were red from the cold, but his expression full of understanding.

"Yes. That's it exactly. I want to be able to take care of the kids and the house on my own."

"But you don't have to."

She stood and stomped her frigid feet. "After David died, it was just Liddy and me. When she married, I was on my own. The first year I lived in a little duplex, took in sewing, washing and ironing, and cleaned for the old fellow who lived next door. I didn't need much. But now I have three kids to think about."

"You do have your hands full, don't you?" He tugged her back down onto the bench beside him. "We'll just have to put our heads together and see if we can figure out a way to help you feel more independent."

"Thanks, but I have an idea or two."

"Would you give me the opportunity to spend more time with you?"

Annabelle could feel the heat in her cheeks. He really was a sweet man. She tucked her hand under his arm again and watched the sunlight shining on the water. This felt comfortable, safe, but she didn't need a man to make her strong.

"Yes. And thank you."

"For what?"

"For listening to the complaints of an old woman and for being kind."

He squeezed her hand. "You're younger than I am. And I cherish our friendship."

"Me, too. Let's go back, I'm getting cold." Her nose was numb, but resolve warmed the rest of her. At sixty-seven she had at least twenty good years to go. There were all sorts of possibilities just waiting for a woman with some feistiness and gumption to make them happen.

THE HOLIDAY BREAK was over and the kids were back in school. Annabelle had the house to herself during the day once again. After all the hubbub of Thanksgiving and Christmas, she looked forward to returning to a routine. Enjoying the newspaper uninterrupted for a change, the phone rang into the silence.

"Hello."

"Mrs. Hubbard?"

"Yes."

"This is Marvel McElroy, Sam Duncan's assistant."

"Yes, hello. What can I do for you?"

"I understand from Mrs. Duncan that you made the bridesmaid dresses for their wedding."

"That's right."

"And that lovely suit you wore as well?"

"Yes. I did."

"I wondered if you might be interested in making the dresses for my daughter's wedding? With the quality of your work, I would pay top dollar."

Annabelle's breath caught in her throat.

"Mrs. Hubbard, are you still there?"

"Yes. I'm here."

"We have six months until the wedding. There are eight bridesmaids and one flower girl. Do you think that would be enough time for you to get them done?"

"If we can get the fabric ordered right away."

"I've already taken care of that. Laurie has chosen her colors and the fabrics she wants. We have only to determine how much is needed. Would you be able to meet with us at your home this evening to discuss it? I have patterns and swatches I can bring."

"Certainly."

"How does seven-thirty sound? Would that give you enough time to have dinner with your family?"

"Oh yes, that'll be fine."

"I was so excited when I saw the dresses you made. Do you think if there's enough time for you to make me one as well?"

"I don't see why not."

"I'm looking forward to doing business with you, Mrs. Hubbard."

"Thank you, and call me Annabelle."

"Goodbye for now, Annabelle."

She hung up the phone and sank down at the kitchen table.

Could this mean what I hope it means? Could I make a living sewing dresses for weddings and special occasions?

She retrieved a pad of paper and pencil from the drawer and started figuring out an estimate of time per dress, including fittings. She started playing with the charge per hour times the number of dresses to see what might make a reasonable profit and not make the dresses too pricy. She'd have to research what bridesmaid dresses were selling for and what styles were popular.

I can't wait to tell Phil. Won't Regina be amazed? This is so perfect. I've got so much to do before the kids get home!

Grabbing a coat and her pocket book, Annabelle headed out to the car, pad, pencil and phonebook in hand. She had all day to shop the stores. The possibilities were exciting. Maybe this was just the opportunity she needed. If it worked out like she hoped, the trust would remain untouched and could be used for the kids, to help them to get a good start in the world.

She backed out of the drive grinning, filled with hope.

About The Author:
Bonnie Tharp

Born and raised in Kansas, Bonnie Tharp spent much of her formative years in her grandmother's kitchen as official taste tester. Although not much of a chef herself, she adores good food and believes all the best discussions happen at the kitchen table.

Bonnie Tharp's award-winning women's fiction novel, *Feisty Family Values*, (written under the name B.D. Tharp), was one of the 150 Kansas Best Books, a finalist for the USA News Best Books of 2010, and winner of the J. Coffin Memorial Book Award for 2011.

Additional publishing credits include magazine articles, essays and short stories for the following publications: *Generation Boom, Women's Focus, Active Aging,* the *Wichita Register, East Wichita News, Sheridan Edwards Review, A Waist Is A Terrible Thing To Mind* (Anthology), *National Association of Women Writers Weekly* and the Kansas Writers Association newsletter. She's had the honor of winning local, state, and national awards for her writing.

Bonnie Tharp graduated magna cum laude from Wichita State University with a bachelor of arts degree in communications, women & minority studies, and fine arts. While living with her husband and a spoiled Brittany Spaniel in the middle of the United States, Bonnie admits that when she's not writing, she's either reading or watching old movies.

CPSIA information can be obtained
at www.ICGtesting.com
Printed in the USA
FFOW04n2054250414
5047FF